┐

FRANCISCAN

**New Pope's Startling Revelations and Sweeping Reforms
Endanger His Life**

Volume I of The Franciscan Trilogy

William R. Park, Sr.

AmErica House
Baltimore

First printing

Cover design by Carolyn White

ISBN: 1-893162-62-1
PUBLISHED BY AMERICA HOUSE BOOK PUBLISHERS
www.publishamerica.com
Baltimore

Printed in the United States of America

He governs by the great cloak,
acts courageously. The red hats
quarrel, create new schisms, and
produce sophisms against him.
They will stain the cloth.
Murder will be perpetrated.
Nostradamus: synopsis

To lost loved ones - I pray that they wear smiles of approval. Also, to my cloistered dear friend whose spiritual counsel lead me from an unfamiliar wilderness into the light, deepening my faith.

Special Thanks:

To my loving wife, Genie, for her patience with my grammar and her valued multi-draft editing. Without Sharon Worthey's unselfish sharing of her writing skill recommendations, The Franciscan would still reside in my computer rather than the Vatican. And to Christen Beckmann, Senior Editor of Erica House Publishing, who put the shine on the apple.

To Debbie,
Stephanie and Will —
Merry Christmas 2000

Love
Grandpa

Disclaimer:

This book is a work of fiction. Names, characters, places, institutions, organizations, and incidents either are products of the author's imagination or, if real, used fictitiously. Any resemblance to actual events and locales or persons, living or dead, is entirely coincidental. Events of papal history, sayings, and those of saints, are common historical knowledge.

CHAPTER ONE

When God first imagined this day in earth's passage, He marked the calendar with an asterisk. It would be a day of monumental events, a day destined to cause chaos, bloodstained treachery, and a worldwide crucible of faith.

The first rays of sunshine struggled to make their presence known to a city deep in slumber. As nature's clock whispered to the sleeping, Rome slowly woke to witness the birth of a new day. Rolling gray clouds, filled with tears of gods long gone, fought to choke back the sun's warmth, anticipating days to come when clouds of the unknowing would rule.

Between lingering nighttime shadows and a few brave rays of sunlight, a lone figure stirred. With a suppressed groan, his body moved, stiff from the dampness of the stone flooring, born of the chill of two thousand years.

Neither the movement nor the muffled sound of a prayerful chant went unnoticed. An alert guard's shout pierced the silence of the Colosseum. "You there, come out! Now! Vagrants are not allowed! Out - before I use my stick!"

From deep within the underground pens where wild animals were once readied for mortal combat with humans, the figure stepped into the dim light of morning.

A second guard arrived, then gasped upon seeing the emerging man. "Please forgive us, your eminence. We didn't recognize you."

Both guards stood speechless as the man, dressed in a friar's plain brown habit, forced a faint smile and gestured forgiveness with one hand. Then nodding a dismissal, pulled the cowl over his head to fend off the chill of an October dawn. He turned left, strolling slowly up the Via Dei Fori Imperiali, and would eventually turn left again at the Forum, heading toward the Vatican.

In wonderment, the guards watched the friar's form disappear. "You fool, Raphael! Didn't you recognize that man? That was Cardinal Domenico Francisco Masone. His picture was on the GlobalNet yesterday, and he's here with the other cardinals to choose our next pope."

Raphael, the guard who had first taken action, responded sheepishly. "Think he was trying to sense the anguish of Christians before they were driven to slaughter? Seems his task isn't much different than the Roman masters. He votes today to throw another Christian to the lions."

In a blessing of their own, they made the sign of the cross. They were unaware of the prophetic nature of their words, and the significance of their chance meeting with a man destined to have a profound effect on their own lives, and the lives of generations to come.

*****

Buldini was a large brooding man well over six feet tall, sporting a disproportionately smallish nose hemmed in on both sides by billowing, fleshy spider vein cheeks. Bushy white caterpillar-like eyebrows clashed with the cardinal's dyed, coal black hair. The red hat neatly concealed a short ponytail.

His hands were a point of pride, adorned with meticulously manicured red fingernails, color coordinated to compliment his hat and sash. Yards and yards of black cloth enshrouding his frame intensified his moon shaped black eyes, held in place by two dark shadows beneath.

Cardinal Alfonso Buldini was head of the Congregation of the Faith, the office responsible for monitoring activities of the clergy, theologians, and faithful followers worldwide, including censorship of those not adhering to dogma.

Systematically, over the past 14 years, using the strength of his office as a shield to mask his ruthlessness through fear, deception and skillful manipulation of papal authority, he had accumulated personal wealth and power unequaled in modern times, mirroring that of the medieval Inquisition. Pius XIII and his successor, the recently deceased Pope Paul VII, both weakened by age, in mind and body, relied heavily on the cardinal, who catered to their trusting natures to become both confidant and unchallenged spokesman for the pontifical office. This unbridled autonomy granted Buldini access to Vatican Bank funds and a priceless treasure trove of antiques, art, and historical relics.

He swivelled his oversized chair for a more favorable view of the Vatican courtyard teeming with locals, religious pilgrims from around the world, and swarms of international media types, then turned to face his small staff. He cast a look as dark and foreboding as the atmosphere within his office, and growled, "The Franciscan, Cardinal Domenico Francisco Masone, must become pope on the very first ballot, as swiftly as the punishment we promised to those who fail to cooperate with us. Go now. Apply pressure on the cardinals. Do whatever you must to ensure our victory. The Franciscan will be mine, as were the others." He slammed his fist on the massive desk. "Go!"

Unaware of the significance of the next day's date, October 4th, his people dispersed to continue their unrelenting persuasion of the cloistered cardinals far into the night. The Holy Spirit would have no part in choosing of this pope... or so they thought.

*****

For Uden Borne, cardinal from the Netherlands, returning to the spiritual bosom of the Church had always been a refreshing and inspiring experience. Until now. The very source of his greatest joy had become his Achilles' heel. Cardinal Borne would be considered a handsome man, except for a prominent, elongated ski slope of a nose which hung over his upper lip like an impending avalanche. His North Sea icy blue eyes and unruly shock of wavy blond hair almost made the nose inconspicuous. Almost, but not quite. To his friends, parishioners, and clergy staff, he was affectionately referred to as Cardinal Cyrano - but never nose to nose. He certainly stood out in a crowd, especially when wearing his beloved brown Franciscan habit. Borne was one of three married cardinals, much to the delight of the throngs that loved him.

However, he was scorned by those who disagreed with the edict by Vatican III that allowed such a marriage. In preparation for tomorrow's vote, each cardinal was assigned a remote apartment to discourage intercommunication until they were summoned to cloister in a sealed-off conclave. Actually, he cherished the silence. It was an opportunity to meditate on the task of choosing the next pope and weigh the consequences that threatened all he held sacred.

From the vantage point of his apartment high above and to the right of St. Peter's Square, he had an excellent view of the Eternal City with its numerous cupolas, spires, obelisks, columns and archways that fueled his imagination, recalling the history of the past twenty-one centuries. He wouldn't sleep a wink all night. The constant gentle splashing of two massive marble fountains would be his only companions and reminders of the outside world.

9

The sun's slowly departing lemon-orange glow outlined the seven hills embracing Rome, reminding Borne of a gigantic slumbering green giant. He wondered if the image was prophetic as he stood leaning against the cold damp plaster wall, gazing out of the single window with legs numb from lack of motion, and made every effort to clear his mind. The bottom of the small window began about five feet from the old uneven wooden floor. One had to stand in order to view anything but the ever darkening sky. To say the room was Spartan would be an understatement. Drab gray in color, it featured a small rock hard bed and flat musty pillow, an extra blanket, a wash basin and mirror, one extremely uncomfortable straight back chair, and desk with a little lamp. And, of course, a crucifix. Under the circumstances, the accommodations suited the cardinal; he deemed it fitting.

Tomorrow, he and the other 118 voting members of the College of Cardinals would choose the next pope. Under normal circumstances it would be difficult to objectively examine a crown bedecked with radiant diamonds and quickly select the most brilliant. He considered the implications of his conscience and the inspiration of the Holy Spirit, and realized he would risk this beautiful life he had enjoyed for thirteen years if he ignored the pressure to cast his vote for Masone.

*****

Monsignor Giuliano Diamante, senior aid to Cardinal Buldini, half dragged his slight frame across the Courtyard of The Sentinel and paused to read his watch before entering the long staggered stairway that would eventually lead to Cardinal Borne's apartment. It was 11:36 PM. He was already exhausted from lengthy rounds of verbal combat with key dissenting cardinals, and this last cardinal would certainly be no less disagreeable.

The monsignor was no one's favorite. Only Buldini knew why he kept the aging 64-year-old bag of bones around. His ferret-like features, set upon a small, slightly stooped five foot four inch form, drew an immediate response of distrust.

Sadly, this unfair image had haunted him since childhood and stunted his personality, as well as his relations with others. However, it had helped to hone his most obvious talent. He genuinely disliked people, and was equally suspicious of everyone in general. In self-defense he had became a

10

master of persuasion and deception. Perhaps that was why Buldini tolerated him; or maybe it was because they had been boyhood acquaintances.

Ascending the three levels of stairs became an almost monumental effort. One step at a time, head and shoulders drooping, he grasped the rickety, seldom used handrail for support and slowly mounted the staircase. His heart was pounding so loud, he was certain he could hear its echo throughout the dimly lit and deserted enclosure.

"Blast it all!" he muttered, stopping to catch his breath and give his weakened knees an opportunity to recoup an ounce of strength. At what he thought was the halfway point in the laborious climb, he nearly collapsed. This time he sat down on the landing where the steps curved, exposing yet another set of steps. He cursed. "Blast you Borne! You would take the most remote apartment. Someday you'll be sorry. Someday. Maybe I could rest for just a few minutes." He thought to himself, *No. Buldini would have me skinned alive if I didn't get to Borne. He's now the key to victory or defeat.* Summoning the last hope of strength, generated out of both duty and fear, he stood up, teetered, then proceeded upward on all fours. It was safer that way.

*****

A loud knock rattled the old door on its hinges and startled Cardinal Borne from meditation. Subconsciously, his mind resisted responding. Struggling against an almost overwhelming urge to deny the intrusion, he forced himself back to reality. Darkness ruled. Dawn still slumbered. Who could be summoning him at this hour? His watch read 12:03 AM.

This time the knock was applied with far more force, echoing throughout the dimly lit, musty scented corridor. Someone was extremely anxious.

Fumbling with the ancient latch and lock, Borne opened the door and staggered backward in utter surprise. "Uden, old friend. It's good to see you again. How are Inge and the youngsters?" came a familiar voice.

With a blend of disbelief and joy, Borne responded, "It's you! And still wearing the Franciscan habit, I see. It's grand to see you too, Domenico. The family's fine - thus far." The two friends, clad in friar's habits, heartily embraced with loud back claps of brotherly welcome.

Borne had always envied his friend's thick curly raven colored hair, now at 54, graced with a hint of silver just above the ears. He often kidded

11

THE FRANCISCAN

Masone that his hair reminded him of an unkempt bed. And despite his vow to forsake worldly vanities, he would give almost anything in trade for that straight Roman nose. Masone was just over six feet, with an average, but muscular build. Large dark olive eyes complimented by the medium olive complexion was stage for an always contagious broad toothy grin. A square set jaw completed the portrait of a man's-man image which he cultivated with guarded pride. His presence opened doors as well as hearts, and the kindly and likable demeanor braced with a air of strength of character drew people to him like a magnet.

Silently closing the door, Borne turned with a puzzled expression, and inquired, "Dom, what are you doing here? We're forbidden to be in contact until later today."

"Well," came the reply, "technically, it is today. You know I always do as I'm told," he grinned. "You're surely aware that Buldini's aggressively bulldozing me into being voted pope on the first ballot. Even if he found out, he won't dare say a word." Uden nodded in agreement.

Masone sat on the edge of the bed and gestured for Uden to join him. "I'll quickly get to the point. You need rest, and I haven't much time. Yet this morning, I have a rendezvous with the shadows of long ago at the arena of death, the Colosseum, then must return before the conclave breakfast."

He continued, not providing the opportunity for questioning. "Dear friend, I need you to vote for me on the first ballot. That's vitally important. We can't allow Buldini's influence time to wane. There's always the chance that blocks of votes would emerge, changing opinions, and the outcome. Now don't say anything! Not just yet. Allow me to finish. I'll explain in due time. We both know Buldini's perverted intentions..."

"Dom," Borne interrupted, "you know I love you as a brother, but I honestly feel Cardinal Mumbwa of Central Africa could best withstand Buldini's pressure. He's strong of mind, will and spirit, and a proven fearless advisory of oppressive leadership in his own country. Mumbwa is best equipped."

Masone agreed. "You're correct. Cardinal Mumbwa has the quality of character and sense of conviction to stand up to Buldini's intimidation. But, there's more at stake here. There's a destiny to be fulfilled. My destiny. The destiny of the Church worldwide." At this point, Borne was not just tired, he was somewhat confused. He stood up, walked to the window, and gazed into the darkness.

12

Masone motioned for him to sit back down and continued, "Let me explain. I've never told this story to another, and it must remain with you in confidence forever. Agreed?" Uden nodded assuredly, still exhibiting a look of confused wonderment.

In hushed tones, Cardinal Domenico Francisco Masone divulged all. "You're mindful that I was born and raised in Assisi in the very shadow of St. Francis' spirit that to this day still hangs heavy within its ancient walls. My dearest friend, his spirit is with us today, October 4th, his Feast Day. The anniversary of his death. This day of the first vote is extremely significant as the trials to come will witness. We will all be tested, and our very lives will be in jeopardy. But I digress. Forgive me. Obviously, versions of the name Francis were most popular in Assisi for a new born male. If one were to call out the name in the town square, seven out of ten young and old men would turn their heads, including a fair number of females. My middle name, Francisco, is not a name of coincidence, nor the remainder of this story. I'm convinced all was by divine intervention, as you will soon learn."

Masone stood, walked to the window, then turned to face his friend. "You see it all began when I was a young, impressionable lad of eight. I was fascinated by the legendary tales of my namesake, so when I could, I'd sneak down the mountain from Assisi and slip into the large Basilica of San Maria degli Angeli that's shelter to St. Francis' 'la Porziuncola.' That's the little church-shrine that he built with his own hands, and wherein he later died naked on the dirt floor. It became my favorite place to hide from the world. I would lie in the tiny chamber room, fully clothed of course," he said with an impish smile, "and pretend to be the saint himself. On one particular day the thought came to mind to visit the church of San Damiano where hangs the crucifix that spoke to St. Francis. As you know, it was in the autumn of 1206, as a young man of 24, while Francisco Bernardone was praying alone, that Our Lord's lips suddenly moved declaring; *'Francis, you see how my house is in ruins? Go and restore it!'*

"Uden, I prayed to Our Lord that fateful day many years ago. And, Iddio mio (my God), I lost myself in His large mournful eyes, unaware if the tears were in the painted eyes or mine. He spoke to me, Uden. I swear!" he confirmed with a raised right hand. "'*Domenico, my house is in ruins. Restore it!'* You can imagine how a boy of eight would react. I ran as fast as my two little legs would go, nearly knocking over three tourists in the church entrance, climbed the hill in Olympic time, and arrived home

13

completely out of breath. That evening I was too excited and frightened to sleep. You are the only person I've ever told this to. In time it became a fleeting recollection. Perhaps to protect my sanity, I unknowingly swept it from my memory."

Masone sat back down next to his friend and continued. "I don't believe the experience was the cause of my calling to the ministry. But who knows?

"After graduation from the seminary, where we met and later became Franciscans, I returned home to Assisi on vacation. One day while wandering aimlessly among the stone streets attempting to recapture my youth, proudly sporting a new friar's habit, and contemplating what the future held for me, it happened again. Suddenly, the repressed memory of the words, '*Domenico, repair it!*' burst with the force of a thunderclap inside my head with such might it tossed me down a narrow winding alleyway. To this day I have an indentation above my right eye from hitting the hard stone wall. When my senses cleared, I found myself lying in a fetal position on the dirt floor of St. Francis' 'la Porziuncola,' my favorite hiding place as a boy. The local priest that was shaking me awake must have thought the young friar covered with dust to be demented. Thinking back, I didn't do a good job convincing him otherwise.

"Rather ashamed, disoriented, and shaking of limb, I made my way to the church of San Damiano to sit and pray for discernment. It had been sixteen years since I faced the wooded Byzantine crucifix with large haunting eyes. It was as frightening as on that first day years ago. My eyes focused on His lips in anticipation, so long, that my mind emptied of all other thoughts. His lips remained inanimate as my mind filled with what I knew to be the direction of the Lord."

Cardinal Uden, now sitting on the edge of his cot, could no longer stand the suspense. "Dom - will you get to the point! I'll believe anything you say, just say it! You're as windy as ever."

Chuckling to himself, the future pope continued. "Patience. I'm almost there. Unlike St. Francis, who for the longest time took the Lord's words literally and proceeded to physically rebuild the dilapidated churches in the region, including San Damiano, I knew instinctively the meaning of the edict placed in my keeping sixteen years earlier. The message, '*Restore it*', was as clear as life itself. To restore the Church, I had to be in a position of supreme leadership and authority."

14

He paused, ran his fingers through his hair, and then resumed his explanation. "Dear friend Uden, for the past thirty years, in patience I have performed my duty to my priesthood, my order and Church authority. However, somewhat like St. Francis I have often been considered an obedient rebel. I frequently moved from diocese to diocese to solve problems of faith for the Vatican; first, always doing what was best in the interest of the people and staying one step ahead of the local bishop. My Franciscan sense of fairness drew the people to me, and this popularity would catch the attention and envy of the bishop, causing him to offer my services elsewhere or promote me to another post far from his district. You know, it's not easy biting one's tongue while pleasing Church authority. You and I, and many of our select group of brothers, have discussed this at length whenever we had the opportunity to meet in private through the years. The cultivated reputation of blind obedience was by design, and is what led me to this appointed time."

Turning, Masone placed a firm hand on Uden's shoulder. "With every fiber of my being, I believe I was destined by the Creator to become pope at this time in history. Now is the time, and I need your help. God's will cannot bear fruit without your vote this morning. You must believe in me. You must believe that you and I are here today by His will and not by mere chance. Cardinal Uden Borne, humanity needs your vote. Please, my brother."

Borne had known Masone for over thirty-five years, and had grown to truly love the man. He had followed Domenico's career with respect and amusement. And he revered Dom's ability to spiritually feed the flock in spite of his superior's meddling, all within the guarded cloak of humble obedience.

Cardinal Masone searched his friend's face for an immediate answer. In Dom, Borne saw a look of strength and unshakable conviction he had never witnessed before and shut his eyes, not to avoid contact, but in an effort to catch his breath. Then, leapt to his feet, turned to face his friend, and in a roaring voice, declared, "Yes! I'll vote for you!"

*****

Upon finally conquering the last few steps to the floor of Cardinal Borne's apartment, Monsignor Diamante was surprised to catch a glimpse of

15

Cardinal Masone entering Borne's quarters. As quietly as his wobbly legs would allow, Diamante stumbled down the darkened hallway, pausing outside Borne's apartment hoping to listen in on the conversation. He strained, cupping his ear to door, being careful not to apply pressure that would create movement of the timeworn piece of timber. Regrettably, the words expressed in confidence were further muffled by the thickness of the door. He wondered how he would explain the meeting of the two cardinals and his failure to reach Borne before the conclave breakfast. The sinking feeling in his chest was relieved by the sudden outburst from within the apartment. "Yes! I'll vote for you!"

His career was saved. Perhaps his life. Why tell Buldini about Borne and Masone? He'd take credit for convincing Borne to vote for Masone. The monsignor's triumphant smile of satisfaction twisted into a grimace with the thought of descending the stairs. Luckily, Masone used the far stairway to reach Borne's apartment level, and would likely leave by the same route.

The monsignor shuffled quietly away. He would fail to hear that the conversation within the apartment concluded with a request from Masone to his friend. "Immediately after the ballots are tallied and I'm confirmed pope, watch for my signal. As soon as you can break away, contact each member of our select group. Do this with the utmost caution. Direct them to proceed in great haste to Rome. Let nothing detain them. Nothing! I will need you and the others with me to succeed."

CHAPTER TWO

Dr. Symon Carpenter stood alone among the bundles of provisions and water bags. He hoped he had estimated correctly for his planned three month sojourn. The doctor arched his six foot plus slender frame, and peered upward. The cave was somewhere in the cliff above him, or so the NASA surveillance scan had indicated. He wiped his brow and let out a deep sigh, and wondered if it had been a wise decision to refuse the helihover-craft pilot's offer to help find the cave and store the supplies. Perhaps he had been too hasty in his quest for solitude.

He was dead tired from his three day trip. The wind was gaining momentum now, whipping mercilessly through rugged terrain, tortured from the beginning of time by the whims of nature. As the sun slowly bid farewell, hiding its warmth behind massive rock formations, beads of perspiration chilled on his forehead. A foreshadowing of the desert mountain evenings ahead.

His small, yet growing ponytail began to toss about in the cool breeze. The experience brought a smile to his face and a mischievous twinkle to his blue eyes. The two dimples that once graced his cheeks in younger days had become elongated deep crevasses in his fifties. They provided character, he convinced himself, just as the hint of silver among the sandy colored strands came to be referred to as blond highlights. Thankfully, his infamous yet playful sense of humor had not left him, though the last six months had tested that most admirable of human traits.

*****

Symon's adventure had begun as soon as he had completed his speech at the International Convention On Ancient Languages in Moscow. He had boarded the plane for Tbilisi in the southern most tip of the New United Republics of Russia immediately after the presentation and had left the hotel without notice to his benefactors. Besides, *Who would miss me?* he thought, and if they knew, the authorities would bar any effort to journey into Turkey.

At Tbilisi he went directly to the train terminal and met an old friend from his early days at the monastery in the English countryside. There would be no time to reminisce. They could do that some other time if all went well.

Peter had made all the travel arrangements and provided the false

17

documents, though Symon balked at the thought of using them. The supplies were ordered and paid for, and the helihover-craft pilot was waiting for his arrival.

With a quick thank you, and a heartfelt hug, Symon had boarded the train for the small seaport town of Kobuleti, then had journeyed by motorcar to Batumi on the Black Sea Russian-Turkish border. Arriving in Batumi with less than three hours sleep in two days, he was met by a joyful heavyset man of questionable nationality, who informed him the supplies were on board, passage over the border was assured, but after that they would be on their own in Turkish airspace. The pilot had timed the Turkish MIT radar sweeps for several days. He had predicted that by leaving in the heat of the day, hovering low and close to the mountains, and avoiding towns as they flew, they would enjoy an uneventful 360 kilometer flight. His assumption proved correct.

*****

So there he now stood, alone, 40 kilometers from the 3,090 foot high Nuruhak Dagi mountain looming to the north. The closest town of any size to his south was Maras. To the north, about 60 kilometers, was the small settlement of Elbistan. His home for the next three months would be a cave, yet to be located in a small mountain range sandwiched between two desolate plains. Large rugged mountains loomed to his far left and right.

He needed sleep badly and did not trust his mind to perform. It was too late in the day to begin his climb to the cave. The cold of the night was already engulfing his body. *I'll eat in the morning,* he thought. *Right now my solar body wrap is all the comfort I need.* Within moments he was warm and sound asleep.

After breakfast, the pinpoint coordinates supplied by another old friend at NASA were right on the nose. The cave was easily found, and the climb was reasonably simple, although it had taken him most of the day to carry the bundles and bags to his new temporary shelter. It would take the remainder of the day to make the cave moderately comfortable, and another before he could call it home.

This isn't so bad, he thought. *If I like it well enough, I just might stay.* Who would know? Who would care? *The children have their own lives. Now I have mine.*

Once a friar, always a friar, was the silent thought of Doctor Symon Carpenter, late of Oxford University. He chuckled to himself, not that anyone could hear. *One step forward, one giant leap for mankind. Or in my case, it's more like 'One step back into the cradle of civilization'.*

His gaze crossed the windswept desert mountains of Turkey, and he recalled Jeremiah's prophecy. *'Her cities are a desolation, a dry land, and a wilderness, a land wherein no man dwelleth, neither doth any son of man pass thereby.'*

He confronted the reality of his current situation and spoke aloud for the first time in three days. "Jeremiah was wrong. Symon Carpenter, a humble friar, doth dwelleth here." Although he had to agree that no man would pass by.

Symon had entered the seminary when he was nineteen at the encouragement of his mother. Not experiencing a full appetite for the priesthood, he had chosen a life cloistered in a monastery as a novice praying for mankind. Although he grew impatient with a life of seclusion, much to his delight and surprise, the monastery possessed a library of ancient history texts that rivaled any university. He had found his calling. Engrossing himself each available hour of every day in endless volumes, he had consumed the knowledge of the past with the passion of a man towards his first true love.

Symon's affection and enthusiasm for ancient history had caught the attention of the abbot, who had teased him endlessly. "Symon, your fire for the past borders on lust." Abbot Parc had soon recognized both Symon's growing uneasiness with their rigid life style and his impassioned craving for further knowledge. One could not serve two masters and do justice to both.

The abbot, being a fair and understanding person, talked at length with Symon. "My son, you have one semester left before you earn your master's degree in English, and in the past four years you've become one of the most learned scholars of ancient history in all of England. You'd make a marvelous teacher."

Symon had remained at the monastery until he received his degree in teaching. As a result of his growing fame in the field of antiquity, and much to the credit of the abbot's influence within the academic community, Symon was offered and accepted a position as professor of Ancient Civilizations and Languages at Oxford University.

Thirty six years later, renowned the world over and beloved by students past and present, he found himself alone once again. His wife of thirty three years had passed away six months earlier. His daughter had moved to America with her husband, and his son to China on a diplomatic assignment for the British government. It was then that he made the second most significant decision of his life, to resign from the university and return to a course of meditation - this time on his own terms. A Franciscan friar in a Turkish cave.

CHAPTER THREE

Christ's raised right hand, depending upon one's interpretation, was either a gesture of blessing or a warning to sinners. Perhaps both. The gentle Holy Mother shared her son's position of glory, surrounded by a sea of human forms, including saints, martyrs, the resurrected and the damned. Monsignor Diamante had always felt awed by the power of Michelangelo's 'Last Judgment', towering 112 feet above the altar in the Sistine Chapel. It was the traditional site for the selection of the new Santissino Padre. But never before had he suffered from the sensation that Christ's arm was about to come down, pointing His finger directly at him. The monsignor was uneasy, indeed.

His job this morning was to supervise placement of the Scrutineer's table below the altar. Also, place cards denoting seating arrangements of the cardinals needed to be set at three long rows of tables, and he made sure the security guard's final sweep of electronic bugging devices throughout the chapel included installation of lead strips to seal windows above. The leading, was an ancient custom - the electronic sweeps, a modern necessity.

All was prepared. He was satisfied the stage was set for the arranged outcome. Still, a sense of foreboding spread from bone to bone as though suddenly stricken with painful arthritis. It was followed by a surprising momentary pang of conscience that he found perplexing. Although he shook off the initial sensation, he could not avoid the Last Judgment fresco. It seemed to hold his eyes captive. Especially Saint Bartholomew, who sat on a rock just at Christ's left foot. Michelangelo depicted his own image and internal torment within the mass of figures. Saint Bartholomew held the flayed lifeless skin of the artist for Christ's judgment. The grotesque, crumpled empty shell gripped Diamante. He was spellbound by the eerie resemblance of the hopeless look on Michelangelo's face in the fresco to the wearied image he had observed in the mirror earlier that morning.

"Diamante!" came the booming voice of Cardinal Buldini. "Is everything ready? Is everyone out? Has the chapel been swept of listening and transmitting devices?"

"Yes, your eminence. But I'm concerned that the cells have not been prepared for the cardinals' cloistered night quarters, as is tradition. For hundreds of years secluded accommodations have been available, so they

21

may live isolated from the outside world until a pope is chosen. I'm afraid we may raise suspicion and provide the media with a bone to chew."

"You let me worry about that, Diamante," Buldini scowled. Then with a cunning smile, he explained, "If you were as successful with Borne as you claim, the normal temporary quarters are unnecessary. If you have failed, God help you. In an emergency the prefab-cells can be erected while the cardinals are at dinner. As we speak, nuns are in the Borgia kitchen preparing for a feast of pasta, choice meats, breads, wine and beers for the planned celebration in the Hall of The Popes. So you see, skeptical one, as usual, I have everything well in hand." Buldini's large frame shook with laughter. Then, deep in a moment's thought, he frowned, forcing the two caterpillar-like eyebrows together as one continuous snowbank ledge, ever darkening the shadows beneath his piercing black eyes. Placing one arm over the monsignor's arched shoulders, in a mighty smothering hug, he whispered, "We'll lock up, post a Swiss Guard, then join the cardinals for breakfast. Relax. All is well."

Diamante wasn't assured. Something was wrong. Something dreadful was about to happen. He could sense it. But what, he had no clue.

*****

It was nearly 10 AM; the cardinals had celebrated mass and enjoyed a breakfast of rolls, sausage turnovers and coffee. The light morning meal lasted longer than normal. This was the first opportunity the cardinals had to renew acquaintances and to inquire about each others' lives. The customary pre-conclave consultations between individuals and blocks of cardinals at private luncheons, dinners and receptions had been eliminated. A deliberate tight scheduling of travel and events successfully restrained socializing. Everyone was forced to stay to themselves, limiting risk of block voting. Buldini saw to that. Unlike John Paul II, who years before had hand picked only the strongest of men to the post of cardinal and those who were in accord with his form of conservatism, Buldini's influence over the last two popes had won out. With alarming success, he had made every effort to have as many elderly individuals appointed whose wills he could bend.

Monsignor Diamante announced a minor delay. There was a problem with the temporary smoke stack assembled in the Sistine Chapel, but extra pots of coffee would arrive shortly. No one seemed to be anxious to get on with the task at hand. Even Buldini took the holdup in stride - much to the relief of the monsignor.

Forty eight minutes later the monsignor returned. The problem was solved. The Commandant of the Swiss Guards had unlocked the chapel door and the choir of The Holy Spirit awaited their entrance. The Secretary of State was conveniently not feeling well enough to perform his responsibility, so Buldini called everyone to order. One by one the cardinals, dressed in scarlet cassocks, capes, and birettas, entered the passageway from St. Peter's Basilica, following the gold papal cross to the Sistine Chapel.

With everyone seated at the long rows of tables, and the choir concluding their hymn, Buldini, below the altar, faced the gathering, and declared in a loud voice, "Extra omnes!" (everybody out). Monsignor Diamante escorted the choir members out. Remaining inside, he locked the door, then tugged on it once. On the other side, the commandant did likewise. Satisfied all was secure, Diamante made a final visual scan of the chapel for unauthorized personnel. Confident the conclave of the College of Cardinals was effectively safeguarded, he confirmed, "Extra omnes!"

The first order of business was always to select the Scrutineers, whose duty it was to receive, count and recount the submitted ballots. At the table below the altar, the small group would perform the lengthy task. If for any reason the number of ballots did not tally with the number of electors, the slips would be burned and another vote taken. The election of the Scrutineer team went rather smoothly, and much to the delight of Cardinals Masone and Borne, Cardinal Mumbwa was selected leader.

A deep reverberating growl within Cardinal Buldini's massive girth registered a complaint that lunch time was fast approaching. A quick glance at his watch confirmed what his stomach already declared; it was nearly one in the afternoon. Due to the leisurely breakfast, the unforeseen chimney repair, and in spite of the swift Scrutineer selection, the morning session had flown by.

Everyone was directed to retire for a light lunch that the good sisters had waiting in the dining hall, and to be prepared to reassemble in the chapel no later than three o'clock. Portable toilets and wash facilities were available in the Borgia Courtyard for the cardinal's convenience. Monsignor Diamante unlocked the door and notified the commandant of their luncheon plans, with orders to lock the door and post Swiss Guards to secure the entrance.

Chatter at the luncheon tables was much more animated than at breakfast. Tension eased as the morning progressed. Only those his accomplices had visited during the night were aware of Buldini's plan for a one ballot success. He felt confident Masone should be a shoe-in. As usual, there were blocks of votes prepared to be cast for various individual candidates in spite of Buldini's influence. Everyone had their favorites. However, from his calculations and estimating the votes of the intimidated, only one person would have the necessary two-thirds plus one tally to be elected. The previous two popes were in their last days when chosen. Even the charismatic Cardinal Masone's age was perfect. His dedication and untiring devotion on behalf of the faithful were well known, as well as his growing aura of spirituality.

This was all well and good as far as Buldini was concerned. It was the cardinal's reputation of humility and strict adherence to Church authority and tradition that pleased him. This was the perceived weakness Buldini relied on.

*****

The chapel was again swept for electronic bugs, and the College of Cardinals took their assigned places. Then the door was locked and secured as protocol directed. Only after each cardinal, in turn, swore to uphold the conclave oath would Cardinal Mumbwa order the ballot cards distributed. He reminded the gathering that when the time came to vote, they must write only one name on the ballot and in a legible yet non-recognizable handwriting. He then administered the order to vote. As though the air had instantly been sucked out of the chapel, only the sound of scribbling on paper could be heard.

Then, a clearing of the throat, a sniffle or two, and numerous audible sighs broke the hush. Several pairs of eyes were noted to be searching Christ's face for some sign. Any sign. Later, many would be heard to say that it seemed a lifetime between the order to vote and the beginning of the ballot tendering.

The process had begun. All cardinals folded their ballot cards once, as prescribed. One after another they proceeded to the altar, knelt to pray, and rose to utter the final oath. "I call Christ the Lord to be witness that my vote is given to whom in God's presence I judge should be elected pope."

24

Each cardinal then placed his ballot on a silver plate held by Cardinal Mumbwa, who, after each card was received, tilted the plate so the ballot fell into a large chalice. After all ballots were collected, a second member of the Scrutineers group took the cards from the chalice and wrote each name down, then passed it on to another who repeated the act. A third person did the same and then announced the name. Several hours passed as each cardinal came forth, proclaimed the oath and deposited his ballot. The ballots were counted for each person whose name had been called. The two groups confirmed each others figures, and the balloting names and numbers were ready to be announced.

Mumbwa examined the list of names and number of votes registered per name, took a deep breath and turned to face the assemblage. His onyx face was as fixed as a Michelangelo masterpiece. For the sake of drama, he paused, closing his eyes as if in prayer. His eyes snapped open; a smile crept across his face. "My brothers in Christ, the most extraordinary event has happened. Truly the Holy Spirit has spoken." He paused again. Pure theatrics; he was relishing the moment. "I cannot recall when last our pope was chosen on the first ballot. Can any of you? He has today, October 4th. Our newly elected pope will hold our faith in his hands, and our burdens upon his shoulders. He will need the strength of all our prayers and the direction of the Holy Spirit and God's blessing if he is to successfully confront the challenges in the days to come."

Buldini squirmed impatiently in his chair. *What's the man doing?* he thought. *It's beginning to sound like an acceptance speech.* Could his calculations have been wrong? Looking in Diamante's direction, he glared.

The Scrutineer leader, setting aside his obvious personal pleasure and mustering all sense of dignity possible for the moment, inquired, "Do you Most Reverend Cardinal Domenico Francisco Masone accept your election as Supreme Pontiff as proclaimed by ballot this day?"

You could have heard an angel's feather fall. All eyes were on Masone. With head bowed, eyes and lips tightly shut, and fists clenched in his lap, he rocked back and forth in his chair. His head nodded involuntarily with the body's movement. Moments passed painfully slowly, as he softly repeated, "Lord, Lord, Lord, yes Lord." The cardinal raised his head, and with teary eyes and a deeply inhaled breath, stood. Fists clenched at his sides, he stood as erect as his tall frame would allow, and firmly declared, "Accepto!"

Instant and spontaneous cheers and applause rang out. Some of the younger and more boisterous cardinals from several of the emerging countries stomped their feet in approval. There were handshakes and hugs all around, along with astonishment at the first vote victory. Cardinal Mumbwa, who had noted he was second in the voting tally, was equally animated, and shook both arms in celebration of Masone's triumph.

"Diamante! Diamante!" barked Buldini, "Don't just sit there like a stone. Gather the ballots for the burning. The world awaits the white smoke, and those outside the chapel door must be in a panic hearing the shouts from within." The dutiful monsignor took the secret ballots to the temporary burner, and soon added the powered ingredient, to be certain the smoke would change to white from gray. The throng in St. Peter's Square and the billions watching television would soon learn that a new pope had been chosen.

Leaving his place at the second table, Cardinal Masone walked towards the altar, stopping momentarily behind the seated Cardinal Borne. Lightly squeezing Borne's right shoulder, Masone leaned over close to his ear and whispered, "Wait for the opportunity during dinner." Upon reaching the altar, he raised his hands and gestured for silence, then spoke. "My brothers in Christ. Please bow your heads in prayer for me, as I pray to our Lord." He turned, knelt and then laid prostrate before the altar and prayed. "Jesus, Lord Jesus Christ, Son of the living God, to whom I love and give praise, have mercy on me, a sinner. Forgive me. Direct me. Protect me. And may the Holy Spirit ever guide me to do Your will. Amen."

Rising, he faced his brother cardinals. "We are pleased and thankful for your vote of confidence. There is much to do. Please pray for me ceaselessly. Pray for our brothers and sisters the world over, that they might succeed in their quest on God's behalf. Pray for the poor and downtrodden, that they be enriched by the gifts of the Holy Spirit. Pray His power touches and transforms the hearts of those with the means to make a difference in the lives of those with less."

Still facing those before him, he pointed behind and upward in the direction of Christ and His mother. "In the name of our Lord Jesus Christ, our Holy Mother and all the saints, especially Saint Francis on this, his feast day, I call on all of you and all those serving the Church to be mindful of 'Supreme lex salus animarum' (The Supreme Law is the saving of souls). This must be our first concern. Make this law paramount in all we do. I beseech you, pray for me ceaselessly that I may fulfill my papacy as willed by the Holy Spirit."

*****

The patient vigilance of the packed crowd of thousands waiting in the square turned to surprised anticipation as the Sistine Chapel's slender smoke stack revealed a thin line of gray smoke. Their reasonably subdued behavior broke into jubilant hysteria as the gray became white against a cloudless blue sky. Cheers of "Viva el papa!" from the faithful echoed into every corner of the world via strategically placed giant GlobalNet screens.

Peter's successor had been chosen. All eyes and the media cameras focused on the basilica balcony. Tailors feverishly adjusted the papal vestments to fit Masone's measurements. The silk white cassock was near perfect. Red-velvet stretch slippers over white stockings were a little too snug, but wearable for a brief appearance. He wore a mozzetta with gold trim worn over his rochet. With white skullcap and sash in place, the new pope was almost ready to greet the world. The final garment to be placed around his neck was the pallium.

The ultimate sign of a pope's pastoral office was a circular band of white wool with pendants in front and back, attesting that the passing of authority from Christ to Peter has been laid on the shoulders of the new pope. Cardinal Buldini walked onto the balcony to do the honors of announcing the new pope. Amid the crowd noise he boomed the name of the elected pontiff over the powerful sound system, waved triumphantly to those below, then quickly retreated.

CHAPTER FOUR

The recently elected pope, admired for his unassuming demeanor and strict obedience to authority, moved onto the balcony disporting a newly unveiled aura of independence, certainty and conviction. Keeping with tradition, he blessed the crush of humanity below, as well as the millions upon millions throughout the world witnessing the formalities via reflective laser view.

His infectious smile beamed affectionately upon the masses, and bore a curious air of triumph, as he gestured for silence. An immediate and collective hush befell the crowd. Intuitively, every heart embraced the sense that today they would be part of a uniquely extraordinary event.

Reflecting, as if to inhale and taste the significance of the moment, the new pope gave thanks in silence. A barely audible whisper escaped his lips midst a breath and a sigh, "Now is the time."

Gripping the balcony rail firmly with both hands, he spoke. "My brothers and sisters in Christ, I, Pope Francis, have received a message from our Lord for the faithful and all the world. It is His will that I disclose its contents one month from today. Until that time, I will be in prayerful seclusion and would entreat you to pray for me during this time. From this very balcony, at 2 PM, in exactly one month, I will share with you, the faithful, and with the world, the message He wishes to convey. Until then, peace be with you."

The multitude in the square melded into a static pool of silence. Not a ripple was seen, nor sound heard. Even the normal cries of children were mute. Anticipations dashed. Disbelief, universal. It was as though his abrupt statement eclipsed the sun, causing mass paralysis among all those within reach of his words.

Turning, not waiting for a response, he briskly reentered the room off the balcony. Facing an equally stunned gathering of high ranking Vatican officials, he pronounced, "We will dispense with the customary pompous public ceremonies and be officially installed in a private mass in my bedroom chapel within the hour in honor of Saint Francis of Assisi's Feast Day. Monsignor Lucchesi will make the official announcement and regrets to the media, and offer my apologies to the people. After the installment I do not wish to be disturbed by anyone for any reason, until I speak to the people one month from today. Understood?"

As he left for his new chambers he turned quickly, reading the expressions on each of the faces gathered before him. Then he thanked them for honoring his wishes without question.

Question him! They stood stone-like, as if frozen in time. Like human imitations of the statues atop Saint Peter's Basilica. Mouths agape, minds whirling. Cardinal Buldini was reported to have groaned, "What the hell is he up to?"

*****

The new pope remained in seclusion, adamantly refusing to favor an audience for anyone, including the now visibly irate Cardinal Buldini. As the next few days passed, Franciscan Friars arrived one by one at the Vatican, traveling from monasteries around the world. They were the only ones Pope Francis would allow in his makeshift quarters in the Archives, located in the very bowels of the Vatican. Before them, nearly buried under centuries of dust, were miles and miles of books, manuscripts, religious and secular documents and writings acquired and accumulated by the Church for well over 2,000 years. Through the millenniums, only a handful of carefully chosen Vatican officials had ever had complete access to this vast wealth of religious and world history. And only then by the personal and direct authorization of the reigning pope.

With the diligent assistance of his personally selected Franciscan brothers, the pope searched through fragile documents as though lead by some unseen hand, making copious notes gleaned from specifically chosen material.

Work filled days and nights flew by all too quickly for the excavators of the Secret Vatican Archives. The global media was in a feeding frenzy. Rumors were rampant. For the Vatican and the waiting world, time passed painfully slowly. Especially for Buldini and his conspiring band of popemakers. What was this new pope up to? This priest from the Franciscan order, chosen to be pope because of his meekness, and humble, unquestioning adherence to Church authority. Buldini's perfect choice. And what had he meant by… "Now is the time"? Now is the time for what?

CHAPTER FIVE

"New Pope Buried In Secret Archives!" Thus read the headline on the front page of the *L'Osservatore d'Italia* newspaper. A brooding Cardinal Buldini read the headline aloud. In silence he mused, *If that were only true!*

Turning his attention to the little band of unmerry-pope-makers, he bristled. "Diamante! I demand to know the names of all the Franciscans who assist Masone in the Vatican Archives, and where they come from. The rest of you, get to your sources. Find out as much as you can about what's going on down there. What are they looking for, and after they find it, what does Masone intend to do with it? Whatever it is! I must know well before the month is up. Before he speaks again from that balcony."

*****

Flipping a set of keys in Uden's direction, the pope said, "Uden, until further notice, you're the Keeper of the Keys to our Vatican Archives. I've already informed the Prefect of the Archives. He wasn't too pleased, but I assured him his duties would resume shortly. Lock the public entrance. We will all enter by the old inner door and stairway down past Pope Hippolytus' statue. Secure all other possible entrances and post twenty four hour Swiss Guards. No one other than our Franciscan brothers and the nuns from the kitchen are allowed to enter and exit the archives, unless personally approved by me."

Cardinal Uden Borne made notes as Pope Francis gave directions. He continued, "Everything should be as informal as usual within our select group. I wish to be called Dom, as I always have been when we Franciscans have gathered together. Only in the presence of others should they use my titles. Dear friend, you have been my strength through the trials of the past few days. When are the other brothers arriving? Paulo Valdarno of Italy is hard at work already. That leaves seven."

The cardinal thanked Dom for having confidence in him, checked his notes, and replied, "Christian Unhlanga of South Africa, Jan Jurewicz of Poland, Karl Kumback of Germany, and Jabal Wasitah of Egypt will be here in the morning. Kim Xinan of China, due to a political delay will not arrive for another day, but both Rico Barcetos of South America, and Nathan

Jordan of America will have flown in by late afternoon today. A working dinner is scheduled for six this evening. Is that okay?"

"Perfect! We have much to discuss. It'll be a long session, so be certain the good sisters furnish sufficient quantities of wine and beer with the meal, including a midnight snack serving. We'll need it. Inform the brothers to drink their fill. They'll be alcohol-free for the remainder of the month," he smiled, cuffing Uden's shoulder. "Advise Kim of his assignment after he arrives. Now what about living quarters? I don't want everyone scattered and isolated. We all need to be within hailing distance."

"Dom, your personal office is located in the Tower of the Winds in the Room of Meridian. We moved several bookcases, containing thousands of documents, to make room for a desk, chair and cot for napping. There's no electricity, but I had lamps brought in to provide adequate light. There's a narrow winding staircase leading to the corridors below. The climb and descent will give you all the exercise you desire," he chuckled, knowing Dom's propensity for physical fitness. "In moments of meditation the frescoes on the walls will relax the spirit. Two represent godlike figures, and the other two, pleasant scenes of past Roman life in different seasons of the year. Just below is the room where Galileo signed his confession. I find that ironic, in view of what you have in mind. Don't you?"

The pope, reading his own notes, barely raised his head, arched one eyebrow in acknowledgment, and nodded ever so slightly.

"Concerning sleeping quarters, a single corridor ramp leads from the Tower of the Winds above a courtyard to the Borgia apartments. Ten solitary cells have been prepared for us. Five on each side of the hallway. You are directly across from my room. Access to the apartments, other than the corridor to and from your office are sealed and guarded."

Dom looked up. "What if there's a fire? It's a possibility, you know."

"Then Swiss Guards are to break down all doors, otherwise, we'd be too easy of a target for our enemies." Dom smiled at his friend's astute awareness of their predicament.

"Friend Uden, as usual, you're right on top of things. And you're correct. Our enemies will grow in number worldwide once our proclamation is made at the end of the month. At this moment, that's not my number one concern.

"There are twenty five miles of documents of every description buried within the bowels of this ancient archive. Countless rooms and corridors are stuffed with cabinets and boxes, rows upon row of metal shelving as far as one can see, all housing the history of the Church and the ages. Records of murders and suspected murders, and indulgences for sins. There are thousands of volumes of requisitions for grace or favors, including numerous documents on Luther, feats of martyrs, conclusions of councils, judicial verdicts. Financial journals, tax and real estate records, claims to palaces, estates, cemeteries, and correspondence from kings and queens to centuries of popes, as well as my predecessor's decrees and letters; they're all there. And who knows how much more? Even his Holiness' Letters to his lover." He waved his hands in front of his eyes, shook his head, and took a deep breath. "Enough! We could go on for hours. We'll learn more as we investigate; as we too become coated with the dust of time."

"Pray brother Dom, answer me this. How in good Saint Francis' name are we going to find what we need in this never ending ocean of clutter? I've been told that it would take a team of experts well over two hundred years to inventory and record the thousands of loose documents alone. And add this to the dilemma. Much of the parchment is being attacked by a fungus that leaves a purplish discoloring."

Dom stood, stretched, then removed his skull cap and proceeded to blow off a small accumulation of dust. "What intrigued me most was the Prefect of the Archive's tale of secret documents that may still be hidden in the walls or obscure passageways of the archives, and the Vatican itself. This was common practice when the city was being attacked. Often the person that hid the records was killed or passed away, and the items forgotten forever. Jan Jurewicz is an electronics genius. I'm sure he can concoct an instrument to discover treasure hidden within any structure. That is part of Jan's assignment; one he'll savor with a ravenous appetite. If we could only trust the Prefect, he could prove to be invaluable to our search. We'll see."

"Your Holiness. Uh. I mean Dom. That won't be the last time any of us make that flub. No matter how close we are, it's difficult to recognize you as pope, the head of the Universal Church, and at the same time call you Dom. I'll work on it. I received a long letter today from Inge. She misses me, and the twins have the measles. She said to be sure and say you're in her prayers. Dom, once all this is over, Inge and I plan on taking a long overdue vacation. Just the two of us." Teasingly, he concluded. "And you can take care of the kids!" Both bent over with laughter, breaking the seriousness of the moment.

*****

Pope Francis sat cross legged on one of the three makeshift picnic style tables that would serve as the sequestered group's dining tables for weeks to come. With a confident smile he addressed his Franciscan confidants. "I thank you all for coming to my aide. Your unquestioning display of loyalty and friendship is most appreciated and will be rewarded via the merits of our endeavor. You all look well, except you Rico. Is that a black eye you're brandishing? Is there something we should know? Would you care to enlighten us all?"

Rico Barcetos was a short man with shoulder length glistening black hair, broad nose and thick lips. His shy reply seemed out of character coming from someone built like a five foot six fireplug. Either he was in awe of the pope, or totally embarrassed at the circumstance relating to the colorful shiner.

The collective mocking snickers from his brothers, including the pope, added to his obvious discomfort. "Holy Father, it happened as we landed in Rome. I stood too soon to reach my bag in the overhead. No sooner had I released the latch, when the pilot screeched on the brakes. The duffel fell into my eye! Now you witness what was my fault." At poor Rico's expense, the group was shamelessly howling, tears filling their eyes. The pope was the loudest, and clearly the ringleader instigating the playful banter.

Seeing Rico was genuinely embarrassed, the pope bounded from the table and gave Rico a big bear hug, then returned to the table. "Rico, we love you! I'm sorry for the teasing. And by the way - as Uden already explained, I thought - you are all ordered by papal decree to continue calling me Dom. We've shared too many good and trying times together to have it otherwise. We all came from different countries and backgrounds, yet we gravitated towards one another at the seminary. Twelve of us entered the Order together.

"Remember the old Abbot? He used to refer to us as Saint Francis' Dirty Dozen. Of course, now there's only ten. We lost Symon to the private academic sector, and Patrick killed in one of those IRA bomb blasts in Ireland twenty five years ago this Christmas. I miss them both." Dom sighed, uncrossed his legs, and shook them over the table edge in an effort to return circulation. "Then there were our clandestine gatherings on various occasions through the years to unwind and debate theology for hours on end. My brothers, we've meant too much to each other, not to be as informal as always. After all, we're going to be in each other pocket for the remainder of this month at least. Agreed? Good! Uden, please ring for the sisters to serve dinner and refreshments. I'm both famished and thirsty."

The jubilant comradery displayed during the meal set within walls covered with aged, musty tapestry and rich frescos painted by the masters, reminded Dom of ancient times when knights assembled to plan an important quest. He prayed these brown-cloaked knights would find courage during the quest he's ordered them to.

Dom rapped his fork on the side of his empty mug to gain attention above the chatter. It was time to get serious. To get down to business. However informal he encouraged them to be, it was he alone who must lead them. Resuming a sitting position on the one clean table utilized as a buffet, he began to explain why he had summoned them to Rome, and why they would be cloistered in the Vatican Archives.

"Drink up gentlemen, for it's milk, water, and iced tea here on out. Our resources must be sharp. Our minds clear. And our energies boundless to accomplish the task at hand. Our deadline is less than a month away. Based on the conversations we have enjoyed when gathered through the years, and considering my recently acquired papal authority, each of you have probably formed an opinion as to what we plan to achieve. And you're all correct in your thinking, to a degree."

Pounding mugs and whispered opinions followed. "Our joint effort in total will have a profound effect on Christianity worldwide. There are those who will praise us. Others will condemn us and do anything in their power to block our progress, even to the extent of doing bodily harm to any one of us. Including the pope. As a precaution, the entirety of our plan will not be divulged to you. The less you know, the less I risk your safety. I'm sorry for this. You must trust me. We cannot take the slightest chance of failure. The walls, halls, corridors, cells, even the privies may have eyes and ears. Jan will do his best to trim the ears, and remove the prying eyes of our foes. Cardinal Uden will pass out envelopes with each of your assignments. Paulo already has been hard at work having arrived first and not wanting to waste a single day. Jan, along with attending to our security, will have other duties. No need to open your envelopes until bedtime. Enjoy each others' company now. There will be time to read your assignments later. Uden, as my second in authority, will answer any questions you may have in my absence. Although I'm sure you understand that he cannot reveal the full extent of our labor in the archives either. Stay as long as you like. A late snack is being prepared. It's been great seeing you and being with all of you again. We'll meet here in the morning for breakfast at six-thirty sharp, directly after mass. Uden will direct you to your quarters across the suspended corridor. Good evening my brothers in Christ. Sleep well, and my God bless and protect us all. I'm already late for my meeting with the Boss."

They all looked at each other in an instant of confusion, then nodded in acknowledgment as Dom's last words sunk in. All remained and conversed until the last morsel was consumed and the last drop of coffee and beer became a memory.

*****

The pope's Tower of the Winds office was only two rooms away from the makeshift dining facility, but mercifully, the fortress-like thickness of the walls muffled the noise of renewed friendships. Besides the desk, chair, file cabinets, and cot, Uden had arranged to obtain the most important piece of furniture, a prayer kneeler Dom had requested. Tonight and in the days and nights to come the newly elected pope would spend countless hours in prayer meeting with the Boss, humbly asking for direction from the Holy Spirit. He prayed for the gift of discernment, and God's blessing and protection for himself, his group and the world. Tonight, his mind drifted along with his eyes upward to the ceiling fresco with its rendering of an ancient compass circled with child-like angels and gods of the four winds. Of particular fascination was the painting of Jacob's ladder suspended in the clouds depicting angels descending from heaven as Jacob lay dreaming. Thinking out loud he whispered, "Saint Francis, pray for me. If it was all a dream, we're all in big trouble."

*****

"Good morning my brothers. From the sounds originating from your cells early this morning, I take it you all slept well? In fact, the snoring and raucous gasps for breath were so loud in the Borgia apartments, I fully expected at any moment to see Pope Alexander VI himself storming down the hallway in search of what woke him from nearly six hundred years of sleep."

The morning was off to a good lighthearted start. Before Dom could inquire, Jan Jurewicz nodded. "The dining room, your office, and our cells are clean. At least for the time being. If we can trust the locked doors and the Swiss Guards, they should remain that way. I'll randomly sweep the areas on a daily basis, just to be on the safe side. Obviously, there's been no time to complete a full and thorough sweep of the archives. An exhaustive search and sweep would take days to complete. However, an unscientific two hour spot check uncovered dozens of such devices. They are here! We're infested with bugs."

He turned and faced his brothers and continued. "It would be my recommendation that we all follow the instructions set forth in our individual envelopes. Go about our business, and not discuss our findings with each other until we meet in either the dining room or Dom's office, and not before I make a secure check each time."

He rumbled his brow and looked at Dom. "This assignment is rather overwhelming considering the vastness of the area, and the importance of the concern for secrecy. I could use some help. At least initially."

Without hesitation, the pope responded. "Jan, you're correct in your caution. Good thinking. Jabal, you've had some experience with sensitive electronic gadgets in Coptic archaeological digs for the Egyptian government. Would you assist Jan?"

The dark Egyptian was of average height, and quite slim. His elongated face and bald shaved head brought even greater attention to his profile. The nose would have made any pharaoh proud. Not as large as Uden's, but beak sharp. With a wide smile, rivaling the width of the Nile, Jabal accepted the additional duty.

"Ah - Your Ho - I mean your Domness. Jabal is so honored. And please forgive my memory, and your wish to be referred to as in the past. Dom. Brother Jan need only point the way."

Suddenly a loud disturbance of shouts, grunts and thuds echoed upwards from the narrow stairway to the Tower and dining room. The men leapt to their feet, acutely aware of impending danger. Dom lead the way to the Tower landing. Laughter was spontaneous. The sight of a giant Oriental dressed in a friar's habit struggling up the stairs with two limp Swiss Guards, under each arm, was more than his brothers could bear. There was hardly room for him, let alone two more bodies.

Plunking them down unceremoniously, this mass of humanity faced the group to explain. "They detained me in China, and I was in no mood to be delayed once again from responding to my pope's urgent call. Dom, I am here!"

Before Dom could move or utter a word, Kim Xinan was upon him. Kim's massive shoulders and chest smothered him with affection while powerful arms embraced and lifted his friend off the floor. The gesture was repeated eight more times, leaving everyone somewhat breathless. The last member of the group had arrived. Late, but with flair.

The pope gathered himself and attended to the still bewildered and chagrined guards. They were unharmed, but their egos were bruised, and their spiritual leader didn't help matters. After soothing their ruffled feathers, he admonished them to be on guard for any further unauthorized intruders. Then he blessed them, sending them on their way with forced smiles.

"Well, now we're complete," Dom emphasized with a fist held high. "Kim, Uden will fill you in on our conversations and provide you with your assignment. Your little escapade brought something to mind. When we're working in the archives or within the Vatican grounds, leave your tunic hoods down at all times, no matter how drafty it gets. We must be able to identify each other, otherwise it would be a simple disguise for anyone to wear our habit and pose as one of the group. This way, if you see a Franciscan with his face hidden within the hood, alert the others and approach with caution. Now let's get to work."

Jan and Jabal immediately left for the archives, sensing devices in hand. Jan's typical Polish features, and ever present smile glowed with anticipation. He was hot on the trail. While it cannot be said that all Poles resemble one another, Jan's strong resolve and gentle character mirrored another of his countrymen. A proud day it was when Jan was sponsored in the seminary by none other than the robust yet spiritually gentle Pope John Paul II.

CHAPTER SIX

The rhythmic lullaby of the leisurely-moving waters of the Tiber river always had a soothing influence on Monsignor Diamante. As a grubby little moppet straying from his home in the orphanage, he would linger on the bridge connecting with the huge brown cylindrical fortress, the Castle St. Angelo, built by Pope Benedict IX in the early 1,000's AD over the remains of Emperor Hadrian's mausoleum. He enjoyed standing halfway, directly over the central arches built in 136 AD by Roman architects, and imagined lying in a boat allowing the current to carry away his fears, sorrows, and loneliness. This evening was no different. But something was amiss. He had sensed it in the Sistine Chapel before, and during the election process. It felt like an itch he couldn't scratch; a soreness in his soul that would not heal. This was inherently felt, yet he was unfamiliar with the sensation. It gnawed on the very essence of the man, no matter how much he tried to ignore it. It wouldn't go away.

The tiny bent figure in black blended with the coming darkness of night. Diamante's mind was as numb as his fingers, toes and nose in the mid-November chill. "Lord - No!" he screamed, and fell to his knees in fear as the bridge lamp lights came on without warning. The monsignor found himself surrounded by ten giant winged angels. Shaking and breathing a sigh of relief, still on his knees and with forehead touching the pavement, he uttered incoherently, "I've seen them a thousand times before, as angels sculptured by Bernini and perched on tall bridge pedestals, but tonight they looked alive. I swear they moved towards me! I'm losing my mind. I'm too old for this intrigue. Buldini will be the death of me yet."

*****

Cardinal Uden's security efforts were paying off. The archive investigations had continued for over a week now, without incident. No locks had been breached, and no information leaked. Buldini became more frustrated with each passing day, and the intensity of his anger directed at his inept disciples grew to a boiling point. He could not infiltrate the core of the Franciscans. The idea of not knowing what was going on under his very nose was a new experience he could not tolerate. Suspense ate at him like a cancer consuming his ego. With a face as scarlet as the skullcap flung at

39

those before him, and with fists waving, he demanded, "Someone do something!"

Diamante timidly half raised his hand for recognition. "Your eminence, there's hearsay that secret entrances and passageways into the Borgia apartments still exist. If one could find a way..." Before he could finish the sentence, Buldini interrupted. "Go Diamante! Go! Discover! Go now!"

*****

So it was that the monsignor visited his favorite boyhood haunt. There was a known passageway from the Castle St. Angelo to the Borgia quarters in the form of an ominous block long, three-story high wall stretching out behind rows of buildings connecting the castle and apartment complex. Unlike the Great Wall of China where a path was designed for the movement of troupes, and as an outlook to observe the enemy, this wall was intended to completely hide those using the corridor built within the wall. If only the concealed passageway inside the structure could speak, it would tell of those who escaped to the security of the castle from the apartments during periods of peril, and of mysterious guests the Vatican desired to keep secret from the curious.

Still shaking from his frightening experience on the bridge, Diamante managed to unlocked the castle. Re-locking the door behind him, he turned and stepped into a darkness like no other, a darkness sired in hell, made dense by the spirits of hundreds of tortured and slain religious prisoners. This castle was one of Christianity's open wounds. His knowledge of every turn and step made it unnecessary to use a flashlight that might jeopardize the mission. He was never comfortable with these surroundings, and tonight's encounter with the angels contributed to a foreboding atmosphere. "Now I know what the inside of an iceberg feels like."

Edging cautiously along the glacier-cold stone walls, he finally came to the entrance of the Borgia apartment walled passageway. The master key worked, and he stepped into yet another dark world, steeped in ancient fact and fiction. Diamante deliberately stayed to the side of the hidden corridor to avoid the light that from time to time spilled-over from the taller buildings to the left of the wall.

"I don't even know what I'm looking for. I might not even recognize it if I saw it," he muttered to himself. His search for secret entrances to the apartments continued until nearly dawn. Drained of energy, but quickened in spirit, the monsignor traced his steps, exiting the gloom of the fortress unnoticed. His search was a success. However, the chill born of the castle's tortured souls, and the eventual consequence of his discovery, would torment and cling to him the remainder of his life.

CHAPTER SEVEN

The land was flat, and he stood in shoulder high green grass with blades as broad as a man's wrist. An eerie feeling of foreboding primeval danger filled his being. He wasn't alone. At some distance, he could see another figure standing under a barren tree, isolated on a gray shrouded landscape that seemed to go on forever.

Looking skyward, he could barely distinguish shapes of large slim white birds with overly large wings and long necks. As the flock came closer, he saw they were flying in tight formation. It was still hard to make out any detail, but he observed what looked like small bits of color within the formation.

To the left, another flock of white birds appeared. Within the V-shape he observed tightly held pieces of twigs, tree stumps caked with mud and debris. To his surprise - attached to the debris was a bright yellow Volkswagen Beetle. Upon seeing the formations, the person by the tree discharged a shotgun. Birds to the left scattered. The broken formation caused twigs, and debris, including the Volkswagen, to plunge to earth.

The first cluster of birds, now directly overhead, opened but held formation, revealing a most beautiful and colorful sight. It was as though they were holding dozens upon dozens of different colored pieces of cloth. The sky was aglow with brilliant colors. It was an indescribable display of beauty.

Symon woke with a start. Shaking his head to bring reality into focus, he smiled when the drab, almost colorless surroundings of the cave clashed with the dream's lasting vision. This was the first dream remembered since arriving, and it was a doozy in living color.

Weeks of silence and prayerful meditation had passed without notice of time. He enjoyed the emptiness, being all too familiar with the pressures and restrictions of the past. Later he would admit that 'the dream' was the highlight of his adventure to date.

He ventured only a short distance from his roost and spent so much time sitting on the lip of the cave staring endlessly across the parched plateau below, that boredom slowly began to seep into his consciousness.

Glancing around the cave, he admonished himself for neglecting a discipline. Until now he had always been neat to a fault - one of the many qualities his mother had attempted to instill. "Pick up your clothes, turn off

43

the faucet, eat with your mouth closed, sit up straight, walk with your shoulders back," were a few of the gems of wisdom that had sunk into Symon's character during years at home. The older he got, the more her persistence was appreciated. No doubt the cave was a mess. Even the spider webs were back. Those rather large crawling furry creatures must have been busy the past few weeks. The day after arriving, he had fashioned a broom from a dead bush and a long crooked tree limb. It now lay where he had left it against the wall, and it too sported a newly constructed web.

Dust flew everywhere as the spiders scurried for cover. He had no fondness for the long legged arachnids, and chased them like a wild man laughing hysterically. *This is fun*, he thought. *I'm glad no one else is around. I'd feel like an idiot.*

All the spiders had disappeared into the thousands of nooks and crannies except one. This brave soul clung tenaciously to the roof of the cave in the far right back corner. That part of the ceiling sloped downward and was no more than nine feet high at that point.

Symon, with eyes riveted on the target, broom in hand, crept forward for the kill. He held the broom at the base just above the brush area. The plan was to squash the critter to the roof with the end of the pole. Almost there now. One quick upward thrust and it would be over. Much to his astonishment, the pole continued to be propelled upward through the ceiling into a chamber above. "Damn!" he shouted. "There's a cave directly above mine. A two story cave. How about that!"

NASA's surveillance satellite scanner had only registered a single hollow, due to the lack of density of the flooring in the upper chamber. Try as he might, the suspected room above could not be reached from his cave's vantage point. The cliffs on either side were too steep, and he didn't relish the thought of making the climb down the way he'd ascended weeks earlier. It would take too much time and energy to attempt to find a way around the mountain, then to the top, and discover a way into the upper chamber. After doing that, he'd have to repeat the process to get back to the first floor cave.

Applying the *what-if*, theory, he thought, *What if I enlarge the opening in the ceiling to allow me to crawl through?* The area was low enough, and with just two large boulders in place, one upon the other, he could stand upright, waist-high into the upper cave. He raised the broom handle and in very little time had enlarged the hole enough for him to squeeze into the chamber above with lamp in hand. The floor was fragile in that area so he proceeded with caution.

As with the lower chamber, daylight coming into the cave opening was sufficient to illuminate the area. Symon could see it was approximately the same dimension as the one below, and it was obvious it had not been occupied in recent time. But even with the thick coating of dust, he could tell that once the cave had entertained visitors. There was evidence of a makeshift table; a long slab of rock had been placed on four flat rocks, each about a foot square. The crude but serviceable top had been shoved off its pedestals.

There was no doubt as to its purpose. Someone had used it as a table, and someone had knocked it over on purpose. The slab top was too heavy to have fallen by itself, and a natural disaster would not have left the rock pedestal intact. He had entered just before noon, but now the light was beginning to fade, and in a matter of minutes any attempt to further explore the chamber would be futile. Symon decided to leave the chore for the next day, and re-entered the first floor via the newly excavated entrance. He chuckled to himself, "I have a room with a loft. Now I can invite company."

For the rest of the evening, the keen investigative mind of the professor of ancient civilizations and languages replaced the meditative friar. He could hardly sleep as his mind raced, mentally flipping through the pages of books memorized on the Assyrian and Babylonian Empires. He sensed that would be as good as any place to start. After all, this was Turkey.

*****

Symon quickly devoured the dry cereal, impatient to have a full day's worth of sunlight to 'pick the bones' of the recently discovered second story apartment. In his haste to begin, he nearly fell. A chunk of ceiling collapsed under his weight and narrowly missed crushing his knee. "Symon you fool! Be careful!" he yelled, chastising himself. "If there were enough poles and thick twigs, I could fashion a ladder, but wood is scarce in the region." Cautiously chipping away the remaining portion of the ceiling, he was satisfied the opening was safe. Scrambling up, he entered the loft apartment.

As a trained archaeologist, he was aware of the procedures for a calculated and meticulous method of sifting for artifacts. There was not enough string to design and implement a grid for the entire area. Instead, using the trusty broom pole, Symon drew straight lines on the dirt floor from left to right, each approximately a foot and a half apart. Then he repeated the exercise from the front of the cave to the back. He had his grid. The entire floor was a checkerboard. For the next three days, using a large metal food strainer, he painfully sifted the dirt in each square without a single find.

*****

On the fourth day Symon was sifting through the back of the cave where the ceiling pitched down to about three feet in height. This was the only remaining portion of the grid left to be examined. The cramped space forced him to lay flat on his stomach. It made for a most uncomfortable working position, and his arms soon tired. To rest, he rolled over on his back. From this perspective, a small opening about four inches in diameter directly above the main entrance was noticeable. The tiny hole could not be detected while standing or sitting.

A shaft of light passed through the hole generated by the noonday sun. He had noticed the beam of light the previous day as it briefly illuminated a spot on the back wall. Unable to determine its source and visible for only a minute, he dismissed it as an unusual reflection. Symon lay there in the dust accumulated over the millennia and tried to remember stories and legends of hidden treasures that had been discovered by understanding the meaning and message of a projected shaft of light. Could it be that simple? Could he be that lucky? Actually, it wasn't simple. If the elusive, shy speck of light did point the way to hidden treasure, it was an ingenious design to conceal something of value.

His "Wow" turned into an "Oh," when he suddenly got up, forgetting about an outcrop of rock overhead. "One knee, one head, what next?" he thought out loud. He couldn't move fast enough. The fragment of light had vanished almost as quickly as it appeared. There was no sense in chipping away aimlessly at the wall. If in fact there was something hidden, it had remained concealed for years, and wouldn't be going anywhere before noon the next day. And Symon had nothing but time.

*****

Another restless night. His adrenaline was working overtime. Excitement was at a fever pitch. His mind sped out of control, conjuring up all sorts of treasure to be found. He missed the anticipation of discovering something unknown. A friar's life of silent contemplation was gratifying and uplifting, and necessary to cleanse one's spirit. But this - this was exhilarating! For the first time in over a year he felt truly alive. "Symon old boy, let this experience be a lesson to you. You made the same mistake twice now. You're not cut out to be a full time friar. Wake up, it's time to live again." He said this aloud, so as not to forget.

Anxiety took its toll. It was six in the morning, and the wait for the next six hours would feel like a week. At noon today, the small ray of sunlight would appear once again and disappear in a few heartbeats. He must be there to mark the spot on the cave wall during its brief appearance. To miss it and wait another day would be unbearable. He was certain his heart couldn't stand another jolt of adrenaline.

Symon had no appetite for breakfast. The next few hours were spent in meditation and prayer, sitting in the sun on the cave's ledge and making notes in his daily diary. At 10 o'clock, curiosity won out. He could no longer stand the wait to climb up into the upper chamber, and did not want to take the chance of missing the light if it appeared sooner than expected. Armed with a chunk of chalk and a hand-size pickax, he carefully climbed into the cave and sat in the center with his back to the entrance, facing the wall. It would be a two hour wait, but that was fine. He couldn't risk missing this opportunity. The only concern was falling asleep. From time to time he moved from a sitting position to kneeling. Sometimes he sat with legs extended and elevated, shaking them to return circulation. Not once did his eyes stray from the wall - not even to check his watch.

It was a tedious undertaking; sitting - staring. Waiting. For a moment his head nodded ever so slightly. In the blink of an eye he was back on target, and not a moment too soon. There on the wall was a bright circle of light. His heart was in his throat, and he tried desperately to jump to his feet, but they were numb from nearly two hours of sitting. He stumbled forward like a drunken man, screaming encouragement to his legs. "Legs don't fail me now!" Upon reaching the wall, he hastily began to make a large circle encompassing the tiny dot of light. Three quarters of the way around the circle the chalk broke on the rough wall exterior, and by the time Symon stood up from retrieving the largest piece, the dot had disappeared. "Thank you God!" he prayed. "All I have to do is complete the rest of the circle. I've got you! If you're really there. Whatever you are."

His hands were shaking with excitement as he raised the pickax, tapping lightly around the edge of the circle. Working clockwise, the point struck hard rock. Nothing there. Before entering the circle which was approximately four feet in diameter, he decided to check the area outside the perimeter. Still nothing. Now, he meticulously began gently tapping within the circle clockwise spiraling inward towards the center. "All right!" he shouted. Two feet inside the circle, the rock wall began to chip away like dry plaster. In minutes an oblong-shaped area was visible in the configuration, the size of a large dresser drawer.

"Whoever did this, I take my hat off to them. What an inventive mind. The rock would have to have been carved out to make the cavity, then a form of plaster created. The material was molded to fill the area and sculptured to look like a natural part of the wall. He, she, or they must have completed the job by throwing fine dry dirt on the wet worked area, blending it into the dust coated walls. Whatever is hidden away, became invisible. Until now! Oh no," he lamented aloud, "I've been here too long. Now I'm talking to myself." Or could he be talking to the ingenious spirit who devised such an elaborate hiding place?

Symon managed to define the outline of the drawer. Now all he had to do was to chip a hole above the center large enough to insert the long pick, and hopefully wedge the drawer face out. He could tell that the face was not too thick. The pick caught the edge, allowing him to apply pressure, but it wouldn't budge. He duplicated the process in four different areas around the facing slab, without success. It was just too snug. The next obvious step was to chip away the area around the face, alleviating any resistance. This worked. Inserting the pick, the slab easily fell out, revealing a dark tomb-like orifice. Symon had visions of a huge nest of black furry spiders, waiting for him to insert his hand.

Gathering courage, he plunged his hand deep inside. "Aaah!" he screamed, yanking his hand out with a jerk. "It did feel like fur!" Every hair on his body stood on end. That wouldn't be attempted again. Not without first seeing what was inside. The flash-lamp was downstairs. That's what was needed.

After retrieving the light, he was ready to try again. On knees and lamp in hand, Symon aimed the light at the darkened opening. It was fur.

No, it was lamb's wool. Taking a deep breath, he reached in and pulled out a bundle. A brief dusting revealed something wrapped in sheepskin. He carefully unwrapped the decaying hide, unveiling what looked like a metallic box the shape and size of a photo album.

The anticipation was overwhelming. The tiny latch flipped open with ease. Resting inside were two separate manuscripts written in what he recognized as ancient Babylonian hieroglyphics. Instinctively, he turned in excitement to show the find to his companions, but of course there were none. In a moment's lapse of memory he forgot he was alone. *What a shame not to be able to share this discovery,* he thought.

The natural sunlight was beginning to fade, so with treasure tucked away under arm, he gathered the tools and climbed back down to the cave below, eager to decipher the writings. Then, pen and pad in hand, he set about the task of reading and recording the manuscript's message. Thankfully, the dry climate of the cave and airtight bundle had preserved the papyrus in extraordinary condition. In the glow of two bright lamps, Symon began to read and record long into the night, frozen with the fascination of the tale being told.

He couldn't bring himself to stop, and it was well into dawn when the last page of the first manuscript was finished. It was extremely old. Symon estimated a date of 415 BC. After breakfast, he began to read his deciphered account of intrigue and adventure.

CHAPTER EIGHT

Pope Francis often felt that he and his brothers were trapped in a temporal rift, prisoners of ancient chronicles, while hours rocketed by, robbing them of precious days. And the once enthusiastic group of dedicated friars were becoming uncharacteristically sullen with each evening's debriefing.

History is a hard taskmaster. Especially religious history. "Pax vobiscume," *Peace be with you*, was Dom's greeting each night as they prepared for working meals. "Or, shall I say chins up? You all look like you were chosen pope instead of me. None of you were. That's reason enough to celebrate. So cheer up, guys!"

Dom's attempt at a joke got a mild ripple of chuckles, followed by nine pensive frowns. "All right gentleman, I too am aware of what reading about our Church's bloody years can do to one's frame of mind. It can have a numbing and disheartening effect. It's quite another thing to study our two thousand plus year history in the seminary with instructors glossing over various reprehensible events, while apologizing for others, and simply ignoring hundreds of years of Church past. Now - in recent weeks we've all read the words and deeds of the clergy, kings, queens, popes and their mistresses from their own hand. Sort of up close and personal. What we've known, and much of what we never knew, has become all too real. It hurts! I feel the pain along with each of you," he admitted, pointing to his heart.

The slender German with chiseled features and short blond Dutch boy haircut was on the verge of tears. Then they swelled in his eyes and silently cascaded down flushed cheeks. He began to sob inwardly, catching Dom's attention.

"Karl, do you want to talk about it? It's obvious, something's tearing you up. We can discuss it privately if you prefer."

Gaining composure, he responded. "No, Dom. It's something all my brothers should hear. I'm experiencing a crisis of faith, but I'll be okay. Not all of you know that I'm a Jewish convert. My entire family is Jewish, and as a youngster was brought up in that faith. In my late teens, after reading the New Testament covertly out of curiosity, our Lord touched my heart. It nearly killed my parents when I converted and left for the seminary. No one in my family has ever talked to me since. I'm dead to them. Dom, you assigned me to investigate the treatment of Jews by the Roman Catholic

Church. Yes, my soul is torn by what I've learned. The injustice and cruelty directed at my forebearers by the Church for the most of two thousand years placed a burden on my Christian faith. The holocaust against the Jewish race by the madman Hitler was a recognized ungodly act. But a holocaust targeting Jews by those representing our Lord on earth is the very opposite of what He stood for. Jesus was a Jew!"

Dom's voice expressed his compassion. "Karl, you have every right to feel betrayed, outraged and disillusioned; and by the way, I was not aware of your conversion. If I had been, we would have discussed this assignment, and perhaps given you another. Please forgive my ignorance."

Cardinal Borne interrupted. "We've all been shocked by what we've uncovered during our joint process of investigation in the corridors and rooms that house records of the good and wicked deeds of those that proceeded us. We cannot deny that the Church throughout history was all too often led by a papacy shepherd more interested in personal pleasure and power than religion. The world has witnessed popes who were madmen, murderers, tyrants, forgers, fornicators, adulterers, warmongers, heretics; perhaps, even atheists. I'm certain much of this will reveal itself and more, as we all pursue our individual assignments. We must keep working if Dom's going to have the information he needs to realize his ultimate purpose - his promised report to the world.

"Karl, I'd like you to seriously consider one fact." Uden emphasized his point with a raised finger. "Then I'll be quiet and let Dom comment further. It's impossible to deny the wrongs of the past, as we cannot make apology for those injustices by simply saying they were a product of their times. Those popes, cardinals, bishops and priests who committed these deeds, had the solemn obligation to follow Christ's example and the spirit of His words. The world during those times cried out, as they do today, for spiritual direction and leadership. Many in positions of authority thought only of themselves, ignoring and prostituting His teachings."

Uden turned his attention from Karl and addressed the group. "Here's what I pray we all weigh in meditation. It's nothing short of a miracle of the Holy Spirit that the Roman Catholic Church still exists, considering so much of its history is stained with the blood of the innocent, and defiled by questionable papal history. The true saints are the laity and clergy. They're the mortar that have held Christ's Church together for most of our two thousand plus years, not the papacy. This is a miracle! God's Spirit must not have abandoned us, though we did not deserve it by our actions. And right now - this very moment in time my brothers, we collectively have been given the opportunity to change the course of history."

Perched cross-legged as usual on the empty picnic table, Dom took up the conversation. "Good advice Uden, and I agree with your analogy. While the past will attest to our share of saintly popes, martyrs, pious members of the clergy, and the religious, those that you so graphically described nearly rent the Church asunder. In fact, their ungodly actions did separate Christian from Christian, and alienated other faiths of God's world. Frankly, I don't blame them for looking at us with distrust. Luther was right. The selling of indulgences was wrong. In 1520 Pope Leo X condemned Luther for proclaiming it was against the will of God to burn heretics. The pope was dead wrong. Too bad Luther didn't stay with us. It was unfortunate he was excommunicated. Brother Karl, if you feel up to it, please provide us with a capsule version of your findings."

"Bless you Uden. I understand your words. Thank you." Karl stood at the end of the table and gave his report. "As we have all studied, the Jewish race has stood the brunt of bigotry, persecution and political domination since recorded time, and during the Crusades, thousands of Jews as well as Christians considered heretics, were murdered in Christ's name with the blessing of the reigning papacy. Let's jump forward now to hear the words and understand the attitudes of six popes from the 16th century to the 21st. In 1555 Pope Paul IV declared Jews 'Christ-killers.' He herded them into ghettos, burning the Talmud and other sacred books. They were dealt with like slaves. Many lost their lives by being burned alive.

"Even in more modern times we read anti-Jewish remarks from the papacy. Pope Pius X said in 1904, *We cannot prevent Jews from journeying to Jerusalem, and we cannot sanction such. The Jewish people did not recognize Jesus, so we cannot recognize them.* In 1965 Pope Paul VI, in effect, corroborated Paul IV's 1555 declaration that said... *After waiting for thousands of years for their Messiah, they killed Him.* "

Dom's expression mirrored the faces of all in the group. They all felt Karl's pain and frustration. Karl continued. "A ray of fresh hope, that Dom, I pray you will follow - no, I know you will, are the brief and brave words of the Pope John XXIII in the early 1960's, and John Paul II's in 1986. Pope John greeted the leaders of the United Jewish Appeal with.... *I am Joseph your brother.* And John Paul in his remarks to a chief Rabbi in a Rome

Synagogue expressed his wrath towards the hatred and persecution of the Jewish people in the past by anyone. He deliberately repeated... *By anyone.* John Paul clearly incriminated some of his predecessors and others throughout history, including the present. His courageous March 2000 apology confession and plea for forgiveness, underscored his determination to resolve the issue."

Dom now disclosed one of the fundamental beliefs of his papacy. "Karl, I believe, as well as you and your brothers, that it was not the Jewish race that crucified Jesus; it was the sins of the entire human race. And, as part of my plan yet to be completed and revealed, we intend to make that perfectly clear to all who hear our voice."

Poor Karl no longer had control over his emotions, and wept openly without shame. His torn soul was comforted upon hearing Dom's words and of his intentions.

Before going on to the next subject, Dom made an observation that set the tone for the remaining revelations. "Karl, Uden, my brothers, I am reminded of one of St. Augustine's often quoted statements, one that is significant to all known and newly discovered findings thus far. *'God has many the Church does not, and the Church has many God does not.'* We can disagree with him in certain areas of theology, but on this, he cannot be challenged.

"Oh, I shouldn't sit cross legged like that, I'm getting too old," Dom complained as he slowly edged himself off the table top and stretched his legs. "We've been putting in 16-hour days for weeks now, and it goes without saying how much your loyalty and hard work is appreciated. Thank you so much. Now - I've got a surprise. Uden, fetch the beer! You all deserve this special treat, but don't become too used to it. This time I'm holding to my word: it's the last until our work in the crypt below is completed. And unfortunately, we're rapidly running out of time."

The earlier somber mood that weighed heavily on the group and twisted their features vanished, replaced with newborn vigor and enthusiasm. Dom didn't become their leader by way of his recent election. He had always assumed that honor. His leadership qualities were infectious, and he certainly knew how to motivate those who would follow his direction. Beer or no beer, they knew his word could be trusted. They were all dying to hear of his new vision for the Church, and were thrilled to be a part of molding that future.

*****

Nathan Jordan was a quiet man from America, where the Church had become more and more liberal on various points of theology and teaching. He stood ramrod tall, a former U.S. Marine who had left the corps to join the seminary many years ago. He still wore the corps' skin-tight crew cut with pride. No one ever quite knew for sure what he was thinking. His long oval shaped face was a mask of someone pondering a momentous, earth shaking issue. Yet, deep in those clear blue eyes, a mischievous boy hid. Though pensively silent on most occasions, when he spoke he went directly to the target, without rhetoric. This was one of those times. He had the pope's ear.

"Dom, before we all retire, I'd like to bring up a subject related to my assignment: infallibility, or rather the fallibility of the pope. You for instance. The subject is too complex to discuss in the remaining time tonight, or to debate for that matter. But I respectfully request you give it consideration, so we may place it on tomorrow night's dinner agenda."

The room became as quiet as the darkened archives below. Gulps of beer remained unswallowed. All eyes were on Dom. Everyone uneasily held their breath. The only one who seemed unaffected by the enormously meaningful and pointed question was Dom, who laughed with delight.

"Brother Nathan, why did it take you so long to shoot your arrow? I've anticipated that question for days. You disappointed me until now. Yes, tomorrow night you'll lead the discussion on the fallibility or infallibility of the papacy, based on your research. And to quell all your curious minds, that is one of the prime issues we will clarify on the balcony when our thirty days of solitude is concluded. One more item before I leave. Then it's prayer time for me. I must confess, as the days pass, it seems I come to rely on His mercy more often. Karl, in due time, you will become the Vatican ambassador to Jerusalem. Similar posts will be assigned to all of you, if you so accept. Now that I've dropped that little bomb for your collective reflection - pleasant dreams my brothers."

The evening was full of surprises and theological intrigue. Dom left them sitting silently with their individual thoughts. Uden appeared privately amused as he scanned the tables to discern each reaction. After draining their mugs they passively headed across the corridor to their cells. Nathan was the first to break the silence with a barely audible observation. "I don't

55

see how I'll get through tonight and tomorrow." That was the catalyst causing a domino effect.

"Wow, me too!" "I wouldn't miss it for the world." "He's amazing!" "What's he got up that friar's sleeve next?" "Buldini will have a fit!" "Ya, isn't that too bad?"

*****

Dom was visibly exhausted, both physically and mentally, though his spirit was always refreshed after laying his burden at the feet of the Holy Trinity. In recent nights he had waited until all had retired before withdrawing to his cell in the Borgia Apartments. He didn't want to expose the group to a fatigued leader. Upon opening the door of the darkened room, he heard a slight crinkling sound as he stepped across the threshold. By now his eyes had dilated sufficiently enough to distinguish a folded white sheet of paper at his feet. He closed the door, picked up the paper, turned on the small lamp over the bed, and embarked on a mystifying reading journey that would play thief to hours of much needed rest. The strange message was written in rhyme, in a fabricated handwriting, and was an obvious warning.

"Beneath a boulder, behind a tree, or out in the open for all to see - his name is Judas. Over the bed, back of the concealed door - for personal gain he became a whore. He shares your vision, your drink and your meal - it's your thoughts he intends to steal. Messages are sent and then received - let it be known you're being deceived. Beware the hostile one without a soul, wickedness and corruption fill that black hole. Elude the nocturnal Pale Horse - or surely you'll join the man nailed to the cross. Like a vapory haze in the night, I'm here and there and then I'm not - heed this warning from a reluctant member of the plot."

Being careful not to awaken anyone and with folded paper in hand, Dom stepped cautiously across the hallway to Uden's cell. Knowing Uden to be a sound sleeper, he turned the knob and quietly slipped in. With one fluid motion he placed his hand over his friend's mouth and whispered, "It's Dom. Don't make a sound. Something vitally important has come up! We need to talk. Keep your voice down. Bring your flashlight to the far end of the room."

They sat on the floor in a darkened corner, like two school chums reading some forbidden magazine by flashlight. If the fate of the Christian world were not so threatened, and religious and political alliances not so fragile, the scene would have been comical.

"Dom, this better be good," the cardinal protested. "My energy is nearly bankrupt. What's so important? What's that in your hand? And why are we sitting here in the dark?"

Handing him the note, Dom motioned to keep his voice down. Uden nonchalantly read the message and looked at Dom quizzically. "First of all, whoever wrote this won't win any poetry prize, and secondly, if this isn't some kind of morose joke by one of our group, I'd say we have a major and critical problem."

Uden returned the note to Dom, who held the light between them so they could both study the note. Dom, looking at Uden, could not help but be amused. "If the circumstances weren't so dire, I'd be laughing right now. Do you realize when you're deep in thought, you rub and pull on your nose? It's long enough, you know."

"You can jest at a time like this?" Uden was indignant. "What a pope you're going to make!"

Dom sheepishly nodded in acknowledgment of surrender. "Okay, let's dissect each paragraph. *'Beneath a boulder, behind a tree, or out in the open for all to see - his name is Judas.'* Obviously the author is telling us a person is hiding, yet seen, and is a Judas. Both a trusted individual and a traitor. *'Over the bed, back of the concealed door - for personal gain he became a whore.'* Now we're being clued there's a secret entrance to the apartments, and the traitor is profiting in some way. The *'Over the bed'* escapes me, unless it's again telling us the person is in bed with us; close to us. One of us."

At this point Uden picked up the interpretation. "I'll try the next two. *'He shares your vision, your drink and your meal - it's your thoughts he intends to steal.'* Again he's pointing a finger at one of our group. Although the person agrees with what we intend to do, he's bent on confiscating those ideas, and based on the previous paragraphs, for personal gain. *'Messages are sent and then received - let it be known you're being deceived.'* Could it be, whoever it is, has already passed on information of our conversations and intent, and our enemies are now aware of our purpose in the archives? It's clear we're being deceived if all of this is the truth."

Dom continued his rendering. "Now the conspiracy becomes all too threatening. *'Beware the hostile one without a soul, wickedness and corruption fill that black hole. Elude the nocturnal Pale Horse - or surely you'll join the man nailed to the cross.'* This is warning of a death threat. The *'Pale Horse'* is the symbol of death. *'Nocturnal'* means the act of murder is planned sometime during evening hours. The warning was left on my doorstep; it's apparent I'm the target. We can only guess who the ringleader without the conscience is."

"Damn it!" Uden raised his voice in anger. "We know darn well who's behind this. It's Buldini!"

In panic, Dom clamped his hand over Uden's mouth, knocking the light from his grasp, adding to the moment's commotion. "Hush! Uden, you'll wake the dead! Sorry for the reaction my friend. It was a knee-jerk response. Here, hold the light and I'll continue. *'Like a vapory haze in the night, I'm here and there and then I'm not.'* Sounds as though our benefactor is someone who can come and go as he pleases. *'Heed the warning from a reluctant member of the plot.'* Uden, we may or may not have an ally in the enemy camp. At least someone who doesn't share the hostile one's taste for murder, yet remains loyal to his leader. If we can believe all this. Either way, we can't take chances.

"Let's sum it up," Dom yawned. They both stood up, stretched, and sat on the edge of Uden's bed. "If you disagree or have something to add, I want to hear it. You're the only one I can truly trust with my life. It seems we have someone in our group of brother Franciscans who is a traitor; a Judas. Someone with whom we've thus far shared our intimate thoughts, ideas that the individual champions himself, yet for whatever reason, is willing to betray, and has done so by informing the opposition of our sketchy plans. The person our poet-friend refers to as the hostile one must be in desperate straits if he has to devise a murder to halt our final proclamation. Perhaps this one has the most to lose. And, I agree. Cardinal Buldini is the most likely suspect."

"Dom, I have nothing to add. It looks like the reluctant member of the plot has done us a great favor. We can prepare to avoid the Pale Horse's sharp hooves, now that we're aware of his approach. But I don't see how we can alter, or in any way vary our archive research. And if we discontinue our evening debriefings, the Judas might become suspicious. I suggest we continue as usual, keep our eyes open, and do whatever possible to fortify the archives, your office and the cells against intruders, sympathizers and foes included. First, we should have locks placed on our cell doors. At least that will keep you out," he said with a wearied attempt at humor. "Then have Jan spot check all areas on a more consistent basis and search for that hidden entrance to the apartment."

From the weak smile on Dom's face, the sarcastic barb had hit its mark. "Uden, do two things for me when we finish breakfast tomorrow, or shall I say, this morning. As you suggest, have Jan put locks on all cell doors, and give each occupant their key. Have him and Jabal suspend their research assignments, taking whatever time necessary to conduct an adequate sweep, concentrating on uncovering any concealed entrances. The more I think about the Borgia Popes and their infamous family members, the more one can envision secret escape routes. Make sure they cover every inch of the walled walkway from the apartments to the castle. Secondly, as soon as you can, contact Cardinal Mumbwa. Thomas is one we can trust outside our group, with the exception of our Judas informer. All cardinals remain in Rome, awaiting their pope's emergence from the secret archives. Mumbwa should be easy to find. If you locate him easily, have a Swiss Guard escort him to my office to arrive at 8:30 sharp this morning, and no later than noon if it takes time to contact the cardinal. And Uden, I wish to have you there with me, too.

"Well dear friend, it's been an interesting night. There's much to do between now and 8:30, and we're still in need of a few hours rest. Based on the warning, you might consider following my lead and place a chair under the doorknob when I leave. I intend to."

CHAPTER NINE

It was a restless and unsettling handful of hours for the new pope. Between a series of disturbing and enlightening dreams, and imaginary footsteps and shuffles originating in the corridor outside his door, he had scant sleep to recharge badly needed mental and physical energies. In fact, for the first time that month, he overslept and arrived halfway through the serving of potato pancakes and thinly sliced prosciuto. He noticed the atmosphere was reflectively subdued. Without a doubt, everyone would just as soon skip the next twelve hours of investigative work and go directly to the promised discussion on the subject of infallibility.

Dom normally took cream and sugar with his coffee, but this morning he drank it black, thinking it might stimulate the senses. He had just dipped a pancake rolled inside a strip of prosciuto, into syrup, when he spied Uden marching in with a worried expression, heading straight toward the empty table where he was seated. Luckily the other two tables were full, and Dom sat alone. They could speak without alerting the others.

"Dom, if you weren't pope I'd ring your holy neck. I'm tempted to anyway! You've scared me half to death. You're never late for anything. You're always ahead of time to fault. When you failed to show up for breakfast, and thinking about the death threat warning, I naturally became concerned. I went to your cell and you were gone. I had just returned from looking for you in your office when I saw you calmly eating breakfast. What happened? The last time my stomach was tied in this many knots was when the twins were born. And by the way, the electronic sweep and search will be underway immediately after breakfast. Locks will be installed by noon. Mumbwa is anxious to meet with you in your office at 8:30. He said to tell you he's looking forward to the opportunity. Now - where were you?"

"Uden, have some coffee. I'm not going to apologize for oversleeping, taking a leisurely shower, and being late. Heck, other popes did what they wanted to do at their whim. Why can't this pope?" Seeing the wounded look on Uden's face, he explained. "Only joshing you, my friend. I truly appreciate your loving concern. My excuse. Exhaustion, plain and simple. I'm eager to examine some interesting scrolls that appear to have been stuffed haphazardly under a cabinet below the Roman scene fresco in my office. There must be thousands of such recordings of events crammed in obscure niches throughout the archives, that haven't been read in hundreds of years and never chronicled. How many could harbor essential knowledge for mankind? I'm beginning to realize that a month is not nearly long enough to provide us with all we hoped to uncover. A hundred years might not be adequate, from what we've witnessed thus far. We can only pray we have sufficient data for a brave new beginning. Finish your coffee, and I'll see you at 8:30."

*****

Borne relieved the Swiss Guard by intercepting Cardinal Mumbwa at the foot of the narrow staircase to the pope's office in the Tower of the Winds. The two cardinals chatted briefly, then headed upstairs. Dom met them at the top landing, and warmly embraced Mumbwa. After rounds of greetings and cups of coffee, they got down to business.

"Thomas, we've been friends and theological allies for a number of years now, and I could certainly use your wisdom and evaluation of what is occurring in the world above the hole we've dug for ourselves in the archives. In fact, you are the only person outside the Franciscans whom we've allowed inside the archive perimeter."

Mumbwa replied with enthusiasm. "Yes, I am aware, and you could toast marshmallows off the heat radiating from Cardinal Buldini's plump redder-than-ever face. I'm told that when he was informed of my audience with the cloistered pope, something he was flatly denied, he nearly had a coronary. It's reported he physically trashed his office in a rage; they say he threw a chair, injuring someone who hadn't yet fled the room. God forgive me for saying so, but it couldn't happen to a nicer fellow."

Dom tried unsuccessfully to curb his pleasure at the cardinal's tongue-in-cheek comment, but managed to continue with a straight face. "Thomas, you were asked to join Uden and me for three reasons. First, we trust you. Second, we want an honest and informed assessment of the present pulse of things within Vatican circles, and around the world. Lastly, we have a significant assignment for you to consider."

Cardinal Mumbwa reacted with spirited animation. "Thank you Holy Father! Your confidence in my loyalty is cherished. Let there never be a doubt. You have it to the death."

Dom stopped Mumbwa's response. "Thomas, as I have instructed the others, when we are together in private, refer to me as you have in the past, as Dom. Continue, please."

"The mood within the Vatican, within all the clergy in Rome for that matter, is a mixture of disbelief, wonderment, apprehension, puzzlement and deep concern. Of course you can imagine how Buldini and others in his camp are reacting. They're already spreading rumors concerning your state of mental health, and of a possible call for your immediate resignation. The world press is in a feeding frenzy and reporting on every rumor slithering off the forked-tongues of your detractors. It's unbelievable! To your benefit, the faithful are silently praying for the success of whatever message you have for them. Considering all the turmoil and unfounded allegations of the past three weeks, without any word from the leader of the Roman Catholic Church, I find this most encouraging. Certainly unprecedented."

Thomas took a breath and continued. "Traditional Wednesday audiences with the pope are canceled. No masses performed by the pope. No pope to meet with various visiting dignitaries and heads of state. The pope vanishes. Can you fault anyone for speculation? Yet, in all the confusion, our constituency from around the world reports that bands of the faithful are holding prayer vigils on your behalf. This is a miracle in itself! They wait with uplifted spirit for your message. One gigantic collective heart holds its breath in confident anticipation. Like I said, it's a miracle! One obvious positive result of all the intrigue and speculation is this: global attention is at its apex.

"When you appear on that balcony next, you'll enjoy the largest viewing and listening audience of any event in the history of the world. And knowing you, I'm beginning to suspect you planned it that way."

"Cardinal Thomas Mumbwa. You favor me with far too much credit," he replied with a toothy grin. "But, as you so astutely surmise, we have been blessed with the best of timing. Truly, a hand stronger than mine has orchestrated the symphony soon to be played. This we fervently believe. We thank you for your candid appraisal of the situation and of course, for your confirmation of loyalty, which is the third reason you were summoned to the Tower.

"Last evening a note was passed on to us by a Swiss Guard. It was a handwritten resignation from Cardinal Berno, citing ill health as the reason for relinquishing his duty as Secretary of State. We're reckoning he could no longer keep up the pace. He's succumbed to the relentless pressures place on him by the head of the Congregation of the Doctrine of Faith. Namely, Buldini. Clearly Berno would rather surrender the position, and keep his health. Good choice, I'd say."

Dom continued. "During the pontiff selection process, Buldini assumed the responsibility of the absent Secretary of State, as you'll recall. With the resignation of Berno, it's imperative we nip Buldini's budding power play before it flowers. This crucial position must be filled immediately. Considering your high regard for Cardinal Buldini, we could not imagine anyone more qualified to be our new Secretary of State. Thomas, you are the strength we need by our side. Someone with the necessary integrity and fortitude to stand tall against all pressures. A loyal confidant to the pope. Within this sealed envelope is the official authorization for you to assume the position this very hour. What say you?"

Cardinal Mumbwa turned to Cardinal Borne who wore a wide grin of approval, then took a deep breath while gazing at the little angels dancing on the fresco overhead. With closed eyes he blessed himself making the sign of the cross, and with all the determination he could muster on such short notice, looked his pope square in the eyes and responded. "You honor me with your trust. I accept. Thomas Mumbwa will become your ears and eyes, and protector. This I swear." And on further reflection added, "Oh my! Now Buldini will really have something to howl about. I'd love to be a fly on the wall when he hears this!" Both Dom and Uden embraced the new Secretary of State.

"Don't smile too much, Thomas," said the pope. "Your first official duty is to take the letter of authorization to Cardinal Buldini, relieving him of his assumed duty. It's I who would like to be the fly on the wall."

The smile vanished, and Thomas' head and shoulders dropped all within the blink of an eye. Just as suddenly, he stood up straight and beamed. "No! What am I afraid of? Thomas Mumbwa is taller, stronger, and handsomer than he. I just won't turn my back on him. Besides, this is going to do my heart good. Imagine, this is the first time an African prelate has been named to the exalted position of running the affairs of the Vatican City-State. My family and country will be proud. I am proud. My life is yours in Christ, my friend."

Thomas noticed the wax papal crest that sealed his appointment authorization, and said, "Your crest looks vaguely familiar."

WILLIAM R. PARK, SR.

"It's probably the capital M that you're referring to. We borrowed it from Pope John Paul II's crest. The M's in reverence of our Holy Mother. We have the same dedication to her as the saintly John Paul exhibited during his papacy. We display the crucifix in the background, and the haloed dove centered at the crossbar denotes the Holy Spirit's presence. The lone dove directly above the M panel pays homage to St. Francis. This papal crest will be unfurled from the balcony in little over a week.

"One more thing before you go, Thomas. Here's a permit pass authorizing unlimited access to the archives. Now you may come and go as you deem necessary in accordance with your new responsibilities. Uden will alert the Captain of the Guards. Welcome to the inner sanctum, and Pax vobiscume."

*****

For the friars laboring within the archive's cold sterile walls, hours moved like a snail slithering across the pages of one of the dusty manuscripts they foraged. No one could concentrate on the search at hand. Thoughts of the evening's discussion haunted and interrupted their quest with each tick of the clock. A fallible or infallible pope? The anticipation was distracting.

Time is relative, depending on an individual's focus of attention. Dom knelt in the light of numerous lanterns illuminating the Tower of the Winds, submerged in meditative prayer. Following a dozen hours of intense reflection on the various elements of his approaching address to the world, the pope felt himself collapsing in the arms of spiritual abyss. To someone fully aware there was precious little time to accomplish so monumental a task, hours travel at breakneck speed. The sheer weight of what he was expected to achieve mushroomed in his consciousness.

He prayed for guidance. "How am I to hear Your words Lord, when You've filled my mind so completely with the details of my charge? My poor mind is brimming over with a myriad of millstones essential for fulfilling what You've asked of me; to the point I have no more room to hear Your words. My cup is too full to hold any more. Lord, I need a larger cup. Bestow upon your servant the capacity to grasp and retain the necessary, while allowing room to embrace Your words in prayer. Amen."

*****

Dom made his way into the dining area, where the group had assembled for coffee prior to dinner. The conversation was restrained, the atmosphere charged. As he strode into the room, the men focused on him immediately.

With eyes wide and grins even wider, the room fell silent. "What!" he said with a frown. "You all look like a chorus line of Cheshire cats on a tree limb. What's up?"

"But Dom, don't you recall tonight's topic for discussion?"

Christian Unhlanga was the tallest South African Dom had ever seen. He was nearly seven foot tall and slender as a riverbank reed, and couldn't help but stand out in a crowd. His physical stature made him self-conscious and shy; he normally hid behind a barrier of silence. But not tonight. Much to the amazement of the others, Christian blurted out - "Are you infallible?" This was so out of character, no one could help themselves. The group, including Dom, broke into hysterical laughter.

"Christian, if I could reach that high I'd kiss you!" replied the pope, wiping tears away. "To be honest, the topic was forgotten in the long process of writing my papal address. However, I'm sure we're all ears and anxiously waiting Nathan's evaluation of his findings on the subject. Of course, we personally have an opinion, and I'm looking forward to hearing if Nathan and I agree. Uden, please inform the sisters we're ready to eat. After dinner and over evening coffee we'll digest both our food and the issue at hand."

A swarm of locusts couldn't have devoured an acre of grain any faster than the Franciscans consumed their evening meal. Dom was hardly half through when the others were refilling their coffee cups, and Nathan stood to relate what was recorded in the archives on the subject of papal infallibility.

"Dom, my brothers, since we're all more interested in what the newly elected pope has to say about this highly volatile and controversial theme, I'll just hit the highlights of my research, omit lengthy commentary, and be as brief as possible.

"Linus was the first recorded pope, reigning from 67-76 AD. Peter, who was never considered a pope during his lifetime, was however bestowed the distinction hundreds of years after his death, making him the first practicing pope. We're fully aware that Peter made numerous mistakes prior to our Lord's crucifixion and after. If it hadn't been for Paul's intervention, Peter might have taken Christianity down the wrong path. In 1869, Pope

Pius IX called for the first Vatican Council. They jointly declared a pope to be infallible. His edict didn't end there. In disagreement with the fifteenth century Council of Constance's decree that a pope is subject to the General Council, he further declared that the Church obtains its faith from the pope, not the General Council.

"Dozens, perhaps a hundred popes, contradicted one another in sundry ways, even charging a predecessor with heresy. For instance, Pope Formosus (891-896) was exhumed after he had been dead almost a year and accused by Pope Steven VII with being elected dishonestly. After the charge, Formosus' body was tossed in the Tiber River, then retrieved and reburied. Now get this. Ten years later Pope Sergius III again exhumed Formosus, and censured him anew. He went for another swim in the Tiber, this time minus his head. Somehow the headless body was found and was reburied in St. Peters.

"In the early thirteenth century Pope Innocent III contended he was subject to no law, even if it was evil, because no one had the right to judge the pope. Later, Pope Gregory proclaimed the pope to be lord and master of the universe. Pope Boniface VII later declared; *'I am pontiff, I am emperor.'* And as others had done before him, he made his nephews cardinals, bestowing land and precious valuables to his family. In fact, several popes had sons who became popes."

Nathan remained standing now, and begun to nervously shift from one foot to the other. "Sex seemed to be a preoccupation with many popes. Pope Benedict IX, in the eleventh century, abdicated in order to marry. The woman he loved was his cousin. She refused him, so he wanted the papacy back. Two popes I came across were murdered in bed by jealous husbands. Still another two were charged with incest.

"Early on, and for almost two hundred years, there were three dozen popes. Many were elderly and feeble, some in their early twenties; a few were teenagers. A number were banished for one reason or another; some murdered. Others were out-and-out fakes. In the tenth century, Pope Benedict V fled with the Church's finances after disgracing a young woman. And, oh yes, he too was slain by an outraged husband.

"At the beginning of the eleventh century Pope Gregory VII enforced clerical celibacy, in effect making harlots of thousands of wives; severing husband from wife, father from children. It's reported that hundreds of faithful wives took their own lives. His excommunication's of kings for personal profit incited bloodshed throughout the world. He was accused with forging and altering Council documents to back his claims. It's assumed many are included in today's Canon Law. He proclaimed the Roman Church has never erred, nor could it ever. And that a justly elected pope is a saint by being Peter's direct successor.

"Here's another bit of evidence supporting the preoccupation with sex and personal fortune. It was Pope Julius II who pressured Michelangelo into making the newly constructed Vatican a grand piece of art. Another accomplishment was to father three daughters in spite of syphilis devastating his body. And for those of you unaware - Julius II was a Franciscan.

"Popes had many schemes for increasing their personal fortunes. Pope John XXII, (1316 and 1334), excommunicated eighty members of the clergy for not paying their taxes, including archbishops, bishops and abbots. And for the right amount of money, you could receive forgiveness for any crime.

"An early Synod in Rome condemned torture. Pope Nicholas I said torture was a violation of divine law. In the sixth century, in spite of Gregory I's ruling that a person's testimony during or after torture should be discounted - torture approved by the pope was the norm for hundreds of years when dealing with those considered to be heretics. As we know, thousands of Christians considered heretics were slaughtered during the Crusades. Pope Urban II, in the eleventh century, declared that heretics were to be tortured, then killed. In the thirteenth century Innocent III had a reported 12,000 Christian heretics killed in one day. Soon after, Gregory IX created the Inquisition, proclaiming it was the responsibility of every good Catholic to find, torture and kill heretics.

"Here's something you'll all be interested in hearing. In the fourteenth century, an angry Pope John XXII said that if the Franciscans didn't cease professing that our Lord and the apostles lived in poverty, they would be burned as heretics. In 1816, Pope Pius VII finally put an end to the practice of torturing heretics.

"We've now witnessed evidence of papal fallibility. In fact, several popes were themselves excommunicated for considered acts of heresy. But here's proof positive of papal err. The 1546 Council of Trent advocated the writing of a new edition of Saint Jerome's original Bible. Forty years later, Sixtus V decided to personally write the new edition. His version was to supersede all other Bibles. It was printed and distributed. Within two years, all copies were found and destroyed. The pope's rendering of the Bible was error filled, and many passages were missing. It was re-edited and again made available."

Nathan saw Dom's right eyebrow twitch, his nose wrinkle, and thought it wise to wrap it up, and not tax his patience any further. "In conclusion - yes Dom, I'm about to conclude my briefing. Here's what three popes said, who reigned between the twelfth and sixteenth centuries, including a saint, regarding fallibility. Innocent III conceded he could be judged by the Church for any sin, even on the subject of faith. Innocent IV agreed the pope could err on the subject of faith. And Adrian VI also admitted a pope can err. St. Augustine once said that when a pope had made a decision, that was the end of it. Still, he disputed several pope's resolutions, and when he failed to change their minds, called in Synods to resolve the situation."

Nathan took a deep breath, made an audible sigh, and ended with a question. "I ask you all to decide. Was Pope Pius IX correct when in1869 he declared a pope to be infallible, or do the deeds of the popes we just unearthed speak for themselves? Please remember, I only disclosed a bit of past pontifical history. Dom, the floor is all yours."

Dom refilled his coffee cup, and while others followed suit, took the now familiar seat atop the vacant picnic table. He ran his fingers through the mass of short dark curls, lowered his head in thought, pausing momentarily, then with a half erect head and upraised eyebrows, admitted, "I'm not in too good a company, am I? The evil, unacceptable and unjust actions of some can overshadow the virtues displayed by many righteous and charitable popes throughout our religious history.

"I say to all now, that within my own conscience, I cannot agree with Pope Pius' claim. All the evidence is in favor of fallibility. I agree with Dante when he said that the papacy's passion for power incited fracture within Catholicism. The pope's claim of infallibility certainly fanned the flames of division. That issue we must very cautiously address, but need more time to study the possible consequences of announcing my opinion, pro and con.

"Thank you, Nathan, for your exercise in papal dissection. While we consider which position to publicly embrace, I've got to wrestle with writing the speech we are to deliver. I'm counting on all of you to give me your thoughts on the subject of infallibility. Place your decision on paper and slip it under my cell door. I welcome your input. Tomorrow evening's topic is also a key element of our address and will be examined by Paulo Valdarno.

Since Paulo's permanent residence is in Rome, he received the first assignment. It was perhaps the most difficult task of all, with so many intangible incidents, blind paths, and forked roads. Interesting? I, for one, look forward to brother Paulo's appraisal of his findings.

"Pertinent to tonight's subject, and before we prepare to turn-in, I'll leave you with two quotes and another possibility to ponder. It was St. Augustine that said something like, *'Any institution owning beliefs that all know to be unsound are apt to get itself laughed at.'* And during the sixteenth century a Jewish Rabbi is quoted as saying, if I can remember it correctly, *'Changing, censuring and denouncing the views and expressions of those who hold beliefs contradictory to our teaching, weakens our own.'* Four centuries later, Pope John XXIII declared *'That everyone has the God given right to worship Him within their own conscience, and to demonstrate their religious beliefs openly or in silence.'"*

Dom slipped off the table with his usual groan, bent his legs a few times, and grinned. "Now here's something else to ponder as you recite your evening prayers. What do you think of developing a representative, democratic, conciliar, and synodal approach to Church government? Of course, the pope would preside. And lastly, what do you think about summoning a worldwide conciliatory ecumenical council encompassing the leaders of all believers in One Creator? These two considerations would no doubt be catalysts providing us with new friends as well as new foes.

"Let me now share with you a boyhood event that has always haunted, yet pleased me. When in my early teens I was called to my grandmother's deathbed. She wished to see me in private, and revealed this story. As with so many of her generation, and those before her, she had been taught that Catholicism was the only pathway to the Father. The night before my visit, she had a dream that she died, thus arriving at a long narrow corridor with numerous doors on either side. On each door was the name of a particular religious denomination or faith. Naturally she choose the door denoting her own persuasion. Once inside, she was surprised to discover all doors opened to the same place. She was so pleased, she told me that now she could die happy. And she did. Grandmother passed smiling that evening."

Dom threw up his hands as a silent message that the session was over, and he and Uden led the way to their cells. When the two were well ahead of the group that lagged behind deep in debate and conversation, Uden turned to his brother and said, "For a minute there I thought you were going to explain your mystical experience with the Assisi crucifix."

"Oh no!" replied Dom. "That secret will remain just that, and will follow us to our respective graves."

*****

Only a few minutes had passed since the apartments had quieted, when a light tap on Dom's door interrupted his prayers. After fiddling with the newly installed lock, he found Uden standing in the darkened hallway. "Dom, do you have an extra pillow? The sisters failed to replace the one I had when they stripped my bed to change linen."

"No, but you can have mine," came a sleepy reply. "I never use a pillow anyway. A rolled up towel beneath my neck is all I need. It helps my jaw and neck ailment. I've been cursed with the problem for years. Here. Sleep well, dear friend."

"A word of caution, Dom. Next time, don't open your door without first asking who's there. Okay? See you in the morning."

CHAPTER TEN

As one could imagine, breakfast was animated. Dom sat down next to Kim and inquired if he had seen Uden. He had not. When Uden had not arrived by the time Dom had finished his first cup of coffee, he asked Kim to see if Uden had overslept, and sent Jan and Jabal to look for him in the Tower of the Winds. *Now it's my turn to worry,* he thought to himself.

Uden wasn't in the Tower. Kim reported that his cell door was locked, and he hadn't responded to knocks. "Kim, come with me," Dom directed. After numerous bangs with the side of his fist and no reply, Dom ordered the giant Oriental to break down Uden's door. The ancient dried-out wood splintered with a resounding crack. If possible, Dom's heart would have echoed the sound. Uden was in his bed. He wasn't breathing, his face already turning blue. The shock was too much, and Dom's knees buckled under him; Kim eased his fall. From a kneeling position and between heavy sighs, Dom struggled to speak. "Kim, inform the group, but tell them to remain calm and to stay in the dining room until I arrive. Also, find Cardinal Mumbwa. Don't tell him of the situation, just that I need him to come immediately. Please leave me now."

The sun seeping through faded and cracked shades created eerie scattered shafts of light. One lay motionless, the other on his knees, with arms enshrouding his fallen brother; his body shuddered with every breath. Exhausted from the ache in his heart, Dom rested back on his heels and fought to control the tears choking his words. "Oh my dear Uden, what shall I do without your strength, encouragement and wisdom in the hours, and turbulent days and years that will surely follow me? And Inge. The twins. How can I find a merciful way to ease their pain? There is no easy way. Oh, I'm so sorry. So sorry.

"I swear that whatever my papacy accomplishes, your spirit will ever be beside me. This I know. You will remain in my thoughts and memory until we meet again. Now, gazing down from God's everlasting day, you can see if we eventually prevail in our quest. Direct me if you can. Redirect me if my path wavers. Continue to be a source of strength. This I pray with all my heart and soul. Our loss is our Lord's gain. May He bathe you with the warmth of His light. Amen."

Dom sadly performed the last rites for the man he truly called brother, and concluded just as Cardinal Mumbwa entered the room. "Dom, they told me what happened when I passed your people in the dining room. Was it his heart?"

"It looks that way, Thomas," he sighed, wiping tears away. "We'll know for sure when the local coroner completes an autopsy. That's the norm here in Rome. I was not aware of any health problem, and I'm not certain Uden would have told me. He was a proud and sometimes stubborn man. Much like me. Thomas, would you see to it that the body is cared for, and prepared for his journey home to the Netherlands. He would want the service and interment to take place close to his loved ones. And, make every effort to keep Uden's passing confidential. I'll take care of my group. Inform the authorities of my desire for secrecy. The Vatican Secretary of State will make the announcement at the right time. Not before. I don't want Inge to hear the devastating news secondhand. She must be told personally, face to face, by someone close to the family. As much as I would like, there's no time for me to make the trip."

Dom covered his friend with a sheet, closed the door, and walked slowly down the corridor; Thomas placed a steadying hand on his shoulder. "Thomas, here's where you can be of further assistance in this matter. You remember Symon Carpenter from our seminary days? Before reverting to civilian life as a college professor, he was the twelfth member of our Franciscan group. Uden was his best friend and confidant. Their families visited each other whenever possible. Symon would be the perfect choice to break the news to Inge. Find him for me. The last word on him was after his wife died, he resigned his post at Oxford and faded into obscurity. We too, were close. Symon is someone I could trust without question. Find Symon. One other thing. I want that autopsy report as soon as possible. And let the coroner know in no uncertain terms that Uden's body must not be violated."

*****

The dining room, once a place of laughter and enthusiastic theological conversation, was mournfully still. Everyone sat in a state of shock, and muted silence, waiting for Dom's appearance.

Long days and even later hours, the weight of the papacy, and now the death of his dearest friend took its toll on Domenico Masone. The once erect frame arched under the burden; his chest fallen from a heart ripped asunder. Each step was slow and deliberate. He would have preferred not to confront them, suffering the pain and loss in privacy. But he was their leader. He was the pope who had a Spirit-given trust to perform. There was no turning back.

He took a deep breath, forced his shoulders back, and lifted his chin high before entering the room; the redness of his eyes could not be disguised.

Dom faced his seated brothers, clasped his shaking hands, and spoke. "We have all lost a dear friend this day, but just as we're aware of Uden's strength and courage, he would insist we build on that knowledge and forge ahead in accomplishing what he gave his life to achieve on behalf of our Lord and Savior. Let us all dedicate our search today in his memory. We'll pass on tonight's debriefing. Paulo's evening accounting will be deferred one day. Prior to dinner this evening we will gather to say mass for Uden's safe passage, and for the spiritual support of his loving family." He raised and shook one finger for emphasis. "One last thing before we return to our assignments. Breathe not a word about Uden's death. It will remain unannounced until we can break the news gently to the family. Not before."

*****

Concentration was hopeless. The advent of Uden's death hung like a leaden shroud cloaking and suffocating any attempt to focus on individually assigned areas of investigation. The dark brown walls, the crusted ceilings and tired floors in the timeworn archives attracted more attention than the weathered books, scrolls and documents. The brother lost consumed their collective minds as the day turned to night. The meal after mass mirrored earlier emotions. Dom, hardly touching his food, bid all a good evening and left to retire unusually early.

The apartment corridor was darker than normal due to a burned out wall fixture, forcing Dom to hesitate until his eyes adjusted. As he was about to insert the key to his cell, he turned and noticed the door to Uden's room was ajar. Pushing the door open, he stepped inside and was taken back by the lingering scent of the man he loved as a blood brother. The ache in his heart deepened, as moisture veiled his eyes. He closed Uden's door behind him, and stepped across the hall to his cell. The scant light, the blinding tears and a quivering hand made inserting the key near impossible.

As once before, he heard the crackling of paper under his sandals. Turning on the light, he counted nine sheets of paper that had been slipped under the door. He had completely forgotten the fallible, infallible opinions.

75

He would read them in the morning, but right now needed sleep to restore his energy. The thought entered his mind, *It's been the worse day of my life. So far!*

He immediately dropped into an abyss and when the first light woke him, he sat straight up, startled by the thought; there were nine sheets of paper. Not counting himself, there were nine brothers. Uden could not have slipped his recommendation under the door today. That left eight. Who had left the ninth sheet?

The count was six for fallibility. One presently undecided, one abstention. And one unsolicited poem which Dom read in horror.

"From beyond the concealed door rode the Pale Horse who came for one, yet sent another the way of the cross.

"On the bed where to lay the papal head, unknowingly rested the other in his stead.

"A venomous vapor he receives, murderously ordained by the father of thieves.

"Peril remains so heed this warning - the Reaper rides anytime, day, evening or morning.

"No pleasure is taken in the design of this plot, an innocent man's death made heavy my heart.

"No more can be said for fear of being found, thus to join him beneath the ground."

"Dear God!" He shouted. "No. No. It's can't be! Uden was murdered. He died in my stead. He died in an assassination attempt on me. Oh, poor Uden, forgive me."

Through misty eyes Dom reread the poem to fully interpret its message. Forcing his breath to calm and his mind to focus, he came to a conclusion. "Through a concealed entrance, yet to be discovered, the assassin came for me, and Uden mistakenly became the victim. The papal head lies on a pillow. The pillow Uden borrowed. Venomous vapor? There must have been some kind of undetectable deadly fumes emanating from the pillow. And since they missed their target, they'll be bolder next time.

"Obviously, the poet's loyalty is torn, yet fears for his life if caught." For the first time in his life Dom felt a rage, a hatred he never thought possible; it scared him, and would be a further source of torment in the days ahead.

Filled with guilt and grief, he clung to his Jesus Prayer, repeating it over and over to center his spirit and calm his person - "Jesus Lord, Jesus Christ, have mercy on me."

Dom entered Uden's room quietly so as not to wake the others. The linens, including the pillow, were missing. It was a good guess the sisters had burned everything the deceased slept on; a superstitious practice. Any evidence of a poisonous pillow was most likely destroyed.

Dom rapped softly on Jan's door. Apparently surprised to see his visitor, Jan invited him in, but Dom placed his finger to his lips, and whispered, "Get dressed. Don't wake the others, and meet me in my office. We have work to do."

*****

Jan carefully maneuvered his way through the darkness across the hanging corridor, past the dining room and to the Tower of the Winds. It wasn't until entering Dom's office that he made his first false step. The only light, struggling to illuminate the Tower office, was at the far end, over the stairway leading down to the archives. The sound of Jan knocking a portable file to the floor jolted Dom out of a prayerful meditation on the kneeler.

Unaware of Jan's arrival, he let out a guttural howl, which in turn launched Jan into releasing an equally frightening yell. "It's Jan. Is that you, Dom?"

"You scared me near to death," came the reply. "I didn't hear you enter. Here, I'll turn on all the lamps and give us some light.

"Jan, you've done an excellent job of security, but recent events suggest that there is a secret entrance to the Borgia Apartments. You must find it, or them. Do whatever is necessary. We don't have much time."

"Yesterday afternoon the latest state of art portable sonar detection equipment finally arrived so we can immediately start searching for hidden wall panels and passages. If an entrance exists, we'll discover it."

Jan left just as Cardinal Mumbwa entered from the archive stairway. Making himself comfortable in the only stuffed chair, he reported. "Dom, there's news about Symon. After resigning from the university he headed off to attend a conference in Moscow, then mysteriously vanished. I just got off the phone with an old student of mine, Peter Yosof, in Tbilisi. By sheer luck, he knew of Symon's disappearance. In fact, he assisted him. Would you believe it? Symon's living illegally in a cave in the mountains of Turkey."

"Yes I would! He always was a free spirit. I must confess, at times I envied his ability to detach himself and his courage to pursue new adventure. Turkey. No, doesn't surprise me at all. It almost saddens me to spoil his fun, but, we need him here. Immediately! Thomas, call Peter and ask him to find Symon and give him a message. Here, I've written down what Peter must relay to him without delay."

Placing the folded note in his cape pocket, Thomas explained the remainder of his phone conversation. "Peter knows you want Symon found, and most likely want him to come to Rome. That much I told him. He estimated it would take two to three days until Symon could arrive. I'll phone Peter right now, if you like, and give him instructions and your message for Symon. It might be best if I use your secured phone, and not the one in my Vatican office. Before I do, two things."

Dom nodded for him to continue. "The autopsy revealed nothing unusual. The cause of death was heart failure, although no sign of heart disease or disorder was evident. 'Just one of those unexpected things' was the coroner's explanation. Second, Buldini's taken care of. Surprisingly, I had no problem at all. It was almost as though he already knew of my new position. And I suppose I have a confession. I actually felt a twinge of disappointment. I was all prepared to do battle, yet Buldini was so conciliatory that it took the wind out of my sails."

Dom frowned and shook his head. "Thomas, make that call, and then we must discuss what I uncovered concerning Uden's untimely death. I also need you to accompany me for a visit to Cardinal Buldini's residence. There are two gray capes hanging behind that partition we can put on. Then we'll slip out the library side door unnoticed."

*****

The two figures blended well into the obscure shadows of buildings silhouetted by the first hint of dawn. The home and headquarters of the Doctrine of the Faith, once known as the Palace of The Inquisition, was a stone's throw from St. Peters. Halfway there, Cardinal Mumbwa stopped abruptly, steadying himself at a stone barricade. Dom had just finished

78

telling him of the botched assassination attempt, and how Uden died needlessly. The revelation took Mumbwa's breath away. "What are you going to do, Dom? Is this why we're heading for Buldini's house? Are you certain he's behind this heinous crime?"

"My friend, at this moment I have no proof, but I'm bound and determined to face him down. The other cheek will not be turned! Not in this case, it won't. Even Jesus openly displayed anger when He physically ejected the money lenders from the Temple. One of the reasons you're with me is to be my conscience, to see to it my own anger is managed. There's a degree of wrath within me I never knew existed. It frightens me."

The huge foreboding mansion loomed on the corner with its brooding facade and bitter history of torture and death in numerous dungeons, home to Cardinal Buldini and the CDF. They found the outer door leading to a small foyer unlocked. However, the two massive black hand-carved doors just inside were locked. Dom undid the cape tie, removed it, and tossed the cape to Thomas. Ignoring both the buzzer and cast iron knocker, he proceeded to fiercely pound on the door with his fist until an aged servant opened it with an alarming wail - "Your Holiness, it's you!"

The old man moved aside as quickly as his weary limbs would allow, arthritic finger pointing to the gold leaf French doors directly ahead. Without knocking, Dom flung open the doors, and strode in with dramatic flare, taking Buldini clearly by surprise. There he sat, stuffed behind a huge seventeenth century dining table, eyes and mouth agape, the remnants of a last spoonful of soft boiled egg dripping down his chin. The room was an antique dealers fantasy: ornate furniture designed for kings, surrounded by dozens of priceless oils painted by the masters of several ages. Dom's attention was focused on the excess of flesh before him, oblivious to the extravagance. However, Thomas absorbed all in sight and made a mental note before turning his own attention on the scene before him.

"Masone, uh, Holy Father, this is quite unorthodox. We simply do not..." Buldini's words froze in his mouth, as Dom seized the edge of the embroidered tablecloth, yanking it sideways. Food, silverware, candelabras, and a chalice of wine all flew in different directions, causing an unholy clatter as they came to rest on the floor. Buldini was so stunned he flung his huge arms upwards and over his head without realizing the circumstance of his action. His balance was lost, and he and the chair tumbled helplessly backward in a thunderous crash. Dom bounded forward, placed his right hand on Buldini's massive girth, and on one knee bent over to whisper words only they would hear. "You unworthy loathsome wearer of the Red Hat. If and when we have proof that you ordered my assassination, and murdered a man you were unfit to be in the same room with, pope or not, I'll personally strip you naked and drag you by that ponytail to one of the dungeons below. There you'll rot until you've finished devouring the flesh of your fellow rodents. Beware Buldini, beware!"

Dom stood up, turned and smiled at Thomas, who was stunned at what he had just witnessed. Throwing Dom his cape, he commented, "If I didn't think it beneath my position, I would have applauded, although I must confess, for a minute there you had me worried."

Dom cast a meaningful look at Buldini, "Thomas, so was I. However, I feel somewhat better now. Let's go."

As they walked towards the door, they passed the frail figure of Monsignor Diamante coming in from an early morning walk. He scanned the shambles on the floor, and his boss still on his back, then peered at Dom and Thomas. His expression queried, "What?" but he remained speechless. Dom looked into Diamante's eyes, nodded, and said, "The elusive poet, I presume?"

*****

When Dom and Thomas returned to the Tower office, a message was waiting from Peter Yosof concerning Symon Carpenter. It reported Peter was having trouble finding the pilot who had flown Symon to the cave. He was the only one who could identify the exact location. Without him, a search would be useless. Peter would do his best.

"Dom, I have a recommendation. After seeing the number of valuable possessions in Cardinal Buldini's Vatican owned villa, I think it's imperative we conduct an itemized inventory in all Vatican held property. The existing Vatican Museum and adjoining building inventories should be included in the investigation, and cross-referenced with Buldini's inventory. The result could prove most interesting."

Dom nodded in agreement. "I like the way you think, Thomas. Include in your inquiry an accounting of the Cardinal's Vatican Bank holdings and any international assets. Also, those of his close associates. Dig. Let's see what floats to the surface." He sighed. "But right now I must get back to preparing our address to the people."

Cardinal Mumbwa hadn't been gone five minutes when Jan burst into the Tower, exploding with excitement. "Dom, Dom, I found it! I found the secret entrance, and you won't believe how complex the passageways are!" Dom followed Jan, who was in a near trot like a hound on the scent of a fox.

"Dom, open your cell door," Jan ordered in his enthusiasm. They stepped inside, and Jan immediately went to the closet, opening the door. "See that small inconspicuous hole in the right front corner? The location is almost unnoticeable. It's practically invisible." Jan leaned over and inserted a bent coat hanger into the hole. With a tug, the closet floor raised up enough for him to place his fingers under the lip and lifted the panel. The entire floor was a hinged trapdoor.

"Dom, let's go to Uden's room." They crossed the corridor, entered the room and went directly to the closet. "You see, the same kind of hole, and below the trapdoor is a short wooden ladder, just like in your room. In fact, each apartment room has the same entrance-escape capability. Anyone in any room could come and go unnoticed. As we all know, there's a high wall walkway leading from the Castle St. Angelo to the Borgia Apartments. At the end a finished closed-in stair structure ascends to the main apartment rear entrance, which is bolted from the inside. Here's where the portable sonar unit proved invaluable. When we scanned the stairs from the end of the wall to the apartment entrance, a framework became visible inside the existing set of stairs. The stairs appear to be a solid seamless structure from top to bottom.

"However, if one places both hands under the lip of the first bottom step, and lifts, the next six steps are hinged on the inside, revealing a second set of stairs within. Taking the hidden stairway upward, I discovered the outside walls of the apartment complex are not singular, but double-walled. There's an approximate two foot wide walkway between both walls, extending the length of the building. This accounts for the extra wide windowsills in the rooms. The same is true of the top apartment floor and the ceiling of the quarters below. Between the two floors, there's a comfortable crawl space reaching to the far side of building. Off both double-walled spaces, and a short distance within the crawl space, are ladders leading into each cell's closet trapdoor. I can only guess that the secret passageway was used in time of peril to escape capture, or to come and go

81

unseen on some clandestine venture. Maybe as a way to smuggle in and out a person of mystery. If you get my drift."

"Good job Jan. This is amazing, and it does answer at least some of the mysteries we've got around here. Dom studied the trapdoor, stroking his chin. "Let's keep your discovery between the two of us for the time being. And, to be on the safe side, why don't you install a padlock on the inside of the hinged stairway. Hopefully that will shore up security measures." Dom slung one arm across Jan's shoulder. "You've been a tremendous help. Right now, I have to return to my notes. See you and the others this evening for dinner and debriefing."

*****

Very little of the meal was consumed this evening, and communication among group members was limited to an occasional request for someone to pass salt or pepper. Small talk was nonexistent. Uden's death weighed heavily on their minds. Dom was the first to raise his voice above a whisper. "Our dearly departed brother would be the first to remind us of our duties. And that would be to go forward with renewed passion. Therefore, while we continue to pick at our food, Paulo, why don't you apprize us of your findings?"

Paulo Valdarno was born in Italy, and before receiving Dom's call, had been cloistered in an abbey outside Rome studying the effects of early day canon law and its application to current Church and secular issues. Slight in build, and nervous by nature, he wore his thinning brown hair in long strands that framed a narrow face. Thick wire brim glasses were slightly skewed, and more than one fellow Franciscan had told him he bore an uncanny resemblance to Pope Pius XII.

Paulo fidgeted with his spoon while he spoke. "Dom, your assignment, what you asked of me, has turned out to be - simply impractical, not feasible. The information was unattainable. The accounting records of history are either fragmentary, nonexistent, or remain buried among thousands - no, millions of books, scrolls and documents within the archives. I can only guess that more records exist in churches, castles, abbeys, and who knows where - in Rome, throughout Italy, and in other countries. Dom, I just cannot do it!" Paulo's shrill voice cracked, as his manner grew more and more agitated. He began to shake uncontrollably.

"Paulo, it's all right." Dom said, his voice lending reassurance to his words. "We really appreciate your efforts. You did more than your share of work this month. I knew your assignment was difficult if not impossible for the very reasons you characterized. But it was an assignment that needed to be explored, and you were the person to accomplish the assignment. You did your job well."

A little color returned to Palo's cheeks as Dom explained. "We needed to know if sufficient records exist to consider returning money and possessions to families who lost their worldly belongings due to conspiracies or unfair exploitation during the Church's darker moments in history. Because of Paulo's fine effort, we have now confirmed that this idea is not feasible. However, all is not lost. We have a plan that will satisfy our original concept of sharing Vatican resources with the less fortunate throughout the world. This will become crystal clear soon enough. Before I bid you all a good evening, and because you are all so deserving, it is only befitting I divulge an account of betrayal, an assassination attempt, and a murder."

*****

Breakfast this morning was considerably more animated than the previous. Each assignment had been concluded, or was near completion, lifting a tedious millstone from their shoulders. They now could relax and wait in anticipation for Dom to put all the pieces of the puzzle in place. He had lifted the order not to discuss their individual projects, so intriguing dialogue prevailed amidst the servings of pastry, fruit, and large platters of pancakes.

An understandable undercurrent of somberness only slightly dulled the edge of outright enthusiasm. After Dom's disclosure and interpretation of the two poems and dreadful consequence, he had sworn them to secrecy, at least for the immediate future. Regardless of that request, no one had it in their hearts to discuss the loss of their fallen comrade.

"Christian, have you seen Paulo this morning? Has anyone seem him?" inquired Jabal.

"No!" Came the overall response.

Jabal persisted. "Dom, I'm concerned. Paulo's frame of mind was not favorable when we retired to our cells last night. He was visibly despondent.

I could hear his pacing up and down in his cell. I think I'll check to see if he overslept."

Within minutes, Jabal returned with a note in his hand, and a look of utter disbelief on his face. "Dom, read this!" he blurted out. While Dom read the note, Jabal went on. "The bathroom at our end of the corridor is locked from the inside, and the shower's been running for hours. Paulo must be in there! We must do something!"

Dom quickly led the way across the bridged corridor to the apartments and the bathroom at the far end.

"Kim, do the honors." With that order, Kim lifted his right foot, and with one swift kick of the bottom of his sandal, the door flung wide. Rico rushed into the steam filled room, reached for the hot water knob in the shower and turned it off.

"He's here!" shouted Rico.

The group pressed forward. When the steam cleared, all viewed the badly scalded body of their friend slumped lifeless, his wrists slashed. Remnants of any blood had long since been washed away, exposing open wounds on both wrists; the single edged razor blade rested on the shower drain. To a man, they gasped in shock. Karl headed straight for the commode, relieving himself of breakfast. Two others were soon to follow. Nathan moaned, "This explains why we were all forced to use the bathroom at the other end of the corridor this morning. This one was locked when I tried, and I could hear the shower, too." Dom made the sign of the cross over Paulo's body and closed the shower curtain. Stepping outside, he read aloud the note written in Paulo's handwriting.

"Holy Father, loving brothers - in death I humbly ask your forgiveness. Paulo Valdarno betrayed each of you and your efforts to revitalize the spirit of the Church, which I too, prayed for. Death visited me a thousand times these past weeks for what I was coerced to do. My father, the entire Valdarno family throughout Italy, would have suffered a crippling disgrace if I had not succumbed to blackmail. Please understand this. Paulo was unaware of an attempt on the Holy Father's life. Before this, I would have soon given my own. Uden's murder leaves me no choice. My life is now worthless. Pray for my soul."

Dom turned to Jan, and started to ask the question, but Jan, anticipated the inquiry. "There's no entrance to either bathroom from the underside. Both facilities were built in later years and hang out over the edge of the outer walls."

"My brothers, I will pray in private for another lost companion. Jan, please inform the Secretary of State. Tell Thomas I wish him to handle the necessary formalities."

Dom turned back into the bathroom and closed the door behind him.

CHAPTER ELEVEN

Nearly a week had passed since Symon's discovery, and he had read the translated manuscripts numerous times. He consumed the written words as a dying man gasps for breath. The mystery surrounding the ancient narrative fueled his imagination and stimulated his craving to know more. While he sat by the opening of the cave, the sun warmed his body, and meditation purified his soul. What could have been Assuri's last words on earth, and the narrative of his days at the Library of Alexandria bewitched him beyond belief.

Somewhere, he thought. *Somewhere between the lines, somewhere hidden within Assuri's journal could be a clue to a far greater treasure. A treasure that has eluded humankind for thousands of years. A treasure that could help answer the question: what was the history of the world prior to the mass destruction in Alexandria of recorded chronicles?* Once again, Symon read the rendering of the second journal-manuscript.

"I, Assuri, a trusted slave of Babylon, journeyed by the great river to the northwest (Symon's note: Euphrates River), *disembarking at a predetermined site before reaching the town of Carrhae. Then west by land over the mountain range to the sea and Tarsus. My beloved master had a relative who lived in Tarsus and who arranged passage by boat to Alexandria. In all, I witnessed ten suns rise and set, and paid homage to the gods for my safety, which was in peril as I will relate."* (Symon's note: Estimating a distance of some 2,000 kilometers.)

"My thoughtful master, knowing all well that I have never ventured far from the city, dispatched two mercenaries to accompany, guide and protect this humble servant on the trek to Alexandria with our most cherished volumes in tow. When the request from Hypatia (Symon's note: A most highly respected female mathematician and astronomer.) *of Alexandria arrived, my master immediately routed a message to inform his dear friend that he would certainly comply. It was an honor to have the writings of our late high priest Berossus' three volumes of the world dating from Creation to the Great Flood copied and preserved in the Great Library at Alexandria."* (Symon's note: About all that is presently known about the volumes is that Berossus estimated the time between the two events to be 400,000 years - a hundred times longer than Old Testament chronology.)

"I was excited beyond belief. The journey would be tedious and dangerous, but my master's description of Alexandria and the library, and Hypatia's beauty filled my being with joy. His entrusting the volumes greatly humbled this person. My love for him grew like a raging river as he told me of rooms upon rooms filled with writings gathered for hundreds of years and valued more than gold."

(Symon's note: There were an estimated 500,000 scroll-books from Greece, Persia, Israel, India, Africa, and many other countries, all comprising the knowledge and history of the world to date. Alexandria was a community of scholars studying and teaching: physics, literature, astronomy, philosophy, music, medicine, biology, mathematics and engineering. The world's first research institute. In the early 300's BC King Ptolemy I wrote: *'To all the sovereigns and governors on earth. I implore you to immediately send me works by authors of every kind: poets, rhetoricians and sophists, doctors and soothsayers, historians, and all others, too.'* Thus began the Library of Alexandria, and for hundreds of years the known writings, including history, were duplicated and stored. The line of Ptolemys, ending with the death of Cleopatra, set out to not only collect every book in the world, but to translate them all into Greek.)

"With Berossus' works slung over my neck, close to my person in a large leather sheep-lined pouch, and my guides aboard, we set sail northwest. The night's encampments were uncommonly dark. On the fourth night, berthed on the bank where the great river sprang streams to both the north and south, I overheard the two men plotting to kill the servant and nip the valued prize. On the fifth night, playing the fool and obedient servant, and after grinding a powder from a known venomous plant, I sprinkled an amount sufficient enough into the wine jug to render them in a death-like state for at least two days. If they survived. They fell for my offering, and drank with gluttonous passion. At first light I left them in slumber, and pushed on, knowing full well they would not follow once they realized I was two days ahead of them.

"The gods smiled on me. Easterly breezes carried the boat to the appointed remote area to disembark as instructed. I piloted the small craft into a cutout bank, and laid the sail pole flat. Using as much brush and driftwood as I could unearth, I concealed my home on water for the past five days as best possible in hopes to once again place it in service on my return. The master's crude map proved true, and the ground journey to the seaport

town of Tarsus was arduous, yet without mishap. His cousin was pleased to hear all was fine in Babylon, and provided a small boat, agreeing for a small favor, to escort me across the great sea to Alexandria." (Symon's note: Mediterranean Sea.)

"Bypassing an island he called Cyprus, we sailed directly south to Alexandria. A short distance from the island, a strange light was sighted, and grew larger and brighter as we approached our destination. I later learned it was the flame from the famous lighthouse of Pharos. Not wishing to be detected, we avoided the harbor and royal port, and the large inlet on the far side of the Island of Pharos. Instead, he chose to dock by the rocky banks outside the corner of the city wall. I was on my own now." (Symon's note: The lighthouse fires blazed and could be seen for 100 miles out to sea. Considered one of the seven wonders of the world.)

"The evening seaside walk was pleasant. Anticipation of the splendid wonders I was to soon savor impeded any thought of how to gain entrance to the walled city. Turning a corner of the outside wall, I was suddenly confronted by a large wooden door and two armed Roman guards. The gods smiled again. The letter of introduction securing entrance to the city and library, as imprinted by Hypatia, proved to be a key to the door and a new world beyond. Once inside, the royal palace and majestic theaters lay directly before me. At this hour no one was about. A short dusty alleyway accommodated me until dawn.

"Hypatia was even more beautiful than my master's vivid description. She was tall and slim in stature. Much taller than me, her lowly servant. Taller than most men in The Great Hall of The Library where I first beheld this vision lecturing to a group of students. Her skin was velvety dark olive. Sable hair was pulled tightly back into a tie behind her neck, and then cascaded outward like a waterfall across her bare shoulders, nearly to her delicate waist. She carried herself with an air of royalty as she strolled to and fro gesturing, making a point here and there. The white cloth that draped the most feminine of curves captured the attention of the audience, rivaling her words. But it was her eyes that mesmerized me. The eyes were the most pale, yet most brilliant color of translucent amber this person ever witnessed. It was as though she could look deep into your soul, and you into hers.

"During the sixteen months I lingered in Alexandria, we became the closest of confidants. At times she made me forget I was but a servant, a

slave on a mission for my master. While the Berossus volumes were being copied and translated, the lovely and learned Hypatia taught me to read and write my own language, as well as introduced me to the writings of Hipparchus, Euclid, Dionysius, Herophilus, Heron, Apollonius, Archimedes, Ptolemy and other renowned teachers. Hypatia was herself a known mathematician, musicologist, and astronomer." (Symon's note: Hipparchus was an astronomer who charted constellations and the distance of stars; Euclid methodized geometry; Dionysius described divisions of speech; Herophilus placed the brain as the focal point of intelligence, not the heart; Heron invented the steam engine; Apollonius, a mathematician, revealed forms such as the ellipse, parabola, hyperbola; Archimedes was considered for centuries to be the greatest mechanical genus; Ptolemy was the forerunner of modern astrology.)

"Hypatia warned me to be certain to gather up the originals of Berossus' writings as each copy was made. It had been the custom, if the owners were not aware, to return copies and keep the originals. In fact, it was not true that part of the great library content was destroyed by fire during the battle with Caesar. True, books were lost in a fire, but only those stored in the warehouses at the edge of the harbor ready to be shipped to their owners. The main library held the originals. Copies were destroyed.

"The time was nearing for my return journey home. It was a sad farewell. Alexandria, its gathering of scientists, poets, artists, scholars and harmonious meld of Romans, Jews, Egyptians, Africans, and visitors from lands afar, would remain in my memory. My beautiful mentor and protector, Hypatia, is now a permanent part of my heart for all time. I shall worship her as a goddess forever.

"But, my heart was heavy. Days before I was scheduled to leave, she came warning of a possible plot to steal and destroy the volumes in my keeping. The intolerant Christian leader and patriarch of Alexandria, Archbishop Cyril, and his followers conspired to drive the Jews from the city. They also planned to destroy all the books they deemed pagan in nature, and that included Berossus' writings. I was in danger. She too, was in danger. Not only was she considered a pagan symbol of learning and science, the Archbishop despised her because of her friendship with the Roman governor. A vengeful Cyril had been, among many others, spurned when he asked for her hand in marriage.

"*My escape route was fixed. Upon arriving from Babylon, being naturally suspicious, I invented a tall tale which would now serve my purpose. As far as all was concerned, except Hypatia, my original journey from Babylon had taken me southwest on one of the fingers of the great river, ending in the desert, upon which I ventured overland to reach Alexandria. As I have written, this was not the actual route taken. It was my hope that they would expect me to return home on that falsely given eastern route, while I journeyed north.*

"*The morning before the arranged escape, I purchased an ass and let it be known that I planned to retrace my steps home two days hence. That night, bidding a sad goodbye to my lady, I left undetected, Hypatia distracted the gate guards. I rode the uncomfortable beast east along the coast 'til arriving at the final tributary of the Nile, then convinced a poor boatman that a fair exchange of the ass for a small sailing boat was in his favor. Afraid for my person and the writings in my care, I hastily set sail north towards the island of Cyprus. Prayers were composed that the gods would see that those who would pursue this lowly one followed the false path east across the desert towards Babylon.*

"*After resting, moored by a large rock on the coast of Cyprus for a few brief hours, I set out again, northward for Tarsus. My master's cousin was kind enough to supply food, and directions to flee north. The plan was to sail the trusty boat up the river from Tarsus, then continue on foot over barren mountains and desert plateaus until reaching water where the great river from Babylon ceases to flow. Then follow the river home. If the gods willed so, the craft hidden on the bank would be waiting my return. As I sailed up river from Tarsus, my thoughts were on those most joyous days in Alexandria.*"

(Symon's note: It was a blessing Assuri was ignorant about the events in Alexandria since departing. All hell broke loose the morning after his escape. Hypatia, on her way to the library was set upon by a Christian mob of Archbishop Cyril's followers, including Egyptian zealot monks from the desert, and pulled from her chariot. They tore her limb from limb, then flayed flesh from her bones, and burned the remains. Thousands of books regarded as pagan, were put to the torch in the days to come. A goodly amount of the history of the known world to date perished in the name of God. This was in 415 AD. It seems ironic that Cyril, in time, was named a saint. The library's final demise came in the mid-600's AD when Caliph

Omar under the flag of Mohammed, ordered the complete destruction of the great library. Scroll-books were distributed throughout the four thousand public baths to fuel stoves to keep the baths warm. It's estimated it took six months to burn all the writings. Only Aristotle's books were spared.)

Assuri's tale continued, *"Discovering a skeletal remnant gave this person lasting chills, and filled my being with premonition. Nights on the open plain were cold. The decision to stop and hide came shortly after I spied a cave on the cliff-side. Approaching the cave from above, I was surprised to find a second well-concealed cave sitting atop the one I had viewed. The top cave is where I found him, and where my home would be until I felt it safe to proceed, although that next afternoon I ventured out long enough to bury his bones on the mountain top. An unfinished message left on a makeshift rock table explained that he was the last member of a secretive scholar-monk society called the Ashkari. The Ashkari monk wrote of hiding their scrolls in hope of preserving their beliefs - but failed to disclose the hiding place. Evidently, he passed beyond before placing his departing words in a ready-made cavity in the cave wall."* (Symon's note: This was the first time I've heard of the Ashkari society.)

"In the ensuing days, I made and executed plans as the Ashkari did; to hide the valued writings of Berossus, for the same reason. On the ninth day, from the vantage point of my cave entrance, a cloud of dust became visible in the distance to the south. They were not fooled after all. They had come for me.

"My life is short now, but time and the gods are still with me. There is time to conceal my own journals, and place them in the opening provided by my Ashkari. Whosoever finds my silver box, let it be known that I, Assuri, did not survive. Let it be also known then, my duty was fulfilled. Copies of the Babylonian High Priest Berossus' chronicled volumes reside for all time in the Great Library of Alexandria. The originals did not fall prey, but died with me."

Symon felt as though his heart and gut were made of lead. An emptiness, only once experienced before, filled his mind and soul, and permeated the entire cave. He could almost sense the tremendous sadness of Assuri's spirit as it grieved and haunted the surroundings. His spirit most certainly was aware of what had happened at the library, and to his beloved Hypatia. Forcing the heavy-heartedness aside, he considered the mysteries before him. *What had become of Assuri's body? I have his journals, but where had he hidden the silver box housing Berossus' volumes? Who were the Ashkaris, and where were the Ashkari-monk's secret scrolls?*

*****

It was hard to focus on the meal that night. A legion of thoughts quelled his appetite. Several hours after sunset while staring into the still darkness of the desert below, he became aware of a hissing sound in the distance. It grew louder. Whatever it was, it was almost upon him. Intrigued, but not wishing to give away his whereabouts by shining his lamp, Symon sat patiently concealed. A voice cut through the sound of hushed hissing. "Doctor Carpenter! Doctor Carpenter, I'm here to take you!" Symon immediately recognized the deep voice of the aviator who had piloted him to the cave a month earlier.

"It's not time," he shouted back. "You're two months early!"

In spite of his girth, it was an easy climb for the younger man. Once inside the cave, he explained his unscheduled arrival. "You're wanted immediately in Rome. At the Vatican. By the order of the new pope himself, Pope Francis. A former Cardinal Domenico Masone, I'm told."

"That's impossible," Symon countered. "Dom, pope? Someone's playing a prank on us both."

"No! No, Doctor. There was a murder in the Vatican. Pope Francis needs your help straight away! There was a second message, one I don't understand. If you were hesitant, I was to say, 'The sky shone with a wondrous array of radiant colors. Don't you think?' Doctor, we need to move fast while we still have the cover of darkness."

The doctor was stunned. Dom becoming pope? Well, that was one matter. But how in the hell did he know about 'the dream', and the sky full of colors? As much as he hated the thought of leaving the caves of discovery, Symon knew his prime responsibility was in Rome. Besides, he now had a question that burned for an answer. Taking only what was necessary, including the two journals and translations, he left tools and supplies for his subsequent return. Before climbing into the craft, he looked up at the cave entrance and said aloud, "Farewell friend Assuri, I will return!"

CHAPTER TWELVE

The time was nearly at hand. Just three days remained to prepare for the most anticipated balcony scene in history. Dom's concentration was torn in four directions: his speech, his and the group's safety, Uden's family, and Symon's arrival.

Dom's attention to his writing was broken by the sounds of Cardinal Mumbwa's voice and shuffling footsteps mounting the stairs from the archives below. "I believe you know this friar," said Mumbwa. Dom stood up, and hurried to the habit-clad man standing on the top step.

After a hardy warm embrace, Dom stepped back and broke the silence. "Symon, it's good to see you."

Symon smiled, "Look at you, you're the pope! How long has it been?"

"Far too long," came the reply. "I was sorry to hear about the loss of your wife. We said a mass for her blessed soul. But right now you're probably eager to hear an explanation of my message, and before I do, I want you to know how grateful we are that you came. We need you. And before this night is over, I want to hear all about your Turkish adventure, and of course, all about that ponytail."

Symon stepped back and pointed his finger at Dom. "I'll tell you all about my ponytail if you'll explain how in the world you became pope."

"Agreed, but let's get comfortable." Each found a chair.

"Dom, at first I could hardly believe the pilot's demands that the new pope, Pope Francis I, the former Cardinal Domenico Masone, wished to see me immediately; then there was something about a murder at the Vatican. But what really fired my curiosity was the message's reference to 'the radiant colors'. That's what fascinated me!"

"All things in their order, Symon. We have much to discuss before we come to that."

Cardinal Mumbwa asked to be excused to continue pressing duties, and the two old friends took time to reminisce and get caught up over cups of coffee before tackling the more urgent issues.

Symon sat in riveted silence as Dom recounted the various events of the past month: Cardinal Buldini's obvious attempt to thrust him into the papacy, the promise from the balcony, the Franciscan search in the Vatican Secret Archives, Uden's murder, and Paulo's suicide. Symon, slumped in his chair, looked at Dom with a glassy stare, shaking his head in disbelief.

"Wow! And I thought I had a story to tell. Incredible! Poor Uden. Poor Inge. I'd give anything to get my hands on this Buldini character."

"Symon, I know what you're feeling, and I came close. Too close. Thomas will fill you in on our recent encounter with Buldini. We'll have to leave it at that until we gather proof of his involvement. Right now, because of your friendship with Uden's family, I want you to accompany Uden's body home, and gently as possible break the sad news to Inge. Besides me, you're the only one I trust with this burden. There's less than three days left to prepare my vision for the Church, and how we intend to interact in harmony with all world faiths. Then we'll see if I crash and burn, or step off the edge and fly. When you return, I hope you'll agree to become my right arm, in Uden's stead. That would please me."

Symon's face reflected his surprise with his friend's request. "Who wouldn't be equally pleased to become the pope's right arm, his confidant and advisor. But Dom, to be perfectly candid, right now I'm a little overwhelmed with what I've heard. I need more time to assimilate the situation. This I will do, however, I'll escort our dear departed friend home, and do whatever I can to ease Inge's pain. Then I'm yours for however much time it takes to implement your vision. You know you can count on me, but you must also understand that I cannot in good conscience promise you a specific amount of time. You see, I have a mission of my own." Symon smiled. "You tell me about 'the radiant colors', and I'll tell you about my cave exploit."

Dom chuckled, and agreed. "Okay my friend, we have a deal. After dinner tonight, just you and I will return to my office and share stories. The group debriefings are over so we'll have time. Our brothers will be surprised and delighted to be reunited with an old friend, and fellow Franciscan. But...we need to cut this reunion short. It's essential I get back to my writing." Dom walked over to his desk, sat down, started rifling through a stack of papers, then looked up. "If you would, get with Thomas, have him provide you with an unlimited access pass, make your travel arrangements, and ask him any questions you need answered. Meet us for dinner at six. And why don't you invite Thomas to join us. It's good to have you with me, Symon. See you tonight."

*****

With the archive search behind them, the men sensed a feeling of relief. As promised by Dom, beer and wine flowed freely, while platters of mixed hors d' oeuvres disappeared at an alarming rate. Preoccupied with the joyful spread of food and drink, the group failed to notice two men in the dining room doorway.

A loud complaining voice interrupted the chatter. "Will you please keep it down, I'm trying to study!" All turned towards the door, and in unison called out, "Symon!" Hugs, handshakes, and questions consumed Symon as the evening meal progressed. When individual conversations once again dominated and Symon's appearance no longer commanded attention, he and Dom slipped quietly away to the Tower office.

*****

A single lamp directly under a fresco of ancient Rome, provided the only source of light, and the shadows added atmosphere to the evening's tales. After a momentary argument as to who would go first, Symon began the account of his adventure in the cave deep in Turkish territory, and elaborated on what Assuri's manuscripts disclosed. He watched with amusement as Dom's eyes widened as he leaned forward in his chair like a school boy listening intently to a tale of high adventure.

"Do you have any idea at all where Assuri might have hidden Berossus' chronicles?" Dom asked.

Symon grinned, delaying the moment, enjoying his friend's excitement. "I have an idea, but nothing I can be certain of….yet. That's why I can't promise to stay for years at your side."

Dom's expression sobered immediately, and Symon regretted his last words.

"If I could trust anyone else, Symon, you'd have my blessing to return to your search. I can only imagine how excited you must be to get back to your cave. If I didn't have the responsibility to restore the Church, I'd be at your side in that cave, if you'd have me. Unfortunately, I must ask for your indulgence for now."

"Okay," said Symon. "Now it's your turn. Explain the message, *'The sky shone with a wondrous array of radiant colors. Don't you think?'* I would have come anyway, but the reference to the radiant colors clinched it. How in the world did you know?"

Dom hesitated in his answer, because he really didn't know. "Frankly, I didn't know. It was a dream I had the night after Uden's passing. You were in it, and I just assumed the imaginable. It seemed to have a mystical quality with far reaching religious consequences. If you indeed experienced the same vision, we can compare similarities and conclusions."

Dom described his dream in the tall thick green grass: the two men, two tight formations of huge white birds, and a shotgun blast that caused the formations to part. "As I interpret it, the archetypal setting is reminiscent of teetering on the edge of a new beginning. I was standing by an old barren tree with a shotgun in my hands. Another person stood some distance away, mostly hidden by the grass. When he turned to look up at the first flight of birds, I recognized him immediately as you, Symon Carpenter. By that time, a second formation of the same white birds came into view high overhead. I shot the gun into the air, but I wasn't aiming at either formation. The blast seemed to represented a disturbance of some kind. As you know, dreams are mostly symbolic in their essence, and that is the way they should be correctly construed."

Symon nodded. "Go on."

"I believe both formations of swan-like birds with long necks and wide wingspans reflect the embodiment of the Church. The second tight formation held within its bosom, dried mud, dead twigs, tree stumps, and a vintage yellow Volkswagen. The mud and aged wood represented a stagnant Church. The Volkswagen symbolized a Church with little power, energy and authority. However, firmly held and nearly invisible within the first flight were minute pieces of every color of the rainbow.

"When the disturbance occurred, both formations broke. The second group scattered, dropping the debris and the yellow Volkswagen. The first group broke their tight formation, but managed to remain intact, revealing and blanketing the sky with a burst of fresh radiant colors. Symon, both groups represented the Church. The one that is, and the one that it could become."

Dom sighed as if tired yet resigned to the inevitable. "I know that I am the one in the dream who caused the Church to show its true colors. And, I am the pope who in the course of a little over forty-eight hours may very well cause a great flurry within Christianity."

Dom leaned back in his chair, as if exhausted. "You were with me during the great disturbance. Until now, I didn't fully realize why, yet here you are with me. That part of the dream has come true, therefore my tendency is to trust my interpretation. What's your reading on all of this?"

Symon took a little time to gather his thoughts, and after a swallow of coffee, responded. "You've answered any questions I had about our mirrored-dream, and I can't imagine the odds on having the same dream in such detail. It cannot be a mere coincidence. We're being directed.

"Dom, there are several schools of thought on the subject of dreams. There are those who debunk the concept as purely random bits and pieces of daily activity and concerns coming together, and becoming disjointed in our subconscious, resulting in a nonsensical dream. Others profess that a dream is nature's way of assisting us in sorting out issues we cannot solve while awake.

"Another camp says it's a way of listening to God, while still another simply defines a dream as a wish of the heart. Even St. Jerome got into the act, and in fact, in the end, contradicted himself. During the early days of the Church, many held dreams as quite sacred. Jerome placed belief in dreams in the same category as witchcraft, sorcery and fortune-telling, and when writing his interpretation of the Bible, warned against them all. But here's the irony.

"Jerome had a staff of scribes assisting him in his Bible rendering assignment, and all was going fairly smooth until he came to the interpretation of one particular passage. He spent several days on a single construction without success. Much to the surprise and relief of the scribes, one morning Jerome began without effort dictating his explanation. When asked by a scribe how, after so many attempts, he could so easily clarify the passage, Jerome admitted that the Holy Mother, St. Peter and St. Joseph came to him in a dream, and explained it all.

"Dom, who knows. You're where you are today, and for whatever reason, I'm here with you. My impression is we shouldn't attempt to analyze it; just accept it, and place it squarely in our Lord's lap."

"You're the same old Symon. I've admired the way you've always cut to the chase, and you haven't disappointed me tonight. So that you are fully aware of how I came to be in the position I find myself in, and what we intend to do about it, let me take you into my confidence."

Dom disclosed his childhood experience with the St. Francis of Assisi crucifix phenomenon, and his calling to *'Restore the Church'*, swearing Symon to secrecy as he had Uden. During the next two hours he caught

Symon up on the results of the Franciscan Vatican Secret Archive investigation, and his plans to restore the Church.

Symon, in complete agreement with what he heard, once again pledged loyalty to his friend and pope, wishing him success in the coming days.

In closing, Dom wished Symon God speed on his trip to the Netherlands, and for a safe return to Rome. They parted as old friends, each looking forward to enjoying the rekindled relationship.

CHAPTER THIRTEEN

The muttering of the fussy old Monsignor Albani grew more vigorous as the final hour before Pope Francis' address was coming to a close. "He will be a sight to see. The beautiful clothes are all laid out, and yet he won't wear any of them except the white silk skull-cap," he mumble under his breath. Throwing his arms up in desperation, he continued to fret, fuss and worry. It was the usually congenial monsignor's responsibility to be certain the pope looked his regal best, and he was not succeeding.

"Your Holiness, you cannot be seen like that! The world is watching. Your image..." Pope Francis cut him off in mid-sentence.

"Monsignor Albani, you have performed your duty well. Please sit down. Have a cup of tea. Relax. The image of a Franciscan Pope is the one we wish to portray. The Franciscan habit reflects the flock's humble servant, and the white skull-cap signifies the office of the papacy. I am as you and as the world will see, a humble friar who happens to be pope."

Various members of the Curia, including Cardinal Buldini and Monsignor Diamante, clustered to one side of the room directly behind the balcony, bedecked in their finest silks. The remaining seven Franciscans in their traditional habits milled around, admiring the festive and age-old trappings that decorate all Vatican chambers. Excluding Cardinal Mumbwa, disdain for the Franciscans on the part of the gathered officials was evident.

Buldini and his group kept to themselves - whispering. The pope's instructions for positioning individuals who would appear on the balcony with him did not ease the tension; it increased hostility. Christian Unhlanga, the tallest, would be placed directly behind the pope. Three Franciscans to his right, and three to his left, all in order depending on height. In the second row, spread to the both sides, came select cardinals representing the Curia. Last, were Buldini and Diamante, situated in what would be the third row, centered behind Unhlanga, effectively obstructing their view of the crowd and television cameras.

It was planned that when the pope approached the balcony rail, Cardinal Mumbwa would step forward between the pope and the Franciscans occupying a space several paces behind and to his immediate right. Members of the Curia were not pleased to be upstaged by the likes of ordinary friars.

Buldini was heard to mutter only one word. "Preposterous!" He tried his best not to show anger, but when the crimson hue of his face matched the color of his skull-cap and sash, all knew.

*****

The pope's unfurled crested banner fluttered in a light breeze. It was unusually comfortable for the first week in November, and the sun shone in all its glory. Looking over Albani's shoulder at the bedroom chamber window, he scanned the mass of humanity below. Thousands of the faithful and curious stood thick as blades of grass in a vast field guarded by towering marble cliffs.

They remembered his promise, and waited patiently for their pope's appearance. As the multitude spoke to each other in muted tones, the drone reminded him of his days as a child in Assisi when on a walk in the fields he knew when he was approaching beekeepers by the buzzing whispers of the swarm. With eyes skyward, he thought to himself, *It's a great day for a funeral. If I'm wrong, God help me!* With a thankful and reassuring pat on the thoughtful monsignor's shoulder, he walked from his private chamber and faced those waiting for him in the balcony access foyer. Eight were smiling from ear to ear. The others, at the sight of the pope dressed so plainly, were rendered speechless. Buldini rolled his eyes in obvious disgust. The pope met his gaze directly with a penetrating stare of defiance. It caught the cardinal completely off guard, forcing his chin to his chest. This ever so brief engagement of warring wills did not go unnoticed by those in attendance.

*****

"It is time, Cardinal Mumbwa. Let's proceed," bade the pope. In place, and in unison, the entourage pressed forward to meet the waiting world among joyous, warmhearted, cheers of welcome from the throng in St. Peter's Square.

With the first hint of the pope approaching the balcony, the St. Peter's crowd burst into a concert of cheers. Once Pope Francis came into full view, the world suddenly turned mute. Shouts of welcome ceased as open mouths no longer formed words. Silence fell over the faithful surrounded by ancient structures. There before them stood a man in a plain brown friar's habit

102

wearing a white skull-cap. Where was their pope clothed in a radiant white costume?

Pope Francis gripped the balcony balustrade with both hands. He sensed their bewilderment, leaned forward and addressed the people. "My brothers and sisters of God's earth, I, Pope Francis I stand before you as a humble Franciscan friar. As your pope, I am more happy to serve you than to occupy the Chair of Saint Peter. Thus my modest appearance. I am one of you. The role of this pope shall be that of a working shepherd to the whole flock. To accomplish this task, we will need the prayers and strength of all peoples. Together we will become as one. Pope Francis needs you!" With that, he opened his arms wide as if to engulf the globe, and the crowd responded wildly.

He could feel the balcony rail vibrate under his hands. "Si, Si! Viva el papa!" echoed for nearly five minutes. Taking advantage of the moment of success, he permitted them to enjoy their jubilation. They understood his petition and collectively responded.

He was aware that a similar response would be taking place in front of a thousand giant reflective-laser-screens strategically situated by the international news networks throughout the world, plus individual TV's and radios. It would be the largest viewing audience in history. Pope Francis became visibly energized and increasingly confident. He continued. "We have much to do in the years to come, and we invite all God's sons and daughters, regardless of their faith, to participate fully in restoring His loving will for all His children. God's love for each and every one of us is far greater than any of our differences. This is the truth we build our papacy on.

"We will begin here in the Vatican to simplify our ways, mirroring Saint Francis, and be joined by all the clergy. We intend, with humility, to lead by example. Do not be alarmed; times have changed since my namesake, Saint Francis endeavored to do his Master's work, so we will not be so dramatic. He once said, *'I would be happy to remain with only a tunic, a cord around my waist, and a clean pair of drawers.'"*

St. Peter's came alive with laughter. The crowd appreciated the man before them. He was perched on a high balcony, yet did not seem above them. This pope was truly one of them. And they loved it.

"As the spiritual head of the Roman Catholic Church, I confess to the world that for over 2,000 years we have erred in various ways and on numerous occasions. Too often, grievously so. The Church cannot right all the wrongs of the past. We cannot compensate individuals; it is a physical impossibility. However, we can do so in spirit, by our immediate and future service to those in need. This will be done in the name of all who have suffered. Our first act is to turn the Pope's Palace and Office behind St. Peter's Basilica into a hospice for abandoned and abused children, and our summer retreats outside Rome will become residency for the homeless elderly. Perhaps they will be kind enough to save me a room."

The confusion and uneasiness caused by the pope's public admission to any wrong generated quite a stir among the crowd. This was done only once before, but not so dramatically. But as his full statement was absorbed into their collective consciousness, the buzz grew into a roar of approval. The gathering of cardinals stood dumbfounded, mired in disbelief. Thomas, Christian, Karl, Jan, Jabal, Kim, Rico and Nathan were aglow with admiration for their friend's wisdom and courage.

"In addition, there are volumes of priceless antique-treasures within the confines of the Vatican City buildings, elsewhere in Rome, throughout Italy, and throughout the world that are the property of the Catholic Church. Our Secretary of State, Cardinal Thomas Mumbwa, will be in charge of performing an up-to-date inventory and evaluation of all possessions. While certain select objects of a spiritual-nature will remain in our keep, the majority will, in time, be auctioned-off to creditable museums worldwide. We wish the world to enjoy what only a handful can now afford to behold. More importantly, the proceeds collected will be dispensed to better the lives of those in need, no matter their race, color, country, or faith; be it for a school, hospital, housing, a church, temple, synagogue, or mosque; or to help save our fragile and endangered environment.

"Saint Francis also said, *'In the leper's disfigured body there was always a person with divine dignity.'* We believe in this principle, and our papacy will follow that truth. Every single person on earth, every one of you who can hear these words, has the divinely given right to be treated with dignity as a child of our Creator.

"Consequently, every person has the divinely bestowed birthright to worship his or her Maker as mandated by their own conscience, and to express their faith in community with others, or in the silence of their own heart."

The pope turned briefly to see what the commotion was behind him, then once again faced his audience. "It seems Cardinal Buldini is fond of the

104

word 'heresy.' We would like to remind him and any others who also presume the same, that within Church history is proof that there's often a fine line between what was once termed 'heresy', and what was in the fullness of time demonstrated to be truth." Embarrassed in front of the world, yet unseen, Buldini stormed off the balcony, literally dragging the bewildered and defenseless Monsignor Diamante by his collar.

"We would further remind our detractors that evil, bigotry, and misunderstandings are not solved by fear, but by truth. And, as stated previously, God's love is far greater than our perceived differences. We all have a single common parent; God the Father. By His Word we are all unequivocally joined as brothers and sisters of one universal family.

"In the spirit of those words, we will, in the very near future, organize a Worldwide Conciliatory Council encouraging the attendance of representatives from all faiths and believers in the One Creator. It's purpose will be to concentrate on our common beliefs, *not differences.* Perhaps if our hearts are changed, as Pope John Paul II suggested, our differences will fade, becoming insignificant in time. Remember, 'Supreme lex salus animarum.' 'The Supreme Law, is the savings of souls', the souls of all God's children, not just those considered Christian. We are all His children. He loves each of us unconditionally. Equally. Can we do anything less? I ask you - can we do anything less?

"While we do not wish favor to any one faith, it is necessary as a demonstration of our genuine sincerity to right wrongs, and relax differences with all faiths. In this example, it is a people that we along with others have persecuted for millenniums: the Jewish race. It is in the spirit of Popes John XXIII and John Paul II, that I Pope Francis, declare it was not the Jewish people that crucified Jesus Christ, it was the sins of the whole human race.

"We will also summon a General Council to discuss the development of a representative, democratic, conciliar, and synodal approach to Catholic government. As part of the General Council's agenda, we intend to reopen and support the argument for women entering the priesthood. This pope finds no biblical evidence barring women priests; the opposite is true. And in the light of our devotion to Our Lady of All Nations, the Holy Mother, logic favors female full participation in the sacraments."

The crowd who had been listening, with respect and fascination, spontaneously bellowed their approval. Although, scattered objections could be heard. With gestures for silence and repeated 'bless you - bless you', the

105

pope continued. "And now to a far more controversial subject, papal infallibility. An exhaustive study of papal history provides contradictory testimony to Pope Pius' 1870 declaration of papal infallibility. This decree, in fact, became a source of an unfortunate and unnecessary schism within Christianity. To the contrary, we agree with popes Innocent III, Innocent IV, and Adrian VI when they acknowledged that a pope can err, even in the matters of faith. Therefore, we hereby revoke Pope Pius' decree, and too, allow that a pope is not infallible; but fallible.

"Now after saying that, you should all know I personally and wholeheartedly agree with and uphold the various dogmas concerning our Blessed Holy Mother Mary. Evidence of my devotion is this papacy's banner-crest unfurled before you. The 'M' is in honor of our Blessed Mother's abiding presence in all our daily lives. Of course, the 'M' was borrowed from Pope John Paul's papal crest.

"Much of what was been unveiled to you this afternoon will be received with open arms and hearts by many. Others will close their minds, aggressively contesting and openly opposing our intentions. Members of the opposition will prove to be those who have the most power and wealth to lose. Watch. In the coming days they will reveal themselves. See who they are. Remember their faces. Remember their names. Pray for them. Pray that their hearts, too, will change.

"In closing, we invite and encourage the faith leaders from every corner of God's earth to contact the office of Cardinal Thomas Mumbwa, the Vatican Secretary of State; provide us with your thoughts for a Worldwide Conciliatory Council Conference, also expressing your willingness to share a united vision to do the Creator's will for the goodness of all humanity.

"And, as well, a similar invitation is extended to every citizen of God's universe who heard our words today. Write or e-mail us. Provide us with your sentiments on any of the topics we articulated. Your input is important. We are determined to listen. We cannot successfully accomplish His will without you.

"In the near future, and periodically, we intend to hold worldwide-town-meeting broadcasts to apprise you of any progress or problems concerning our shared undertaking.

"Our Creator's promised message is in the form of a loving Father's petition to His children - 'Rebuild My House!'. The house is the earth, our home. 'My House is in ruins. Rebuild My House,' He commanded. Today you have witnessed my humble attempt to comply with His will as understood. Join us. Pray for our success.

"When Saint Francis died, he left written words for his Franciscan brothers. Those words are my prayer for you. *'Il Signore ti benedisca, e ti custodisca; ti mostri la suo volto, e diati pace.'* *'The Lord bless you and keep you; may He show you His countenance full of compassion. May He turn His face upon you, and give you peace.'"*

Raising his right hand and making the sign of the cross, he blessed the throng of faithful in St. Peter's square. The pope made one final statement before turning to leave the balcony - "May God grant you that peace."

*****

His speech was only ten minutes in length, but between the extremes of fractured silence, excessive jubilation, and moments of noisy disjointed confusion, his balcony appearance lasted nearly twenty-five minutes.

Thousands remained, refusing to leave the square for well over an hour, loudly discussing what they just witnessed. Their pope covered a lot of ground in such a short period of time. Centuries, even millennia, flew by effortlessly.

As expected and later reported, Pope Francis' address was received with mixed emotions. Traditionalists were outraged, but reserved, awaiting further in-depth justification on some points of controversy. Most in the mainstream were encouraged. The clergy were split. The Catholic Women's Coalition, ecstatic. Other Christian domination's were outwardly pleased, as well as the eastern and middle eastern faiths, although the latter took more of a wait-and-see attitude. Others were suspicious. The Israelis were humbled by what they considered the pope's brave sign of reasoning and a genuine kindness towards their people. Unforeseen were days of disruptive street protest rallies, often resulting in bloodshed in countries where the dignity of human rights and worship were still woefully wanting. These accounts deeply saddened and disturbed the pope.

CHAPTER FOURTEEN

Cardinal Mumbwa and the special group of Franciscans struggled within themselves to contain their enthusiasm. Dom was, before all other things, pope, and they fought to keep that first in their minds - at least in public. They looked forward to the meal Dom promised to share with them that evening.

Pope Francis acknowledged his friends with a nod and a sigh as he passed them heading purposely for the Curia Cardinals, who looked to be in complete disarray and at odds with each other.

"Why I've privately thought that to be true all along," one was explaining.

Another, "Someone with courage enough to say it was inevitable, and long overdue." Still others joined in with a chorus. "It's heresy plain and simple!"

As the pope drew closer, several moved towards him, hands extended, with words of praise. Yet another group lingered and congregated, ignoring his presence.

"Gentlemen, your attention please," said the pope. "Since none of you were consulted concerning the content of our address, we certainly understand your surprise. If you feel ambushed, no one will fault you. The amount of research necessary and the constraints of a self-imposed time limit did not allow for debate. We anticipated your concerns and anxieties; therefore, please assemble in the administrative office promptly at nine tomorrow morning. Bring whomever you wish, and if necessary we'll adjourn to the conference room. Cardinal Mumbwa has a copy of my speech for each of you. Take it. Read it. Pray over it, and be prepared to discuss your areas of apprehension. We'll set aside the entire day. Oh yes, someone may wish to inform Cardinal Buldini that his presence is desired, if he so chooses. I'm looking forward to a spirited meeting in the morning. Pax vobiscum."

Turning on his heels, the pope headed to his living quarters, and pointed to the beaming crew of friars. "See you all for dinner at seven in the Tower Hall, and thanks for your hard work and support. This is just the beginning!"

Before he could say another word, Cardinal Mumbwa called out from a small office doorway, "Your Holiness, there's a long distance phone call for you. It's Symon. You can take it in here." The pope's pulse and footsteps quickened as he headed towards the office.

*****

"Symon, thanks for the call. How's Inge and the family?"

"Dom, it's something I wouldn't want to repeat," came the reply. "Escorting my best friend's remains was bad enough. Explaining the circumstances of Uden's death, and consoling his widow tore my heart out. But before we get into that, and we can talk about it in depth when I return to Rome, Inge wanted me to express her feelings to you. First, she wanted you to know she watched your speech, and to tell you Uden would have been so very proud of you, as she is."

At this point in the conversation, silence ruled as both were overcome by emotion, and attempted to compose themselves. With tears choking their voices, the dialogue continued for another five minutes. Symon explained that Inge did not want Dom to feel in any way responsible for Uden's death. She felt Uden gave his life doing the Lord's will, something he would have gladly done willingly. She was proud of him, too. Finally, Symon closed by saying, "I also want to echo Inge's sentiments. Dom, you did a masterful job today. And putting any detractor on notice that the world will be watching them, as well as the worldwide fireside chat commitment, was a stroke of genius. I would have liked to have seen Buldini's face when he was singled out. That did my heart good."

The pope had the last words. "Give Inge my love. Tell her that Uden, she and the twins are in my perpetual prayers. And Symon, have a safe trip. We're looking forward to having your full participation. May God bless you."

*****

"How did it go with Symon?" asked Thomas.

"It was a tough assignment," replied the pope. "He'll be heading to Rome on the morning flight. I see by the note you placed on my desk during the call, that the computers are inundated with e-mail messages from every corner of the globe, and all phone lines are aglow. No doubt this will continue for some time, if not permanently. We're certain to be swamped with mail during the next month, and thereafter. Manning the computer and phone lines twenty-four hours a day, as well as sorting mail would be a good job for our seminary students, don't you think?"

"Dom, you're so tactful, yet correct. Calling for volunteers to do work for the Holy Father will have them crawling all over one another. There won't be any lack of helping hands. It's getting close to dinner time and your celebration feast with the group, so I'll take my leave. This time I'll have to pass on your dinner invitation. There's far too much to do before the conference tomorrow. Due to the overwhelming and immediate response to your speech, we are in dire need of a system to organize the incoming messages by category. I'll have something for you to review before we gather with the cardinals. It's been a memorable and stimulating day."

*****

In an office at the far end of the Vatican, overlooking a picturesque patio garden, sat a silently brooding Cardinal Buldini. The darkened room was also inhabited by a handful of equally sullen conspirators. No one said a word. No one dared. The veil of gloom was torn by a deep grumbling sound of Buldini clearing his throat, preparing to speak. "How could I have been so wrong; so blind? Masone fooled everyone. Humble parish priest be damned! Adherence to Church authority and tradition; double dam! That man's a maverick! He's like an out of control runaway freight train, and must be derailed. He'll pick all our pockets before he's through, and he'll give it all away to the poor.

"Diamante, contact the assassin. He failed before. Maybe he can make up for his blunder. It was I who discovered that Paulo Valdarno's father had been embezzling funds from the Vatican Bank for years. This we held over Paulo's head, blackmailing him into betraying his companions. Sergio, your buddy, the little weasel, deserted us after the assassin's attempt missed its mark. Neither one will ever see a red cent from me. Since Sergio's long gone, it's up to you to find and contact the hitter. Tell him we'll double our first offer. The one he never received."

In the dim light, Buldini could not see the look of pain on the monsignor's face. "But your eminence...," he pleaded. "I don't know the assassin, or where to begin to search for him. I don't even know what he looks like, if anyone does. Or his name. When I think of him, I shudder.

111

He's so evil. He may have left the country after what occurred, and perhaps killed Sergio to shut him up. I don't think it's wise to try again."

"You're not paid to think little man," came the abrupt retort, dripping with venom. "This is push or get pushed time. Old friendships are out the window. Do what you're told, or death may be visiting you next. I'm not going to lose everything I've garnered these past fourteen years. Not for anyone. Not for any reason. Is that clear?" A browbeaten Diamante left the room midst undertones of jeers, sneers, and sarcastic quips from the others. His uncharacteristic and obvious distaste for their recent maneuvers had held him up to ridicule and distrust among his peers, and to the worriment of the cardinal.

*****

A teasing, polite and restrained applause greeted the pope as he entered the scene of the Franciscan's recent internment, the Tower of The Winds makeshift dining facilities. As he stood before them, silence fell across the faces of the remaining seven. Then, without warning, shouts of 'bravissimo!' raised the rafters. They took turns congratulating and hugging their beloved friend and leader.

"I see you've already gotten into the liquid spirits," he teased back with a playful chuckle. "Eat, eat and drink heartily my friends. If you think you've toiled long and hard this past month, think twice. This papacy will come under attack from within at any moment. There are plots being fashioned, lies fabricated, and unholy alliances forged as we speak. And, there's little doubt that my very life is in danger from inside and outside the Church. Thomas informed me that the majority of early incoming comments from around the world are positive. Of course, there are criticisms as well. We expected that. However, it's those who are unusually voiceless that trouble me the most."

Speaking on the behalf of the group, Karl took the initiative to assure their leader. "Dom, to a man, we pledge our undying support. You tell us what you want us to do, and we'll do it."

Dom smiled with an expression of someone thoroughly pleased. "I knew we could count on the loyalty of each of you. Thank you, and bless you all. But right now let's set business aside and enjoy the meal and comradery."

During the latter course of the meal, Dom revealed the content of his phone conversation with Symon, including Inge's understandable sorrow. They were all delighted to know that Symon would be joining them, and in effect, would assume Uden's role within the group. Over coffee, he outlined the various assignments he had in mind for each person. Kim, the Oriental giant, and master of numerous martial arts techniques, would become like a second skin to Pope Francis, his bodyguard. Jan would continue to be in charge of security and surveillance within the Vatican buildings and grounds, working in tandem with Jabal. Jabal would be the outside man, developing civilian and clerical informants, coordinating safeguards with Jan. Karl was to keep his finger on the pulse of any incoming communiqués from Israel, or the American Jewish League. Christian, Rico and Nathan were to oversee and coordinate the efforts of seminary students aiding Cardinal Mumbwa. After evening prayers honoring their fallen comrades, they departed for their new and somewhat more elaborate living accommodations close to the pope within St. Peter's Basilica grounds. Tomorrow the pope would encounter the Red Hats.

THE FRANCISCAN

CHAPTER FIFTEEN

It was eight in the morning and Cardinal Mumbwa and the pope had been deep in conversation for the past half-hour. The office was sizable, but they decided to retire to the conference room once the cardinals and their guests began to arrive. Kim resembled a tall granite pillar guarding the office entrance.

Mumbwa stood while Pope Francis sat on the corner of a large desk. "Thomas, your plans to coordinate and organize the incoming communications are excellent. And, by the way, Christian, Rico and Nathan are available to assist you in directing the seminary students. You have far too much to do to be bogged down with those duties. The inventories must be started as soon as possible. More volunteer students will be needed to perform that task. And, your personal investigation into Cardinal Buldini's finances is a priority. Perhaps this is where Symon could be of value. He's an unknown in Rome, and could nose around covertly. Have him intercepted at the airport this evening, and in the cover of darkness, Jan will meet him at the castle. He'll have already unlocked the secret stairway to the Borgia Apartments, so they'll be able to enter unnoticed. Two can play at that game. Right?" Dom continued to talk as he moved behind the desk and sat down. "I'll meet with you and Symon in the old Tower office at nine tonight. I have a few more items to complete before facing the cardinals. Why don't you join those who have already arrived."

Thomas frowned, and briefly wondered what was behind the secrecy of Symon's return, then put it out of mind. "Dom, I'll do my best to feel out the mood, and drop back in just before you make your appearance. And, one other thing before I go. Reports are not good in countries where there have been accounts of unrest. Your call for the rights of human dignity has induced protests from various governments worldwide, often with disastrous results."

The pope thought for a moment, and with a painful expression said, "This concerns me greatly. We never foresaw this, and yes, we must do something about it. Have Monsignor Lucchesi announce our first broadcast papal worldwide chat to his media contacts. Insist those countries involved with protests participate by allowing the broadcast reception. Have him personally explain to the heads of state that it is my intention to ease tensions in their countries, nothing more."

"The broadcast is fairly soon after our address, but necessary. We'll do it in three days."

*****

The conference room was filled to capacity. Scarlet and black, black, and white dominated and obscured the plush blue seats. Local Curia Cardinals, their monsignor aides, and male secretaries fidgeted like a nervous herd of cattle before a lone figure in a plain friar's habit and white skull cap. The pope sat with his head bowed as if in meditation, playing on every advantage of drama possible. Then, looking up, he glanced across the room, attempting to make eye contact with each member of the clergy. At last he stood to speak.

"Gentlemen, thank you for being prompt, and for coming. This gathering is off the record, so please feel free to speak your minds. I intend to do the same. Nothing said will be taken as disrespect to the papal office. We are all here to do our Lord's work. Is that not so?" He gestured with open hands, "Who will be first?"

A cardinal in the third row was the first among many to rise to his feet. The pope acknowledged his question. "Your Holiness I am Cardinal Shahpur from India, an old yet still emerging nation. Meaning no disrespect, and while I do agree with your direction for the clergy to closely imitate Saint Francis' way of serving God's children, rather than many of the excessive examples evident today and in past Church history, my question is this. Are you personally threatening the exalted position as St. Peter's direct successor by your plain attire?"

"A reasonable question," answered the pope. "To the contrary. It is my researched opinion that a more modest approach to preaching our Lord's gospel would be more effective, and appreciated by our flock. Rather than talking down to the people, we should be talking to them eye to eye, just as Jesus did. And, my simple habit sets that example. In my opinion, it will not make me any less their pope.

"The last part of your comment concerning St. Peter's successor brings up an interesting theological point we could debate some other time. As you're aware, St. Peter was not considered pope until two hundred years after his death. And here's the most interesting fact that has been overlooked by most students of early Church history. Our Lord's statement, *'Tu es Petrus, et super hanc petram aedificabo ecclesiam meam, et portae inferi non praevalebunt adversus eam.'* '*Thou art Peter and upon this Rock I will build My Church and the gates of hell will not prevail against it,*' was argued to be interpreted quite differently by the Great Fathers of the Church, including Cyril, Augustine, Jerome, Origen, and others. For them, it was Peter's faith, or the Lord Himself in whom Peter had faith, that was the Rock upon which the Church is built. In other words, and I believe rightfully so, Jesus is the foundation of the Church. Not the papacy. The pope is just a tool, among others. But, as mentioned, we can debate that intriguing theological challenge at a later date."

While many of the attendees smiled in approval, Cardinal Mumbwa included, the reaction of others was the equivalent of pouring gasoline on an ant hill and then lighting the fire. They were on their feet not knowing which way to turn. Their secretaries were frantically scribbling away.

The pope still standing, called for order, and when all was reasonably quiet, he asked for the next question. "Holy Father, I am Cardinal Pelayo of Naples. Although I am of the mind for a more democratic Church government, as it once was long ago, I cannot envision women participating fully in the sacramental practice of the Church. Jesus did not ask women to become apostles. It was men only. The Church did not create the male priesthood. Jesus did!"

Pope Francis nodded his head in recognition of the statement, and answered. "I understand your conviction on the subject of a female priesthood. However, there is no evidence that I could find that Jesus ever suggested that women should not participate fully in spreading His message. There is evidence there were female missionaries spreading the gospel. And He, against the norm of the times, outwardly befriended and associated with women the male population shunned. Some were considered outcasts. His actions leveled the playing field, if we can look at it that way. And who was it He first appeared to after He rose again? Women.

"Cardinal Pelayo, let me ask you this question. Considering it logically from our Lord's point of view, and taking the Jewish male view of women two thousand or so years ago, what would have happened to His ministry if He chose a few women to join the band of apostles? I'll answer for you. It wouldn't have gotten off the ground, and most likely He would have been crucified before His time. Certainly the women apostles would have been killed trying to preach in the temple. It just wasn't feasible at that

117

time in history. He did, however, go out of His way to honor and show equal respect to women through other avenues. If He came back today and selected women along with men to serve, that would be excepted, don't you think?"

Cardinal Pelayo was about to open his mouth, but the pope continued. "My good cardinal, it's very much like the Church's long stand on a celibate clergy. I remember as a youngster visiting relatives in Chicago with my parents. We watched a TV debate where a representative from the Catholic clergy argued the case for celibacy against a lay person who recommended providing a priest with the option to wed. At the time, I was unaware the priest was lying to millions of viewers. His rationale in favor of celibacy was the same as your argument against women priests. It was Jesus' direction.

"We know from Church history that celibacy was not made mandatory until the twelfth or thirteenth century. It was implied prior to that, but never enforced. When the pope put his stamp of approval on the concept, it caused heartbreak throughout the Church. His mass annulment of all married priests literally made widows of wives, and orphans of children. It was ignored if a member of the clergy had a woman on the side, so to speak, as long as it wasn't his wife. Making love to one's wife was then considered a sin.

"Jesus' apostles included married men, even the man later considered to be the first pope. Re-read Paul's first letter to Timothy, chapter three. It is here where Paul outlines the qualifications for a bishop, including the ability to manage his children, and the provision to be married only once. No where can it be found, or insinuated our Lord was unquestionably anti-marriage for the priesthood. And, what one pope did, another pope can undo. The member of the Chicago clergy said, 'What Jesus commanded, no pope can undo.' As we just mentioned, Jesus did not make the law, a pope did. Consequently, a pope did declare the option to marry some years ago. Obviously, logic dictates all the reasons our Lord could not have married. Therefore, his chosen celibacy is understandable and no longer a subject of debate.

"Lastly, if we can honor a woman in the manner the Church has exalted our Holy Mother, even to the point of considering her a co-redeemer with her Son Jesus - cannot the same gender enter the priesthood?"

As Cardinal Pelayo sat down slowly, joining the others now talking to each other in hushed tones, Cardinal Buldini stood defiantly in the middle of the assembly waiting to be recognized. The room fell silent, all eyes on the pope.

"Welcome Cardinal Buldini," said the pope. "I didn't see you enter, although I can't understand how you'd be missed. You have a question, or did you want to make another heresy claim?"

A mixture of groans and giggles swept the room as Buldini strove to gather his thoughts. "Yes I have!" came the answer. "I and others in this room, throughout the Vatican, and elsewhere within the Roman Catholic Church believe you have overstepped your authority, and vigorously condemn and challenge your judgment."

Un-perturbed, the pope replied with a toothy grin. "Coming from you, this doesn't surprise any of us. Based on current papal authority and power as the leader of the Roman Catholic Church, does anyone here deny a pope has the jurisdiction to declare changes in, or present new teachings? If not, then your challenge and condemnation is misguided. Therefore, irrelevant."

The room went silent, except for the sound of shuffling feet, and an occasional cough. All eyes targeted Buldini, waiting for his response. The cardinal stood with teeth clenched. He knew as did the others that Pope Francis was within his given authority. No one spoke in opposition. "Well then," said the pope. "Please take your seat. And I suggest you recall my words to you the last time we talked face to face." Buldini turned beet red as he remembered the words of warning the pope had whispered to him as he lay on his backside amid his breakfast meal.

The deep-seated and genuine dislike for Cardinal Buldini tugged and gnawed at the pope's conscience and was quite bothersome. It was something he prayed about daily. It just wasn't like him, he thought.

Pope Francis stood, stretched, and motioned for everyone to remain seated. "Perhaps yesterday's unbridled display of unfettered papal power will prove to demonstrate the need to convert the present dictatorial form of Church government to a more democratic assembly." This comment drew a harmony of 'yeses' from the group. "Well now, at least we found something we can all agree on. And on that note, let's adjourn for lunch."

*****

Taking advantage of the lunch break, Cardinal Mumbwa and Pope Francis met in the pope's office off of the conference room with bodyguard in tow. Kim had stood quietly inside the doorway during the proceedings and sensed for the first time his leader's animosity towards Cardinal Buldini, although the reasoning escaped him. He resented the cardinal's blatant verbal attack on the pope, and had been eyeing Buldini suspiciously since that moment. Like everyone else in the room, he wondered about the contents of the message the pope had imparted to Buldini when they last met.

"Thomas, we must intensify our investigation of Buldini's finances. We need some sort of dagger to hold to his throat."

"Dom, the inquiry is underway. Paulo's father is the second ranking official at the Vatican Bank. He's pulling all Italian and international holding records on Buldini. We should have the report in a few days. The father is aware of his son's suicide note, and revealed his own part in Paulo's death. He will do as we ask; pay back the money embezzled in return for our silence. I agreed. Once we have reviewed the findings, and with your written authorization will, without notifying the cardinal, freeze all his assets."

"Good show Thomas! By the way, did you happen to spy Monsignor Diamante in the meeting? I didn't. And it's the first time I haven't seen the little fellow sniffing behind his master."

Thomas thought about it, and said, "No, come to think about it. Did you miss seeing your 'elusive poet'?"

"Oh, you caught that comment coming out of Buldini's quarters, did you?" inquired the pope. "I'll explain that to you one day soon. Right now there's no time. I've had another thought as to how to utilize Symon. You'll remember we agreed to use him covertly. What do you think of Symon attempting to infiltrate Buldini's cave of demons?"

Thomas frowned and shook his head. He had been afraid that Dom had this in mind all along. "Dom, that could be dangerous. If anyone would recognize him, his life could be in jeopardy. We've already lost two. Let's talk it over with Symon tonight."

*****

The pope's counter challenge to Buldini's criticism quelled any other serious questions doubting his authority. The remainder of the afternoon was devoted to a more courteous debate on forming a new style of Church rule and structure. Even his detractors seemed eager to participate. All went well. The pope thought it was a good beginning, and made certain Cardinal Mumbwa played an important leadership role in the discussions. Towards

120

the end of the day the group even found time to briefly examine the proposed Worldwide Conciliatory Council. At this point the debate took on a more heated tone. So that the congenial mood would not be spoiled, the pope called for adjournment, promising another meeting on both subjects within a week. He was bothered by the afternoon absence of Buldini and several other cardinals under his influence. An outright and public schism within the Church could prove detrimental to the pope's plans for Church revitalization. The bank investigations and Symon's successful efforts were crucial.

*****

'My house is in ruins; restore it!' The phrase ricocheted throughout every crevice of Pope Francis' brain as he waited for Symon's arrival. The Tower office was dimly lit as usual during the pope's meditation and prayer sessions. But this night, 'the phrase' dominated his thoughts, making quiet reflection impossible. For the first time since his election, he was having second thoughts. Did he misinterpret 'the words' as St. Francis had in the beginning?

Was he moving too fast; attempting to accomplish too much, too soon? What little concentration he could muster was shattered by the voices and footsteps as they approached his office from the direction of the hanging corridor.

"Thank heaven it's Symon," he said aloud.

"Thank heaven is right!" roared Symon. "That plane bounced all over the Roman skies as we attempted our landing. Thought I'd wear out my beads!"

"Symon, it's so good to see you. We have much to talk about. What do you think of Jan's secret passage?"

Before Symon had a chance to respond, Jan, who accompanied Symon to the Tower, proudly began to explain to Dom his addition to the hidden stairway entrance. "Dom, you have to hear this," he said. "You instructed me to install a padlock on the inside so no one could enter from the castle wall. Right? Well, there's a problem with that. If someone wants to leave the apartments, as Symon may, it cannot be locked or unlocked from the outside - until now, that is."

Symon, enthused by what he had seen earlier, entered the conversation. "Dom, it's ingenious! Jan replaced the padlock with a hidden spring-loaded

121

push button lock, one on the inside, one on the outside. Just press and hold for three seconds, and bingo, it releases the bolt. The flush with the surface button on the outside is concealed beneath the outer left side lip of the fifth step. No one would ever suspect, let alone recognize what it was. Jurewicz, the British Intelligence Service could use your genius."

"I need him first!" Dom demanded. "Jan, as usual, a job well done. Thanks. Why don't you join the others. You've probably missed dinner, but if you're lucky they may have saved you a morsel or two. God bless."

Turning to Symon, he continued. "Your trip was a heart-breaker, I know, and we do want to hear all about it. But first, we have a rather dangerous mission for you to consider. Thomas should be here shortly. He's running a little late, and it's necessary the three of us discuss it together. Before you arrived, I was weighing my actions of the past few days, and frankly I'm fearful.

"Fearful my reading of our Lord's direction to 'rebuild my house' may be unfounded. Maybe it's merely stage fright. I'm not sure. When St. Francis heard the words, he incorrectly thought it meant to physically rebuild the rundown churches in the area of Assisi. He thought small. Our Lord intended him to rebuild the Church universal.

"After all that has happened in recent days, I'm concerned I thought too big. I construed the reference to 'house' to mean earth; God's house. Spiritually, it is in ruins. My intentions were to build and solidify the faith, trust, fairness and love within Catholicism without alienating other Christian dominations. I had hoped to encourage a dialogue with them, based on truth and our mutual beliefs. Hopefully baring our Catholic soul, as I did, would be accepted as an expression of friendship to all faiths under one Father, easing their long held suspicions of the papacy. From early indications, we are cautiously optimistic." He sighed. "I just wish it could have been without all the bloodshed."

"Hold your ground my friend," encouraged Symon. "From what you've told me, your life from boyhood to pope has not been one random consequence after another. There's truly a divine finger pointing the way. You are personally accepting more responsibility than you should be expected to shoulder, yet you're handling it admirably. You're understandably apprehensive. Who wouldn't be? Remember this. God will not give you a burden He knows the two of you cannot manage successfully. In my opinion, you're doing everything correctly. You're praying and asking for guidance, then thinking all your moves carefully with passion for all. Pray for those killed protesting for the God given dignity of all the Father's children, for they can be honored as modern day martyrs. Their deaths were unfortunate. Only their killers are responsible."

Their personal thoughts were disrupted by a sudden bright light over the landing from the archives stairway. The welcome but tardy Cardinal Mumbwa had finally arrived. After a brief report as to the nature of his delay, including the surprising disappearance of Monsignor Diamante, the three tackled the seriousness of Symon's perilous assignment. Symon was versed on Buldini's outburst on the balcony and his conference challenge, as well as the circumstances of Dom's recent words of warning to Buldini. Symon was grinning from ear to ear as Thomas explained what he planned concerning Buldini's finances.

Dom had been completely briefed on all important current events and now outlined his thoughts on Symon's covert activity, including Thomas' misgivings. "Jabal's assignment is to mingle with members of Rome's clergy, as well as the secular community to identify those that may sympathize with our objectives and are willing to secretly keep us abreast of the mood of the people and schemes of any suspected enemy. However, Jabal is one of us, and known, especially to a segment of the clergy. So his success may be limited, yet the attempt necessary.

"On the other hand, you Symon, are a relatively unknown entity in our clandestine equation. The information you could gather from contacts would prove invaluable. Change your name and your appearance slightly, and only you would know who you are. And, you've got the perfect hiding place, the Borgia Apartments. Of course, you'd be provided with keys to the castle. What do you think 007, are you up to it?"

"Wait! Hold on there Dom," Thomas chimed in. "This is not the movies. This is real life where real characters can die. Two already have. Symon, we're fairly certain that Cardinal Buldini is the mastermind behind the attempt on the pope's life, resulting in Uden's death. And he's indirectly responsible for Paulo taking his own life. As of this date, there is no indication as to who the actual assassin is, although we're also fairly certain we know who warned us of the impending danger. Don't we Dom?"

"All right Thomas," said the pope. "I'll give you my reasoning as to why I think Monsignor Diamante is our 'elusive poet.' About ten years ago, I was loaned to the Monastery of St. Catherine on Mount Sinai to assist translating and cataloguing the remainder of over 3,000 manuscripts uncovered by workmen way back in 1975. The project began immediately after discovery, but was subsequently abandoned due to a combination of lack of interest and funds. The assignment was enjoyable. It was like stepping back in time. The monastery was akin to a miniature walled city with a dozen or more red tiled buildings. The small fertile and green garden outside the main entrance was a picture perfect site for quiet meditation. The entire tranquil scene lay in the shadow and protection of a harsh mountain side. The only drawback was insufficient housing. And this was when and where my and the monsignor's paths converged."

Dom turned to Symon and said, "Thomas knows Diamante. The little man's appearance and lack of social graces do not encourage fellowship. In fact, his first impression repels relationships. Therefore, he has learned to dislike and mistrust everyone. Sadly, he became a very lonesome and much maligned individual. After I came to know and understand the man, my heart went out to him."

Dom once again addressed them both. "Since St. Catherine's had a lot of extra bodies there for the research, they were already over-booked and the monsignor was denied lodgings. I spotted him sitting alone having breakfast and decided to join him for coffee; he looked so forlorn. At first he seemed distant, unwilling to even make eye contact. As you know, I can be persuasive.

"After a few minutes of priming the well, he mentioned needing a sabbatical. There was something about his conscience that was confusing him and threatened his commitment of loyalty. He refused to take me into his confidence no matter how hard I tried to convince him that it would help ease the inner tension. However, I did persuade him to share a room with me until another was available. My room was large enough to accommodate a cot. He gladly accepted, and in time became quite neighborly."

Dom chuckled to himself. "Gentlemen, much to my surprise he fancied himself a polished poet, and beamed with fatherly pride when I read aloud those poems he shared with me. I must confess they were atrocious, and his handwriting was equally bad. When I read the warning poems I recognized the phrasing and penmanship of Monsignor Diamante. There's no doubt."

The Pope got up, poured himself a cup of coffee and returned to his chair. "After he opened up to me in confidence, the hardened and unsavory persona melted away. He later revealed that I was the only one he could recall ever treating him so kindly; like an equal. Perhaps he's now returned the favor. I seem to remember, he once asked me why I slept with a rolled up towel under my neck in lieu of a pillow. Obviously, he was aware there would be an attempt on my life, and even if he knew the assassin planned the deed, he would have assumed I would be safe. The pillow wouldn't be used. No one, not even the assassin could have foreseen Uden's unexpected involvement. I'm convinced Diamante is what he claimed to be: *'a reluctant member of the plot.'*

"My intuition tells me the man's conscience is wrestling with his loyalty towards his domineering boss, *'the hostile one without a soul.'* Thomas, find a photo of the monsignor to show Symon, just on the chance he might discover his whereabouts. If you do Symon, approach him with caution and compassion. Tell him his roommate from the Monastery of St. Catherine wishes to renew that friendship."

Thomas and Dom looked at Symon for his response, and he didn't hesitate one moment. "Sounds like a hoot to me. Always did enjoy a good espionage thriller. But, I've got a small problem from the start, clothing and money. Or, rather the lack of same. I left my Moscow conference clothes and luggage with Peter in Tbilisi and made for the cave with my habit in a small bag, wearing one set of civilian duds. That's it! I even had to borrow a coat from Thomas for my trip to take Uden home."

"You'll need several changes of clothes, money to purchase whatever disguises you feel necessary, and money to live on, plus a sufficient amount for entertainment and bribes," Dom surmised.

"I can see you're really getting into this Dom," said Thomas. Symon was failing in his attempt to stifle his laughter. Thomas continued. "I've anticipated Symon's eagerness to accept this assignment regardless of the danger and my warnings, including the need to financially support this cloak and dagger escapade. Here Symon, this should be more than sufficient to get you under way."

"I've been dealing with the wrong banker all these years," teased the pope. "Next time the Church needs funds we'll call on the Bank of Africa. Okay, Symon's assignment is set. He does it his way, developing a plan as he goes. What we need now is a way for him to contact us, and a way for us to contact him. How about this? The light is out in the far corner of the Borgia Apartment corridor. Under the bulb area there's a large brass bowl ornament that unscrews. I know because I accidentally removed it by mistake when changing the bulb. There must be a short or something; it keeps burning out. Well anyway, we can exchange messages by placing them in the brass bowl. Symon can check it every night, and so can we. And, if necessary, Jabal can also contact Symon on the outside in a covert manner so as not to raise suspicion."

Thomas yawned, and said, "Okay my conspirators, the day's been long, and the evening's provided more intrigue than these old bones could ever imagine. I better get going and check in and see how our seminary volunteers are progressing. Dom, remember your meeting with the eastern-block ambassadors for breakfast. It'll last approximately two hours. Then there's the luncheon with the American Congressman, his wife, and several representatives from Ireland. The afternoon is open for you to work on tomorrow's Wednesday audience speech. And don't forget the early dinner with eight local museum directors. If nothing else, we're going to fatten you up.

"Give me six months and you'll resemble Pope John XXIII - in girth. And you Symon, take good care of yourself. I've come to like you, your courage and sense of adventure. We need you with us through all of this. I'd hate to lose you, too. I can't possibly hold the reins on His Holiness here all by myself. It takes two, or more. May the Holy Spirit be with you."

*****

The two Franciscans sat quietly for over an hour, reminiscing about their seminary days, their infrequent long sessions discussing and debating theology with the group of twelve, and the opposite paths their lives had taken until now. Their mutual dream revelation surfaced during the conversation, prompting Symon to reveal a dream he had some months ago after questioning his own faith resulting from his wife's death.

"Dom, as you know, even though I returned to civilian life as a professor, and later married, I remained true to my faith. After Lynn passed away, I questioned it all; I felt so alone. A few nights later a dream set me back on track. In the dream there was an altar. Not high, just three steps from floor to the top. Sitting on the floor of the altar was a golden crucifix. Suddenly the crucifix transformed itself into a monstrance, housing the exposed Holy Eucharist. Then, over the altar a cloud appeared, and out of the cloud came a voice saying, *'The Holy Seed.'* At that point the monstrance transformed into four capital letters with the appearance of brilliant pure ice. The letters spelled out the word L-O-V-E. I woke immediately and remembered that in the Old Testament God spoke to the Jews from out of a cloud. All doubts vanished.

"That evening I sat on the back porch speaking silently to God, thinking - *'I'm so alone. It's too bad that we, those still on earth, can't contact loved ones that have gone on, and vice versa.'* Later that week, sitting on the same porch, staring at the heavens enjoying the warm calm evening, a familiar fragrance suddenly filled my nostrils. I shook my head. *'No, it couldn't be,'* I told myself. Then the fragrance repeated itself ever so briefly. There's no mistaking the unique aroma of the scent I came to love for thirty three years. Within my heart I knew it was God's way of answering my reflection, and letting me know I wasn't alone. Lynn came when I needed her.

"It's just after that experience that I made the decision to return to the monastic way, and made plans to find my cave in the desert. And now look at me. I'm a Vatican spy!"

They both got a big laugh at the 'spy' reference.

"Symon, right now we need some rest. We both have a big day tomorrow. Hope you don't mind being isolated with the Borgias. Pax obiscume, my brother."

*****

The musty odor of hundreds of years hung heavy in the dark corridor of the Borgia Apartments. Symon had his choice of rooms. It would not be at the far end close to where Paulo had ended his life, and he couldn't bring himself to enter the cell where Uden had given his life. He finally decided on the room closest to the bathroom just off the entrance from the Tower walkway, facing St. Peter's Square.

As he lay deep in thought, the notion of ghosts past and present wandering the dark corridor had a smothering effect. He found it difficult to breathe; his chest heaved, struggling to pull in more oxygen. "What have I gotten myself into?" he said aloud. "I wish I were back digging in the cave. Lord help me!"

CHAPTER SIXTEEN

The closet trapdoor opened with ease, but the descent down three short steps was quite a feat for a tall man. "You either need to be a bloody contortionist or a pygmy!" Symon complained, as he bent over nearly on hands and knees. Crawling backwards to the double wall, he finally had room to stand and stretch his frame, but it was still a tight fit as he edged his way towards the hidden stairway. "People must have been tiny in the fifteenth century," he continued to fuss.

The doorstep latch sprung open, releasing the bolt and unfastening the outer stairway. As Symon pushed up on the underside of the stairs, a humorous thought struck him. *"If someone's standing there, I'm going to have a heart attack! I'll have the shortest spy career in history."* Much to his relief, he was alone on the wall's hidden walkway to the Castle St. Angelo. The wall passageway was several city blocks long, and by the time he reached his destination, the sun was already awakening. He had slept longer than expected, and now had to hustle to get in and out of the castle before the guards arrived for their daily tour of duty. Symon slowly opened the castle door facing the Via della Conciliazione that lead directly to St. Peter's Square.

Like any good spy, he lingered in the harbor of the early morning shadows. Once his eyes adjusted from the blackness of the castle to the new dawn's light, he stepped tentatively across the avenue, then over the meandering Tiber guarded by rows of towering stone angels perched on the ancient bridge of St. Angelo. It was too early for the Little Sisters of Charity Thrift Shop to open, but he remembered a coffee shop in a secluded alleyway off Rome's fashionable shopping area on Via del Corso leading to Trinitade Monti and the Spanish Steps. It was only one and a half kilometers, and he could use the exercise. Perhaps the cool refreshing air would clear his mind of the premonition that all of Rome was watching him, knowing what he was about.

*****

Symon didn't usually like coffee much, but for whatever reason, this morning he enjoyed the stimulant. In fact, he consumed five cups over a two hour period. "I'll never sleep tonight," he fretted. Earlier, a block and a half

129

away, he had passed the Thrift Shop on the walk to drown himself in coffee. In the window, on a one armed, headless mannequin, he saw a jacket like the one he had always longed for as a youngster. That would be his first purchase. The dark navy blue seaman's jacket with the large collar, and all those buttons, would finally be his. If they had a matching wool knit cap, his childhood vision would be complete.

Thoughts of the jacket brightened the morning gloom. The promised sun had begrudgingly submitted to the pressure of a sky dominated by ominous gray clouds rapidly enveloping the city. Before long the weather would become bitterly cold, and the jacket would provide welcomed warmth.

As he plotted his next move, the jacket gave him an idea for his cover, as it were. He decided to become a recently retired British seaman named Jonathan St. John. Johnny for short. To test his new identity, he engaged in conversation with the waitress, explaining that he had left ship in Naples and came to Rome where he always enjoyed the people, the food, the history, and charming female companionship. He was never much of a flirt as Symon Carpenter, but being Jonathan St. John, that was a horse of another color. With some amusement he thought to himself, *I think I'm going to enjoy my alter ego.*

Ah. The jacket was still there. A bell on the glass door drew the attention of a petite old lady dressed in traditional nun's habit. "Mother, please take the jacket out of the window; I wish to purchase it if it's a 42-long. And, do you have a wool knit cap to go with it?" The coat was a small, but luckily she had several in the back room, and she knew one would surely fit him.

There was also an ample supply of caps. Symon chose a light gray rib-knit turtleneck sweater, black wide-wale corduroy trousers, and a broad black belt with an unusual silver buckle to complete his new persona. Then he selected several shirts, socks, and a perfectly fitting pair of well worn thick soled black shoes. He decided to pass on the used underwear. This he would buy new.

After convincing the little sister that if she allowed him to use the back shop to change clothes - it was getting cold outside - he would leave something in the money jar for the convent upkeep. With his own clothes and newly purchased items neatly crammed in an old duffel bag, and looking like an old salt of the sea, Symon headed in search of the costume shop the sister said was only two blocks away.

The permanent beard, the shopkeeper assured him, would only come off with a special solution that he would gladly sell. Symon stepped back from the rest room's dingy mirror to admire his altered appearance. With cap in place, cocked at a defiant angle, a now lengthy ponytail, the beard, and jacket collar pulled up under his ears, he spoke quietly to the mirror's reflection, "You're one handsome bloke! All you need is a black eye patch. No - Dom wouldn't ever let me live it down. Better leave well enough alone."

*****

Giuseppe Zacchia had the appearance of a kindly village priest with a thick drift of snow white hair, a matching short cropped beard, and a faraway look in his eyes. It wasn't until he spoke that one's initial opinion was dashed. The jagged tone of his voice, combined with the curl of the upper left corner of his lip, changed his demeanor entirely. Buldini had called him, 'the chief inquisitor', and Giuseppe came by the nickname honestly.

Monsignor Zacchia's primary roll in Buldini's household was as investigator and protector of his master's interests. Matters of religious consequence were of no concern. His future prosperity was directly connected to the cardinal's good fortune. He enjoyed the fruits of his labor to the extreme, and was not hesitant to do whatever necessary to keep the status quo. Zacchia was a man who kept to the shadows within the Vatican. Very few knew the extent of his ties to Buldini, which enabled him to operated most effectively.

"Well!" came the angry and impatient voice of Cardinal Buldini. "Where in the hell did Diamante disappear to? It's as if he fell off the face of the earth, that little toad."

"I'm working on it your eminence," came Zacchia's quick response. "My informants are searching everywhere. We've spread ourselves thin, also attempting to run down leads to the identity and whereabouts of the failed assassin. We have little to go on in either case. Diamante's one thing, but if we're unsuccessful with the latter, it would necessitate engaging another hitter. Someone equally as nameless as the first, and that may take awhile."

"I don't want excuses, Monsignor Zacchia. You're paid a high price for results, not alibis! And what do you mean Diamante's one thing? He has enough information to bury me under the Vatican, including you! He must be found! We need to know his intentions. Is he merely unhinged over his chastisement, or has he decided to defect, planning to cripple me in revenge? He must be found and silenced if necessary."

"Your eminence, we will achieve both tasks. This very evening, disguised as a civilian, I will meet with my most trusted operative, Agapito. He's from Rome and has been on the streets for two days now. I will see what he has unearthed and will report accordingly."

Buldini's and Zacchia's arranged meeting in the Vatican Mosaic Workshop behind St. Peter's Basilica did nothing to satisfy either party. Both remained frustrated with the situation, and with each other. Zacchia was the one person in Buldini's group that the cardinal could never manage to completely intimidate, and that bred suspicion and mistrust.

*****

"I think my first outdoor Wednesday audience and message went well, don't you think, Thomas?" questioned the pope.

"Yes!" was the emphatic reply. "You're an overnight attraction. I'm told there were thirty percent more people than the normal Wednesday crowd. Thousands were turned away, but stood outside the square in the streets surrounding the colonnades hoping to hear your words. The most interesting report came from the crowd control guards. Apparently a much higher percentage of people of differing faiths were in attendance. You've become quite a curiosity. And our people mingling with the crowd report an extremely positive reaction to your simple attire. In earlier history the faithful enjoyed the grand and elegant trappings from medieval times that in a sense gave them the feeling the head of their Church was above all others, thus, somehow making them special. However, it also was responsible for the feeling of a great gulf between the papacy and the average man and woman.

"No doubt the mystique of God's presence on earth in the form of the pope's holiness has proven to be effective. Simply put, the love and respect for the papacy remains, but now the people feel you are one of them, understanding their everyday material and spiritual needs. They always felt they could touch former popes, but only from afar. You, on the other hand, they feel they can touch, shoulder to shoulder. Your candor and aura of confidence, trusting God's love for His children, is as personal as a handshake. Dom, you're off to a brave start, but there are mountain ranges before us."

"How well I know," sighed the pope. "The mountains give me no fear. Failing the community of God terrifies me. Their blind faith in their pope compounds my terror. Meeting my own Waterloo is one thing; shepherding them to an unfortunate heartbreaking conclusion is my greatest fear. The thought of failing God and His people is consuming me. I pray continuously throughout the day and night for His guidance; for success. Faith in Him is unwavering. Faith in this imperfect mortal is questionable. Symon and I discussed this subject at length recently, and his advice was sound and encouraging. Yet, the doubt in myself remains. Perhaps that's part of being human, and a safeguard compelling us to remain humble."

"Ha-ha!" burst Mumbwa's familiar husky laugh. "As usual, you paint yourself into a corner, and then in the same breath design a way out. Just have half the faith Symon and I have in you, and you'll succeed. And when you do, it'll take the two of us, and all the angels in heaven to keep you humble. Speaking of Symon, any word on his first twenty-four hours as James Bond?"

"No. I checked the globe under the light in the apartments this morning, and no message. However, Jabal informed me earlier that he intends to leave Symon a note tonight. He thinks he's discovered a weakness in Buldini's armor, one that Symon should investigate. Which reminds me, did the letter over my signature and seal go out to the clergy and the Vatican staff?"

"Yes, this morning. As you dictated, it directed them to search their consciences and join a voluntary effort to closely adhere to the spirit of St. Francis' example of service in their individual communities. They are to respond back directly to your attention within three weeks, outlining their voluntary action. As stated, you were leaving it up to each to observe St. Francis' standards as independently interpreted, and if the global endeavor is lacking in substance, a mandatory papal decree will be issued with a uniform code of performance.

"And Dom, Paulo's father called with the results of his inquiry into Cardinal Buldini's finances. He, somehow, has managed to accumulate millions of dollars in cash. An amount is in the Vatican Bank account, and the bulk in several banks worldwide. To our benefit, the banks outside of Rome have agreed to cooperate with whatever we wish. I've given instructions to freeze all offshore holdings, and two thirds of his available cash in the Vatican bank. Everyday withdrawals will not alert Buldini unless he cashes a check, or checks totaling three hundred thousand dollars or more. Or attempts to make a withdrawal from one of the other banks. Monthly statements will not reflect the freeze issue. The father will notify me immediately if a large check is written or a substantial amount of cash is drawn on any account. The safety deposit box holds various interesting documents, including deeds to buildings thought to be Vatican property, one being the Casa Santa. Buldini's living quarters and official office of the CDF, with all its elaborate trimmings, valuable paintings and antiques we witnessed not too long ago belong to him; so says the deed. It seems we've just scratched the surface of the biggest Vatican internal scandal uncovered in several hundred years."

Dom shook his head in disbelief. "My two elderly predecessors played right into Buldini's greedy clutches, and he milked their trust for all it was worth. Evidently, he expected to continue to harvest from the meek, namely me. Wasn't he surprised? Great job, Thomas. Continue to dig his hole, and ask Paulo's father to send you copies of all documents and statements.

"Walk with me to the broadcast studio. We can talk along the way. I've got an hour before the little red light comes on, and we once again address the world. Which brings me to the question, did Monsignor Lucchesi manage to convince everyone to allow our transmission to be received?"

"All said they would allow reception, but reserved the right to discontinue the broadcast if they regarded your remarks inflammatory in nature. The monsignor is a good negotiator. Changing the subject, Dom, does Kim follow you everywhere?"

Looking over his shoulder, Dom winced. "Oh, my yes! Well, almost everywhere. I love the big man as a brother, but honestly, he's becoming like a hair shirt. You want to get rid of the darn thing, but at the same time, you realize it serves a purpose."

The Vatican Broadcast Studio was state of art, including a replica of the pope's official office. There he would deliver the first of many worldwide-chats. Monsignor Lucchesi and his global broadcast connections advertised this event extensively. In spite of the short notice, another vast worldwide audience was expected.

During his twenty-minute chat, Pope Francis provided an update on his last talk. He also explained the essence of the meeting with various museum directors regarding the disposition of Vatican treasures.

Then he sketched out the details of the recent conference with cardinals representing the Curia, including consideration of a more democratic approach to Catholic Church government, the formation of a new World Council, and women's place in the priesthood. He announced the content of his letter to the clergy worldwide, and warned that several of his proposed changes were already causing internal conflicts. Also, that Vatican lawyers were reviewing plans to convert Church owned retreats and buildings for use by those most in need. This was all background for the real reason for the broadcast: to address those suffering physical oppression, and spiritual strife.

*****

The pope made his televised plea. "To all who live in a land not yet enjoying full freedom and to those who rule. We appeal to you to consider that cooperation between individuals and their governments is the basic principal of social order. It is the beginning point for harmony. People, we are now entering a new era when physical violence is perilous, and unnecessary.

"Please. Discontinue your demonstrations that have led to the loss of your loved ones. Trust in your Creator's power and loving nature. Trust in me when I say, give God a chance. Unite your prayers for the changing of hearts. We will pray with you. The world will pray with you.

"Put down your weapons. Take up words. Form those words into petitions and prayers to your Father in heaven. He can hear His children's cries. He can see His children's tears. He can feel His children's pain. Trust. Give God a chance.

"And to those who continue to discriminate wherever you live, may we remind you of the words of saintly Pope John XXIII, paraphrasing. *'Truth calls for the elimination of every trace of racial discrimination, and the logical and intelligent recognition of the sacred principle that people of every status or state, are by nature equal in dignity.'* This we believe. Pray all our hearts are changed in time.

135

"One last observation before we all go back to our everyday lives. Pope Francis represents the Catholic Church, but he is also a brother to all people as each one of you are - with one universal Father. Therefore, we must never forget that different faiths project different images of the Creator, and provide fresh ways of thinking about what is beyond our understanding. No single human instrument of the Father owns all the answers, no matter how faithful.

"Our spirituality can be deepened only when our understandings are broadened. We need each other. We are more likely to hear the Divine melody when we are listening to, rather than berating, each other.

"Thank you for the millions of positive comments, including your respectful challenges. We will make every effort, with God's help, to live up to your faith and support. We'll talk again soon. Peace be with all of you."

*****

"Dom, why is it you gravitate to this, the scene of your month long self-imposed incarceration in the Tower of The Winds?" Thomas asked. "You have several other options, all more comfortable and better lit."

"I'm not certain," came the answer. "There's just something that draws me to the Tower and Borgia Apartments. Perhaps it's because it's where we all worked so diligently and shared camaraderie. Perhaps because it's where I last enjoyed the company of my brother, Uden. I can tell you it's not because of the frescoes in the apartment's outer rooms. They're almost sacrilegious. Pope Alexander IV's family symbol, the bull, looks down in defiance from the ceiling in the fourth room. The pope's daughter Lucrezia, depicted in the portrait of St. Catherine is certainly borderline. The fresco in the fifth room is most distressing. The painting of Pope Alexander kneeling before The Resurrection fresco with a young Roman soldier considered to be his son Cesare, along with another son, the brother whom Cesare later murdered, is utterly outrageous. If they had been in any of our sleeping quarters, none of us would have enjoyed a moment's rest. But, I guess they're part of history - good or bad.

"I had hoped we'd run into Symon as he came in for the night. We haven't heard from him in two days. Jabal left him the message I told you about, and I included a short note to meet us if we were here before he turned in."

It had been a most trying day, and both men were talked out. A silent pensive mood set in. Suddenly, the dim light projecting into the darkened office from the temporary dining area was blocked by the outline of a figure dressed in black. Startled, both men jumped up, knocked over their chairs, and assumed a protective stance. Their unexpected response, in turn, alarmed the intruder, who gave off a bloodcurdling cry.

"Dom, Thomas, it's me! Symon. The Vatican spy has come out of the cold, and this is the reception I get?" Dom composed himself, turned up all the Tower lanterns, and looked at Symon in wonder.

"You gave us both a start. From the looks of you, we thought Buldini had sent the grim reaper himself to do us in. You missed your calling. You'd make a great theatrical performer. Spy, I don't know; movie star, maybe. We wouldn't have recognized you on the street."

Thomas joined in. "The beard and mustache becomes you. And I like the seaman's jacket. As a youngster visiting the ports on the African coasts, I always envied the rugged black coats they wore. You have to tell me where you bought it. A black man would look more handsome than some pale Brit," he said with a guilty grin.

Symon spent the next half hour filling them in on the past two days of familiarizing himself with Rome; its haunts and its people. He reported on the mixed, yet mostly positive feeling towards the pope's speeches among the citizenry and members of the clergy. Thomas' assessment was much the same, with the exception of the pope's worldwide chat. Symon's news was more current.

"It's both interesting and intriguing," Symon said. "The people, thinking I'm from afar and not cognizant of recent papal events, are more than anxious to fill me in on everything. They actually want their feelings known. Dom, they love you for your openness with them. They feel you've taken them into your confidence. You're the prime topic of discussion throughout the city, be it churchyard or the seediest of taverns. Although not all totally agree one hundred percent with everything at this point, I believe they would follow you anywhere. And just in case neither one of you has viewed the global channel in the past few hours, it's reported that the protesters and their repressive governments have called a truce. At least for the time being. You should be pleased with that outcome."

"Thanks for the information Symon. The truce is the best news of all. But what about Jabal's message?"

Symon took the note out of his inside chest pocket to get the name right. "This gets a little complicated. It involves a Monsignor Zacchia, a shadowy associate of Cardinal Buldini. Jabal has been in contact with some Ethiopian Seminary students; the seminary behind St. Peter's. The Mosaic Workshop is close by, and while walking to the square, they overheard a small portion of a conversation between Buldini and a Monsignor Giuseppe Zacchia. All that they could gather was that the monsignor was to meet another to discuss something the cardinal emphatically insisted be done. Zacchia's an obscure character around the Vatican City and Rome. I'm to meet Jabal on the Via Portico d' Ottavia. You know, that's where the big open air fresh produce market is located. I was there yesterday. He's to apprise me of all he's learned thus far. I'll take it from there. And by the way, my name's Jonathan St. John. My acquaintances call me Johnny."

The laughter of the three men broke the tension of the moment. After a brief but serious warning to Symon by Thomas, they headed to their respective evening lodgings. Dom and Thomas descended the archives staircase, through the musty corridors, then on to the Vatican buildings beyond. Symon wandered to the seclusion of his Borgia cell, trying desperately to ignore the creeping loneliness. He hadn't experienced this feeling of emptiness alone in the Turkish cave, and the emotion puzzled him.

*****

The aromas of fresh cut flowers, fruits, vegetables, and pungent smells of Roman breakfasts in the cool morning sun, along with sounds of dozens of early shoppers, had quickened Symon's spirit. With coffee cup in hand, he leisurely made his way between and around the stands of produce and customers. The cheerful colors of the flowers, the patron's clothing, and flapping awnings of outdoor cafes were in stark contrast to Symon's cave mountain view. Though he longed to follow Assuri's trail, the excitement of this covert assignment and the sights that filled his senses this morning stimulated his imagination. Then it hit him like a bolt from the heavens. *How would Jabal recognize me?* he thought in a panic. *Only Dom and Thomas know. That was dumb of me! Some spy.*

He decided it would be wise to sit at one of the outside cafe tables where he could get a better view of the open air market in hopes of spotting Jabal. Then he'd find a way to alert him of his identity. The prearranged time of contact came and went, and Symon was becoming mildly agitated. *The best laid plans,* he thought. Customers finished with their shopping began filling the empty chairs and tables - and still no Egyptian in sight.

"My master tells me you are in need of female companionship, my fine seafaring friend," came a voice from the table directly behind Symon. Startled and offended, he started to turn, when the voice commanded him; "No! Do not acknowledge my existence, brother Symon. It is I, Jabal. Several blocks away at the foot of Via Catalana is the main Jewish Synagogue. Behind it is the tiny Church of Our Lady of Heavenly Mercy. At this time of day it will be deserted. There's never any service, so we can talk freely. I'll leave now. Meet me inside in fifteen minutes. There's much to discuss." Jabal left immediately, leaving Symon with his thoughts.

*****

"Greetings brother," Jabal said with a Nile wide grin. "Did my salutation get your attention, Johnny?" As Symon's eyes adjusted to the dimly lit church, he wondered how Jabal recognized him, and how he had come to know his nickname. The fumes from the recently stained timeworn wooden floors filled his nostrils, triggering a dull throb in his sinuses.

"Yes! You commanded my attention. How in the bloody heck did you know it was me? Was it that obvious?" Symon demanded an answer.

Jabal would have loved to lengthen Symon's curiosity, but time was in short supply. "It's elementary my dear friend. Dom versed me on last night's meeting in the Tower, including your excellent disguise, and new name. He requested I meet with him first thing this morning. That's why I was so late. Forgive us."

"Well, no harm done. Except a sudden headache. So here we are. Did you see the inscription on the side door that faces the synagogue across the street? If Dom knew, he'd have a bloody seizure. Sorry for the bloody this and bloody that, but I'm trying to get into character."

Jabal shook his head and said, "No. I came in the front door."

"Jabal, you won't believe it. In this day and time to allow this kind of racism to exist, especially so close to the Vatican, and on a Catholic Church door is inexcusable.

"I can read Latin and Hebrew, and the inscription is in both languages. It's taken from the Book of Isaiah, and reads; *'I spread out my hands all the*

139

day unto a rebellious people which walketh in a way that was not good after their own thoughts.' The censorious implication is plain, and no longer should be permitted to remain as a symbol of a division of two faiths. Jabal, you have to alert Dom as to the message on the door, its intent and my personal feelings on the matter."

"Symon, I too am appalled, and will do as you ask. But right now, to the business at hand. You're aware of the extent of information obtained from the Ethiopians, which was limited. However, since then I've been fortunate to add to what we already knew. Especially concerning the elusive Monsignor Zacchia. Basically, he's a very cunning agent in Buldini's service. As a member of the Vatican clergy, and when necessary, undercover as a private citizen, he probes into any present or foreseeable unrest within the faithful or private annoyances concerning Buldini. Whatever negatively affects the cardinal, would eventually impact Zacchia. Therefore, he's extremely dangerous.

"The Ethiopians said the monsignor was to meet someone to help him accomplish whatever it was the cardinal was so worked up about. I've been able to find out that Zacchia enjoys frequenting three taverns. It's a pretty fair bet you'll find him in at least one of the three. One is called Hemingway's Mistress. The monsignor likes it because he's fond of thinking he resembles the author, and enjoys their ravioli stuffed with artichokes and anchovies spread on bread. It's at the end of the produce market opposite the Piazza di Biscione. You walk down into a cave-like tavern that in ancient times was a theater. Coincidentally, it's a stone's throw from where Caesar was murdered on the Ides of March."

"That's comforting to know," Symon cringed.

Jabal continued. "One last point of information. Take the fifth bridge to the left of the castle and cross over the Ponte Sisto to the market. Christian martyrs were often thrown into the Tiber from this bridge, and Romans say, *'It's good luck to see a white horse, an old woman and a priest all crossing at the same time.'* So be on the watch. We need all the luck we can muster.

"Another watering hole favorite of Zacchia's is a German tavern, the Gerhardt Tolz. It's behind and to the left of the Castle Saint Angelo on Via Vitelleschi. The neighborhood is small with ancient buildings and medieval dwellings, called the Borgo. The tavern's been serving since the middle ages, and Zacchia likes to consume tankards of German tap beer.

"The third is a 1760 establishment called Nero's Coffeehouse, one half block from the Spanish Steps on the Via Condotti. They feature several rooms with marble tables and walls lined with oil paintings. It's a perfect place for private meetings. Here, I've written down the names of the taverns and addresses. Good luck."

"Jabal, when this is all over you could moonlight as a Roman tour guide. As for me, after making the rounds of taverns in hopes of encountering Zacchia, I'll end up in the pope's ward for homeless alcoholics. It would be most helpful if you could find out a day, time, and place where a suspected meeting was going to take place. I'm certain my liver would thank you."

Jabal reciprocated in kind with a typical high pitched Egyptian laugh. "Yes, Johnny, I will do as you ask. Remember, the monsignor does resemble Hemingway with a mane of white hair, and closely cropped matching beard. He's about five foot ten with a barrel chest. His upper lip tends to curl when speaking. He shouldn't be difficult to spot. Check the lamp in the apartment tonight. If I have anything new to report, there will be a message. May the Holy Spirit watch over you my friend. Good-by."

After Jabal left, Symon took the opportunity to light five candles. One each for Uden and Paulo's souls, one for Inge, and one each for the twins. He also spent the next half hour in prayer before the statue of the Blessed Mother, asking her to intercede on his behalf with her Son. He prayed for Dom's success, for forgiveness, and for protection in the days ahead.

CHAPTER SEVENTEEN

Christian, Rico and Nathan discussed recent findings of the seminary students, who were gathering incoming phone, fax and letter messages concerning the pope's worldwide chats. Their individual reports were zealously delivered, and although the results were significantly favorable, three to one, the pope's mind was elsewhere. The words of his colleagues lacked the power to penetrate an unconscious barrier. He was preoccupied with the presumed disappearance of Symon Carpenter.

Just that morning, both Jabal and Thomas had voiced their uneasiness with the fact that there had been no word from Symon in three days, and there was no evidence he had returned to the apartments. The notion of losing the person who had taken the place of his best friend, Uden, and the thought of another forfeiting his life, tormented Dom's soul. He was unable to concentrate on other important matters. Thankfully, Thomas was there to take note of the student reports and would later refresh the pope's memory on the accounts.

Obviously distracted, Dom thanked everyone for their participation and effort and apologized for his lack of attention, explaining his concern for Symon's safety.

*****

It was nearing 10:30 PM. A worried group of four sat in the pope's makeshift Tower office, anguishing over Symon's failure to return to the apartments. "I've checked the hidden stairway latch mechanisms, and they're working perfectly," Jan reported.

Jabal, visibly shaken, felt personally responsible for Symon's well being. "It's my fault! I was his outside contact, and should have been aware of his whereabouts at all times."

Thomas, too, felt accountable. "If it's anyone's failing, it's mine. I've had a bad feeling from the start, and should have insisted that he refuse the assignment."

Dom, hearing about all the self-deprecation he could stand, interrupted. "Stop it, all of you!" he said with a wave of his hand. "Symon's a full grown intelligent adult who's quite capable of taking care of himself. Accepting the

143

task was his decision, and he did it eagerly. There could be a perfectly good reason why Symon hasn't contacted us or returned to the apartments."

"Your faith in me is flattering. And yes, there is a perfectly good reason for my so called disappearance," came a voice out of the darkness from the direction of the dining hall.

A cry of "Symon!" passed everyone's lips, followed by a flood of questions. "Where have you been?" "Are you all right?" "What happened?" "Tell us all!"

And a final second question by Dom.

"Forget the faith I have in you. Don't ever go more than two days without finding some way of leaving us a message, or at least let us know in advance of a known prolonged absence. That's a direct order from the pope! The only exception would be if you're bound and gagged somewhere." The lightheartedness of Dom's last remark fell on Thomas' deaf ears, who found no humor in the situation and let Dom know with a piercing look of disapproval.

Sensing a flash of tension between Thomas and Dom, Symon explained the reason for his belated return. "First, I'm touched by everyone's concern. Truthfully, it really is Jabal's fault." All eyes were on the jaw-fallen Egyptian. Laughing, Symon continued. "Yes, it's true. Brother Jabal provided me with a list of taverns Monsignor Zacchia frequented, and I felt duty bound to follow up on that lead. I've spent more time in taverns the past three days than in all my years up to now." Realizing he was the brunt of Symon's ill timed joke, Jabal managed a weak snicker. Thomas still could find no humor in any of this and did nothing to hide his disfavor.

Symon looked directly at Thomas and said, "Cardinal Mumbwa, your genuine concern for my safety is appreciated. Be assured there's no one here more interested in the success of my mission, and for my continued well-being than Symon Carpenter. But if I become so distracted by the seriousness of it all and lose my sense of humor, I'll sacrifice the necessary calm to survive the ordeal. And I respectfully suggest you do the same."

Thomas looked at Symon intently with jet black eyes and then managed a brief but understanding smile. He nodded in acceptance of Symon's suggestion and gestured for him to continue his account of the last three days.

"Unfortunately Monsignor Zacchia was nowhere to be found. However, on my third visit to Hemingway's Mistress, and for those unfamiliar with local watering holes, that's the name of one of Zacchia's favorite taverns, I encountered a gentleman named Agapito. Jabal had informed me he is one of Zacchia's trusted informants.

"You see, I've spent most of the time in all three taverns the monsignor favors, and at different hours of each day. During the extended visits I made sure to become buddies with the local tipplers, freely buying drinks for those who would listen to my tales of the seven seas. In short, I've become very much a celebrity, earning a rousing *'Yo Johnny'* whenever crossing thresholds of sour smelling establishments. On second thought, it's more likely the free booze made me so popular."

Symon leaned forward in his chair and almost in a whisper, continued his tale. "Late last night at Hemingway's I overheard a conversation with a bloke I've primed with shots of Irish Whiskey downed by tankards of ale for the past few days, and this rather nasty gent named Agapito. The latter is completely bald with a layer of skull skin so thick it's actually wrinkled in large folds over each ear, bending the tops outward. His earlobes looked remarkably like oversized grapes, with golden loop earrings. Quite a character. Dangerous, I'm sure.

"Agapito was showing a small thin piece of stone to my new found drinking buddy. It turns out Agapito bought what he thought was a priceless authentic ancient relic, intending to resell it for a goodly profit. My buddy had spied me swaggering through the door. Ten minutes later he waved me over, and introduced me as a retired seaman who, when having the opportunity, dabbled in archaeological finds. The bald one pocketed his treasure as I approached the table, but after several rounds of drinks that I purchased, and a string of lies bolstering my cover, he began to loosen up. And, at the prompting of his friend, he presented me with a palm size slab of stone."

By now, everyone sat on the edge of their chair, and leaned forward. "Inscribed on the stone were five rows consisting of five letters each written in Latin. I recognized the artifact immediately as a well known archaeological puzzle. The same inscription has been found on the walls in England, Pompeii, Mesopotamia, and elsewhere. For years, experts have attempted to decipher its meaning with little results. The letters are designed to be read both backwards and forwards. Many consider it to be of Christian origin. The letters can be arranged in the shape of a cross and made to read

PATER NOSTER (Our Father) in Latin, with extra A's and O's representing Alpha and Omega. To this day, it remains a mystery.

"Agapito seemed to lose interest in the item when he realized it was a well known artifact. He then considered it useless because it was something he couldn't directly benefit from. I offered him a fair price with the excuse that while it's not valuable, my hobby was archaeology, and I'd love to study the puzzle now that I have leisure time. Another round of free drinks and he agreed to meet me tomorrow night at the German tavern, the Gerhardt Tolz, to finalize the transaction. It's one of Zacchia's three favorites, and just behind the castle. Hopefully, it will help cement confidence in me as a new drinking buddy, and perhaps lead to meeting Monsignor Zacchia."

Symon leaned back in his chair and relaxed. Obviously the interesting part was over. Everyone followed suit. "It's been necessary to rent a small hotel room. It wouldn't be wise to leave the taverns late at night and walk back to the castle. I imagine that you might find me floating in the Tiber along with some former popes. Besides, I feel it's important to establish a temporary residence to complete my cover in Rome. That brings you up to date on my activities the past days and the possibilities ahead. I'll maintain the hotel room, but will make every effort to return to check messages in the apartment whenever possible. It might be smart if Jabal and I meet at the Church of Our Lady of Heavenly Mercy at least every other day. Jabal and I can work out the details later. Dom, could we talk privately?"

*****

After everyone said their good-byes and good-lucks, Symon elaborated on his decision to establish residence outside the Borgia Apartments. "Dom, it's true I felt Johnny's cover would be more believable with a local address, but there was a dual motive, one I knew you'd understand. From the hotel I can phone Inge. Something that couldn't be done with any secrecy from a Vatican office phone. We talked at length the first night. She told me to tell you to keep up the good work, and you'll always be in her prayers. The twins are taking their father's death pretty hard, and their immediate spiritual and psychological needs help Inge cope. She has a cause to channel her energy and sorrow: the boys. I promised that when my work in Rome is complete, I'd come for a visit before heading for Turkey. You do understand?"

146

"Yes my friend, I do understand. And it was a wise move to rent temporary quarters. Just be sure you give Jabal your address. Do me a favor. When you talk to Inge next, ask if she is in need financially. We can help if there's ever a problem. Also, assure her that the boys' education will be taken care of as well. Thank her for her prayers, and remind her that she and the boys are ever in my mind and petitions to the Holy Mother."

As Symon got up and turned to leave, Dom grabbed his sleeve. "Symon, before we part, I'm sure you'll be pleased to note that when you meet Jabal at the tiny church, you'll find the door facing the synagogue with the obnoxious message has been replaced. The original will be kept in one of the museums as an example of our religious intolerant past."

*****

The clothes-clinging haze of cigar and cigarette smoke, mingled with the stench of the tavern's centuries old wooden floor, often drenched with spilled beer, and now covered by a soggy coating of sawdust, quickened Symon's sense of drama. The dimly lit interior of the German tavern mixed with gregarious sounds of laughter were successfully transforming Symon Carpenter into the character of a worldly old salt.

"Let him go back to the Monastery! Whatever I got, I got myself without praying to his God!" Symon roared, hoping to get the attention of Agapito who he noticed approaching his table of hangers-on. "No pope has ever done me any good. The last two were worthless old men, and the new one sounds like a wimp. It's time to do away with the papacy. That's what I say!"

Symon was relieved as Agapito's presence halted the beginnings of what could have turned into an all-out ugly brawl. While many within earshot soundly voiced their agreement, the pope did have his loyal followers. They were now in a hostile mood and growing more irate by the minute. Agapito's appearance had the same effect on the tavern patrons as the unexpected arrival of a fox in a hen house. Those already on their feet, ready to do battle, scurried back to their tables, hiding behind their mugs of ale. Agapito motioned for Symon to follow him to a secluded corner table.

"Johnny, you'll get your kidneys carved around here with that kind of talk. The tavern may be full of alcohol soaked downtrodden low-lifes, but most are Catholics that somehow identify with the new pope. Better watch your tongue and your back from now on. Are you ready to deal?"

Symon pulled a folded newspaper page from his inside jacket pocket and slowly shoved it across the table top within Agapito's reach. Opening the crinkled sheet, Agapito counted the bills and smiled in satisfaction. He reached in his own pocket, and placed the small stone slab inside the paper, refolded it, and slid it back to Symon.

"Johnny, you're a rascal, but a generous rascal. Let me buy you a tankard, and you tell me what your beef is with the popes."

Symon hadn't prepared for this part of the charade and had to reach deep within to find courage to slam everything he had believed in all his life. "It's not just this guy, it's religion in general. I gagged on it until I was nine, and then ran away from home to live on the open sea. It's been a great and profitable life, and I've never let God get in the way. There's money in ports around the world. I put my trust in the sea, and jobs of a mercenary nature filled my shore time and pockets. But, that's my business. I've said too much already. Thanks for the drink, and it's been good doing business with you. Hope our paths cross again. Ciao."

Without another word, Symon left Agapito to his thoughts, skirting around table after table until he reached the door. Stepping outside, he found himself surrounded by an angry group of men and women brandishing their bare fists. It was obvious they were bent on making him pay for his blasphemous remarks. He hadn't foreseen a confrontation and braced himself for the rush of a lone figure waving what looked like an ancient dagger. The gathered crowd was also taken by surprise and stepped back so as not to be part of such an outrageous act. Their intention was to teach the stranger a lesson, not to take his life.

Symon somehow managed to grasp the wrist of the assailant's knife wielding hand. Their bodies locked in a vice-like clinch as the two men struggled to throw each other to the ground. Symon could feel the attacker's hot breath on his neck and heard his wrathful cries of vengeance. As they spun one way, then another, the man's words softened as he whispered, "My brother, you are far stronger than you look. Later, look into your pocket for a message. Now strike me and make it look true."

Jabal loosened his grip on Symon's free hand, allowing a surprisingly powerful right cross that sent him reeling into a row of tavern garbage cans. The would-be slayer, blood streaming from his nose, jumped to his feet and quickly vanished into the darkness of the moonless night. The crowd dispersed just as conveniently.

Symon, ever the actor, played the scene to the hilt. He remained with fists clenched, shaking his shoulders and arms as if to loosen taut muscles, hoping his trembling legs would not betray him. As he turned, there stood Agapito with arms folded and wearing a wicked grin of approval. Before stepping back into the tavern, he flashed a thumbs up sign in Symon's direction. At that moment Symon felt secure in the knowledge that he had not only won the fight, but now was all he appeared to be in Agapito's mind: a rascal, seaman, mysterious mercenary - and one proven to handle himself when the chips were down.

The street lights lost their duel with the moonless night as darkness prevailed. The figure dressed in black was consumed by the night, as if swallowed by some nocturnal beast without a body. Only his ashen features and shaking hands were faintly visible. Symon was completely drained by the harrowing experience, and a fatigue, never felt before, insatiably devoured his energy. He sat on the steps of the tavern's loading dock for a period of time he would not later recall. He was numb. Thoughts could neither enter nor leave his consciousness. The clatter of a garbage can lid overturned by a scampering rodent broke the spell. Symon was once again himself. Almost.

Still feeling weak from his ordeal but clear of mind, he decided it would be wiser to stay the night in the Borgia Apartments just blocks away rather than to chance another encounter walking to his hotel in the dead of night.

*****

No message. The globe on the corridor light was empty. Halfway to his room, Symon stopped in his tracks and thrust his hand into the side pocket of his jacket. "I have a message!" he gasped. Until now, he had all but forgotten Jabal's muffled words during the scuffle. "Later, look in your pocket for a message."

With the cell door locked and the curtains drawn, Symon read the crumbled note in the glow of a small lamp over his bed. *"Brother Symon, please forgive the handwriting as I write hastily and in the dim light of a shop window. I followed you this night and from a distant corner of the*

149

tavern heard your irreverent words, as did everyone else. When tensions grew, I joined others, who had left to gather in wait for your departure. Sensing the crowd was determined to enact bodily harm on your person, I promptly devised a plan to intercede. I pray we were successful in our attempt.

"Monsignor Zacchia is in Stuttgart on business and will be away from Rome for a reported four days. Let us meet again the day after tomorrow at Our Lady's Church, say 2 PM. Hope I did not hurt you too badly during our mock battle. Forgive me, brother."

Symon reread the last two sentences and began a laugh that started in the vicinity of two weakened knees and slowly made its way into his lungs, releasing an uncontrollable roar that caused pain in his aching muscles.

"Hurt me? Wait 'til I see the new shape of that classic Egyptian snout. Hurt me indeed. But, thank heaven Zacchia is out of town for a few days. It'll give me time to dry out and give my liver a breather."

Symon needed a good night's rest, and much to his surprise, slept until ten the next morning. Although he woke refreshed of mind, his muscles screamed in silence. They were so sore it even hurt to put on his socks.

CHAPTER EIGHTEEN

It was noon and the Via Portico d' Ottavia marketplace reminded Symon of a bustling, humming beehive. The colorful outdoor café umbrellas sheltered a crowd of festive patrons from a brilliant sun and a cutting fall breeze. He had already visited the little church where he would later meet Jabal and was pleased with the replacement door facing the synagogue.

As he sipped the third cup of coffee, his mind wandered; he was no longer conscious of the sights, sounds and smells surrounding him. Events of the past few months flashed before him: the wrenching decision to leave his professorship - the hazardous journey from Moscow to the desert cave - the startling discovery of Assuri's journal - the unexpected summons to Rome by the pope - Uden's murder - Inge - and the birth of a new and perilous personality, Johnny, seaman and mysterious rogue. It was all rather overwhelming. The memory of his serene world of campus life was doused by the sudden creation of a new world that smacked of surrealism. Shaking his head in an effort to clear the cobwebs of confusion, Symon thought to himself, *I can hardly believe this life - but I'm here, and will follow His will, if it is His will. Time will prove us right or dreadfully amiss.*

*****

Symon was deep in prayer when the sound of the church door opening broke his concentration. He was prepared to defend himself. Whirling around, he gasped aloud, and covered his mouth with both hands. Before him stood a man whose face was masked with what appeared to be a plaster cast from the bridge of his nose to his upper lip. His eyes, though penetrating, shone expressionless, peering out of two gray circles.

"Think carefully, my friend before you say a word or utter another sound," warned Jabal. "You may find my present appearance humorous, and while I understand the unavoidable circumstances of my aching injury, I cannot detect a trace of whimsy in the situation. Therefore, tread lightly."

Symon was filled with remorse at the pitiful sight of his friend. "Oh my, Jabal, I'm sorry," he said apologetically. "How bad is it?"

"The nose is broken. Twisted to one side is a more accurate description, and my upper lip is split nearly corner to corner. As you can see, both eyes are as black as a camel's heart. You, Symon Carpenter, for a scrawny Englishman, launch a potent clout. The nose has been set, the lip stitched, and by early spring I will be as handsome as ever, perhaps more so." Jabal's attempt at humor brought a trace of a forced yet painful smile to his only visible lip, hopefully signaling an ease of tension.

Feeling helpless and remembering Jabal's note stating he hoped he had not hurt Symon too badly, Symon desperately tried to stifle the growing impulse to playfully challenge Jabal. It was hard to keep a straight face. Thankfully Jabal made it clear he wanted to proceed with the business at hand.

"I take it both you and your liver are well rested these past two days?" Jabal inquired, not waiting for a reply. "There is little new to report. Zacchia is still out of the country, and rumor has it he may take a few extra days at an undisclosed location. Interesting. Since I cannot show my nose in the Gerhardt Tolz Tavern - someone may add two and two and identify the attacker as one of the pope's confidants, Nathan has replaced me for prospecting information. However, I'll remain as your main contact. Rumor also has it that your heroic stand in the face of a crazed knife slashing foreigner has put you in good standing with your former accusers. Lord knows why! If they only knew."

"Jabal, please forgive me," Symon pleaded. "It really wasn't my fault. Your action took me completely by surprise, and until you spoke, I felt my life was in danger. My striking out was a spontaneous reflex. I did not purposely hurt you; it was an accident. Can't we forget it ever happened?"

Jabal nodded slowly. "I forgive my brother. Forgetting is more difficult. The object of my Egyptian pride throbs with every breath, and I fear when healed I will more closely resemble a European. God forbid! What hurt almost as much was Dom's reaction to my appearance and the explanation for same. He could barely contain his amusement. Thomas on the other hand became quite sullen. Clearly, there is a foreseeable fracture in their alliance. While they both desire the same end, Thomas would prefer a more conservative approach, whereas Dom is venturesome and perhaps too reckless in Thomas' mind. Pray do not read me wrong. The cardinal remains dedicated to Dom's vision for the Church, and to Dom, his pope. But when discussing our covert operation, he is mindful of the two deaths and the ever present danger to all of us. It is this that guides his judgment."

Symon let a minute pass before responding. "Thank you brother, for your forgiveness. It eases the heaviness in my heart, and be certain that I will pray that your Egyptian pride is soon restored to its original splendor." Before Jabal had an opportunity to say anything, Symon placed his finger to his lips, then continued. "Dom and I suffer from the same brand of humor. By instinct we seem to find humor in most everything, and in times of stress we often use it as a form of protection, or a vehicle to lighten the weight of a serious situation. As I just now did, praying on the behalf of your nose. All too often we're misunderstood, frequently accused of displaying a devil-may-care attitude towards an individual or subject. It's just our nature, and hopefully in time friends come to understand that quirk. Others, it leaves somewhat befuddled. Believe me brother, in the past year humor has helped me survive.

"Jabal, we need to do something to reassure Thomas before sparks do fly. I too, believe he's loyal to Dom, but he's also his own man. I'd like you to contact Thomas as soon as you return to the Vatican and ask him to break bread with me in my Borgia Tower room, say seven o'clock. And let's stay in touch via the lamp. I have some personal housekeeping chores to do while Monsignor Zacchia is away, and I'll drop in on my new found fans at the German tavern tomorrow night. Perhaps Agapito will be there. We wouldn't want him to forget me, would we?"

*****

Voices from an open window of the third story apartment building on the outskirts of Paris could now be heard over street sounds of vendors and children at play. "Hush Ma-Ma! Everyone will know of our dirty laundry. Why are you so upset to keep watch over your grandchildren? You know that since Pa-Pa and Charles died I must make a living for all of us. I've invested day and night for over a month making my jewelry. Now I have the opportunity to sell the stock. A department store in Rome is renting me a very nice booth."

She was no more than 5' 3" with an almost boy-like figure and delicate squared shoulders. In her frustration she turned quickly to shut out the prying ears of the neighborhood. Her movement to the window was that of an athlete, but with grace of an ex-ballet dancer. A short cropped pixie hairstyle framed her face, highlighting large blue eyes, smallish nose, and full lips. The mother looked older than her age. Tiny in stature like her daughter, but with an aura of sadness worn as a penance. She was the sole survivor of

153

the auto crash that claimed the lives of her husband and son-in-law four years ago, and she continued to condemn herself for not perishing as well.

"No, no, no, my child! It's not our little ones. I love them dearly, but I get so lonely when you're gone - and then the ghosts from the past come in the night," her mother argued. "Annette, when you go, you are gone so long, just like Charles used to do. And now you're going back to Rome so soon?"

"Ma-Ma, sometimes you act as the daughter and I the parent. Get over the past. I have. If business is good, you know I must stay to sell all the stock, and sometimes that takes weeks. Christmas is coming soon, and it will be the best of timing for me to sell gift jewelry. Now please go down and call the children for supper. My jewelry cases are packed, but not my clothes. Be a good grandmother so I can pack in peace. And remember, as we have often talked, if anything were to happen to me, quickly go to the bank security drawer and empty the contents. There is a letter addressed to you and the children. Follow the instructions within."

*****

It was nearly seven o'clock; time for Cardinal Mumbwa to arrive. Symon and Dom had been deep in conversation for over an hour. Symon did most of the talking. Dom listened to his friend with an open mind, though the subject matter troubled him somewhat. "You must be completely open with Thomas. Trust him. He's a good man and a necessary ally. Tell him about the spiritual phenomenon you experienced as a child in Assisi. And about the incident that happened on your first visit back home as a young Franciscan.

"Yes, even explain the interpretation of our shared dream. He needs to be convinced you're being led. The disturbing events of the past two months, along with what he construes as your lighthearted attitude, must be fully explained. We cannot afford to lose Thomas as our closest confidant. He's one of the keys to our ultimate success. You're mindful of all of this; I know you are. Open up! I'll do my best to rationalize your seemingly eccentric sense of humor."

"Symon, are you there? It's so dark in this corridor I can hardly see. Turn on the lights, the apartments are secure. Jabal said you invited me to dine with you this...oh Dom, I didn't know you'd be here, too. What a pleasant surprise."

Cardinal Mumbwa looked at them both, and remarked, "What's wrong? You two look so serious."

Symon wasn't sure he had gotten through to Dom since there was no reply to his appeal for disclosure. Throwing caution to the wind, he made the decision to begin the conversation while setting a small table with bread, an assortment of cold cuts and beer. "Enjoy, my friends!" And with that, he laid all his cards on the table. He began to explain everyone's concerns about the obvious tension between the cardinal and his pope, including the nature behind what Thomas misconstrued as a tasteless sense of humor and disregard for danger.

Thomas remained silent throughout. Symon sighed, lowered his shoulders, and motioned with his head toward Dom, then nodded in Thomas' direction, as a way of saying, "It's your turn; I've done all I can."

Thomas sat without displaying the slightest hint of emotion. Symon held his breath, pleading with his eyes for Dom to do something. Anything. Minutes passed before they both realized Dom was absorbed in prayer. The two exchanged glances. Symon seized another gulp of air, and both sat patiently for Dom.

As his eyes opened and his chin lifted from his chest, a smile crossed Don's face as if amused by a personal joke. Symon and Thomas stood as Dom rose from his chair and walked toward Thomas. The pope gestured with his left hand for Symon to be seated, halting within an arm's length of the cardinal. Placing both hands on Thomas' broad shoulders, said, "My friend, your wisdom, strength and complete dedication is valued. I need you. We need you. The Church needs you. Symon has, in his straight forward manner, convinced me to take you completely into my confidence. That I will do presently. But first I am concerned with the fact you misjudged what Symon so tactfully termed my eccentric sense of humor. His interpretation is correct, and won't argue with his analysis. Nor will I apologize. My sense of humor has been with me since birth - it's in my genes, you see." Dom released his grip on Thomas' shoulders and returned to his chair.

Thomas sat spellbound for the next forty minutes. Neither food nor drink was touched as Dom told his story in detail; his path to the papacy, as he referred to it - including the shared dream resulting in Symon being summoned to Rome after Uden's murder.

"I cannot walk away from what may well be the direction of the Holy Spirit. That in itself may constitute a sin. I must play out the script handed me, even if my life is forfeited for the good of the faithful - for the good of all. This is Symon's attitude as well. I'm painfully aware that I could be wrong in my understanding of being led to a certain destiny, and I pray for discernment. Even if I'm wrong, I pray my efforts will bear fruit. You and Symon are the only living people who know about what has been disclosed this evening. No one else should ever hear a single word. This you must promise. Thomas, considering all that you've have heard - if it had happened to you, what would you have done?"

Cardinal Mumbwa sat motionless with the exception of his eyes, which exhibited wide amazement as they darted wildly from Dom to Symon and back. He was not conscious of the fact that his legs had grown numb, and nearly stumbled as he attempted to rise. Symon caught his arm and steadied him.

"I suddenly feel my age," he quipped. "You see, I too sport a sense of humor. Quick Symon, a glass of ale before my tongue dries up and flutters to the floor." Then turning to Dom, he declared, "I'm deeply touched by your confidence in me and humbled that you have trusted me with such a profound secret. You have my pledge of silence.

"Gentlemen, may we eat? I'm famished," Thomas said as he began making a sandwich. "Let's talk. I'm very disturbed to realize that everyone misunderstood my position concerning our current situation, the unfortunate fatalities, and the ever present dangers. It's in my nature to be cautious, and overly concerned. The children in my diocese lovingly call me grandfather for this very reason. It is also in my nature for my face to reveal my feelings. It's spontaneous! I have no control. It just happens, just as your sense of humor surfaces without warning."

"Well Thomas, I'm pleased Symon slyly arranged this timely get-together. And I do feel better you're now fully aware why we are doggedly proceeding on our present course."

"But I'm not finished Dom," Thomas blurted out in a rather excited tone. "You know nothing of my dream. When you were describing your spiritual episodes and the shared dream, I could hardly contain myself. As a young boy in my native village, I was exposed to various superstitions. Although most everyone was Christian, at times it was confusing. Christian tradition often became interwoven with ancient tribal practices. We never knew where one began and the other left off. Like the Christians of old, before Jerome's Biblical interpretation intervened, our people placed much stock in dreams. Certainly Carl Jung and Morton Kelsey provided contemporary direction in the area of discerning dreams and their purpose."

Thomas was now on his feet and became quite animated. "Dom. Symon. An identical dream has invaded my slumber at times throughout my entire life. As a youngster I could not relate to the event depicted. In later years as I became more knowledgeable in our faith and its hierarchy, I realized who the dream's black man was dressed in beautiful trappings, and who he represented. He was the pope, and the black man was me! I too, felt destiny was calling, especially when we were all in the Sistine Chapel together.

"Originally I was elated with the dream's prediction. Now - I'm fearful and weighed down by the implications."

Dom had a mouthful of sandwich, so Symon spoke for both. "Thomas, it's a proud dream. Look how far you've come and how much you've accomplished since leaving your village. Everything's on track. Someday you may become pope."

It was then that it hit Symon. He suddenly understood Thomas' feeling of impending doom. He just had to say the words. "It's Dom, isn't it? Since you were voted second in the balloting, if something happened to him, chances are you could be voted pope on the next go around. That image is what has you so wired. You're afraid the dream may come true."

Dom finally washed down the mouthful and chimed in. "Wait! Wait! Both of you. I could easily pass away of normal causes, or retire at an early age. Either way, Thomas' dream could be fulfilled. Let's not get carried away here." Thomas stood facing them both and spoke with animated gestures.

"Dom, I looked for you earlier to tell you about the report relayed from the airport authority. You were able to elude Kim's protection. By the way, Kim's beside himself, fearing for your safety. A few hours ago there was a hostage-taking, a killing and a suicide at the de Vinci Airport. As it turns out, he was a terrorist bent on killing you. The man was spotted by a customs security guard while taking a gun made of undetectable plastic out of his carry-on bag and concealing it on his person right after disembarking a plane from Paris."

"What happened? Who was killed?" Symon demanded to know.

"A guard was killed. A brave young woman was taken hostage, and the terrorist shot himself rather that be taken into custody. The head of security told me the entire episode. The guard that spied the gunman drew his own weapon and ordered him to drop his gun while also alerting other security force members. The terrorist reacted by grabbing a passenger. He held her around the neck to shield his body, and then shot the guard through the head. By then several other guards arrived and trained their weapons on him. However, they couldn't shoot for fear of hitting his hostage. Moments after the standoff, this courageous woman brought the heel of her left shoe down forcefully on his instep. As he cried out in pain and surprise, she spun away quickly, and the officers opened fire, hitting the man in the shoulder and both thighs. Escape was impossible, he chose to end his life by shooting himself in the chest."

"Thomas, what makes the authorities think he came to murder me?"

The cardinal explained. "As he lay dying he shouted in a yet to be deciphered Arabic dialect. At least it sounded like Arabic to those close enough to hear. Then he spoke in broken English before expiring. He bragged that others would come, perhaps already here, to kill the infidel pope who threatens to eradicate their faith. That's all he said. That's all we know at this point. When the airport authorities looked to find the woman who acted so bravely, she had disappeared into the crowd. Apparently she was whisked through customs during the aftermath of the confusion. The only clue is that one of the passengers remembered her dropping a case of costume jewelry when being seized by the assailant. There'll be no follow-up on her. She isn't wanted for anything except a thank you from the authorities."

"Well, I guess we have more than Buldini to be concerned with. Would be assassins are coming out from under their rocks," Dom reflected in an ominous tone. "We had better boost our own security. Thomas, tell Nathan to be in my office by eight in the morning. No - ask all the Franciscans to join me, you included. Symon, continue your efforts, but be even more alert and suspicious of everyone you come into contact with. Our enemies have multiplied. To what degree would only be speculation at this time. May the Holy Mother protect us all."

CHAPTER NINETEEN

Contrary to the advice of Jan, his security advisor, Dom enjoyed sleeping with his small balcony's French doors wide open. Falling asleep and awakening to the gentle rhythm of the cascading fountains in St. Peter's Square had a therapeutic effect on his psyche.

He had been awake for over an hour, lying in bed and listening to the sounds of Rome as it too, awoke to prepare for a new day. Echoes of a steady stream of tiny commuter cars racing to enter the city reverberated softly throughout ancient stone structures, in contrast to the harsh clicking heels of the Swiss Guard's shoes on cobblestones directly below his lofty windows facing St. Peter's Square.

Drowsily, Dom sat up and swung his legs over the side of the bed, inserted his feet into waiting slippers, and reached for a bathrobe that hung on the closest chair. After showering, he headed for a private chapel, just beyond the bedroom, for morning prayers.

*****

As he left the chapel, he heard a scuffling of feet coming from the hallway outside his bedroom suite doors. He opened the door, and much to his surprise, there stood Kim, jostling with one of the kitchen cooks for the tray of coffee and Danish.

"Whoa there," ordered the pope, "we wouldn't want to spill a single drop of this delicious nectar. John here makes the best tasting coffee in all of Italy. Thank you John, I'll take it from here. Kim, join me for coffee on the balcony and breath in the fresh air of coming winter. It's exhilarating!"

The two men stood basking in the warm rays of a bright morning sun. It was a beautiful beginning to the day in spite of a slight chill. Pulling the shawl collar of the heavy robe around his neck and ears, Dom stepped forward to the balcony rail. Kim sipped his coffee, looming like a mighty oak directly behind him. Three Swiss Guards finishing their late shift spied their pope and waved. Dom leaned forward over the rail to return their friendly gesture. At that exact moment, a flock of pigeons roosting on the far ledge of the basilica facade decorated with huge statues of the saints, rushed to flight, scattering in all directions. Dom heard something crash behind him and quickly turned to see Kim's coffee-cup shattered on the balcony floor.

159

Dom stood frozen in disbelief as Kim clutched his upper chest. Blood oozed slowly from between his fingers. "I think I've been shot," he said softly.

Then reaching forward with his left hand, he roughly dragged Dom behind him like a rag doll, protecting him with his body. "Dom, get in the room before they fire again."

Dom was in greater shock than Kim, who took charge and ordered Dom to call security, Jan, Thomas, and the Vatican physician. During the next few minutes, Dom collected himself, stripped Kim to the waist and applied a thick compress to his upper chest wound, successfully stemming the flow of blood.

*****

"He's extremely fortunate," said the doctor after dressing the wound and diagnosing the damage. "Your friend's excellent physique saved his life. The unusual mass and denseness of his pectoral muscles denied the bullet entry into the chest cavity. Luckily it was of a small caliber. The lead is still lodged inside and will have to be extracted as soon as possible to avoid possible infection. He's lost very little blood thanks to his Holiness' quick actions - and should have a speedy and complete recovery. I'll give him an antibiotic and be on my way. Bring him to my office within the hour."

Thomas and Dom looked at each other in complete amazement, unable to grasp the reality of what had just happened. Jan had already left the room to check on what the security agents might have found. Dom was first to break the silence. "I would have been killed if I hadn't leaned over to wave at the Swiss Guards. My head would have been roughly where the bullet hit Kim.

"It's only a guess - but a muffled sound from a rifle with a silencer could be what startled the pigeons on the ledge across the square. Kim, did you happen to see anything? My eyes were looking down."

Kim thought for a minute, and the image of a small figure formed in his mind. "Yes. There was a nun. The pigeons caught my eye as I felt the sting in my chest. Just beyond the birds I recall seeing a blur of what appeared to be a little nun."

"She was probably on her way to work at the Gift Shop at the foot of the dome," Thomas offered. "No. Wait. The shop's closed this week for electrical repairs. No one should be up there this time of day but the workers. In fact, the entire area is curtained-off."

Jan burst into the room, but before he had the opportunity to speak, Thomas apprized him of the mysterious nun. "That's what I was about to tell you," Jan cried out. "The guards said a nun bearing a basket of long loaves of bread for the workers was allowed up on the Terrace of the Saints. She never came back down. They found a rope tied around a concrete pillar and hanging down the side of the south wall hidden from view. The nun must have been a gymnast! Several tourists reported seeing a nun with a pronounced limp walking just outside the south wall. That could be our man. The rope was some twenty feet short, and the would-be assassin would have had to jump to the sidewalk below, possibly twisting an ankle. They lost sight of the limper in a bus load of tourists. Security guards found the spilled basket of bread. Two long thin loafs were split and hollowed-out. That's probably how the weapon was smuggled past the guards. The bottom line is, we lost her."

"I warned Buldini what I'd do!" Dom said angrily. His complexion darkened, and his olive eyes revealed a hardened glare never before witnessed. Setting his squared jaw with resolve, he stormed out of the room, obviously heading for Buldini's Vatican office.

"No Dom, no!" Thomas shouted to no avail.

It was some distance from the pope's bedroom on the far north side of the Vatican complex to his destination, and he covered the span in record time. His unruly curls bounced, and the bathrobe flowed as he sprinted through corridors, down flights of stairs and across marbled floors filled with gawking tourists, Thomas in hot pursuit.

"Genevieve, is that who I think it is?" asked a bewildered husband from America.

"Yes, that's Pope Francis himself. In his bathrobe - would you believe? Wait 'til the girls back home hear about this!"

The large wooden doors to the cardinal's office burst open with a loud bang, knocking over and smashing a priceless bust of Caesar that once sat on a pedestal against the wall. Startled, Buldini jumped to his feet, as well as three of his aides. He would not get caught again sitting down like the last time the pope had seized him.

With the agility of a cat, Dom vaulted over a footstool and sprang at Buldini, clutching his capped vestments to the cardinal's throat with his right

161

hand, and grabbed his ponytail with his left. Buldini stumbled backward, his chin pushed up by the pressure on his neck, and the hard yank on his ponytail drove the back of his head into the window behind the desk, shattering a pane of stained glass.

"You remember what I said I'd do to you, you slimy slug? You're a murderer! A disgrace to the Church and humanity! You tried to have me murdered again. Just now! Now it's my turn, I'm going to...."

Before he had the chance to finish, Thomas arrived and grabbed him from behind. He wrapped both arms around the upper part of Dom's body and tried desperately to separate the two men. Buldini's aides, gaining a trace of courage, approached Thomas and the pope. They were stopped dead in their tracks by a throaty growl coming from the doorway. The sight of the mountain of a man bracing himself in the door frame with one hand while holding a blood stained towel to his chest with the other, drained them of what little backbone they had mustered.

"Let's go now before something more serious happens. Come on Dom! Jan, you take Kim to the infirmary as the doctor ordered. Dom, we need to leave," Thomas implored.

"No! This buffoon in cardinal's clothing must be stopped. He must go! I demand his immediate resignation - or else!"

"Your Holiness," said Buldini, wiping blood from a small cut from behind his left ear. "I haven't the slightest notion of what you're talking about."

Thomas interrupted, and dragged Dom by the sleeve of his bathrobe towards the open door. "Dom, let's discuss this after you've had the opportunity to calm down. Making such accusations and decisions under present circumstances is not wise. Come on. We'll take the back way to your quarters. This time without scaring off any of the visiting tourists."

*****

Upon entering his bedroom, Dom collapsed on his knees, cradling his face in his hands. "Thomas - what is happening to me? He's right, I - I reacted like a madman. I ran wild though a crowd of visitors, just like one of those demented popes centuries ago. In my nightclothes, no less. This isn't like me. At least I never thought so. I'm not even close to acting with the dignity expected of a present day pope. What am I to do?"

WILLIAM R. PARK, SR.

Thomas helped Dom from his knees and into a comfortable chair, closed the bedroom doors, and seated himself. "You've been under a tremendous amount of stress. What you're trying to accomplish within the Church, the reforms, and being challenged by dissenting members of the Curia is in itself taxing, if not downright overwhelming. Your best friend was murdered in your stead. A Franciscan brother committed suicide as a result of our efforts. There have been signs of forthcoming attempts on your life - like the airport situation.

"In fact, we're all in danger, and now this morning's incident. What ten men could hold up under the weight of it all, never mind one human being? You know my friend, deep within everyone of God's children sleeps a dark side that waits to be awakened by something never before experienced. For some, thankfully, that something never surfaces in their lifetime for them to encounter. Others, depending on the circumstances, handle it in stride, or lose control to varying degrees. It's only natural.

"I confess - the pious and kindly Cardinal Mumbwa has had his own demons to deal with at times. And hasn't always handled them successfully. You've discovered what triggers your hidden dark side - Buldini, unfairness, and the lives of your friends. But Dom, you are not like others any more, you're the pope. And now that you're aware of this weakness, you must pray for strength to go beyond any hold darkness has on you."

Dom found solace, strength and wisdom in the cardinal's words. "Of course you're right," he said, as he stood up and began pacing the room. "Cancel whatever appointments there are for me today; I have a lot of soul searching to do. And I don't wish to be disturbed by anyone until dinner. But I want to know about Kim's condition as soon as you hear something."

He continued to pace and circle the room, forcing Thomas to strain his neck one way and then the other. His next decision would bring about the success or failure of his papacy.

The furrows left Dom's brow. With a new air of confidence, he said, "Thomas, we have a handful of cardinals over the voting age of eighty. I need their names and diocese locations. They will be retired and replaced. Chances are they were hand-picked by Buldini, along with a number of others, and recommended to the last popes to receive the title of cardinal. We need their names as well. Many, if not all, will need to accept an early retirement. We will need our own wearing the red hats. It won't be easy. They'll fight us every inch of the way. But I am pope - at least for now.

163

Tomorrow we'll start with Uden's replacement in the Netherlands. Then, since you're here, we'll need a cardinal in your place back home. Give me your recommendations. And, we should consider the progressive thinking Bishop Medici of Milan. The Vatican stationed the bishop as far north in Italy as possible. He's been passed over time and time again in lieu of other less deserving. It's his turn."

Their conversation continued for another five minutes, and as Thomas opened the door to leave, Dom had the final words. "Thomas, I'll never be able to thank you enough for your friendship, loyalty and words of wisdom. Everyone - even a pope, needs to be reminded he's merely flesh and blood with ordinary failings, and ever in need of the direction of the Holy Spirit. No - perhaps more needful."

*****

"He what!" The words snapped heads and popped eyeballs throughout the smoke filled tavern. The sudden burst of emotion surprised even Symon, who now wished he could shrink to an unnoticeable size. He had entered by the back kitchen door, hoping to remain as inconspicuous as possible; he remembered the events of several nights ago. He sat in an empty corner of the bar, trying to look nonchalant, as if nothing just happened, and toyed with his drink to avoid eye contact. After he was certain that the memory of his eruption had passed, he resumed his whispered conversation with the seafaring-looking man perched on the stool next to him.

"Dom physically assaulted Cardinal Buldini, and bloodied him to boot?"

Symon questioned Nathan in amazement. "Why? Damn, I miss all the excitement."

Nathan had assumed a seaman's disguise similar to Symon's in order to walk freely in Symon's tavern hopping footsteps. He planned on passing himself off as an old shipmate of Johnny's to avoid undo attention. The typical navy blue knit cap was pushed back as far as it would go on his close cropped crew cut without falling off, and the thick oversized wool sweater successfully hid the man within. A newly acquired, store-bought, droop-handle mustache completed his cover.

Symon sat riveted on every word as Nathan accounted in detail the assassination attempt on Dom's life - Kim's superficial wound - the disappearing nun - and Dom's clash with Buldini.

"Wow! I can't say as anyone could blame him. It's a good thing Thomas was there to intervene. Nathan, you're not privy to all the specifics as to why we're certain Buldini was behind Uden's murder, but believe me, he was. I can understand Dom's anger, especially after this second attempt. He has so much on his mind, and now this, too. I feel sorry for him. No doubt Buldini will make good use of the incident to his advantage. It's good pabulum for the propaganda he'll feed the College of Cardinals and the Vatican Curia."

THE FRANCISCAN

CHAPTER TWENTY

Pope Francis called an emergency meeting of the Vatican Curia for 10AM, and any visiting cardinals. At 9:30, Buldini and his assistants were still engaged in his office, mulling over a possible reason for the unexpected summons.

"Are you all deaf, dumb and blind? Don't any of you nitwits have an idea of why he's called this meeting? What am I paying you for? You're all worthless! And what about the attempted hit on the man? We had nothing to do with that - this time. Who was it, and where in the hell is Zacchia? And while we're at it, is there any report on the whereabouts of Diamante?

They all looked at each other, each waiting for one or another to speak first.

"Well," Buldini bellowed, "we don't have all day! Angelo, you first."

Angelo squirmed in his chair; beads of perspiration appeared on his brow. "Your eminence, all any of us could discover about the meeting is that Cardinal Mumbwa spent the night pouring over files of those that make up the College of Cardinals. That's all we know."

Another found the courage to speak. "Since Monsignor Zacchia is still vacationing and didn't tell us where he would be, we know nothing about the latest attempt on the pope's life. However, the talk is that Cardinal Mumbwa received a message for the pope from a coalition of religious leaders representing faiths of the Middle-East. They wanted to assure His Holiness that there is no organized plot to silence him. They did admit knowing of the individual that threatened the pope at the airport, and who later killed himself.

"The fact is, he had spent the last six months in a mental institution and was released just four weeks ago. The message went on to say that as far as their own investigation went, it seemed apparent the would-be assassin acted alone, was a religious fanatic, and to ignore the man's allegations concerning a team of assassins   targeting the pope. They found no evidence of an organized conspiracy."

"Well, at least we know something," Buldini said sarcastically. "I guess the subject of Diamante's whereabouts will have to wait. It's time to head for the meeting."

"But your eminence, the monsignor was spotted," came a weak observation. "One of our informants described a man fitting Diamante's description lurking around the Castle of St. Angelo two nights ago, but when approached, he disappeared into the shadows."

"Why wasn't I informed sooner?" Buldini inquired. As before, his question was answered with blank stares.

If someone had been holding an electric bulb in their hand, with the energy generated by the uncertainty of the meeting's purpose, it would surely have glowed brightly. Buldini was determined to work his plan to undermine the pope's credibility, regardless of what Pope Francis said this morning. His assistants were strategically seated throughout the small conference room next to cardinals known to be loyal to the pope, or considered on the fence. They made discreet reference to Cardinal Buldini's heavily bandaged head, giving an account of the pope's uncalled-for attack on their beloved cardinal. Buldini was playing his part by tenderly cradling his head from time to time, as if in some difficulty and pain.

As the pope, Thomas, and the Franciscan staff entered, anticipation of the unknown filled the room. Kim closed the door with a jolting bang, then stood guard, pointedly staring a hole through Cardinal Buldini. Unlike the last time they were all together, when the pope stood before them on their level, as previous popes had always done, this time he took the elevated chair looking down on the group seated before him.

A gentle rap on the door aroused the stillness of the moment. "Kim, you may open the door, that's probably our newest cardinal-to-be, Bishop Medici of Milan. I asked him to join us," explained the pope. "Ah, good bishop, please be seated. So happy you could make it on such short notice."

The room immediately flamed with mixed emotions. While everyone expressed surprise, they were somewhat divided in their response. Both frowns and smiles saturated the room. The pope took a quick frown and smile count and was pleased to note that the smiles outnumbered the frowns.

The pope stood, then knelt before the assembly, saying, "Let us now all ask our Creator for guidance in what we are about to attempt to accomplish in His name this day. Join me in a silent prayer." They all complied, and when the pope finally rose to be seated, they in turn took their seats. The pope, however, did not sit down. Instead, he walked up the aisle to the third row and stopped directly in front of Cardinal Buldini, who visibly flinched. He reacted instinctively based on his recent contacts with the Holy Father. The cardinal, to no avail, attempted to get to his feet, but he fit too snugly in the plush chair, and the firm but gentle pressure from the pope's hand on Buldini's right shoulder easily prevented him from doing so.

Cardinal Mumbwa, who was seated on the first row closest to the door, was a split-second from leaping to his feet with the intent to restrain the pope if necessary. Kim took two steps forward. Fully aware of the bad blood between the two, everyone held their collective breath.

With his left hand, while soberly inquiring about Buldini's injury, the pope tore off the huge bandage and held it high so all could see clearly, and said, "My, my, you're a quick healer. Not a speck of blood, and one can hardly notice the slight scratch where the reported four inch long and inch wide gash once was. It must be a miracle."

Turning quickly, he headed for his chair, enjoying a private grin while his back was still to the group. With satisfaction, he soaked-up the snickers that moved like a wave throughout the room at Buldini's expense. Uncharacteristically, Buldini sat mute, displaying no emotion whatsoever. Deep within he raged. What vexed him the most was that the pope benefitted from the encounter. The cardinal took advantage of the next three hours of the pope's session to mull over his new plan to remove Pope Francis from the papacy, along with his Franciscan brothers, and Cardinal Mumbwa.

"We've had our little fun; now to the business at hand," said the pope with a subtle grin. "But first, an update on the issues we discussed during our last get-together. The Vatican's first auction to sell some of our precious antiques to raise funds for special humanitarian projects went well. I'm pleased to report that in all but three cases, museums throughout the world were the recipients of objects. Thankfully, the three private individuals who purchased items, in turn, donated them to museums in their countries. You are encouraged to inventory such works of art that may be in your possession, or are aware of elsewhere. See to it that a list is given to Cardinal Mumbwa."

He paused, smiled, looked directly a Buldini, and continued. "Recently Cardinal Mumbwa and I had the pleasure of visiting Cardinal Buldini's home at which time we observed numerous expensive works of art and century's old antique furniture, sculpture and household items. I'm sure that many of these items that were listed as Vatican property during the last inventory conducted some fifteen years ago, will certainly be donated by the cardinal in time for our next auction to help the less fortunate.

"Our plea to the clergy of the Catholic world to more closely adopt the examples set by St. Francis is moving along, though more slowly than we had hoped. The most encouraging deeds are those of priests and bishops, and a handful of cardinals who have voluntarily given up their diocese owned or supplied cars. They will go to and from places of work or service in their own private vehicles. A great number, who, due to personal or family wealth, have given or willed property to children's homes, the elderly, and for the benefit of the terminally ill."

Pope Francis pointed to a person sitting in the front row. "Our visitor, Bishop Medici, has set a sterling example. When we first recommended that we all search our consciences concerning St. Francis' service to the community, the good bishop took immediate action. He had been living in a large home he purchased with his own funds. Keeping one bedroom, private bath and office, he opened the rest of the residence to provide shelter for three homeless elderly couples. Knowing how Bishop Medici likes to eat, it wouldn't surprise me if he personally interviewed the couples applying, to determine which three wives were the best cooks."

Allowing his audience the opportunity to congratulate the bishop and the laughter and conversation to subside, he continued. "Speaking of examples. We, everyone of us in this room, should become examples of our saint's life by simplifying our own. Therefore, the personal limousines we enjoy, as well as the fleet stationed at the Vatican, will become part of the next auction."

"What!" "Why?" "Outrageous!" "Unheard of!" "What are we supposed to do now - walk?" "You're right. He's gone mad!", were some of the many comments to be heard, along with a smattering of - "You can count on me, your Holiness."

Signaling silence with both hands, he went on, drowning out the remaining protesters. "Yes, it is unheard of. We're setting a new standard. Walk? Yes if you wish. Cardinal Buldini, like many of you, live just a few blocks away from your Vatican offices. The walk will do you good. Besides, most of you are affluent enough to own your own cars and are not too old to learn to drive. God help the pedestrians of Rome." Many of the cardinals and their assistants were on their feet, loudly protesting the pope's directive. Kim took another two steps closer to the fray. The remaining Franciscans were also on their feet, standing their ground. All the attention was on the cardinals and their present dilemma.

Stealing a glance at Cardinal Mumbwa, the pope winked and mouthed the words, "We're separating the wheat from the chaff." Thomas sat rather relaxed with a smile on his face, legs crossed at the ankles, and hands folded on his lap. Without moving or directing attention to himself, his two thumbs popped up, giving the pope the 'thumbs-up sign of approval.'

"Gentlemen. Gentlemen. We're not through yet," the pope said, trying to restore order. "Wait until you hear what we have next for you to consider."

That seemed to get everyone's attention, so he continued. "This time please do me the courtesy of not interrupting. We will take whatever time necessary to answer any and all questions when we're through. Thank you. We have a number of cardinals, including two here today, that are past the age of voting for a pope's successor. All those that fall into this age category will be retired with a comfortable yet sensible income. If they wish not to retire but continue to contribute to those in need, their support will be greatly appreciated."

The cardinals were in collective shock as the pope continued. "We also have an additional number who are below the stated age, and who for various reasons, will be offered an early retirement plan. Cardinal Mumbwa will now pass out the list of retiring princes of the Church. Within two weeks, their successors will be announced and brought to the Vatican to be presented their red hats."

After hearing the pope's words and reading the list, Buldini could no longer hold his tongue, nor his temper. "No!" he screamed. His face was blood red. His arms flayed about wildly. "Most of these men I proposed be installed - and they were."

"That's correct," answered the pope.

Buldini's assistants desperately tried to calm their master down, but to no avail. He continued to rave on. Militantly stepping to the front of the room, he was quickly met by Kim. The pope waved Kim away, who hesitated for a moment, then reluctantly obeyed.

Puffing himself up, he turned to the group, raised his arms, and with clenched shaking fists shouted, "You see, here is proof this man is not fit to be pope!" Pointing his finger at the pope, he continued screaming. "He's mad. He attacked me twice, and now this, along with all the other radical changes he's proposing for the Church. He's insane! He must be stopped! Who here is with me? If you are, leave with me now."

There was a lot of instant soul searching going on among all the cardinals. Some had previously made up their minds to challenge the pope with Buldini leading the way. Others were not so sure. This group wanted to know more of what the pope proposed to do, and how he intended to accomplish his goals. Many, fully aware of Cardinal Buldini's reputation, thought he was the one who was insane, and wished not to be associated with him. At final count, approximately one-third of those attending followed Buldini. To those who remained, the pope said in complete sincerity, "Thank you for your continued loyalty to the Church. There's no doubt in my mind that most of what we have recently proposed must weigh heavily on your hearts, and in addition, that I personally must earn your trust and loyalty."

*****

For the next hour and a half Pope Francis provided an update on the continuing reaction to his series of broadcast worldwide chats. He reported that comments by religious leaders and the laity were overwhelmingly positive. What pleased him most was that the religious unrest, persecutions, and bloodshed that had followed his first chat had ceased and instead a peaceful calm prevailed.

The pope's final comment concerned the development of a new democratic Catholic Church government. "Gentlemen, we need to form a committee, if you will, to give focus to the subject of how we can formulate a more pro-democratic administration within the Church; we must eliminate the present outdated dictatorial makeup to which we are subject - including the pope.

"It was Pope Innocent III in the thirteenth century who claimed to be above all laws, and soon after, Pope Gregory declared himself lord and master of the universe; other such claims followed by future popes. Thankfully, we have become a little more humble than they, but not so one would notice by the way we conduct the business of the Church. We are but simple men of flesh and blood who strive everyday to serve the perceived will of our Creator, and the community of God's sons and daughters we minister to, and serve.

"I'm inclined to disagree with Pope Pius IX, and agree with the Council of Constance's edict that the pope is subject to the General Council - in principle, that is. We do not wish to diminish any pope's spiritual or managerial authority. The Church needs a leader with jurisdiction to shepherd the flock, but not with absolute power to rule independently.

"Cardinal Mumbwa has been given the responsibility to work with you to elect committee members whose job it will be to develop and recommend standards for the implementation of a new democratic Church governing body. The approved system should include input from all administrative branches of the Church, from the pope to the laity. All should have the opportunity to express their views on subjects relevant to their spiritual needs. Elective representatives from the grass roots will provide recommendations to their local priests, who in turn will report to their bishops, who, after consultation with their priests, will provide the governing cardinals with the consensus.

"The new Council of The General Assembly will be made up of members representing all countries, and will be presided over by the Secretary of State. The Council's major responsibility will be to consider and vote on necessary issues. The result of the votes will be presented to the pope for his review. After careful deliberation, he claims the right of authority to approve or veto any resolution. His veto can only be overridden by a majority vote percentage yet to be determined by the recommending committee. In the event of an override, the pope may express his opinion to the worldwide Catholic community at large, and after presenting his case, the entire matter may again come to the attention of the council. Each vetoed subject should be given a reasonable amount of time for further worldwide deliberation and prayer before the issue is decreed. The committee will also recommend a time frame for such an appeal. Whatever the outcome of a final vote, on any subject, the pope retains the right to offer his personal opinion, although not binding, for consideration by all members of the body of Christ."

Pope Francis made a final comment before turning the floor over to Cardinal Mumbwa. "This directive is not meant to handcuff the committee's recommendations. I'm merely providing food-for-thought; a beginning point for the process. To be fair, those who earlier chose to leave this meeting must be contacted and considered for committee duty as well as all cardinals.

"Since we will be retiring a number of cardinals and installing new members within the next two weeks, keep this in mind. Until then, work with Cardinal Mumbwa on forming the rudiments of our new council and its duties, and reporting structure. Actual committee members could be selected when appropriate. Thank you for your participation. I leave you now to attend to your new responsibilities."

CHAPTER TWENTY ONE

It was as though the world was coming to an end, and the lone figure looking out of the upper balcony window was the last surviving human. Lightning flashed from every angle ripping the pitch black fabric of the heavens, suddenly illuminating the city and skyline in a brilliant display of energy. Then just as unexpectedly, it drowned the surrounding hills, dwellings and their inhabitants in utter darkness; repeating the scene endlessly. Aware of his own existence while beholding the awesome power of God's creative force dramatically diminished the self-worth of the observer. He felt so isolated. So insignificant - and so helpless.

"Jan would come unglued if he knew you were standing in front of your balcony window, your Holiness," came a familiar voice from behind him. The darkness of the pope's bed chamber could not mask Symon's distinct English accent and soft deep voice.

The pope remained facing nature's mighty display of force. "You know my friend, this is the loneliest job in the world. And on a night like this, I not only feel alone, but also helpless. You want the job Symon?"

"Not on your life! Oops. That didn't come out right. Sorry. No. Even before this adventure is but a memory, I'll be happy communing with the spirits of yore, with Assuri the Babylonian servant in my cave. You want to come?"

"Oh, don't entice me. If I only could. Get thee behind me." The pope turned and faced his tempter. "Thanks for coming so late at night. I felt it would be safe coming from the Borgia wing the back way. His Holiness needs someone to talk to in confidence, and you're my closest friend.

"And you know, this 'holiness' thing bothers me somewhat. One day a mere human is just that, and within hours he becomes holy. I don't feel any different than I did months ago, with the exception of the enormous pressure of the position His Holiness holds in the world. But that cross we must bear."

Symon added his own thoughts on the subject. "I'm pleased to hear you question the obvious. It's assumed the Holy Spirit's grace chooses the one to wear the fisherman's ring. Unfortunately, no matter how hard we and God try, it seems that whenever man becomes involved, our free will gets in the way, and too often greed and personal agendas overrule the Holy Spirit. How often have we heard conversations by voting cardinals discussing who should become the next pope. 'That one's too young. We don't want someone who'll be around too many years. We need someone who will only live but another eight or so years.' Or the discussion goes like this. 'No, he's too conservative. No, he's too liberal. No, he's not Italian.' And on and on. What ever happened to, 'He's the best person to lead the faithful?' Sure, we've had popes that we can genuinely claim were holy men. But as you and I are both so painfully aware, far too many were just the opposite. There were men and women too numerous to count throughout history and the present, both religious and lay people, that deserve to be called holy. Most of whom were never even recognized as such, and most probably preferred it that way. But, don't get me started. You didn't ask me up here to discuss if I thought you to be holy, or not. What's bothering you my friend?"

The pope reflected for a moment and admitted, "Well, to be completely honest, I guess I was more lonely than anything else, and needed companionship. As of late, I can be lonely in a room packed full of people. Maybe that comes with the job."

They both stood by the window and peered out into the darkness. Symon stroked his beard, then said, "The job of being a spy isn't much different. Of course, a spy can quit whenever he wants. It's not so easy for a pope. The weight of the job, instead of lightening up, has only increased for you. And, I'm aware of the fact you're wrestling with your conscience concerning your anger with that scum bag Buldini. It's not the time for me to lecture you on either subject, we've already been there. So, how can I help?"

"You already have; being here helps. Just before asking Kim to bring you, I slept for two hours and had another of those dreams."

"Don't tell me you saw birds and Volkswagens again?"

For the first time in several days the pope displayed a genuine grin. He sat down, and left Symon standing at the window "No. No. No birds. No automobiles. Prior to falling asleep, I prayed for guidance to deal with my growing anger towards Cardinal Buldini. I asked to be forgiven for this weakness.

"Earlier this evening I met with my confessor and received our Lord in Holy Communion. Now the dream. Two people were standing side by side before an altar. There was an almost blinding light coming from the far side of the altar obscuring my view so that the two figures were seen as silhouettes.

"The strange thing was that one was male and the other female. Then a voice emanating from within the light said, *'The last time we met, I blessed both the abused and the abuser.'* What do you make of that?"

"That's a strange one," Symon conceded, scratching his head. "The man and the woman is the confusing part. I would think the message is for you, but two people? What has the woman got to do with you, if you are in fact the male? Perhaps you're not in the dream at all. I'm stumped."

"Well, I finally came up with something that you can't easily explain away. Here's my take on it," Dom said, as he joined Symon by the window. "We are all both male and female to a degree. That is, we all have similar mixed traits. A particular mannerism, a physical quality, or emotion, are but a few heterogeneous traits both sexes share. Now hold that thought. Remember our early-day Latin, and teachings at the monastery? I was seeing my Anima - Animus sides. My female - male sides that make up my being. I was both the abused and the abuser before the altar. We were blessed, thus forgiven; forgiving me completely."

Both men were startled as a flash of lightning crackled just outside the balcony window. The hair on the back of their necks stood at attention as the security lights throughout the Vatican City flickered and died. Seconds later, the backup generators kicked-in, once again illuminating ancient buildings.

"I always knew you had a flair for the dramatic, but that was going too far. Dom, did you plan that little display of fireworks just to convince me He was on your side? You really didn't have to, you know. I'm beginning to feel safer with the thugs at the tavern than with the pope."

"Your sense of humor is priceless my friend," Dom laughed. "And speaking of the tavern, what's the latest?"

"Things are picking up. Jabal left me a note in the light fixture this evening. Zacchia's back in Rome. Maybe now I can arrange a meeting through my contact with Agapito and learn more about Buldini's involvement in all of this. And what he's got planned for you next."

"Symon, be extremely careful from now on. He became fiercely aggressive during this morning's session of the Curia, and there's no telling what his demented mind may cook up next. We're threatening his very existence here in the Vatican, including his financial future. He's becoming increasingly dangerous."

"I'll watch my back at all times," he agreed. "As you know, Nathan is now involved, masquerading as an old seafaring chum. We've cooked up some intrigue of our own, and if everything goes as intended, Agapito, Zacchia and Buldini will be bloody excited about what they learn from my old buddy about my unsavory background."

"I'm not even going to ask what," Dom yawn. "Sometimes ignorance is bliss."

"Popes and spies need their sleep," Symon said, taking Dom's yawn as his cue, and turned to leave. "I'm certain your anger towards Buldini has been forgiven. We're all human, even a pope. You get some much needed rest. That's what I intend to do, and tomorrow night, it's back to the taverns for Jonathan St. John. Better known as Johnny to his newly acquired mates."

*****

The cock hadn't crowed three times yet and Cardinal Buldini, his assistants, a handful of informants, and the elusive Monsignor Zacchia were already deeply involved in concocting a new scheme to rid themselves of the troublesome pope. Well before dawn they began arriving, one by one, through an obscure side door of Buldini's augustly decorated residence-office close to St. Peter's Square.

Monsignor Zacchia was the last to arrive, but the first to feel the sting of the cardinal's tongue. "Where in the hell have you been! You were due back a week ago. Much has changed since you left, and you were needed here, not elsewhere. What's your excuse?"

Fearless of any reprisal, Zacchia looked the cardinal straight on, and in a calm patronizing tone replied. "Don't get me mixed up with one of your lackeys here. Zacchia doesn't report to anyone. You and I are equal as far as I'm concerned, and I've got the skeletons in the closet to prove it. Don't ever forget that - your eminence. Now, if you want your new plot to have the slightest chance to succeed, I suggest we cut the bull and get on with it."

If the fire in Buldini's eyes could have been hurled in the monsignor's direction, he would have been fried to a crisp, along with anything and anyone in the general vicinity. As much as he hated the man and would kill him twice for embarrassing him in front the others, Buldini knew he had to handle Zacchia with kid gloves. He needed him too much. Zacchia was right; there were skeletons in the closet, and he held the key. For right now.

He sucked up his bruised pride and began to lay out his revised plan to destroy Pope Francis. "We must both save and slay the pope. First we must do everything in our power to save his life by discovering who the shooter was that made this last attempt."

"What!" - shouted an enraged Zacchia. He stood, walked around the table, and then returned to his seat, somewhat calmer. "First you wanted him dead. We've been frantically trying to find the first assassin to convince him to return and finish the job he was hired to do, but failed. Now you want us to save his life by finding and eliminating this shooter, whoever it is. I thought you ordered this latest hit. Make up your mind, damn it."

"You see what you miss by not paying attention to business. No, this time we had nothing to do with it. That's what you're here for. Put your people to work. Find out who it is, and stop him before he tries again. And before you shout 'why?', hear this. No matter how hard the papacy tried to have both attempts on the pope's life hushed-up, the word's out. And there are those within the Vatican and elsewhere that are beginning to look suspiciously in our direction, including the local Italian police. My animosity towards him is no longer a secret. If the next attempt is successful, the police will be knocking down my door. That is, if I were to survive the wrath of those damned Franciscans. This is serious. Do you understand?"

"Yea. I'll get my people on it immediately," Zacchia barked angrily. "I've got a lot riding on your continued survival. We all do. News has just come my way that may solve our problem. After tonight's meeting with Agapito, I'll know more, and I'll fill you in on my idea soon after. All right - assuming we save his hide, what's this about slaying him? Make sense of that."

"Ah, here's where the second part of my plan comes in. We don't literally take his life, we destroy his reputation. We slay his character, along with those closest to him. And the African must go down with them. Haven't you ever heard the rumor of the serpent-worshipers who lived and studied at a remote Franciscan Monastery in England?" Heads shook in unison. "No? Well, I guess you've never heard about their ungodly homosexual orgies, either. Or about their pact with the evil one himself to destroy Christianity. Can any one of you learned gentlemen guess who their leader is, and who his disciples are?"

"You don't mean it!" came a cry of astonishment. "It can't be. You don't mean - him?"

"Yes! Cardinal Domenico Francisco Masone and his band of Franciscan cronies. We're speaking about the righteous and popular Pope Francis."

"I don't believe it!" Zacchia firmly replied. "There's never been any report about such an outrageous charge. I know, it was I who personally did the background check on Masone before you selected him to succeed Pope Paul VII. He's squeaky clean. No one even remotely suggested such a thing. It's unheard of."

"You're correct," Buldini said with a wicked smile. "But they will hear of it. We'll let the word slip out, won't we now? Those of us here in this room will anonymously leak the shocking news, as will our operatives in every corner of the globe. When we're finished with the Franciscan and his Homo consorts, he'd wish he had played my game; just another puppet pope like Pius and Paul."

CHAPTER TWENTY TWO

Within the hour Symon had hoped to encounter the mysterious and elusive Monsignor Zacchia. And now this. The note made little sense, but he knew immediately who the author was and that his security was breached. A poem composed that poorly was proof that Monsignor Diamante was still among the living and that he was aware of the secret passageway to the apartments.

Agapito and Zacchia would have to wait. Jan needed to be alerted to the breach, and it was essential that Dom be given the note right away. Symon quickly retraced his steps back up the hidden stairway, hopeful the meeting in the Tower of the Winds office was still in progress.

Barging unannounced into the Tower from the darkened corridor walkway was a mistake Symon would not soon forget. He was blind sided the moment he placed his foot into the room by someone from just inside the doorway and enfolded in two of the most massive arms he had ever seen.

Lifted well off the floor and with his feet flaying about, he angrily demanded, "Damn it Kim, turn me loose!"

The gentle giant, not taking too kindly to Symon's tone of voice, tightened his grip and began shaking him from side to side while joining in the laughter that rocked the room at Symon's expense. Then, just as suddenly as he was grabbed and hoisted off the floor, he was unceremoniously dropped, landing in a heap at Dom's feet.

Embarrassed and indignant, he jumped up and spun around to face Kim. With fists clenched and the character of Johnny embedded in his personality, it looked for a moment as if Symon was about to foolishly challenge the mountain before him.

"Better think twice my friend. He won't go down as easily as Jabal. I'm betting he won't go down at all," came the advice of the beaming Egyptian. "Someone get the iodine and bandages with Symon's name on them," he continued to tease.

Defending himself, Symon responded, "I may be crazy enough to put my life on the line for Dom, but not insane enough to tangle with Kim. The move was merely a reflex action, just as it was with you Jabal. Remember? I have important information, and this is no time for levity. My cover's been blown. The hidden stairway is no longer a secret. And there's a message for Dom from Diamante."

181

Dom had been sitting quietly taking it all in, until Symon broke the news. "Explain yourself. This sounds serious. And where's the message from the missing monsignor?"

"Tonight's the night Zacchia was thought to be meeting Agapito at the tavern, and I planned to be there fifteen minutes ago. But when I was about to unlatch and lift the hidden stairway at ground level, I noticed a piece of paper slipped under the bottom step so it would be only visible from the inside."

"Someone knows about the stairway and secret passageways into the outside walls and apartment closets. If that person has had the entrance under surveillance for any length of time, he may know of Symon's undercover work as well. Symon's in grave danger. He can't continue," Jan surmised.

"Wait. Let's think this thing through before we scrap all that Symon's accomplished. If the message is truly from Diamante, we may be in luck. Let me see the paper," Dom asked.

Dom read the note to himself. "I agree, this has to be from Monsignor Diamante. It's his disguised handwriting, and the same poorly written prose. Much like the others. Couldn't be from anyone else." He then shared the message with the group. *"The carpenter sealed the entrance to keep me out - tho he's still observed out and about. Fear not - all your secrets this unworthy one will hide, for now and forever I'm on your side.*

"A weak link will soon be severed and spirited away - his words will bury the pope, they're hoping some day. A Pale Horse is on the loose - the hostile one is as evil as ever, but fears the casualty would cook his goose.

"Look for me not, since neither good nor evil can find the hole - for there concealed is the frightened mole."

Shaking his head, Dom continued. "I do wish he'd come out and say what's on his mind in a simple straightforward manner. This bad poetry is hard on the ears. But at the same time, I'm thankful for his messages.

"Okay - here's how I interpret this, his third contact. He obviously knows who Symon is; he called him by his last name in the first verse. In addition, he must have recognized him while in the guise of Johnny St. John. Although Diamante seems to know much about our business, he's assuring us that he won't expose our intent. And I'm inclined to believe him."

Jan was silently mouthing no, no, no, then spoke up. "Dom, we're taking a major risk with that attitude. You can't mean you believe that little weasel? It's a good thing Thomas isn't here, he'd go ballistic."

Jan wished he could take back his words. Dom looked visibly upset. "First of all, Jan, the man can't help his appearance, so enough of that. Yes, I do believe him. Even though he's afraid for his life, he's been willing to contact us and supply what has turned out to be valuable information about Buldini's past and planned actions against us. As far as how Thomas would react to my belief, he and I have come to an understanding, and when all is said and done, any final decision must be ultimately mine. Even in protest, he would agree. How about you?"

Jan, embarrassed, nodded meekly.

Dom realized how Jan reacted, and mouthed a silent - "It's okay." Then continued. "There's a warning of a coming event. A weak link, as he calls it, will be severed and spirited away. That sounds as though someone close to the papacy, one of us perhaps, will be killed. No. If that individual's words will bury the pope, he must be kidnapped first. So now we have a possible abduction. And also, the Pale Horse is on the loose. The Pale Horse was the assassin in the other poems. On the loose could mean that no one is controlling him, including the evil one, Buldini. Buldini fears the casualty, the killing of the pope, would cook his goose. There have been others besides ourselves that have pointed fingers at him accusingly. He's well aware of that, and can't afford the pressure if I were assassinated now. Maybe he was right when he said he knew nothing of the latest attempt when Kim was wounded on my balcony.

"The poor monsignor's holed up somewhere, taking his life in his hands to contact us, even to go out in public. He's probably in some sort of disguise, too. I'm inclined not to pursue his whereabouts, but to honor his request. Let him come to us."

"I agree with everything," Symon said, "though I'll be looking over my shoulder a little bit more from now on. Well, I'm off to the tavern. There's still time to catch two big fish at the local watering hole. Nathan will fill you in on his part of setting me up as a villain anxiously waiting for another payday."

*****

183

The usual stench of sawdust soaked in spilled spirits and day old vomit made the unrelenting waves of stale nicotine almost welcome. Symon took a long deep breath prior to swaggering through the tavern entrance, and then nearly tripped while attempting unsuccessfully to step over a slumbering patron. The body moaned as it tipped from a sitting position with its back to the door frame and legs sprawled across the threshold, to resting on the bottom step, in a fetal position blanketed with the malodorous sawdust.

The tavern was unusually crowded, but the mishap at the doorway had drawn far too much attention and laughter for his liking. He had hoped to enter unnoticed through the rear entrance, but a full blown donnybrook had been taking place just outside. In fact, in the very spot where he and Jabal had fought. His attempted at an inconspicuous entrance failed miserably.

Squeezing in between two rather burly local ladies hanging over their bar stools, Symon ordered a tankard of ale. While engaging the lovelies in idle conversation, he nonchalantly peered about the room for his prey. He was unable to spot Agapito or Zacchia. The tavern was too thick with bodies and smoke. Unknown to Symon, eyes had followed him the moment he had entered.

Symon was about to order his second tankard when he felt a heavy hand on his shoulder and heard the words, "We have one for you at our table Johnny, and someone who'd like to meet you." How could he have missed spotting the duo, he questioned himself. One was as hairless as a cricket ball, and the other sported as much hair as the albino werewolf of London. Zacchia indeed looked like Hemingway.

"Johnny, this here's a friend. Say hello to The Author. He's heard all about you from yours truly, and your old shipmate. By the way, his name's not really Author. We call him that because he looks a lot like Hemingway, don't you think? For now, he's The Author to you."

Playing the tough seaman role to the hilt, Symon coldly replied, "He could call himself King Author for all I care, as long as you two have that tankard you promised. I'm getting bloody thirsty. So what are you up to my unfeathered friend?"

"You'll get your ale and a lot more if you play your cards right," Zacchia said, returning Symon's cold stare. "For someone who's wanted for questioning in various countries in connection with a number of assassinations, you're pretty smug. We know all about you and how you've made your money, then cleverly managing to escape detection aboard the next departing ship."

"Ya, and there's one loud mouth bloke of a shipmate I should have taken care of long ago. And might still. Is he here tonight?" Symon asked looking around the room. "So you think you know all about 'ole Johnny, do you? So what?"

Agapito looked concerned, apparently remembering how well Johnny had handled the threat to his life in the alleyway, as well as the gruesome tales revealed by his 'shipmate.' Layers of flesh above his eyebrows furled up as he made an effort to temper his new friend's growing animosity towards the one who lined his pockets.

"Hold on there, Johnny. No need to become hostile. Here, your brew's arrived. Miss, while you're at it, bring us another round on your next trip in this direction. We can all be friends. Just cool it. Johnny, we've a proposition for you. A way to make a great deal of cash."

Angrily, Symon stood up and shook his finger in Agapito's face. "I'm retired. Remember? This old sea dog's not interested in any more blood sport activities. I didn't live this long by taking long shot chances. It's over with. See ya sometime when you're in better company." Picking up his tankard, Symon started to walk away from the table. Zacchia nodded in Symon's direction, and Agapito responded by grabbing hold of Symon's jacket sleeve. He roughly snatched it from Agapito's grasp, stepped forward within an inch of the bald head, and placed his hand on an imaginary weapon in his pocket. Marshaling as menacing a look as possible, he calmly said, "The last person that placed a threatening hand on me limped away with a smashed nose. You're bigger, but I've got an equalizer. Am I clear?"

"Okay Johnny, you're tough. But are you smart as well? Do business with us, and you'll get paid handsomely. Refuse and the authorities get a tip about an international fugitive. What do you say now, tough guy?" prodded the monsignor. Symon now turned his attention in Zacchia's direction and decided to play his trump card, unaware of the possible reaction.

But he felt it would be worth the outcome. "I'll tell you just how smart I am, Monsignor Giuseppe Zacchia." Both seated men wore stunned expressions. "And I'm aware of who your boss is, the head of the CDF, Cardinal Buldini. You want me to continue?"

185

"Please sit down, Mr. St. John. You've made your point. Let's talk this over like gentlemen. Forget the fugitive stuff, you obviously have us at a disadvantage. What more do you know, and how?" Zacchia inquired.

Deep within, Symon breathed a sigh of relief as he slowly slipped into the chair opposite Agapito. Looking into the dull emotionless eyes of the big man, he said, "Nothing personal. You took me by surprise, and I don't like surprises. Okay?" And put out his hand as a gesture of bygones be bygones. Relieved, Agapito responded likewise.

"Some secrets have a life of their own, while those who spill the beans lose theirs." Symon offered, gulping the last drop of ale and signaling the waitress for another. "Agapito here had an operative named Sergio, who hasn't been seen for some time now. I tell you this; right now what's left of him is feeding the fish down stream in the Tiber. You see, Sergio was the only one who knew the identity of the person who botched the first assassination attempt, and the hitter was aware of Sergio's loose lip, especially when primed with booze. That's how I came to know so much about your dirty operation, just by listening to tavern gossip. Plus, by what you might call an information network among assassins. They might know who's getting hit, but never know who got the assignment. Like anything else, the work is competitive, and sometimes they have to bid on the job. Works out fine. But, there weren't many interested in knocking off the pope."

Agapito agreed. "Yea, Sergio couldn't stop bragging when he was in his cups. He made the contract and got what he deserved. If I had found him, I would have broken his back, the little rat. And you're right about Sergio. He is missing."

"Enough talk," Zacchia growled. "Johnny we have a job for you, and we'll double what we were going to offer."

"Monsignor, you don't have enough money. There's no love lost for the man, as Agapito can tell you, but this is one I'll pass on. I'm not taking out the man. Besides, I told you before, I'm retired. End of discussion."

"Wait. Wait. You've got it all wrong. We want you to find the shooter who just made the attempt on the pope's life, and take him out. We don't want the pope assassinated," Zacchia whispered.

Apagito leaned forward and hissed, "No, we're going to assassinate his character instead."

"Damn you, Agapito" Zacchia shouted, slamming his fist on the table top. "Shut your mouth! You're as bad as Sergio, and don't ever forget his fate. From now on, you let me do all the talking. Understood?

"Listen Johnny, here's the deal. Just like they say, it takes a thief to catch a thief; we figure the same goes for shooters, hit men, however they care to be called. Make sense? If so, there's $100,000 up front for you, and another $100,000 with proof of death. What do you say to that?"

Everyone remained silent while the waitress served the next round, then Symon responded. "First of all, it'll take $200,000 up front. One never knows how these things will play out. The corpus may never surface. You'll have to take my word in that case. And, since I'm taking out one of my own, which is frowned on within the network, it'll cost you another $100,000 when it's over. No questions asked, just the payment. And keep this in mind. Don't even think of stiffing me on the payoff, or I'll do the next three for free. And you can imagine who the three targets would be. Agreed?"

"Agreed. Meet Agapito here two nights from now, and he'll have your starter fee."

Symon pushed back his chair, got up, and headed back to the bar without another word. Just a nod of acknowledgment. He had placed his hands in his pockets, hoping no one noticed how badly they were shaking.

Now he really did need a drink. He asked for a whisky chaser to go with the ale one of the ladies ordered for him. Much to his chagrin, the ladies had saved a seat right between the two of them, and he still had to squeeze in sideways in order to make it to the bar stool.

Five more minutes was all Symon could bear. His stomach was doing flips from a combination of nerves and booze and he felt as though he was drowning in the tavern's nauseating odors. He slipped off the stool and out of the door without a word to anyone, and headed for the Borgia Apartments to leave a note for Dom in the light fixture.

Exhausted both physically and mentally, he no longer cared if Monsignor Diamante was lurking in the shadows. Besides, Dom seemed to trust him, and the old fellow was probably already fast asleep by now.

After writing a lengthy note explaining the events of the meeting with Zacchia, Symon decided it would be wise to limit further nights within Vatican walls, and instead stay at his hotel room so as not to draw undue attention.

*****

Jabal approached Dom's bedroom suite door at 6:30 that morning, knowing he would be awake and would want to read Symon's note as soon as possible. Although Jabal did have a problem convincing Kim to allow him within two feet of the entrance, let alone knock. "Don't you ever sleep, you big ox? You're taking this personal protection thing too far. This is important! Now let me by," Jabal protested.

"Jabal, have some coffee. And Kim you come in, too. Sorry, coffee's all we have - no tea," Dom offered while unfolding Symon's note. "Well, this is both encouraging and disturbing," he commented after reading it to himself. "Listen to this. I'll just hit the highlights and will fill everyone in on the details at our 9 'clock briefing. Jabal, make certain Thomas is notified. It's vitally important he be there.

"It seems that Symon did in fact make it to the tavern in time to meet Zacchia. Nathan's stories about Symon, I mean Johnny, did the trick. They're convinced he's an unsavory character that they can buy to do their dirty work.

"Much to his surprise they want him to help save my life, not take it. That surprises me, too. He's convinced that Buldini was behind the first attempt on my life, but not involved in the last. And now Symon has a contract to find and dispose of the assassin before he has the chance to strike again. They've taken him into their confidence, which is good, but at the same time places his life further in danger. He's taken the precaution of staying at the hotel indefinitely."

Jabal interrupted. "We'll have to devise another way to stay in contact with him and exchange information. Neither Nathan nor I can be seen anywhere close to Symon from now on."

"You're right, Jabal. Let me know what you recommend. Now here's the disturbing fact. Symon said he learned that since they can't afford the negative publicity of my bodily assassination, they've planned to somehow assassinate my character. We must be prepared to counterattack the minute whatever it is they plan to do surfaces."

After Jabal and Kim left Dom alone, he reread Symon's last three sentences. *"One positive thing came about as a result of tonight's meeting. In two days I'll be given the necessary funds to finance my continuing pursuit of the mystery of the Babylonian slave."* This Dom didn't understand.

188

"Between you and me, my friend, I don't know how much longer I can keep up this charade and survive." This Dom understood, and felt heavy hearted.

CHAPTER TWENTY THREE

The Giardini Vaticiani, the private gardens between the basilica and the museums, took on the appearance of a land fashioned of blown glass. An unseasonable chill had dropped the temperature below freezing and the dew covered trees, bushes, flowers, and the pope's vegetable garden glistened in the early morning glow. Warming rays drew irregular patterns on the manicured lawn as the frost thawed in some areas in the face of the sun, while other sections of the gardens still sparkled, hidden by the surrounding foliage.

The figure treading through the winding garden pathways stopped and called out, "Your Holiness, where are you?" Not receiving a reply, he continued on, stopping from time to time to repeat the appeal. Completely frustrated with his failed search, he sat down on one of the many stone benches to rest. The cold bench and the morning chill were about to send him retreating to the warmth of his Vatican office when he heard the faint sound of a chant. It seemed to come from the direction of the papal beehives. "It's me, Thomas. Dom, is that you? Answer me. Please."

"Over here Thomas. Come join me," came the reply. And there sat the pope in his brown habit and white skull cap, saying his rosary, seemingly oblivious to the glistening wonderland around him.

"Aren't you freezing, sitting on that icy bench dressed like that?" Thomas inquired.

"No, not at all. I've got my papal thermals on," he joked. "You ought to get you a pair, Thomas. What's on your mind this fine sunny morning? You look to be in such a rush. Sit down. Let's talk. We've plenty of time before breakfast and our first meeting of the day. I've been in meditation for over an hour contemplating some of the mysteries of creation. Want to hear my conclusions?"

"I'm all ears, but we don't have time. I've moved up your day by half an hour to accommodate your meeting with three of the cardinals. They requested more time with you. I didn't think you'd mind. We'd better leave."

As the two walked back through the maze towards the Vatican offices, chattering away, neither were aware of the serious charges that would soon be leveled against the Franciscans and would shake the very foundation of Pope Francis' papacy.

*****

The day was filled with various meetings with museum directors, the monsignor in charge of clergy adherence to the pope's austerity program, and three questioning cardinals who mirrored Cardinal Buldini's defiant challenge that Pope Francis was overstepping his authority. All in all, he thought the day leaned in his favor.

As usual, Dom met with his Franciscan brothers and Thomas for dinner at six o'clock. The conversation was spirited and lighthearted until Jan noticed Karl was absent. No one had seen him all day. Jabal confessed, "Karl was bound and determined to see the door that Dom had removed from the synagogue. I warned him that you ordered us to all stick together for reasons of safety, but he wouldn't listen. It's my fault for not stopping him or at least telling someone. He changed clothes and headed in the direction of the museum warehouse."

The poet's words echoed in everyone's thoughts - *'The weak link will be severed and spirited away.'* The room fell silent. Wide eyes were riveted on their leader, who nodded in Jan's direction.

Understanding the meaning, Jan said, "Jabal and I will get on it right away." Both men immediately left the room.

Dom followed them, muttering to himself, "This could be bad, real bad."

Thomas caught up with Dom, suggesting, "We need to contact Symon right away. Perhaps Rico could be adequately disguised and pass a message on to Symon."

*****

The sharp thin blade sliced through both hair and fabric as the grunts, groans and muted cuss words flowed freely. "He was right. The glue on this fake beard just won't turn loose."

Symon's own beard had grown sufficiently in length, and he decided it was time to remove the fake, but the thought was easier than the actual removal. Pulling on the fake as hard as he could without yanking out any of his own whiskers, while at the same time using a straight razor to cut off the

192

fake as close to the glued fabric as possible, reminded him of an ancient form of self-flagellation. It hurt.

"Pope Francis, you're going to owe me big time," he said, as he surveyed the damage in the rusted old hotel mirror.

Symon was preparing himself for that night's meeting with Agapito and the $200,000 down payment. He felt uncomfortable with the thought of taking the money and shivered as a chill shot like lightning up his spine. With the fake beard gone, at least he felt more like himself, though he was no longer sure just what that felt like. His own beard was now about the same length as the fake, but with more of a smattering of gray. "In the dingy tavern light, no one would ever notice," he convinced himself.

*****

Dazed and disoriented, Karl sat up from a fetal position. Questions rushed to fill his mind. Had he gone blind? What had happened? Where in heaven's name was he? And why was he here - wherever *here* was?

Shivering from a cold that seemed to threaten his very soul, Karl stretched out a tentative hand. "I can't even see my hands in front of me!" He managed to stifled a scream. Karl repeated the exercise of covering his eyes with his hands and then holding them a few inches before him, straining to see ten fingers, but to no avail. He closed his eyes and shouted - "God give me strength! Help me Lord!"

His words echoed eerily. "Karl, pull yourself together," he told himself. "Rationalize your situation. There's a very powerful echo, and the floor seems to be made of large stone bricks." Wobbly and unsure of his footing, he struggled to his feet, arms outstretched for balance and protection.

Taking short deliberate steps, with arms extended, he shuffled straight ahead from the direction he was facing. After some ten feet, his hands hit a solid object. "Feels just like the floor, solid rock." Groping his way along the wall, hand over hand, he learned his prison was a windowless room made of stone bricks. He couldn't even find a door. "No wonder I'm so cold," he sighed.

"I'm in a stone box. That's why there's no light. Thank God, I'm not blind after all. We've got that settled. Now Karl, compose yourself and calmly consider your situation."

He sat down, back to one of the walls and took a deep breath, letting the air out slowly. Besides his heartbeat, he heard what sounded like water slapping up against the side of something solid. "Okay - I'm in a dungeon, and close to a body of water. Probably the Tiber, which won't help pinpoint my location since the river wraps itself around and through Rome like a discarded holiday ribbon. I could be anywhere. But the questions remain - how and why?"

Karl closed his eyes and attempted to piece together what he could remember prior to waking up in his black stone box. His first deduction was correct. He hadn't been in the darkness for any measurable length of time. He wasn't hungry. And he did remember changing his clothes, having a quick snack, then after a disagreement with Jabal, heading in the direction of the Vatican Museum warehouse to see for himself the ancient door Pope Francis had removed from the church.

The guard at the warehouse had been quite friendly, perhaps too friendly, now that he thought about it. He was ushered right in without being asked for his authorization credentials. Forgetting that he was in civilian clothes and accustomed to going where he wished in his habit, the no-questions-asked access should have alerted him to possible danger. On second thought, though too late now, he admitted to himself that he had been extremely careless. "Dom warned us all, and I should have listened to Jabal," he said, disappointed in himself.

The last thing he could remember was stepping a few feet into the warehouse with the security guard a step behind. The building lights had suddenly gone out, and that's when he had felt something soft with a spicy aroma brush his nose.

Karl had no way to judge the passage of time without a point of reference. Pure black gave birth to a timeless environment. Five minutes or two hours could have passed without notice if it were not for his complaining stomach. The rumbling declarations of hunger seemed to bounce off the ice cold stone walls in concert with unbridled laughter. "I'm in unknown peril and the simplest of sounds tickles me silly. Already, I'm going mad."

In time, he found that silence and complete darkness was the perfect sedative. Karl fell fast asleep within minutes of sitting with his back to one of the walls. He jumped up, startled out of a deep sleep by the sound of stone scraping on stone, and steadied himself by clinging to the wall for balance. Just as he had been blinded by the blackness, the bright light now pouring in from the opening seemed to sear his eyes. Facing the entrance, he shielded the pain with his hands, trying desperately to make out the identity of the figure outlined in the sunlight. A lifetime seemed to pass before his captor spoke. "Look at the little Homo Jew. Have a nice nap? Ready for some fun?"

THE FRANCISCAN

CHAPTER TWENTY FOUR

Poor Monsignor Albani, he fussed and mumbled to himself but it was useless. His Holiness just wouldn't listen. "Just like last time," he whispered softly, hoping not to be overheard.

The pope was about to greet and install his new and carefully selected cardinals-to-be. The site for the noon ceremony would be at the foot of Saint Peter's Basilica steps facing the square so that their friends, relatives and daily visitors could participate in this most solemn of events.

The monsignor had tried in vain to properly dress the pope in traditional garments for his basilica balcony presentation to the world. He wouldn't listen then and he wasn't willing to listen now. Resting both aching arthritic knees on a colorful but timeworn Persian rug, Albani fidgeted with the length of the pope's Franciscan habit, while continuing to plead his case. "But Your Holiness, it's just not done. It's a formal, serious and stately moment in the history of the Church, and you must be regal in appearance. Don't you understand?" he sighed in frustration.

"First of all, my serious friend, please refrain from tugging on my hem. You're like a little gnat. Granted, a well meaning gnat, but nevertheless a gnat." Reaching down, the pope gently grabbed hold of the monsignor's shoulders and picked him up to a standing position.

The sound of both Albani's knees cracking reminded the pope of his boyhood and the sound of a baseball hitting a bat, and it tickled his irreverent funny bone. Composing himself, after slapping his thighs with both hands and bending over with laughter, he tried to ease the monsignor's obvious discomfort.

"Please pardon my outburst. I haven't enjoyed a good hearty laugh for some time now. Your knees did the trick. Soak them in the tub later and tell 'em them their pope thanks them."

Monsignor Albani collapsed in an uncomfortable wooden straight backed chair. His mouth hung open in an expression of despair, and his hands hung helplessly over the padded arms. As if appealing for spiritual help from some long past resident, sad and exhausted eyes slowly searched age-old tapestries, ornate gold leaf molding, and scarlet colored drapes that seemed to support the four corners of the pope's dressing room. He finally gave up when his eyes came to rest on a large painting of Pope John. Even this pope's jolly expression seemed to smile and mock him. Both popes were in agreement. How could he argue with both and win?

Yet still, the wise old monsignor had one last trick up his sleeve that might work. He turned his attention to the pope who stood patiently with arms crossed, waiting for some sign of life. With eyes that would rival that of a Basset Hound, he said rather sheepishly, "I respectfully submit that Your Holiness should at least wear his symbol of authority for this high ceremony, the pallium - the circular band of white wool with front and back pendants. It would look handsome with your white cap, white waist cord, and in contrast with the brown of your habit. And, it would please me so much."

"Who could resist the excellent advice of someone who is without doubt a sound and clever negotiator. You've convinced me. The pallium it is," agreed the pope. "Let's get on with it," he said with a muted chuckle.

Kim poked his head in the door to inform Dom that participating Church dignitaries had assembled in the outer room and were waiting for His Holiness' appearance. "And by the way, Cardinal Buldini is present," Kim said in a surly tone. "And one of Cardinal Mumbwa's assistants is demanding to see you before the installation. He seems extremely agitated. Almost hysterical. He says it's of the utmost importance. Shall I have him wait?"

"No. Show him in. If he's that distraught, we had better set him at ease. We wouldn't want to be responsible for a heart attack. Perhaps Thomas sent him with news of Karl." In his haste, the archbishop nearly knocked poor Albani to the floor as the tiny man retreated from the room. Pope Francis had his back to the door gazing out from the large floor-to-ceiling window. He had pulled the heavy curtain back to view the milling throng standing or taking their seats below. The general public, thousands of them, stood behind the waist high crisscrossed portable white wooden fences. In row upon row of white chairs sat members of the clergy. Priests, nuns, monsignors, bishops, archbishops and cardinals were seated like wax figures, eyes affixed on the door where the pope would exit the basilica onto the outside steps. Even the first row of soon-to-be princes of the Church sat motionless. This was to be a joyous occasion. What was wrong? Puzzled by the expressionless stares on the faces of the clergy, Pope Francis turned to greet the archbishop.

"It's horrible!" cried the archbishop, whose tears streamed down his grief stricken features. He immediately fell to his knees while roughly taking

198

the pope's hand in an attempt to kiss the fisherman's ring. Sobbing profusely with his lips still glued to the ring, he repeatedly uttered, "I'm so sorry Your Holiness. I'm so sorry. Forgive me for bearing this horrible, unspeakable news. Thomas sent me. He'll be along as soon as he can."

Pope Francis had to grab d'Angelo's wrist firmly with one hand and with the other, pry his ring hand loose from the archbishop's impassioned grip. He was reluctant to stand and face the pope, so Dom was forced to drop to his knees in order to look at the archbishop eye to eye.

The pope's mind raced in anticipation of all the horrible events that could have brought the archbishop to his present state. Had they found Karl or Symon's body?

"Jules, compose yourself," ordered the pope. "Quickly. Tell me what appalling news has you so distressed. And, what's keeping Cardinal Mumbwa? Where is he?"

"He's talking with various media sources about the breaking story Your Holiness. He's trying to determine the origin of the slander. It's in this afternoon newspaper's special edition, and both the radio and television stations have frequently interrupted their scheduled programming with a news bulletin concerning the alleged scandal. Oh it's horrible - unthinkable."

Pope Francis had exhausted his patience. As he stood up, he dragged the archbishop to his feet and shook him, trying to get him to focus on an explanation. "Stop it man, stop your babbling! Now listen to me. What scandal? Who's involved? Is someone injured? Have they found Karl? Tell me without another whimper - right now. Do you understand?"

*****

It was as though he was drowning in a sea of darkness, an emptiness completely void of even the tiniest seed of light. Time was meaningless. He felt as though his life was somehow suspended, and he now floated freely in space. He wondered if God had forgotten his servant. But his training and intellect assured him that if God had indeed forgotten him, he would no longer exist, and he did still exist; the chill that racked his body attested to that fact. At some point in time, whenever that was, his captors had stripped him naked.

A blinding flash of light spun Karl around so as to avoid the impossible glare that ripped the veil of darkness. Before he had the

199

opportunity to think clearly, a voice said, "Here's the devil, Jew boy." And just as suddenly, he was once again smothered by the hard black void.

He was alone again, so he thought, with his prayers, secure in the knowledge that his friends would never cease their search for him. It was important to his sanity that he retain that thought. Any moment now, the stone wall would open with shouts - "Karl, it's us, we've found you! You're free!"

"Who's there? I can hear you breathing," he whispered aloud, "and I can smell you." It couldn't be the devil, he thought. The scent's too sweet. Sulfur didn't smell like that. "Who are you?" he demanded to know, as he staggered in all directions, unbalanced, with arms extended.

The sound of breathing was now much closer, and the sweet aroma made him feel somewhat light-headed, almost giddy. It reminded him of lying in a field of wild flowers as a youngster, bathing in their fragrance awakened by the early summer sun. The high mountain valley was his hideaway to read what was forbidden, yet called to him and stirred his soul.

In a desperate try to seize the unknown, Karl lunged forward with arms spread and hands wildly searching the darkness. He touched something. Something that the nerves in his finger tips immediately relayed to his brain - it felt like soft, warm liquid velvet. The sensation startled him. He jerked his hands away, and clutched them to his chest in shock. Swaying one way and then another, he struggled with the overwhelming feeling of being crushed by the weight of the darkness, the unknown, the sweetness that filled his nostrils and seemed to engulf his very essence - and 'the touch' that left him gasping for breath. From somewhere deep inside, he found the courage to slowly reach out with his right hand. It was still there, whatever it was.

He hesitated, then allowed only the very tips of his fingers to explore the object before him. With much trepidation he cupped his fingers on what felt like a velvety smooth domed surface flawed only by a small protruding firm node. As he instinctively applied the slightest of pressure, much to his astonishment, the object swelled, filling the palm of his hand, and rose as it advanced towards him. "No! No!" he cried aloud. "Lord give me strength to overcome the weakness of the flesh."

Karl stepped backward and turned away in shame, squeezed his legs tightly and placed his hands to his groin. "Go away," he shouted helplessly, as he felt the faint pressure and the fullness of both silky breasts gently grazing his bare back, and her fingernails as they traced a line on the side of both thighs from his knees to his buttocks. He couldn't defend himself; he was frozen by fear of the unknown, and confounded by the strange sensation that was quickly consuming both mind and body.

He was shaking violently, not from the cold, it had since held no power over him, but rather from the experience that was absorbing his willpower. A warm spine-tingling sensation energized every nerve-ending in his frame, and as her tongue and moist lips slithered up and down the back of his inner thighs, he found he no longer had control of his body. His legs were parting with every second. His hands guarding his manhood were now by his side. He was being devoured, both body and soul. He was totally helpless.

She was before him now. He could hear her heavy breathing and feel her warm breath stirring the hairs on his chest; the sweet smell was intoxicating. "No!" he screamed. "I'll not sin again!" She was deaf to his plea and confession. The temptation continued as she painfully traced the crossbar of a crucifix from his right nipple to his left with her fingernails. She held both of Karl's hands fast at his side, while her mouth left a line of saliva that started from under his Adam's apple, worked its way down his chest, and stopped just below his navel. Karl stiffened and straightened his body from the once hunched over position. As she made her final attack, he sucked as much air into his lungs as humanly possible and held it until he felt he would burst.

Once again blinded by the blast of light, Karl turned to protect his eyes. He heard the patter of bare feet on stone, and just as suddenly as his personal demon had appeared, it disappeared, swallowed by the light.

She stood naked and shamelessly before three men in a cave surrounded with human skulls and remnant bones of the long dead. Two wore black hoods to hide their identity. The third was a bald man with large looping earrings. He gruffly demanded to know, "Well, is he or isn't he?"

She laughed, "He's not dead, and that wasn't rigor mortis that set in. No, he's straight - no pun intended. He knows what a woman's all about. He's been there before. Believe me, if anyone knows, I do. How 'bout my due.' "

The bald man nodded to the hooded man behind her, and he promptly placed his arm around her neck. She made a little bird sound, then crumpled to the floor. Later that week, on an inside page of the local newspaper, was a story about the naked body of a woman in her late twenties that washed up on a small sandbar down stream of Rome on the Tiber River. It went on to say that the authorities expected foul play, and were investigating a possible homicide.

CHAPTER TWENTY FIVE

Those waiting in the great hall outside the pope's ready room were fast becoming concerned that the noon hour was upon them and the pope was still behind closed doors with Archbishop 'd Angelo. Everyone was well aware of the message the archbishop was delivering; the news ran like hot lava through the Vatican pipeline.

At the very moment church bells tolled noon, the ready room's double doors swung open with such a force that Kim hadn't the opportunity to jump clear, and the right door nipped his left elbow. Without a change of expression, Pope Francis touched Kim's arm and gave it a squeeze, then stopped in stride to confront his friends and foes. Those sitting sprung to their feet, and those standing in small groups spun around to face His Holiness.

He stood silent, hands on his hips, and made eye contact with each member of those before him. As his back teeth ground together, the muscles on either side of his square jaw pulsated, and his eyes became dark soul searching daggers. Finally, his gaze rested on Cardinal Buldini, who shifted his bulk rather nervously and noticeably. The pope, not taking his eyes off of Buldini's, nodded as if to say, that enough is enough - the time has come.

The spell was broken by the noisy and abrupt entrance of Cardinal Mumbwa. Ignoring all in attendance, he stopped directly in front of the pope and said, "Your Holiness, it's imperative that we talk, now. Jules has apprized you of the problem, but I have the latest."

Without looking at Thomas and with a face cast in stone, he replied with a curt, "Later," and headed down the marble stairs. Then he turned to exit the main doors opening onto Saint Peter's Square. The others scampered in haste to keep up with the leader.

*****

A hush fell over the crowd in the square when the pope appeared in the entrance guarded by two huge iron doors. The only sounds were the distant drone of Rome's traffic and the splashing of the square's giant dueling fountains. Pope Francis hesitated, allowing his entourage to catch up, before descending the steps to stand before the seated clergy. Forcing a smile, he stepped forward, blessing those gathered for the ceremony.

On about the tenth step down, the crowd's expression of restraint turned into one of horror and disbelief. Most were too stunned to utter a sound. Screams were trapped in a thousand throats, but all managed to point upward towards the basilica's dome, and behind those slowly walking down the steps.

Wooden chairs being tipped and flung aside clattered on the stone laid square, as the assembled clergy leapt to their feet, anticipating the worst. Confused by the crowd's alarm and unaware of the danger, they turned all too slowly to avoid the coming peril. Kim, who was several steps behind the group, was the first to hear a dull cracking sound. He turned and looked up. The huge concrete crucifix that had rested on the left shoulder of the gigantic statue of Christ, standing at the center of the row of saints, broke loose. As it tumbled, it struck the peak of an architectural structure and burst into sizable chunks, showering down on the pope and his unsuspecting group.

Kim sprang forward, taking several steps at a time, and just as his shoulder was grazed by a large jagged piece, he gave the pope a mighty shove. The force of being struck gave emphasis to the thrust of Kim's hands, and he literally propelled the pope through the air.

Pope Francis somehow managed to land on his hands and knees. Rolling over onto his backside and ignoring the pain of bloodied, skinned hands and knees, he was grateful to see that most of the group was spared injury. Kim was on his feet, briskly rubbing his shoulder. Cardinal Mumbwa was bent over and holding the back of his leg where he took a hit in full fury, but motioned that he was okay, as did Kim. To Kim's left lay Cardinal Buldini. He lay flat on his back, his belly pointing to the heavens, his legs in the direction of the basilica and head towards the square. Blood trickled down his forehead from a deep scalp wound.

Pope Francis gingerly got to his feet, wiped his bloody hands on his sides, and gritted his teeth while he pulled away the torn fabric that was embedded in the flesh of both knees. "Kim, if you're okay, see to Buldini; he's beginning to move, but needs assistance. Put a compress on the gash and take him to the infirmary. And Kim - take good care of him. You understand me?" Quickly surveying the fallen debris before turning his attention to his dumb struck audience, he said, "Thank God. This could have been disastrous."

Thomas, favoring his right leg, hobbled over to where Buldini sat upright on a step. He held a handkerchief to his head and looked quite

204

shaken. "Kim can care for him. Thomas, I need you here," ordered the pope. "We'll go forward with the installation proceedings." The remainder of the group, also shaken but unharmed, were brushing small dust particles from their formal costumes and assuring the pope they were unscathed.

The crowd stood petrified with hands to their mouths. The clergy remained on their feet, chairs scattered about. Everyone anticipated the pope's words as he limped down the stairs towards the throne-style chair that was placed for his ceremonial use. Upon reaching the appointed spot, he took the microphone, looked at those directly before him and said, "Please be seated. This is your finest hour. And may I please be forgiven for sitting - I seem to have injured both knees."

The same whispers spread like a wave from person to person as His Holiness sat holding the mike - "Look at his hands and knees." Twice the mike nearly slipped from his hands smeared with blood, and both bloodied knees were bared for all to see. He pulled down on the large scooped sleeve of his Franciscan habit to use it as a glove in order to hold the mike in his right hand, and motioned for silence with his left. A collective "Oh!" filled the square when they saw the palm of his raised hand, which looked as thought the entire palm had its skin peeled off.

Reacting to the people's obvious concern, he wiped his hand on his lap and then held it up for all to see. "You see, it looks a lot worse than it really is. I'm fine. Really." Then he looked down and lifted the bloodied and torn skirt of his outfit and remarked with a toothy grin, "But I'm afraid my tailor is going to be extremely upset with me." The air was filled with good natured laughter.

The smile quickly disappeared and was replaced with a serious expression. "Guests, members of our religious orders, and cardinals-in-waiting. We really did not stage this little episode to command your attention. It is, however, an example of a number of similar situations we will now reveal to you. The timing for full disclosure is right, considering the advent of today's reported scandalous and false accusations against the papacy.

"I'm pleased to see the media is out in full force this afternoon. What will be revealed to you for the first time, will be broadcast on the Global Net worldwide." Teams of camera crews and reporters scurried around, jockeying for the best view of the pope, anxiously waiting to report the breaking news live.

A hush came over the crowd as Pope Francis stood to speak. From the grimace on his face, they knew his knees had stiffened and he was in pain. But he continued. "What you have witnessed a few moments ago, was the third such attempt on my life since my inauguration." A gasp arose from the crowd.

"Yes. A third attempt. The first assassination undertaking came soon after my election to the papacy. Sadly, Cardinal Uden Borne of the Netherlands was mistakenly murdered in my stead. Next, Kim Xinan, a Franciscan friar from China, took a bullet in his chest that was meant for me. And as you just saw, once again, he risked his life and came to my rescue.

"Since we made the decision to follow Vatican II's and III's direction of opening the doors and windows in hopes that fresh air would clear the musty bonds of timeworn tradition, we've been repeatedly attacked. The papal order, especially to those in the Church hierarchy, to ardently follow the spirit of Saint Francis' service to all the sons and daughters of the Creator, I believe, was the catalyst that drove the enemies of Pope Francis to this end.

"In addition to the personal physical attacks, they have now stooped to assaulting me on another level - that of a well organized and orchestrated international character assassination. I am not the only target of this shameless and unholy effort. They have also assaulted the reputation of my faithful Franciscan brothers and that of the hallowed monastery from which we sprung."

He turned and laid the hand held mike on the chair's seat and picked up the clip-on, and attached it to the large collar of his habit. Once again he turned to face the audience and cameras. Taking a deep breath, he fell to his wounded knees and stretched his arms upward toward the heavens. His normally handsome and welcoming features were twisted in an expression of suffering.

From the piercing cries of those in the crowd, you knew they, too, inwardly felt the stabbing pain. A small pool of blood became visible at the corners of both knees.

Pope Francis bowed his head. Moments passed agonizingly slow as he prepared himself to set the pain aside. Once that was accomplished, he raised his head and spoke. "My brothers and sisters, I now kneel humbly before you and the world - and before our Father in heaven. And as our Creator is my witness, I say to you simply - there is not an ounce of truth in the vicious lies that are being reported. My Franciscans and I are innocent of the slanderous accusations being leveled. They are, as I have explained, part of a plot to discredit this papacy. Those responsible are the ones who stand to lose the most, financially, if all of our announced innovations would come to fruition."

He stopped abruptly, lowered his head once again, and took another deep breath. Many of those in the square were now openly weeping at the courage and compassion of the pope. He looked straight at the audience, and continued through gritted teeth.

"I need your help to survive this trial by fire. I need your prayers of support. I need you to believe in me." His head dropped to his chest, and his body wavered slightly as he attempted to steady himself while his hands gripped his thighs.

Two Swiss Guards dressed in their colorful pantaloons and polished helmets seemed to appear out of nowhere; their capes flowed and their swords clattered as they ran to assist their pope. He tried unsuccessfully to stand on his own. All the strength in his knees had abandoned him. Each guard placed a hand under his arms and sat him on the chair. Squaring his shoulders, he raised his head and looked at his benefactors. He recognized them both as the two guards that Kim had unceremoniously hoisted up the Tower stairs, and whom he later mildly chastised.

"Thank you guys. I owe you one," he said softly.

The heart wrenching scene that played out before their eyes was far too graphic for many of the faithful and bystanders. Women swooned, and tears flowed freely. Even the most hardy found that holding back the flood was impossible. The sight of the bleeding, shaken, and physically weakened man of God, genuinely pleading for their prayers and their trust, was more than their hearts could bear.

An ear-splitting chorus of "We believe! We Believe!" filled Saint Peters' Square and echoed throughout the ancient marble columns and walls. Thin glass windows vibrated with the joyous sounds of commitment. Unnoticed, the defeated yet defiant face of Cardinal Buldini glared from out of the Vatican infirmary window. His head throbbed from the blow, and he suffered a possible concussion. But it was Pope Francis' moral victory that gave him a riveting headache.

The people's chant, "We believe! We believe!" continued long after the pope gestured for silence. Finally it subsided to a gentle rolling murmur.

The sight of His Holiness painfully attempting to get to his feet forced a hush from the once boisterous but adoring crowd.

This time Cardinal Mumbwa took charge. With a firm but gentle hand, he held the pope in his seat, then leaned over and whispered, "If you insist on going through with the ceremony, you had better stay seated or I'll have Kim carry you bodily to the infirmary - right now. You don't have a choice. Understood?" Pope Francis saw a combination of determination and brotherly concern in Thomas' eyes, and smiled assuredly.

"You win, my friend. Besides, I'm too weak to argue. But, I have one more request of the people. Then we can proceed with what we are here for." Bloody hands once again gestured for silence. A hush befell the crowd.

"Thank you for your most heartfelt response to my appeal for support. This pope will never forget you or this day. Now I have still another request of all of you. In addition to the attempts on my life, the murder, and falsehoods - days ago, one of our Franciscan brothers, Karl Kumbach, was kidnapped and remains missing. Obviously, we suspect the same evil force that is bent on sabotaging the papacy to also be responsible for his abduction. Upon completion of today's installation of cardinals, and before you disburse, guards at each exit will hand out a photograph of Karl for you to take home. Please, if you would, when you go about your daily routine, be on the lookout for this most valued friend of the Church. If you have any information, simply call the number at the bottom of the photo. By no means attempt to do anything on your own. Merely make the call. Now - where are my red hats?"

*****

The remainder of the installation ceremony went as planned. Cardinals-to-be lay prostrate before Pope Francis as vows were exchanged. Upon completion, one after the other, they stood and approached the chair to receive the most coveted symbols of their new responsibilities and authority - their red hats. One by one, the pope presented them with their prized possession, as each in turn, conveyed a brief but personal message to His Holiness. Mercifully, the ceremony was over. Immediately after blessing those in attendance, the pope motioned for Cardinal Mumbwa to approach the chair. With labored breath and clearly in much discomfort, the pope whispered to Thomas, "Get me out of this chair and to the infirmary, but in a manner that leaves me a shred of dignity. I won't be carried. I can walk with some assistance - but slowly. Ever so slowly."

"Kim's still with Buldini. Probably won't let him out of his sight. Nathan and Jan are here now to assist you. One at each side. Once inside Saint Peter's, away from the public, they'll carry you to the doctor's office. From the pained look on your face, you're hurt more than you'll admit. You'll need plenty of rest."

"Thank you for your advice Doctor Mumbwa, but none of us have the luxury of rest. There's too much to do. We have a comrade missing, and there's no telling what kind of torment he's having to endure on our behalf. An assassin is still on the loose, and must be found and stopped. Symon needs some help. And believe me, my painful performance today will only buy us so much time. Our detractors will counter that effort with a new barrage of lies. We need to be prepared for that. And our plans for the Church need immediate attention. No. No my friend, there'll be little rest for any of us - including me. Have everyone meet us in the Tower office at seven this evening. We'll have a snack prepared for a working meeting. Now, Nathan, Jan - away with me."

CHAPTER TWENTY SIX

Loud voices rose outside a small private office where the pope often withdrew from official pressures and prying eyes. "I don't care if the Vatican City is considered a sovereign state, and His Holiness is its sovereign ruler. He's my responsibility. He's been the target of an unknown or several unknown assassins, and I, the Chief of Police of Rome, was never informed. This is unacceptable. I demand to see him now."

Kim defiantly barred the door as Thomas tried without success to convince the chief that all was under control. In fact, his excuses for not calling in the local police only fanned the chief's flame.

"Chief Santini, please keep your voice down. His Holiness has had a very trying day, and the pain from his wounds is considerable. He's not able to receive visitors until his condition has significantly improved. Surely you do understand."

"You haven't convinced me, Cardinal Mumbwa. I'm going in. And if that mammoth monk doesn't move aside, it'll be the second time this month he's gotten shot. Do you understand me, cardinal?" The intercom buzzer on the desk just outside the office droned repeatedly, until it became annoying. Thomas turned a deaf ear, refusing to push the reply button.

"Cardinal Mumbwa, will you answer that damn thing!" the chief shouted in frustration. Thomas knew it was the pope buzzing and did not want to answer. Especially not with the chief within earshot. But the buzzer wouldn't stop. It was obvious the pope was also becoming frustrated. Against his better judgment, he pushed and held the button.

"Chief, I can hear you behind thick doors and do appreciate your delicate situation. You have every right to be concerned, and you have my gratitude for your sense of duty. However, Cardinal Mumbwa is correct. I am presently in no condition to discuss such a weighty dilemma. Allow the cardinal and me a few moments in private, and he'll explain everything to you in detail. Thank you for being so understanding. Bless you. And, oh - for your information, Brother Xinan is not a monk, he's a friar."

Whether it was the tone of stress in the pope's voice, his agreeing with Chief Santini, or the blessing, or all of the above, the chief looked satisfied. Thomas, on the other hand, seemed not to share his mood. Scowling, he disappeared behind the large wooden carved door. "Now before you say a word, Thomas, hear me out. I'm in too much pain to argue. It's always a

211

pleasure I look forward to, but not just now. Tell the chief all we know - but nothing about Buldini's involvement, Symon's assignment, the Borgia Apartment trap doors and secret entrance, or anything related to the elements of our own investigation. Tell him very little or whatever you think he needs to know about Uden's murder, Paulo's suicide, and Karl's suspected abduction. And one more thing. Don't mention Monsignor Diamante. Any questions?"

"No, I've got it all. This is just the way I would have handled the situation. Forgive me for doubting your judgment. I was just overly concerned - as usual."

"You're forgiven. Now do me a favor. Ask the doctor to come and see me within the hour. The bandages on my knees need to come off. They're sticking to the open wounds. When the scabs begin to form and then the gauze removed, it'll cause them to bleed again. The wounds need air to heal, not bandages. I'm the pope, not an Egyptian mummy."

*****

"Kim, so help me, if you bump my knees against another piece of furniture, I'll crown you with my cane," Dom warned. "You're big and strong, but you're also a klutz. A loyal klutz, but nevertheless, a klutz."

The smiling Oriental gently placed his patient in his chair behind the desk in the Tower office. He bowed in jest, followed by a sweeping hand, knowing full well that his friend's expression was nothing more than a term of endearment, and not spoken in anger.

"I never saw a bald headed nurse before. Especially one with such broad shoulders. Leave me now, so I can do some work before the others arrive in about an hour. And Kim, thanks for your physical support. It really is appreciated." As usual, only one lamp was lit. Just the way he liked it. But this time it was somehow different. The darkness and silence mingled with the musty scent of centuries gone by, creating an unusually pensive mood. Shadows seemed to leap from one fresco to another, and his thoughts moved just as freely.

Looking over his shoulder at the kneeler in the corner, he spoke aloud. "Lord, you'll have to accept me in a sitting position; I'm in no shape to come to you on my knees." Closing his eyes, he began to sing a soft prayer chant

212

as he rocked his body slowly back and forth in rhythm with the cadence of the chant.

*****

In an almost trance-like state, time seemed to stand still, yet fifteen minutes had passed when he was startled by the muffled sound of a cough that sat him upright in his chair.

"You'd better be a friend. If not, you've got me. I'm too stiff to move, or to defend myself."

"If I were who I'm reputed to be, you'd be mine," came a familiar voice from out of a darkened corner of the room. "You're quite literally, a bloody sitting duck. I came in five minutes ago, but didn't have the heart to interrupt you; I love that chant so much. Haven't heard it in years."

"Oh Symon, I'm relieved it's you. I thought for sure my reign was about to be a short one."

"Word came to me that you had called a meeting for tonight, and after the episode earlier today, I thought it would be wise to join the group. The TV in my hotel room is on its last legs, but it served it's purpose. I must say, your performance under extreme duress was truly magnificent. You made me proud to be called your friend." He grinned and took a seat by Dom's desk. "I'm sure that Uden was applauding from on high. Now - don't you think it's time we shared another one of Assuri's writings? I told you about his journey to Alexandria and timely escape to the cave, then his unexpected discovery of the mysterious and previously unknown Ashkari monks. Do you have time to read Assuri's two page summary of Berossus' written account of Creation?" Symon waved the pages in the air.

Dom snatched them up. "Symon, you know I do. Your cave adventure and find has whetted my appetite. I envy your return and continuing search."

"Just remember Dom, Berossus' works are still missing." Turning on the overhead lamp, Dom settled back in his chair to read Assuri's words aloud.

"This Journal is for whoever shall discover it, so that they may, and all who read here, will know that this servant has done everything possible to perform his appointed charge as ordained. Even so, to his likely and premature demise.

213

"I, Assuri of Babylon, attest to our late master, Berossus, a Babylonian high priest, and his impressions of Creation, of which he chronicled in the three volume History of The World, and thus was entrusted to my person for replication at the Library of Alexandria.

"As my life may be at an end, secreting my person from those bent on my capture and destruction of the writings in my possession, I have, for the first time in my life, risked to read master Berossus' account of Creation.

"Of particular interest is his discerning of the origin of mankind after land arose from the depths of the never-ending sea. Berossus' words are difficult for a lesser learned person as myself to comprehend, so, out of necessity, will attempt to replace commentary with my simple understanding."

"He accounts: "Mankind was then, in time, formed of the very nature of the earth, as is written by the ancients long before our time. The tale of the Hebrew's 'first man and woman', and as told in various forms by others, is actually symbolic truth of the 'conscious-awareness' of the first who walked the earth, and of their existence, of who they were, and the stirring of the Creator in their hearts...and of right from wrong. Good from evil, as we understand it in our time. The sudden awareness of their nakedness in The Garden, recounts that point in ancient annals when we became aware of who we were. A new breed of human emerged with sufficient intelligence to understand and deduce.

"Before the advent of 'conscious-awareness', humans were, though fully human, animals in nature. Unaware of their actions. They loved, hunted and fought only to survive. Procreated of passion alone. Slew their kind without remorse, unaware of a final end to life. Unaware of the meaning of life itself.

"This new awakening of intelligence is further borne out by the Hebrew tale of Cain slaying his brother. For the first time in recorded history, we became aware of a murderous action, of the consequences of this act, and of death itself.

"Intelligent awareness along with the dawning of the 'human-conscience,' soon spawned the inherent yearning to know and revere a superior being. This new sense-of-self and the element in which they existed cried out that since they themselves could not have created all they could see and grasp, something, someone greater must have done so. And, that

someone so powerful, must be appeased, if not feared. Thus, a rudimentary, yet deep-seated form of religion was born.

"The newly emerging race went forth among the tribes of the lands, teaching, carrying the message and the meaning, and intermeshing their blood, morality and faith with those that came to live with them. Thus creating our most ancient ancestors of old. Measured in seasons, so vast as to not comprehend."

"Symon, this is amazing. Assuri's opening paragraph is written as if he had expected to die and was writing about his responsibilities prior to that death."

"If you'll remember, he wrote of seeing a cloud of dust on the horizon and knew that the trackers were just a day or so away. He became aware of his destiny, and was prepared for the worst. Which I assume, came. But that's something we cannot be certain of. For all we know, he could have been brought back to Alexandria. That's a mystery I'm determined to solve - if I survive my stint in Rome."

Dom gritted his teeth, got up slowly, hobbled over to his friend, and fondly slapped him on the back. "Have patience my seafaring friend, we're nearing the end of our trials. I can feel it in my bones."

Symon looked up at Dom and with an impish grin, played off those words. "Well, if you don't mind me saying so, that's either old age or arthritis. Probably a bit of both."

"You're probably right. What I wouldn't give to get my hands on Berossus' History of The World. Do you think it still exists?" Dom asked, walking stiffly around the desk to his chair.

"Whether Assuri survived his captors or not, he hid the chronicles before they arrived, or much earlier. His Journal attested to that. Of course, they may have tortured him until he revealed the hiding place. But it's my guess, considering his loyalty to Berossus and his writings, that the secret would have died with him. Yes, I think they existed and are still out there, just waiting for me. And if I'm so blessed, you my friend, will be the first to read the translations."

Dom reached across the desk to Symon. "Here, you had better put this away. The others will be arriving soon. Thanks for sharing Assuri's notes. The adventure involved in the exploration and discovery of such important and ancient documents is exciting beyond words. May the Father bless you and your search."

*****

Thomas turned on the stairway lamp and the other lights as he entered the Tower of The Winds makeshift office. "Now we can see not to fall over the furniture."

The Franciscans filed up the stairs one by one, minus Karl and those who had already lost their lives. Thomas refused to count Karl amongst those gone. Right behind them trailed the sisters carrying the evening meal. They proceeded to the dining hall to set the tables, while the men remained in the Tower to conduct the business at hand. Why had the crucifix fallen? Where was Karl? And, what was new concerning the scandal?

"Jan, you first," ordered the pope. "What have your sources learned about today's attempt on my life?"

"The upright just below the crucifix' crossbar had been weakened, and apparently a small explosive charge attached to that area. Each of the guide wires steadying the structure had been cut, and there was powder residue at the spot of the fracture. Since no one was seen on the upper walkway at the time, it's assumed that the explosive was detonated from a distance away. However, one of the Swiss Guards reported that when he checked the walkway at closing time last night, he found a lone tourist milling around and had to ask him to leave.

"Now here's the interesting part. He described the person as being short and small in stature, with a full beard. At the time, he thought nothing about the incident. That is, until after discussing it with others that had conducted the investigation of the balcony shooting. When he learned about the nun with a limp, he put two and two together. The small bearded tourist walked with a decided limp."

"At Thomas' suggestion, we'll continue with our own inquiry, but will also cooperate and coordinate our efforts with Chief Santini and his men," Jabal said as he nodded to Jan. Rico, Nathan and Christian all spoke at the same time, expressing their desire to help. But Dom quickly interrupted.

"I know that the three of you feel as though you could contribute more, and that it's difficult not being in on the chase. But each of you are providing valuable assistance to Thomas and the work being done with the university

216

students you supervise. Gathering and reporting on the results of our efforts to contact and maintain a positive rapport with world religious leaders, is equally important; if not more so."

It was Rico's turn. "But Dom, one of us could be cut loose to help in the search to locate Karl. There's no telling what he's having to endure."

"Everyone's concerned," Dom said, responding to Rico's plea. "There's a search underway by several local law enforcement organizations, including our own Vatican staff and independent sources. Right now, there's not much more we can do until someone finds a lead to follow up on. Knowing Karl, he'll find a way to survive. And besides, you have the added responsibility as Jabal's fill-in contact with Symon."

Up to this point, and as usual, Christian hadn't said a word, he had only listened. Then he stood, faced Dom and said, "With respect - I cannot, within my conscience, sit idly and allow one of our brothers to bear his burden without personally taking action. After my work is completed, doing Thomas' bidding, there are hours left in my day and night. Sleep is of no concern.

"Unless you order me otherwise, it is my intention to conduct my own search for Karl. There are those within Rome's black community that may open up to me, a fellow countryman. Perhaps they've seen or heard something that could help us to find him. It's worth my effort. Again, this is said with the deepest respect."

"No! I won't hear of it," snapped Thomas. "We've already lost two, and now another is missing. And Symon, Jabal and Rico are exposed to whatever danger there is waiting. When will this end?"

Dom raised his hand and shook his head. Then with a sense of pride in his brothers, a smile crossed his lips. "It's called friendship, Thomas, and we won't attempt to stand in the way of the expression of that virtue.

"Christian, if I weren't the pope, I would have spoken as you. I understand. You have my blessing. Thomas will appropriate some suitable clothing. It won't be easy finding clothes to fit someone of your height. Report any clue to Thomas, but under no circumstances should you follow up on your own. Agree to those terms, or forget it."

"You have my word. Thank you."

Before Thomas had an opportunity to vent his opinion, Dom changed the subject.

"Thomas, what's new with this outrageous scandal?"

217

Thomas squinted his eyes at Dom as if to say, 'You won another one.'
"Well, nothing, really. Your words to the world today were convincing, and our contacts report that there's a universal belief that your papacy is being targeted by those in opposition to your reforms. The day was saved, but the scuttlebutt is that a new rumor has surfaced. There's hearsay that proof of the charges against you and your Franciscan aides will soon be revealed. So we're not out of the hen house yet. The foxes are still at the door. One positive result of your plea on bloody knees is that communiqués are pouring in from the clergy around the world; they are pledging themselves to Saint Francis' example of service to the community."

"Well, there's a ray of sunshine after all," sighed the pope. "Now how about dinner? We've nearly forgotten about that. Hope it's still warm - I'm famished. Kim, your arm please."

*****

After the meal and after everyone had left, Dom and Symon continued their earlier discussion. Kim dutifully sat on the bottom step of the Tower stairway, giving them some degree of privacy, but at the ready to assist Dom to his bedroom.

"Dom, I couldn't believe it. They handed me a package wrapped in brown paper, filled with one-hundred dollar bills, totaling the promised $200,000 fee."

"Yes, I know. Paulo's father notified Thomas that Buldini's representative had made two one-hundred thousand dollar withdrawals in the past few days. I've given Thomas the authority to freeze all Buldini's assets with the exception of ten thousand dollars in the Vatican City Bank. The remaining banks and investment firms where he has holdings are aware and affirmed the freeze request. The fur will fly when he attempts to cash anything over that amount in the Vatican City Bank, or any amount anywhere else."

"I guess that means I don't have a chance of getting the other one-hundred thousand, right?" Symon kidded.

Dom furled his brow and bit his lower lip. "There's a little grain of a mercenary in your soul, Symon. Two-hundred thousand isn't enough to bankroll your expedition in the Turkish desert?"

"Who knows? Assuri's and the Ashkari's trail may lead me to other exotic and mysterious lands and adventures. Oh, and another thing, you should be aware that I've deposited the money in the very bank from which it came, under my real name, Symon Carpenter. I've made Inge the primary beneficiary, just in case I don't survive this little escapade. Which reminds me, I had better look like I'm earning my money. Agapito and Zacchia will be demanding an everyday accounting of my progress. I'm meeting them tomorrow night, so I'd better formulate a plan to pacify their thirst. Dom, I'm not ashamed to tell you that my bones are speaking to me, too, and I don't like what they're saying."

CHAPTER TWENTY SEVEN

Less than two kilometers from Saint Peter's stood the ominous monk's chapel, Santa Maria dell'Orazione e Monte, built in 1576. It was here that monks collected and buried the unclaimed. At one time there were various passages to and from the Tiber. Today, only one such passage remained unsealed, and two of the large underground halls for storing corpses were again in use.

The night was moonless, the air damp and cold. Two figures headed their small craft silently around the bend in the Tiber, just south of the Castle St. Angelo. The river mirrored the dark sky and appeared as black as the heart of the boat's passenger. They clung close to the walled embankment to avoid being seen. Once the outline of the dimly lit Ponte Sisto bridge was sighted, they anchored. The large figure wrapped in a hooded cloak stepped onto the worn and slick stone walkway, and was met by a man who had been waiting in the shadow of the rough stone wall.

"This way your eminence, and mind your head. The entrance way is low."

"You idiot," grumbled the hooded man. Keep your voice down, and don't ever refer to me directly. Understand?"

In the darkness they couldn't see the inscription over the facade lined with skulls. It read, *'Me today, thee tomorrow.'* A few feet into the cave-like tunnel, a thin strip of light glimmered from around a sharp corner. They headed toward the light following the voices of their accomplices, who hovered over a blindfolded naked man bound to a chair.

The moment the two late arrivals appeared in the entrance, the one with a shock of white hair and matching close cropped beard issued a stern warning. He pointed to his rotund companion - "No names - ever. Understood?"

A bald headed man nodded his acknowledgment, as did the others. Then they all huddled in a far corner, out of earshot, to discuss the fate of their prisoner.

"Has he cracked? Will he expose the Franciscans as a group of Homo blasphemers, and the pope as their leader?" questioned Zacchia.

"Not as yet," Agapito answered, shaking his head. His golden earrings swung to and fro. "He's stubborn. Everything has been tried just shy of a beating. All he does is pray and shiver. Endlessly. The only statement made thus far is, 'I'll die a martyr in Rome, just like Peter.' Do we have your permission to use more drastic means?"

"No. Not yet. Let's see if a few more days in the gloom and chill of solitary confinement will loosen his tongue. If he's not ready by then to follow our script in front of the video camera, you can start with his fingers and genitalia," he said as he removed his hood and grinned. Buldini walked around the chair and kicked it with such force that Karl's head snapped back and forth. Karl grit his teeth, his head slumped forward.

"But your..., aren't we just wasting time? Let me start on him now. He'll be squawking like a crow by morning."

"There's time, there's time. Don't be so impatient to inflict pain. Our operatives are already spreading the rumor that there's proof of our allegations. It's going to shake the very foundation of Masone's short reign. The Jew will provide that proof, and then we'll broadcast it to the world. This morning's near disaster and the pope's pathetic plea was most effective. It provided us both with more time to achieve our independent goals. Send word in three days. If the Jew is still unwilling to cooperate, then he'll seal his own fate. This is the last time we'll meet here. I can't take the chance of being seen. Put him back in isolation and leave him alone. Let's see if he has a change of heart."

The sound of falling pebbles and a rustling noise startled the men. As they spun around, one of the many skulls tumbled to the floor with a clatter and rolled, coming to rest at Karl's feet.

"It's just rats - happens all the time," Agapito assured them. "We'll replace it with his," he said, jabbing a finger at the quivering man in the chair.

*****

Symon could hardly tolerate the suffocating odor of stale smoke and spilled beer. He thought he'd never get used to it, and longed for the sweet desert air. At that moment, he vowed never to set foot in another bar once it was all over. But he had to admit that the thrill of danger was welcome, compared to his previous academic lifestyle. He was just now, after all those years, finding out things about himself that he never knew existed. And he was beginning to enjoy the new and more venturesome side of Symon Carpenter.

He had already finished his second tankard, and there was still no sign of Agapito. If it were up to him, he would have left right then and there. From behind him came an arm with a tankard of ale attached. A waitress placed it on the bar in front of him, and whispered in his ear. "That young lady at the table by the door bought you this. She said she owed you one."

Her smile shone brightly through the thick and odorous film, and it was aimed directly at Symon. He could see the sparkle in her eyes in spite of the haze. Undoubtedly, she was one of the most attractive woman he had ever seen, but he didn't recognize her. He hadn't seen her in the tavern before. And, what did she mean 'she owed me one?' Curious, he left his bar stool and headed toward her table. Short cropped, yet stylish hair, framed an inquisitive child-like expression. Her large blue looking eyes complemented a full sensual mouth.

His puzzled look gave him away. Shrugging her shoulders slightly, she pursed her lips, and softly purred, "You've forgotten me so soon?"

"I apologize miss, but I can't imagine anyone forgetting you..., no, wait, you're the woman from the department store."

"That's right. I sold you my last pair of garnet earrings to send to your friend. They were my favorite. It was truly a labor of love, designing and making them. I'm sure it'll be her favorite Christmas gift. By the way, my name's Annette, and the drink is because your sale put me over my quota for the holiday season. Won't you join me?"

"Thanks,...Annette. It would be my pleasure," he said, pulling up a chair. "I'm Johnny. But, I have to tell you, I'm waiting for someone. It's business, but it shouldn't take too long. Then it's my turn to buy you a drink. Okay with you?"

"Do what you have to do. I'll sit and nurse this drink, and wait for you to finish. I can't celebrate without company, now can I?"

"Well, speak of the devil, there's old baldly now. You'll have to excuse me. I won't be long." He winked at her before heading to the shadowed booth Agapito selected.

*****

The hushed conversation lasted less than five minutes. Agapito didn't seem surprised that Johnny's pursuit of the unknown assassin was proceeding slowly. It had only been a couple days since he had received the blood money.

But he warned Symon that action would be expected soon. When Symon explained that he had to cut their meeting short, that there was a lady waiting for him, Agapito laughed and cheered him on. "Go. Go, Johnny boy. She's a fine looking little filly. Go."

"Signora, un bicchiere di vino bianco, si," Symon said in his very best Italian, a school-boyish attempt to impress.

"No signore, vorrei un bicchiere di birra, grazie."

"So you prefer beer over wine, Annette?"

"Not really. But I've always enjoyed the taste of a good German beer. Tonight, I'm in a beer mood. I'll have just what you're drinking. And now that we know that a French girl and an Englishman can both speak Italian, you'll have to excuse me; I need to use the powder room. Be right back."

When Symon politely stood up, he noticed just how small a figure of a woman Annette really was, and that she walked with a noticeable limp, favoring her right ankle that was wrapped in a support bandage.

CHAPTER TWENTY EIGHT

"He's missing! What'd ya mean he's missing? The pope just can't be missing. Where and when did you see him last? He was in no shape to go anywhere. Kim, speak to me and make sense," demanded an extremely distraught Secretary of State.

His Oriental features froze in a look of panic as Kim forced the words in response to Thomas' questions. "Late last night Dom called me to help him get to his Tower office. He said that he needed to do some serious thinking and needed the peace and quiet of the secluded office. Once we arrived, he insisted that I leave him. He instructed me to go to my quarters, and said that he'd call when I was needed. My shoulder hurt, so I settled down on my bed, and fell asleep until five this morning. I've been looking for him ever since. He's no where to be found. What are we going to do?" he wailed, wringing his hands.

"Pull yourself together man, you're destroying your image. He must be somewhere within the building or on the Vatican City grounds. Did you check the gardens? He often walks there early in the morning."

"Thomas, I told you - I've looked everywhere! Jan, Jabal, Nathan, everyone, has been searching for the last three hours. He's missing. That's all there is to it. He's missing. I've failed him. I should have stayed with him last night. Instead, I fell asleep."

The door to Thomas' office flung open and a group of wide eyed, worried looking searchers rushed in. "He's nowhere!" Jan announced, throwing up his hands in surrender. "We've looked everywhere. None of the staff and none of the Swiss Guards have seen him. What do we do now?"

"Excuse me, Cardinal Mumbwa. Excuse me," came a shy sounding voice from the doorway. "I don't know if it's important, but one of the electricians that were working in the archives below the Tower of the Winds just reported that a pair of his work overalls, a shirt, cap and work gloves are missing. He left them there last night, and now they're gone."

*****

"Thomas will boil us both in oil. I should never have let you talk me into this. And after he gets through with you, he'll flay me alive."

"Let me take care of the cardinal. I've felt like a prisoner ever since I was elected. Nearly every minute of every hour is scheduled for me to perform some duty, or to meet some boring dignitary. And it seems like every cardinal or bishop is telling me how I should think about this or that subject. I've got a specific job to do, and it's nearly impossible to accomplish when you're a prisoner in your own castle. It's more like a jail, and Symon, you broke me out."

"Okay. You handle Mumbwa. But I'll tell you what. I'm staying clear of him until he's sane. Because he's bloody ballistic by now. And poor Kim, if he had any hair, he would have pulled it all out by now. And you owe the workman a new pair of overalls. You've got blood on the inside of the legs."

Dom thought about it and agreed. "Yeah, you're right. Guess it wasn't fair to any of them, but the walk among the people, the shops, and the restaurants last night and this morning renewed my energy. It was something I very badly wanted. Even the pain in my knees cooperated."

"Be honest with me, my friend. I noticed that your knees collided with the walls several times in the tight quarters of the Borgia escape route. And kneeling on the short steps climbing down from the closet trapdoor must have hurt like blue blazes. I'll curse the day that I returned to the apartments to leave a message about the lady with the limp, then bumped into you and agreed to your scheme. Thomas may kill me before Zacchia has the chance."

Symon's hotel room left much to be desired, but both men were used to cramped cell-like quarters. Sure, the bed was lumpy, and the yellow and orange wallpaper grated on one's senses, but it served its purpose. It was a place for Symon to establish a false identity and residence, and now a haven where Dom could relax and hide for a few hours.

With his feet up on a worn-out, cracked leather hassock, Dom tried to conceal the throbbing ache in his knees and the fact that the scabs had once again torn loose and were bleeding. "Tell me more about this Annette woman. Do you really think she might be the assassin? Sounds farfetched."

Dom had the only chair in the room, so Symon sat crossways on the bed with his back to the wall. "Yes. The more I think of it, the more convinced I am of the possibility. Look at the facts, though only circumstantial. Remember the shooting at the airport? The cornered gunman took a hostage, who, at the right moment, freed herself and sprang to safety. The police marveled at the woman's courage and agility. Annette admitted to me that she was that woman. During our conversation she also told me that in her younger days she had been both a gymnast and a ballet dancer."

Dom interrupted. "And you did say she was small in stature. That means she could have gotten in and out of the Borgia hidden passageways with ease. Unlike us. That also means she could have murdered Uden."

"It's beginning to look that way my friend," Symon sighed. "More evidence is that the shooter who missed you and hit Kim was forced to drop some distance while escaping over the wall to the street below. The rope was far short, and when the person in the nun's habit jumped, he, or perhaps she, twisted an ankle. If you'll recall, several tourists saw a nun hurrying away, limping badly."

"Well Symon, I guess when you put two and two together, you come up with your new friend, Annette. Where do we go from here - the police?"

"No. Not just yet. We need more tangible proof. I walked her to her hotel after we met and had drinks. And don't give me those eyes, that's all we did. She's staying at a small boarding house just around the corner from the department store where she sells her handmade jewelry. This is what I'd suggest. Have one of our people keep an eye on her whereabouts. Shadow her wherever she goes. Your life may depend on it. I'm to meet her again for drinks tomorrow night, so I'll see what more I can learn. We know that she was in Rome during the balcony shooting attempt on your life, and also during the falling crucifix incident. Have the police check to see if she's listed as entering Rome through customs at the time of the first attempt and Uden's death. She seemed to be such a sweet person. Very outgoing and likable. But one never knows what motivates someone to do what they do."

"Sounds like a plan to me. This is amazing; the suspected assassin just fell into your lap. Figuratively speaking, that is. And speaking of motives, mine was to walk the streets of Rome. With that accomplished, it's time to warn the troops of my return. If you don't mind, I'll spend the rest of the day in your good company, and with your help, return tonight the way I left. I'll call Thomas and assure him I'm okay, and to call off the search that I'm sure is going on as we speak."

"You know, in those overalls, shirt, cap, and gloves, and shuffling as you do because of your knees, you could pass for any of the locals. Want a little adventure? How about visiting Gerhardt Tolz's Tavern with me later this evening and have a tankard of German brew? It'll help you relate to what I've been going through for the cause. You know, visit the scene of the crime. And the castle and Borgia secret entrance is just a short walk across

227

the street. What'd you say to that? Who knows, you might even get a glimpse of the lady assassin."

"Count me in - but right now I better call Thomas."

"Just one more thing before you call. Tonight, I'll see you as far as the inside castle wall entrance. After that, you'll be on your own. It'll be easy going from there on, except for the tight squeeze once inside the double walls of the apartments. There's no way that I'm taking any chance of running into Thomas. And for heaven's sake, don't ever admit to him that it was me who broke you out."

*****

"Don't everyone talk at once," Jabal demanded of five very excited Ethiopian students. They were part of Thomas' volunteers gathering incoming messages. "You," he said, pointing at the oldest looking of the group. "You speak. Slowly."

"Brother Jabal, it was us," motioning to himself and the others, "who informed you of Cardinal Buldini's and Monsignor Zacchia's hushed conversation in the Vatican Mosaic Workshop. We overheard it all. It concerned the disappearance of Monsignor Diamante and the unknown assassin. Remember?"

"Yes I do. What do you have for me now?"

"We were saddened to hear of brother Karl's disappearance, and decided to do our part in the search for him. The men in our village are noted for their tracking skills and the ability to be invisible while on the trail. So, we split up to watch the movements of Cardinal Buldini, Zacchia and a few of their known associates."

"Good God man, come to the point. I don't have all day."

"We think we found him!" he shouted excitedly.

"Why didn't you say that in the first place? Where? When? Spit it out!"

"My assignment was the cardinal. Late last night, around midnight, he left his home in disguise, and walked to the water's edge under the Bridge of Angels, where he met another who had a small boat. Together they drifted only a short distance. It was easy for me to follow unseen along the darkened street parallel to the Tiber. The cardinal left the boat and disappeared into the shadows just below the Santa Maria dell'Orazione e Morte. I waited for nearly an hour, and he reappeared. One of the men flashed a light in the boat so Buldini could see to enter. There were at least three others with him now, and by the dim light I could recognize Zacchia by his bushy white hair. It was impossible to hear their conversation, but both Buldini and Zacchia were talking together under the cover of darkness, they were up to no good. I read that the old chapel is where bodies were buried, and that there used to be cave entrances from the Tiber. I'm certain that's where Karl Kumbach is being held."

*****

Forced from utter darkness to bright light in an instant, Karl squeezed his eyes tight. He stood stiff with his head held high and with hands by his side, fists clenched, challenging the blinding light, and waiting for the blow that he was certain would come, knocking him to the floor.

"Thank God we found you!" came a joyful shout.

At the sound of Jabal's welcome voice, Karl collapsed in the arms of one of the students who had arrived by his side, just in time to cradle his exhausted body.

*****

"Karl's safe, warm, and in his room sleeping. He's endured a terrible ordeal, and the doctor said, under the circumstances, it was a miracle he survived as well as he has. There are no lasting problems. He just needs plenty of rest and nourishment. And as for you...Your Holiness, I don't even want to know the whole story," Thomas said, shaking his head in sheer frustration. "If I wasn't so sure that you needed me, I'd be out of here. But your little disappearing act has convinced me that you're badly in need of all the help you can get."

"I knew you'd see it my way," Dom laughed. "What do you think of the lady assassin theory?" he asked, changing the subject.

"It makes sense. Besides, it's the only lead we have. The chief phoned to report there's no movement on his part. We need to follow up on your information. And, soon. Any thoughts?"

THE FRANCISCAN

"I've been giving the subject much consideration since I returned to the Vatican City. You do realize I stepped onto foreign soil, Italy, without permission, even though I'm Italian. Sounds strange doesn't it, yet true?

"Thomas, have the five Ethiopian students come to my office in an hour. We should take advantage of their proven initiative and special talents. You and the others be there as well."

*****

The short walk from the Ethiopian Seminary to one of the pope's offices in the Palace of the Government, located directly behind St. Peter's Basilica, was a somber one, yet charged with anticipation. "Why would the Holy Father want to see us?" one student asked. "Cardinal Mumbwa already thanked us on his behalf."

Their steps echoed on the marble floor, adding to the mystique of the moment. One of the many secretaries directed them to a set of long ornate wooden benches, and they sat with backs straight as rails. No one said a word. Their eyes consumed all they saw: the oil paintings of long dead and forgotten pontiffs and dozens of faded, yet still beautiful tapestries; but it was the ceiling frescoes that took their breath away. Their wait was only three minutes, but seemed like an hour.

"Pope Francis will see you now," whispered the secretary, startling the students. They looked at each other, and with a collective gulp and a deep breath, they timidly entered the office. Cardinal Mumbwa and the Franciscan aides were all present, and thankfully, wearing warm smiles. The pope sat behind his desk and motioned for them to enter.

"Gentlemen, please forgive me for not standing to greet you, but my knees have suffered a relapse," the pope apologized. Thomas released a low, "Un-ah" - which triggered a prompt and prickly glare from Dom.

Nodding their understanding, each took their turn kneeling and kissing the fisherman's ring. Then, they stood like stone columns before his desk, waiting for him to speak.

"Gentlemen, gentlemen, please take a seat. Relax. We," gesturing towards the seated Franciscans, "are most grateful for your discovery of our brother's whereabouts. No doubt, you saved his life. We won't forget this act of loyalty. But, you're all here today because we are in need of your support in another matter."

WILLIAM R. PARK, SR.

The pope's words eased their anxiety and piqued their interest. Leaning forward in their chairs, they listened intently.

"There's a possibility that the person responsible for Cardinal Uden's murder, and the last two attempts on my life, is a woman. The suspect has a jewelry booth in one of Rome's department stores, and lives in a rented room around the corner from the store. Her first name is Annette. Tonight she will be having drinks at a German tavern called the Gerhardt Tolz with a man named Johnny St. John. The tavern is approximately one-half a kilometer from the Vatican grounds, in the old Borgo district."

The mention of Symon's alias caught Thomas off guard. He flashed Dom a questioning look, but Dom continued before the look could turn into something more. However, it didn't take Thomas long to resolve in his mind how Dom had learned about the suspect's identity, and to unravel the mystery of the missing pope. Stealing a quick side glance, Dom knew from the look on Thomas' face, that he and Symon were in big trouble.

The oldest of the students, and their obvious leader, stood and approached the front of the pope's desk. Bowing slightly, he said, "Holy Father, we, your humble devotees, are at your command. I am Jima Hosaina, my brothers and I merely await your instructions."

Dom smiled and motioned for Jima to be seated. "We appreciate your devotion to the Church. Jima, here's what we have in mind. The department store, her rooming house, the tavern, Saint Peter's Square, the basilica dome entrance, and statue ringed facade walkway, all need to be watched. This woman, Annette, her every move requires watching and reporting. Each of you will be supplied with her physical description and a communication device to stay in contact with each other and with both Jan and Jabal. They, in turn, will report to Cardinal Mumbwa or myself. Needless to say, she cannot become aware of your surveillance." Until now, Jan had been sitting quietly, but now stepped forward.

"You already know Jabal Wasitah. I'm Jan Jurewicz. Jabal has your electronic equipment is in the next room. Jima, you and your brothers come with me, and we'll discuss your assignments in depth."

Pope Francis struggled weakly to his feet, with a helping hand from Kim. "We will be forever thankful for your help. Be extremely careful. Do not take things into your own hands. It's just too dangerous. Leave that up to Jan and Jabal. May the Holy Mother protect you." He blessed them as they were leaving.

"One last thing," Thomas said, just before they left. "The man His Holiness mentioned, Johnny St. John, pay no heed to him. He's of no interest to us."

Then, after they were gone, Thomas frowned, and turned to the others and said, "I'd appreciate it if you would leave Dom and I alone for the next hour or so. He and I have a very important matter to discuss."

CHAPTER TWENTY NINE

"Shut that damn window!" bellowed Buldini. "Those damned carolers make me sick. They're serenading their beloved pope, not me. I don't want to hear it, and I don't want to be reminded of him."

Buldini, Zacchia, and four of their cohorts sat around a small conference table in the cardinal's residence-office a block from St. Peter's Basilica. The traditional sounds of a joyous season rode on a brisk wind blowing across St. Peter's Square. A group of school children were singing Christmas Carols under Pope Francis' balcony, their voices drifted unwanted into the cardinal's open window.

Buldini sank back into a fine Italian leather chair. It molded to his considerable mass, making it hard to tell where the chair began and he left off. Monsignor Giuseppe Zacchia, and the others sat in uncomfortable straight back wooden chairs, much to the monsignor's obvious displeasure. Buldini made a mental note to have Zacchia watched more closely. He seemed more discontented than usual.

Just as one of the aides closed the window, they heard a soft knock. Buldini nodded to the person closest to a secret panel, who rose to comply with the cardinal's command. Before the door to the hidden alleyway could be opened, the cardinal cautioned, "Wait! Ask who it is."

"Aldo," came the reply. "Agapito sent me with a written message. It's for Cardinal Buldini's eyes only. He said it was important that his eminence read it immediately."

The aide took the note, locked the panel door, and then handed it to Buldini, who, upon reading it, held his breath and scowled fiercely at Zacchia. Zacchia, unaware of the content of the message, scowled back.

Cardinal Buldini fought to get out of his chair. The effort added to his anger and a darkening shade of red crept across his face. With lips clamped tight and cheeks puffed, he narrowed his eyes and glared at Zacchia. Then he crushed the note in his right hand, brought his arm back, and flung it into the monsignor's face. The paper wad hit Zacchia in the forehead with such a force that it bounced back, landing in front of the cardinal. Within a split second, Zacchia was on his feet, flinging the chair aside. "Who do you think you are, you bloated piece of cheese? If my funds weren't tied in with yours, I'd slit that blubber you call a throat. What's gotten into to you? What did the note say?"

Buldini flipped the balled note back to the monsignor. "Read it for yourself. No - read it aloud. You and your men have failed me once again. And now we could lose everything."

Unfolding the note, Zacchia read the short two line message aloud.

"J - bird flew the coop. Rumored to be safe in gilded cage."

Four puzzled expressions looked to Buldini for an answer. Zacchia instantly grasped the meaning of the message.

"You fools," Buldini said in disgust. "It means the Jew is gone! They found him, and he's back in the Vatican. The question is how they knew where he was being held, and who leaked his whereabouts?"

Zacchia threw the note in the air, and as it floated down to the table top, he angrily shouted an accusation. "Things are becoming too complicated. In time, the trail is going to lead to our front door. We should have had him killed as we had planned in the first place. Now this. And they've brought Chief Santini and his agents in to help. It's all your fault Buldini, not mine."

The cardinal was still standing when there was a knock on the office door. An ashen faced secretary walked in and handed Buldini a long white envelope. He read the enclosure, turned pale, and plopped back into his chair with a thud. He looked at Zacchia with mouth agape and eyes wide in disbelief.

After the reaction from the first message, not even Zacchia was willing to be the first to speak. Everyone waited for the cardinal to compose himself. "Giuseppe - you, you won't believe it," he stammered. "I sent my man to draw a sum of money, and he comes back with this," he said, waving a sheet of Vatican Bank stationary. "This is a notice that until further review of my bank account and holdings, no amount may be drawn over ten thousand dollars.

"They say that a computer glitch has frozen numerous accounts and until it's straightened out, those involved are asked to be patient. They say it may take a week or more."

"Patient, hell! My funds are there - with yours!" yelled Zacchia, pounding the table. "Something's fishy about all of this."

"What's that guy's name you gave two hundred thousand to - Johnny? Find him and get the money back," Buldini demanded. "We may need it until all this is straightened out."

"It may not be that easy. He was given the money to do a job. A job you wanted done. You don't just cancel a contract and ask for the money back. And from what I've witnessed and been told, the Englishman's no one to stiff - and those were his exact words. He warned and threatened us all."

Once again, the office door opened. Buldini's house butler, as old and feeble as he was, burst in, trembling as he tried to speak, but seeming unable to get the words out.

"You're interrupting. Get it out old man, and go."

Embarrassed and frightened, the old man blurted out the words, "Your eminence, the movers are here - and they're taking most of everything! What shall I do?"

"Movers. What movers?"

"They say they have orders from the Vatican, signed by the Secretary of State. And they have an inventory list of paintings, furniture and artifacts that they claim belong to the Vatican Museum. The head man, a big Chinese looking bruiser, said they were only on loan and were now going to be donated at auction. According to the list, they'll take nearly everything in your personal living quarters - and mine."

The cardinal sunk deeper in his chair, and weakly motioned the old man to leave. He swallowed loudly, went into a coughing spasm and turned beet red. As he clutched his chest with his right hand, he pointed a shaking finger at Zacchia with his left and wheezed, "Forget the two hundred thousand. Offer the Englishman whatever he needs to finish off Masone. Now! I don't care what it costs, we'll find the money. I want that man dead."

*****

Pope Francis sat next to Karl's bed, encouraging him to stay in bed and to rest.

"Dom, I'm fine, really. I've had enough rest. Besides, I'm too excited to sleep. The fact that I'm still alive has strengthened my spirit. I was prepared to die. Now I'm wide awake and ready to talk about my ordeal.

"Where's Jabal and the others that were with him? They saved my life." Jabal, the Ethiopians, Thomas, and the other Franciscans had been sitting in prayerful meditation for hours outside Karl's bedroom door. Upon hearing the words from within, they rushed to fill the small cell-like room. Karl smiled at the sight and said, "You remind me of sardines in a can. But I love you all."

Karl got to his feet and made his way to Jabal and those who'd rescued him. After giving thanks and plenty of hugs, he sat back down on the bed, and with tears streaming down his cheeks, he confessed, "I truly thought I was going to die."

Rico was the first to begin the questioning. "Jabal said that you were standing naked in the dark the three entire days you were missing. That's not humanly possible. And you were freezing. How'd you survive?"

"Well - yes, I was standing when they found me. And I was naked and without sunlight all of the time I was in that cold stone stockade. I think focusing on my chanting prayers was the single element that helped me to survive. The fear and depression would have been too much for me to handle otherwise. Maybe my life as a kid growing up in the mountains of Germany also helped. For years I would go barefoot on the farm and even take long walks in the forest. Often, in the winter, I'd walk barefoot in the snow if my mother didn't catch me. I still walk barefoot when I can," he admitted.

Showing the bottom of his feet, he said, "See how thick the callous is? They didn't know that." Karl's expression made them laugh.

It was Christian's turn to ask a question. "Did you not sleep for three days?"

"Yes I did. Often. I was exhausted, cold, hungry, and the chant was trance-like, so I'd pass out. When I felt it coming on, I'd hunch down so as not to fall too far. After some time, and I have no idea when that was, the chill of the floor would revive me. Then I'd begin the process all over again."

"Can you tell us anything about your captors?" Thomas inquired.

"Unfortunately, no. When they entered my stone cell, the light blinded me, and when they took me out, I wore a blindfold. One time, perhaps it was the day before I was rescued, they took me out and tied me to a chair. There were many voices. It's as though they had visitors, but I couldn't make out what they were saying. The blindfold was also over my ears. Sorry. I'm no help."

"That's all right Karl," Dom assured him. "You've been through more than your share of trials. There won't be any more questions today. You get some sleep. That's an order from your pope. And besides, we have a pretty good idea who was behind your kidnaping. He's beginning to pay for it right now - and it won't be the end for him. But it's close."

As everyone began to leave, Karl leaned forward and whispered to Dom, "Will you please hear my confession?"

CHAPTER THIRTY

The suddenness with which the early afternoon wind whipped through the narrow streets and spacious shopping squares surprised both the shopkeepers and their patrons. An unexpected chill forced a slowdown of all normal activity. Customers filled the taverns and coffee shops to their capacity in an effort to keep warm and to avoid Nature's latest ambush. Then came her crowning achievement. Within an hour, the wind subsided, and was replaced with an unusual combination of a fine mist, and a fog that seemed to hug the earth with great passion, refusing to let go. Ancient buildings seemed to float magically, suspended in a surrealistic world, waiting for the first footsteps of its inhabitants. The pavement remained deserted. It was as though no one could find the courage to be the first to venture into the cloud that rose knee high out of the depths of Rome's legendary past. One frightened woman, peering through a shop window, was heard to whisper, "It looks as though only Dante could have carved that scene."

On a once deserted street corner where people were just now beginning to defy the bizarre conditions, a bent figure swayed, seeming to appear out of the enfolding cloud. He was clothed in rags, dragging one twisted foot, and with his left hand clutched to his waist, he wildly swung his right arm as he moved.

Most of the passers by shunned the pathetic shape and gave him a wide birth as he shuffled along, holding to the sides of buildings for balance. Next to the doorway of a small obscure hotel, he stopped, and with a thud, slipped down into the cloud. Only his shoulders and head remained visible. His jet black hair stuck out at all angles from under a well worn, filthy gray cap. The wiry dark beard and smudged features cried out for soap and water. His limp left hand struggled to grab hold of the ever moving right arm, and with the energy of both working together, made an effort to cup clasped hands to form a begging symbol.

And there he sat, consumed by a cloud, with his hands raised and cupped, his head in a constant up and down motion hinting to those few that passed by, to fill his palm with coin.

He made a hoarse grunting sound as the hotel door swung outward and clipped him on the shoulder, narrowly missing his head. He dropped the only coin he held. "Sorry mate," came the reply of the man leaving the hotel.

"Didn't see you there. Here - buy yourself a bath and a dinner," he said, pulling a few bills out of his pocket.

The beggar's words, "You've gotten pretty cheap since you came into all that money - haven't you, Symon?" spun him around. Cautiously approaching the sitting man, Symon leaned over for a closer look and blurted out in amazement. "Rico, is that you?"

*****

The pope shook his head and smiled at Thomas. "I think Rico really took the assignment to contact Symon incognito, seriously. Did you see his get-up? He missed his calling as a Latin actor."

"Yes, and we should all take it so seriously. Symon must be made aware that the pressure we've placed on Buldini will make him most unpredictable and even more dangerous. Karl's rescue, the knowledge of the frozen accounts, not to mention that we cleaned him out of his prized possessions, will no doubt force him to change his plan of attack on the papacy. A poison snake, when cornered, will often make a reckless attempt to survive. We must be prepared when he strikes next."

"You're right as usual, Thomas. And by the way, has Chief Santini uncovered anything more about Symon's lady friend, Annette?"

"He phoned earlier, and yes, she was in Rome during the time of the first attempt on your life and Uden's murder. She left for France soon after, but returned as was noted by the airport incident. Her full name is Annette Bordenave. Interpol has no data on her, but her late husband was under suspicion regarding four assassinations in the past seven years, although there were no serious clues involving him directly. He was known to be in the general area during all four occasions. The last time, he was reported to be vacationing there with his wife."

"Well, the plot thickens, Thomas. Is Rico also aware of Mrs. Bordenave's background?"

"Rico was informed about every detail. And he has instructions to make it clear to Symon that the danger level has increased tenfold. Symon was right when he said that I was frightened that my childhood dream might come true. I pray whenever there's a free moment that everyone will be safe, and this terrible ordeal will end soon. You, in only a short period of time, have made monumental strides. No one else could have accomplished so much so soon. Especially with the pressure Buldini and his College of Cardinal cronies have brought to bear."

Dom shrugged his shoulders, as if to say, maybe so. "Buldini, we must still contend with my friend, but the college is now in tow with the early retirements and new appointments. That's one obstacle we've overcome. But I must confess that the ill rumors that seem to have taken on a life of their own and refuse to die, trouble me. And Thomas, don't trouble yourself with my early demise. There's far too much to be concerned about."

"Holy Father - Dom, as hard as I try, I cannot flush the dream of my becoming pope from my memory. The event's so vivid. Let me tell you how the dream ended. You already know that as a small child in my village, I had the dream of being dressed in clergy finery. Later, I became aware that the man in the dream was the pope, and that the man was me.

"I was so taken by the dream's promise, that I looked for proof of the possibility. So, one night soon after, before falling to sleep, I prayed to God to answer the question, 'How is this possible?' That night I woke up every hour on the hour with the numbers *one, thirty-seven* ringing in my head each time.

"From one in the morning until five, I woke and looked at my rusted old alarm clock. Each time, the small hand was on the hour.

"Up until that time I hadn't really read the Holy Bible. We had only heard some of the stories as told by the elders. In fact there was only one Bible in the village. Upon wakening, I remembered the story a missionary told of how a saint received answers to his questions he posed to God. They were granted him in his dreams. The answers were found in scripture verses he was given while asleep. I was convinced that *one, thirty-seven* was a chapter and verse, but had no idea in what chapter the answer could be located.

"The village Bible was in the safe keeping of an elder who was once an assistant to a missionary who had lived his last years in Africa. My pleading to see the Bible, and the fact that I had been an altar boy when the missionary visited, persuaded the old man to part with his prized possession - with one condition. The book could not leave his house. It had to be read in front of his makeshift altar, and only on Sunday. I agreed. It was Wednesday - Sunday seemed like a lifetime away."

"Did you find the chapter, passage and verse?" Dom inquired with great interest.

"Not immediately. But for some reason I was certain that the answer was in the New Testament. There were only three chapter ones with thirty-seven verses. One was Mark 1:37 which said, *'And when they had found him, they said unto him, all men seek for thee.'* That didn't fit. Remember my question was. 'How is this possible?' (that I could become pope). The next was John 1:37, *'And the two disciples heard him speak, and they followed Jesus.'* That didn't fit either. The third was a charm."

At this point, Dom raised his hand and stole Thomas' thunder by supplying the words. " *'For with God nothing shall be impossible'* - Luke 1:37."

"That's right," Thomas said with conviction. "And do you want to guess the name of the missionary? It was Father Luke! Do you see now why I'm so concerned about the implications of this dream? I pray that it doesn't come to pass."

"Well, with all your precautions, and with the support and protection of our Franciscan friends, it probably never will. So rest easy. Let's move on to events we mere mortals can effect."

*****

Symon was well armed with warnings of possible dangers that lay ahead. Rico had done his job. The fog had lifted, and people were once again enjoying the end of what turned out to be a pleasant day. Symon was thoroughly amused by his encounter with Rico the panhandler. The short stroll to the tavern gave him time to prepare mentally for what the evening might have in store for him. He was still deep in thought when he sat down at the bar. There were the usual 'Yo Johnny' salutations from the regular customers, but no sign of Agapito or Zacchia. He did recognize two of their unsavory goons. They were eyeing him suspiciously from a partially hidden table in the right hand corner of the bar. "What are all the smiles about?" inquired the bartender. "Win a lottery? The usual?"

"No. Never won a thing. And, yes, the usual. As for the smiles - they aren't smiles, they're frowns. In all this smoke, you can't tell a smile from a bloody grimace."

Half way through his first tankard, he noted that two more of Agapito's thugs had entered the establishment and joined their partners in crime. From what he could see of their hand movements, heavy conversation, and numerous glances in his direction, it was apparent that he was the object of a rather heated discussion. He drank slowly, hoping his attention to Agapito's group wasn't too obvious. Symon shrugged his shoulders to ease some of the tension in his body. Whatever was going to happen would benefit his inquiry or place his life in grave danger. Either way, there was no doubt that Buldini was directly behind the order. "Buy a girl a drink sailor?" was accompanied by a soft touch on Symon's shoulder. With his attention and thoughts on what might occur later that evening, he jumped.

"We're a little jittery tonight, are we?" came the response to Symon's nervous reaction. He recognized the joyful sound of Annette's voice and turned to face a smile bubbling with enthusiasm. How in the world could someone so sweet sounding and so innocent looking be a cold blooded killer, Symon wondered?

"Annette, forgive me - my mind was elsewhere. You gave me a start. Yes, certainly I'll buy you a drink. I'll order, and you commandeer that table over next to the wall."

He pointed to a small table close to the front door, one that had a good view of where Agapito's men sat glaring. He approached Annette with drinks in hand. With the pretext that the chair she was sitting on would be better for his back, he asked if they could switch places; he wanted a clear view of the door.

The conversation was light, mostly consisting of the day's activity at the department store and her sales. As it turned out, she had only enough jewelry left for two more days, then she'd be heading for home. Sales had been better than expected. He had been silent for the most part, nodding now and then.

Symon grappled with the fantasy of Annette the assassin and Annette, the child-like creature across the table, within arm's length. He continued to tell himself that she'd probably killed Uden. Rico had informed him that the Ethiopians had her every move under surveillance. That meant that when he was with her, he too, was being watched. Under the circumstances, it was a comforting feeling. As in his meeting with Monsignor Zacchia, he now had to make the decision whether or not to play a risky hand with this cunning female. But now that would have to wait. Agapito was entering the door. He spied Symon and motioned him to a table in the corner, six tables down from him and Annette.

"Business," said Symon, getting up. "This won't take long." She nodded in agreement.

"See you're still working on the little pixie," Agapito said sarcastically, not giving Symon an opportunity to reply. "We've got to talk. Forget the shooter. He's no longer of interest to us. To earn your money, you must take out the 'man.' You know who. Otherwise, we get the two hundred thousand back. If you don't agree, the money's due on call. Now!"

Symon leaned across the table, his head right next to one dangling earring. "We've discussed this before. I said no then, and the answer's the same. No! Your boss hired me to do a job, and I was paid in advance, even if the kill wasn't proven. This we all agreed on. Either way, the money's mine. You both were warned not to jerk me around, and you bloody well better remember."

"So you're refusing to do the 'man' and to return the money? Is that your final say?"

"You got it right, matey."

Agapito's bald head turned a darker shade of red as he walked over to the table where his men were seated. An apprehensive Symon Carpenter walked slowly back to his table where Annette waited with an inquisitive look on her face. Immediately after Agapito sat down, two of his men walked smiling towards the door with their eyes locked on Symon, then left.

"The business didn't go well?" she asked.

Symon decided to play his card with Annette. At this point he had little to lose. "The business I'm in isn't conducive for making friends. Lasting friends, that is. And there's never any chance for a 'thank you' for a job well done. Actually, I reluctantly came out of retirement for this one. Which brings me to you - Mrs. Charles Bordenave."

Her blue pools became wide-eyed oceans as her mouth dropped open, and her high cheek bones blushed. In a voice almost without breath, she uttered, "How? How do you know my husband's name?"

She was about to get up when Symon reached across and held onto her hands, saying, "Please stay. I knew him by reputation only. We sometimes traveled in the same circles. Stay, and I'll explain everything."

She stayed, but the wary expression remained. "From time to time," he said, "those of us in the same international profession, would hear rumors about others. We often passed on jobs to them, if the circumstances were not right for our success."

"But how'd you place me with him? He's dead, you know."

"Car wreck. I heard. Sorry. Just prior to his death, you and he were vacationing in Spain. I was called in as a backup in case the job wasn't consummated. In such cases, the alternate receives half pay. Not bad for doing nothing on a paid vacation. When we talked the first time here at the tavern, I thought you looked familiar. After a few well placed phone calls, my memory was proven correct. You're Annette Bordenave."

"So where do we go from here?" she asked.

Symon lowered his head as if in thought, looked up, and then replied. "Look, you're a pretty woman and I like your company, but you're leaving town and so am I. Let's leave it at that. What you're doing here besides selling jewelry is your business. Mine has just gone up in smoke. You have nothing to worry about. I'm the one who spilled the beans about myself. But I have to warn you, the authorities have been tipped that someone's hunting without a permit in Rome. Catch my drift?"

With his confession, he had hoped she would open up, and make a slip that would reveal her plans. Maybe even ask for help. But she proved smarter than that. There was too much a stake.

Annette smiled softly and stroked his hand. "Johnny, I'd like to get to know you better, but I'm leaving the day after tomorrow. Thanks for having the faith in me to tell your story. It's safe with me. Maybe we could get together sometime in the future. Here, I'll write down my home phone number and address. How about walking me to my flat?"

Symon was disappointed. The knowledge that he might know she was a hunter hadn't moved her in the least. His last hope was that perhaps he could pry a bit of helpful information out of her on the walk to her room. A nagging thought crossed his mind. What if she planned to eliminate him, figuring he knew too much already?

As they stood to leave, she put her arm through his and squeezed slightly. If she hadn't been who she was and the circumstances were different, he would have enjoyed the moment. The night fog was closing in rapidly, causing bright halos to form around the lights on the antique street poles. The damp chill drew her closer to him as she snuggled for warmth. All in all, it was a pleasant walk. The conversation was congenial.

They had strolled less than a kilometer when Annette suggested they cross the Ponte Cavour. Then it would be a straight walk down the V. d. Corso and a short walk to her flat. Half way across she stopped to watch the bridge lights as they created strange shapes on the surface of the fog blanketing the Tiber. The afternoon's unusual street phenomenon was repeating itself at the river's edge. As with puffy white clouds against a brilliant blue sky, the lights played tricks in the billowing fog below. Mischievously, leaning up against his body, she pointed to images of a cat, a horse, and... She stopped in mid- sentence. The lights on the bridge suddenly went out, and running footsteps sounded coming from both ends of the bridge.

Instinctively, they pushed each other away, turned, and strained to see the on-rushers. Although the bridge lights were extinguished, the glow from streets on either side, provided Symon and Annette some degree of illumination. They could distinguish their attackers. Agapito's men, who had left early, were coming from the direction in front of them, while the other two bore down on them from behind. As Symon prepared to defend himself from the two coming from behind, Annette confronted the two attacking from in front. The last thing he heard her say was, "I would have loved to have gotten to know you better, Johnny."

The first man grabbed Symon around the neck in a choke hold, but before the second man could arrive to help, there was a loud thud from behind. And in another instant, Symon's attacker's head turned to the right and snapped. He collapsed in a heap on the wet pavement.

"Fear not, Doctor Carpenter. I'm Jima. I'm here to protect you. Jabal took me into his confidence and told me all about your mission."

"You're from the seminary?" Symon responded, forgetting for a moment about Annette. Then quickly remembering, shouted, "Annette, are you okay?"

Two bodies lay on the bridge where Annette had stood. One man was on his back with legs apart. The other lay face down in a pool of his own blood.

Annette had disappeared. "Jima, did you see what happened? Was she hurt? Where did she go?" Symon asked. He was completely baffled.

"Yes, doctor. She struck swiftly. One man grabbed her from behind, and the other was preparing to strike her from the front. The one on his back had his testicles crushed with a swift kick. He passed out from the pain. Then, she spun around to face the man that had held her, and with the palm of her hand, drove his nose bone upward, piercing his brain. It's a little known and quite deadly defensive move. He died instantly. In the darkness, and the confusion, I lost sight of her, but I did hear a splash."

THE FRANCISCAN

CHAPTER THIRTY ONE

Captain Santini's frown made Symon squirm in his chair. He was in his mid-forties, salt and pepper hair with a matching walrus style mustache, and a large barrel chest. While he dared not smoke a cigar in the pope's presence, the stench of cigars past had permanently impregnated the bristles of his upper lip.

"You, Doctor Carpenter," he said in a stern tone, "are lucky to be alive. Your undercover venture was foolhardy at best. If it were not for His Holiness' intervention, you would have spent the night in the lock-up as a murder suspect. We do have dead bodies."

"Now don't be too harsh, chief. Symon was only following my direction," interrupted the pope. He decided to change the subject. "Tell us, is there any sign of the Bordenave woman?"

"Not as yet. We've staked out her room and the department store, and have notified authorities at the airport, bus depot, train station and border crossings. She can't get far. And you doctor, don't get in our way," he warned with a wave of his hand. "Incidentally, your friend Agapito and his associates, those who are still alive, have vanished. He's an extremely dangerous individual. But, we'll find him, too."

Bowing slightly towards the pope and avoiding undue eye contact with Symon, the chief excused himself, promising to keep them up-to-date on any breaking news - then left by the side door of the pope's main office.

"Whew!" Symon said wiping his brow. "For a minute there, I thought I was in big trouble with the law. He's right you know, people are dead, and I was right in the middle of the fracas. Jima's anonymous phone call brought the police running. It's a darn good thing he left before they arrived on the scene. He wouldn't have gotten off as easily."

Dom leaned back in his chair, stretched and let out a sigh of relief. "Symon, you too, almost gave your life for me, as Uden did. I'll never forget what you've done. Your undercover exploit helped connect Buldini with the attempts on my life, and you identified the assassin. If you ever decide to leave Vatican employment, I'm certain Scotland Yard could use a man with your talents."

Symon chuckled at the thought. "My friend, first of all, I didn't know I was officially employed. When do I get paid? And second, Assuri's calling my name. Once all the loose ends have been tied up, I'm out of here and heading back to the cave." He paused, frowned, gently shook his head, then continued. "But I must admit, my emotions towards Annette are mixed. What she did to Uden and her attempts on your life cannot be overlooked. She must pay to the fullest for her crimes. But she saved my life. There's good in her, I know that. It's such a shame. Such a waste." Standing up, Symon paraded back and forth in front of the pope's desk like a fashion model and asked, "Is this seaman's outfit the real me, or should I be wearing Franciscan brown?"

Dom grinned. "Desert Khakis would be my choice."

*****

Flickering candles cast moving shadows on the bare walls where works of art once gladdened the eye of the beholder. Faded walls revealed their former resting places; the images of square and oblong shapes hung like ghosts upon the walls. A single chair, a large fabric draped canopy bed, and a ragged antique foot rug beside the bed were all that remained of the once luxurious bedroom suite of Cardinal Alfonso Buldini.

A tall slender figure, stroking a long goatee, stood peering through wire rimmed glasses at the enormous lump beneath the plush comforter. It rose and fell with each laboring and whimpering breath.

"What's your prognosis, doctor?" asked the bushy haired man slouched in the chair. "Will he survive?"

"Yes, I believe so. But his heart has been damaged. Starting today, he must change his lifestyle if he is to survive. That means the way he eats, and he must stay calm at all costs. He's way over weight. His cholesterol count and blood pressure reading are both off the chart. For some reason, he's suffered some sort of mental shock that brought on his present critical condition. Combined with his poor physical health, it's a wonder he's still alive."

"Thank you doctor. I'll take it from here. I and my associates will see to it that he abides by your instructions. And we'll call you if you're needed." The door boomed shut; the sound echoing in the empty bedroom suite.

"Your eminence, the doctor has left. Are you awake?" inquired Monsignor Zacchia. Not receiving a reply, he continued. "Good. Rest, and we'll talk later this evening."

As the monsignor turned to leave, a hand reached out from under the bed covers and tugged at his sleeve. "Don't leave me," he gasped, "they took everything."

"You don't have to remind me. Remember Alfonso, we're joined at the hip as far as our major holdings are concerned. And that has me edgy."

Mustering all the energy possible, Buldini propped himself up on one elbow, and shook his fist. "Look at my home. It's barren. He's ruined it! My holdings are frozen. You allowed the Jew to escape. Then your damned assassin took our two hundred thousand dollars, killed three of your men, and maimed the fourth. While I lie here on my deathbed, you fail me at every try. You've been worthless to me!"

Angered, Zacchia's neck arteries bulged as he verbally assaulted Buldini. "You keep that up, you sickly beached whale, and I won't wait for you to have another heart attack. I'll have the pleasure of putting you out of your misery myself. I've got money of my own stashed away. You're really not needed. If you'll recall, my network of contacts blanket the globe. I could disappear anywhere in the world, assume a fresh identity, never be found, and begin a new career amassing my own fortune."

"You could save us both right now if you'd only have that bastard killed!" screamed Buldini.

Zacchia sneered back. "Agapito has three men that he feels he can trust. They're keeping an eye on the Vatican, hoping for an opening to thrust a dagger. They'll notify him if the opportunity arises, and then he'll do the job himself. In the mean time, keep screaming like that and you'll never have to worry about the outcome. You'll be dead."

*****

The warm African climate and plush greenery hadn't prepared Thomas for the morning chill and mystical appearance of the ice covered trees and shrubs in the Vatican Gardens. The locals had remarked that they couldn't remember a colder November and December. Leafless winter branches of the aged trees encased in ice, seemingly frozen in time, especially fascinated him. The grotesquely twisted branches glistened in the early sunlight, blinding him, making it near impossible to see when taking the path heading directly into the sun. As the brilliant orange ball appeared over the horizon, the branches glowed as though they were on fire. It lasted only for a few moments, but the vision reminded Thomas of Moses and the burning bush. A moment later, they turned to gold, then just as quickly, back to silver.

"I'm wearing my Vatican long johns," he said smiling, waving to the figure sitting on the stone bench fingering his peasant rosary. "Did I interrupt your morning prayers?"

"No. You're welcome, Thomas," Dom said, returning the wave. "Just finished saying my rosary. Happy to learn about the long johns. You're a fast study."

Thomas grinned. "Thought we'd get an early start. You've got a full day of meetings and appearances, and there won't be much time for me. Thought we could set an agenda for a late night one-on-one session. We need to talk about your Christmas Mass homily, and then the New Year's Eve balcony speech. Have any thoughts?"

"Frankly - no. I've had too many other thoughts swirling through my poor head. Let me list 'em for you. Maybe you could ease the weight. The assassin, Annette, is still on the loose. The chief tells me there's been no sign of her, which could mean she never left the city. She's still out there and extremely dangerous. On top of that, Monsignor Zacchia's accomplice, Agapito, has disappeared. And he's equally dangerous. To make matters worse, Symon just left me. Don't know how you missed seeing him unless he didn't want to see you. Well anyway, he's gone back on the streets to see if he can find Annette, to stop her. Couldn't talk him out of going. You know by now how stubborn he is."

"Yes. Just like someone else I know. If Chief Santini finds out, he'll be irate. Maybe even have him picked up and jailed."

"We can't do anything about that now. Want to hear the rest?" He paused, waited for a response from Thomas, not receiving one, he proceeded. "Here goes. Received a phone call from our old abbot, Father Parc. Now we know where Buldini's rumor is receiving its new legs. Kevin O'Connor was a young Irishman who wanted badly to join our small group of friends at the monastery. There were twelve of us, and we wanted to keep it that way. Besides, we already had one Irishman. He resented the fact we didn't welcome him, and now he's getting his revenge. He was recently interviewed by the news media, and while he didn't come out and lie, he insinuated the charges against us could be true. He went on to say we met together regularly, in secret. And that we were often seen hugging each other. That's just the misinformation needed to whip the media into a feeding frenzy."

"Dom, I'm glad you mentioned that. It explains why several of the religious leaders who had planned to meet with us after the first of the year, have canceled their commitment."

"Can you blame them? I'd consider the same move if I were them. It's true, we did meet removed from the other seminary students, but it was only to discuss theological points of view, which you cannot successfully do in a larger group. As for the hugs, there's a loving feeling we all share for one another, and being comfortable with our own individual masculinity, never gave it any thought. You've witnessed our joyful greetings."

Thomas stroked his chin and nodded once. "Unfortunately, I'm not the one we must convince. In today's world, suspicion runs high. People are quick to assume the worst, especially when they're spoon feed by tabloid prone elements of the worldwide media. Negative actions of those we entrust with our lives have failed the people, hardening and disillusioning them, creating mistrust, even in the most sincere of men and women."

"Thomas, at times the weight seems unbearable." Dom placed his elbows on his knees, lowered his head, thought for a moment, then sat upright. "Friends have died and have been injured because of me. Peace truces we've been able to secure are threatening to crumble, and bloodshed could resume at any time - because of this rumor. And there's so much to do, yet so much of my time is spent from hour to hour with mundane, and politically inspired meetings. I feel as if I'm being smothered, stalled, unable to fully accomplish the work I came to do, and all too often I'm provided with advice by those with their own selfish interests in mind."

Thomas felt his friend's pain and frustration, but knew in his heart that Dom must face his task head on. "I know. I know. We've had this discussion many times, my friend, and you know the answer. You must hurdle the obstacles, regardless. We'll see if we can't eliminate a number of meetings and appearances, using your Christmas responsibilities as the reason. But we can't be seen as running away from public view, or hiding from the pressure."

"You're right. But if we don't find a way to put an end to the growing rumor, Buldini will have won, and the Church will have lost. We cannot rely on the people's positive reaction to the falling crucifix for much longer. I must do something dramatic to overcome this lingering adversity."

251

Dom let out a loud sigh, he had made a decision. "Thomas, please leave me now. Cancel all my appointments for the next two days. It's necessary I return to the scene of a certain day in my life. I must be alone to pray and to have the solitude that will allow the Holy Spirit to guide me. Don't be concerned if you don't see me during this period; I'll be in good hands."

Thomas put both hands on top of his head, locked fingers, and asked. "You don't mean return to where this all began? You don't mean Assisi?"

Smiling, Dom stood up, looped one arm around Thomas' neck and tried to allay his fears. "No, not Assisi, although that would be nice. No, but yet another place where I spent time preparing to receive the responsibility I now endure. Thomas, you must trust me."

CHAPTER THIRTY TWO

Midst the medieval gems and baroque examples of Rome's multi-colored tapestry of architecture wandered the nondescript figure of an ordinary working man. He appeared younger in years than a life of hard work would suggest. His well-worn dungaree straps hung from his shoulders as his body moved with ease within the garment. A workman's cap tugged tight down over his forehead, and the shirt collar pulled up under his ears effectively concealed his features. One gloved hand clutched a worker's lunch pail. Yet he acted more like a sightseer than a local. He often stopped and lingered to admire the fountains and remarkable statues that arrogantly seemed to thumb their noses at modern society. At other times he stood before shop windows, not to admire their contents, but rather to study the reflections upon the glass.

The workman stopped to admire the Chiesa di Santa Maria in Aracoeli, the church consecrated in 591 AD by Benedictine monks, later taken over in 1250 by the Franciscans. Legend says that on this sight the impending birth of Christ was predicted to the Emperor Augustus. From the steps of the church he could now see the unmistakable figuration of his final destination. Standing out against an ever darkening sky loomed the oval shaped ruins of the Colosseum.

The tree lined Via de Fori Imperial led straight to the Colosseum. He had a critical decision to make. Take the shortest distance between two points and risk danger, or walk through the ruins of ancient Rome spread out to his right, risking even greater peril. The potential of an ambush among the ruins that lay in the heart of the city was far more imminent than an open assault on the street with onlookers. Either way, his life was in jeopardy. On four separate occasions, looking at mirrored reflections, he had noticed the same two suspicious men watching him from across the street. From the steps of the church, he once again spied them leaning against a tree, looking in his direction. There was no doubt; they were targeting him.

He had only taken a few steps when he noticed the Curia. It was the building that during the Roman Empire had housed six hundred wooden chairs covered with soft padded cushions for the senators, who held the fate of the world in their hands. A near fatal lapse of memory perhaps, or mere curiosity, he now became a stationary target that almost cost him his life. A chip of marble from the building flew, creasing the skin just below the workman's right cheek. Blood slowly trickled onto his chin.

Several people along the avenue witnessed the attempt on the old man's life, and screamed, running for cover behind trees. Their shouts distracted the would-be assassins, giving their target time to compose himself and dart among the cover of the ruins. In hot pursuit, they both fired at random, hoping to hit the fleeing man.

As he ran, dodging and zigzagging among the fallen columns and strewn pieces of relics, he glanced over his shoulder. He was in luck. They hadn't as yet reached the entrance of the Roman Forum ruins. As he watched from the vantage point of a rectangular brick edifice, mainly to catch his breath, the two men suddenly appeared and ran straight at him. They had wisely anticipated his next move and had run up the street. Then they cut across to the next group of ruins in order to head him off.

They hadn't yet seen him. As he turned to run, he stumbled over a small broken piece of marble and fell to his hands and knees. Clamping his lips tightly in a desperate attempt to muffle a cry of pain, he rolled over, held his knees, and lay in a fetal position listening for the sound of footsteps.

Luck was still with him. They too had to pay attention to where they were running, which made it hard to search for their target and watch for scattered debris. The coming darkness was also on his side. Gritting his teeth, he stood, looking down at his pant legs. Stains of fresh blood were visible. The healing scabs had cracked open.

His only hope was to reach the safety of the Colosseum and hide among its numerous arches, entrance ways, and underground passages. It would be empty. A new addition to the continuing restoration made it off limits to everyone. First he must make it the rest of the way to the Colosseum. The only objects between him and safety were a string of trees on either side of a winding dirt path. In spring and summer the leaves would have been good cover, but the trees were bare. He would be exposed. If he stayed, they would eventually discover his whereabouts. It was now or never.

After a short prayer to the Holy Mother for protection, he sprinted down the path towards his only chance of survival. It wasn't until he reached the massive ruins of palatial homes of the Emperors on his right that bullets started to fly. At first they nipped at his heels, then whizzed overhead, coming dangerously close. Ducking behind a giant marble archway, bullets chipped away at the base of the structure, making it impossible for him to move on. They had his range. His legs were weak from fear, and his knees throbbed from the pain. He placed one hand over his chest in a fruitless attempt to suppress the thumping of his heart.

Moments went by. It was silent except for the street traffic a hundred yards away. He chanced a peek around the corner of the archway. Nothing. He was not encouraged. It was almost dark now, and they could be advancing towards him, and he would never know until it was too late. Perhaps the silence meant they were reloading their weapons. If so, this was probably his last opportunity. One last dash for his life, a hurdle over a small wire fence, and he'd be home safe.

He took a deep breath and pushed off of the archway to gain momentum, sprinted in long loping strides, cleared the fence with ease, crossed the paved street and then disappeared into the darkness and depths of the Colosseum's many passageways.

Minutes later Dom sat on the ground with his back to a wall and his knees pulled up tightly against his chest. He held his breath and listened.

Again, nothing except street traffic. He was about to relax, when he heard the sound of gun fire in the distance. Strange. His pursuers had been using silencers.

*****

It was close to midnight, and the overalls and flannel shirt could no longer keep out the evening chill. The hours of solitude had helped Dom to sort out priorities and clear his mind of negative forces. He had enjoyed this time to himself. Although he was reminded of the legend of the monk that threw himself into the Colosseum arena to protest the deadly battles between men, and men against beast. The crowd grew so angry, they killed him. Would his fate be similar, he wondered?

Using Karl's mind-over-matter technique to ignore the physical demands that cold holds on a body, he began a soft and melodious chant. For him, time seemed to stand still. The night went on. In a trance-like state, he failed to noticed the figure approach him from behind.

*****

Hearing shouts coming from Cardinal Mumbwa's office, Chief Santini hesitated, not knowing who was in the office or if he should intrude. He decided waiting was the best choice, so he sat down, hopeful that one of the secretaries would soon return and announce him.

Symon and Thomas stood in front of the cardinal's desk, nose to nose, the veins on both men's foreheads and necks bulged and pulsated with every animated gesture. The Franciscan crew dared only look at each other and shrug their shoulders. No one had ever seen the two men this agitated.

"How in the bloody hell could you let him out of your sight, never mind let him go? Why didn't you stop him? You idiot!" shouted Symon.

"Stop him? Ya, just like he could stop you from going out on the streets again. And who are you calling an idiot, you English... You English....,"

Thomas clamped his mouth shut, spun around, and walked behind his desk. Still glaring at Symon as he sat down.

"Symon," Jan interjected, "once Thomas informed us of what Dom might be planning, we watched the Borgia secret passage and the castle entrance."

"That's right," said Jabal. "It's not Thomas' fault. He did all he could under the circumstances. We love Dom, but he can be hard headed when he puts his mind to it. You know that."

"Kim, where were you?" questioned Symon. Then, before poor Kim could respond, he added, "Sorry, we shouldn't be blaming anyone except the man himself. Darn him!" he snapped, slamming his palm down on Thomas' desk.

"Tell him what you learned, Nathan," Christian urged.

"He must have snuck out with the workers who are refurbishing our antiquated electrical system. The man Dom borrowed work clothes from was paid for the garments, but Dom never returned them. Instead, he had them washed and must have kept them for such a move. We figure he merely walked out when they left for their lunch break. As smooth as you please."

A rap on the door created a welcome halt to the highly charged atmosphere. It was a secretary announcing Chief Santini.

"Cardinal Mumbwa, we've made an arrest," he announced, puffing up his chest. "In the process, two have died, another in critical condition, and one in custody."

"Is one Annette?" Symon demanded to know.

Santini eyed him suspiciously and frowned, pulled on his mustache and reluctantly answered. "No. The woman has seemingly vanished into thin air. She's no where to be found. Our best guess is that she somehow escaped the city without our detection."

The mention of her name triggered Symon's memory. Annette had given him her home phone number. He kept that knowledge to himself.

The chief continued. "If I may. There was a report of shots in the Roman Forum ruin area. A concerned citizen who witnessed the incident phoned the police. Three patrol cars were dispatched immediately and arrived within minutes. In fact, the two shooters were still on the site when they arrived. There was an exchange of gun fire. One of our men was slightly injured. One of the gunmen was killed; the other was mortally wounded but able to speak."

"What have you learned, chief?" Thomas asked, leaning forward in his chair.

"He was hired, along with the man who died, to kill an old man dressed in work clothes. He had no idea who the target was. Only the dead man knew."

Kim could no longer sit silent, and blurted out, "Did they kill the old man?"

"I'm coming to that. The man could hardly speak, but he did give us the address of a third assassin. He passed out before he could answer any more questions and is in a coma at the Charity Hospital. So we have no information concerning the condition or whereabouts of the target. We swept the area for the old man and for signs of blood. There was a small smudge of what could have been blood on a broken piece of column, but we can't be sure until the results come back from the lab. It was fairly dark during our sweep, so we could have missed something. We'll continue the search in the morning light."

The word 'blood' curdled everyone's stomach. They all looked at each other with eyes crying out in panic. Thomas was the first to speak.

"Chief Santini, we believe the target to be His Holiness, Pope Francis."

The chief was both stunned and angry. He jumped to his feet about the same time Symon did, but got his words out first. "Why in God's name wasn't I contacted?" he shouted.

Then Symon. "Thomas - what in the hell are you doing? Now you're brought the outside police in on this. We're a sovereign nation. There'll be leaks to the media, and all hell will break loose."

Chief Santini looked as though he was about to slug Symon, thought better of it, and instead, placed his clenched fists by his sides and faced him directly. "For your information, he's my pope, too. I'd lay my life down for him at the drop of a hat. There won't be any leaks from my end. Englishman."

Thomas was quickly losing control of the situation, and had to do something fast. He got up, stood between the two men, and spoke directly to Symon. "Gentlemen, please calm down. We need each other. Symon, the chief has more legs and eyes than we have. We need all the assistance we can get at this critical time. Wouldn't you agree?"

Symon hesitated, then nodded. Fear for his friend was clouding his judgment. The chief went on. "We surrounded the apartment where the third assassin was holed up. He surrendered without a whimper and became quite talkative. Within minutes he fingered Agapito's location. Agapito had a small apartment directly across from Tiber Island. The screeching of our vehicle's tires must have alerted him. As we prepared to surround the building, an officer who knew Agapito by sight, spied him running for the Ponte Palation. If he had reached the bridge, and under the cover of darkness, we might have lost him, so I ordered one of our sharpshooters to take him out.

"Our fugitive was some distance away, and had already made it to the bridge by the time my man had an opportunity to get off a single shot. The bridge lights gave us an edge. At the exact moment the shot rang out, Agapito dove over the railing and into the murky Tiber. By the time we reached the spot on the bridge, there was no sign of him."

Santini paused a moment, pulled on his mustache, thought about lighting up a cigar, but put the craving aside. "Since the hit could not be confirmed, it was speculated that he had escaped by entering one of the underground drainage canals. In 600 BC, great drainage canals were built to divert seven underground streams below the location where the Colosseum was constructed. To this very day, a drain still functions in the area."

"Yes - yes," Rico broke in. "Forget the tour of ancient Rome. What happened next?"

"Well, the banks on both sides of the river were searched with no luck. The current is pretty swift in that spot, and if he were hit, his body would have been dragged down stream. And that's where we found him, caught on a twisted piece of driftwood. There was a small bullet hole to the right and just below his left shoulder blade. Agapito was dead before he hit the water."

Everyone thanked the chief for a job well done. Even Symon. Santini pledged full support in the search for the Holy Father, and assured Thomas that no leaks would come from his office.

After he left, Symon made an effort to gain Thomas' favor. "Thomas," he explained, "that was Jonathan St. John speaking to you, not Symon Carpenter. I've played the character for too long. He's a part of me that must be buried forever. Please accept my hand in friendship."

The two men shook hands and hugged each other.

*****

Startled by the touch on his shoulder, Dom's heart nearly burst from his chest. His hands instinctively covered his face as he shouted, "Lord no!" His worst fear had come true; his luck had run out. They had found him. It was over.

"Forgive me Your Holiness. I didn't mean to frighten you. It's me," he said, turning to face the seated man, shining a light on his own face so he could be recognized. "It's Raphael. Raphael Carcassonne, the guard," he said, pointing to himself. "It was I who first discovered you here in the Colosseum months ago, the morning of the day you were chosen pope. Remember?"

Dom's head and shoulders bent forward in relief. He took a long deep breath and looked up at the smiling guard. "It wasn't your fault, but you nearly scared me out of my wits. It's so dark in here, how did you know it was me?"

"When you made the dash across the street, the Colosseum security lights illuminated your face. Your cap flew off halfway across. I recognized you immediately. Here's your cap," he said, handing it to the man he loved and held in the highest esteem.

"Why didn't you contact me sooner?" Dom asked out of curiosity.

"It wasn't my place to question why you were here, but I thought that you might be running the way you did for a good reason. It was a surprise to see you. Maybe you were being chased. So I waited in the shadows to see if anyone came. There were flashing lights and shots fired, coming from the direction of the old ruins. I thought it best to stay where I was. After everything settled down, I searched for you and found you here."

"Well, I'll never forget you now for sure, Raphael," he laughed. "You're a good man."

Stooping over to assist Pope Francis to his feet, the guard made an unusual request. "Your Holiness, you must follow me now. Giuliano has something for you."

"Giuliano?" asked the pope. "Giuliano who? And why?"

"Monsignor Giuliano Diamante. He says he has something of great value to you. Something about - *'I'll save your papacy.'* "

The pope was both puzzled and cautious, but agreed to go with him. As they walked down the dark and twisting passageways and out into the street, always keeping to the shadows, and then towards the area of the ruins, he asked pointed questions.

"How did you come to know the monsignor, and where are you taking me?"

Raphael answered the questions while carefully picking his way though the darkened ruins. "Giuliano and I were together at the orphanage until I was adopted. Poor fellow, no one ever wanted him. Well, you know. It was he who obtained this job for me eight years ago when I was down on my luck. My family owes him a lot. And, we're heading to the far end of the ruins to the Temple of Saturn. In ancient times people honored the god of the harvest and prosperity during the Saturnalia holiday in December. They gave each other gifts of clay figurines. It's never been recorded, but many of the dead followers were buried in a secret catacomb beneath the old temple ruin."

"What do you mean, never recorded? Just how do you know all about this? And, once again, why are we going there? I need to have some answers right now, before we go any further."

Dom stopped and crossed his arms, and waited for answers. The hair on the back of his neck felt prickly. He was standing in the approximate spot where the assassin's first shots nearly found their mark. The sting under his cheek reminded him of just how close he had come to being the late Pope Francis.

Raphael seemed edgy. "Please have faith in me, Holy Father. Monsignor Diamante awaits you in the catacomb. I've hidden him there, away from his brother. About eighteen months ago, while helping to clear shrubbery roots from spaces between the building stones, I discovered an entrance hidden by debris and wild brush. It led to a yet unknown catacomb. I've kept it's secret until now."

"Brother? What brother?" was all Dom could say.

Ignoring the question, Raphael continued on. "It's estimated that there's some thirty miles of catacombs throughout Rome, and a half-million people interred, all together. The Carcassonne Catacomb will add to that total," he bragged.

The climb down placed a strain on his knees, but he was determined to follow Raphael's lead. His light cast strange images on the walls painted with scenes of everyday life and people offering gifts to the god, Saturn. Figures appeared to shimmer and sway with each movement of the lantern-light. The unknown is always unnerving, even for a pope. Time and the elements had taken a toll on the paintings and inscriptions. Some had fallen off in bits and pieces through the centuries. Others he could clearly make out and read their Latin messages.

"We're almost there," warned Raphael. "Be careful of the footing for the next few feet, and watch your head. The ceiling slopes down just ahead. The soil beneath the temple is landfill, as it is under the Colosseum. There used to be a swamp all along here. Emperor Nero had it filled in. Although the footing is fairly solid in this area, enough to accommodate a small catacomb, the aged existing drainage system sometimes plugs up, diverting seepage in this direction. We're here," he announced proudly.

"Giuliano, it's Raphael and His Holiness. Open up."

On either side of an arched concave rested the bones of the long dead, stuffed into small cavities to harbor as many of the faithful as possible. With a scraping sound, the back of the concave moved inward, exposing an opening filled with light and the weary smile of Monsignor Diamante.

"There you are Giuliano, my old poet roommate, we've been looking all over for you. May I come in?" Dom added with his familiar toothy grin.

The small cave-like room had a few of the comforts of home, including a makeshift bookcase filled with works by famous poets. There was a cot, portable toilet, chair, battery operated lamps and cooker, wash basin and jugs of drinking water.

Diamante noticed the pope looking around the room and said, "Forgive my manners, Your Holiness, please take the chair. My needs are simple. Raphael brings me food and water from time to time, and even empties my portable every other day. The temperature down here is constant, and warmer this time of year than above."

Dom sat in the rickety chair, welcoming the opportunity to rest his aching knees. The two men sat on the cot. He caught the monsignor staring at his clothes, and responded. "Don't even ask. It's a long story and not important just now. You tell me your story. Why are you living like this? What's this about a brother? And, what do you have for me that will save my papacy?"

Monsignor Diamante stood up as tall and as straight as his stooped frame could, and addressed the pope. "First, I have prayed for your safety, and am blessed that you have survived and are with me this evening. I will answer your first two questions with one answer. Because of my brother." The monsignor's next statement visibly stunned the pope. "My brother is Cardinal Alfonso Buldini." With the pope's mouth still agape, he explained. "When I was but a baby, my family packed me off to an orphanage. They were well respected and influential. When the doctor told them I was misshapen and would be stunted for the rest of my life, their ego won out over love. They abandoned me, but privately provided for my keep.

"Four years later, Alfonso was born. When he was eight, he overheard our mother and father discussing the amount of funds going to the orphanage each month. He listened and said nothing. The next day, unbeknownst to our parents, he set out for the home to find his brother. The brother he had never known about, until then. All he knew was that my first name was Giuliano. They had changed my last name. Talking to boys playing in the yard, he discovered only one boy was named Giuliano. He was the one sitting on the swing by himself.

"Alfonso was so thrilled to have a brother that my appearance made no difference. He visited whenever he could. We became fast friends. The orphanage could have dismissed me on my sixteenth birthday, but since they were receiving funds, they allowed me to stay on as a gardener. Some years later, Alfonso announced that this would be his last visit. He was entering the seminary at the insistence of our father. That was the last I saw or heard from him until he showed up four years later, and said that he had made arrangements for me to enter the seminary. He had become a favorite of the archbishop, who agreed to sponsor me. I gladly left the only home I had ever known."

"Your brother showed compassion then. What happened that made him the cold-hearted person he is today?" inquired the pope.

"That's hard to say, Holy Father. The only answer I have is in the old saying, 'power corrupts.' I know that my appearance and the way I was rejected and treated by society made me the way I was. It was self-defense. But, in the last few years I've noticed a change. My conscience gnawed at my soul. The final transformation came on the morning of your election, when I was alone in the Sistine Chapel. Our Lord's finger pointed at me, and I was a new person.

"It was soon after my brother had worked his way to the top of the hierarchy in the Church, that he brought me to the Vatican, made me a monsignor, and his assistant. The change in him was apparent. Greed ruled. He was my brother, and he had been good to me, so I did as he ordered."

"Giuliano, why did you make the attempt to help me by writing those poem messages?"

"As I said, I was a changed man, and even though I no longer condoned his methods or ambitions, he was still my brother. My loyalties were torn. That's why you received the death threat warning. After learning of Cardinal Uden's death, I knew I could play no part in his sinister assassination plan. Later, in front of other members of the plot, he took out his frustrations on me. Even threatened me. That's when I disappeared. I feared for my life. Remember, the last message told you I was a mole in a hole? Welcome to the hole."

"We will be forever grateful for your new found loyalty to the Church, my friend. Now, what is it that you have for me?"

Diamante reached under the cot and pulled out a large faded yellow envelope, and handed it the pope. "This will expose Cardinal Buldini and his plot to have you assassinated, as well as his part in the kidnaping of Karl Kumbach."

Opening the envelope, the pope said, "I don't understand? What's on this video tape?"

"Holy Father, although I was in hiding, I knew all the secret entrances and concealed passageways in his Vatican and home offices. This, he forgot.

And, taking advantage of that knowledge, I spied on his meetings with Monsignor Zacchia and the others. That's how I learned of their plans, and later, where Karl was being held prisoner. I hid in back of the open vent behind the large tapestry that hangs on the wall along side his conference table. I heard my brother tell Zacchia to meet him at the monk's chapel next to the river at midnight. The one where they used to bury the unwanted of the city in ancient times. There was no time to alert you, so I decided to arrive earlier and watch. I entered from the street side and discovered a small storage room behind the underground hall where Karl sat naked, strapped to a chair. There was an opening where skulls and bones were lined up along a ceiling-high shelf encircling the hall. On the chance of securing possible evidence, I brought my video camera with me. Your Holiness, I taped everything!"

"Explain. Everything," the pope ordered, now sitting on the edge of the old chair.

"I began taping even before my brother and the monsignor arrived. Agapito and his men talked about the failed attempts on your life. They stopped when the visitors entered the hall. For some time, my brother wore a hood to hide his face. Zacchia, chose not to hide his. At one point, my brother tore off his hood. He spoke of the plan to force Karl to lie in order to confirm the rumors they had spread to the worldwide media. Your Holiness, Karl was brave, and would have died before he spoke ill of you, his order, and his brothers."

"Yes, I know - go on."

"My hands shook at one point, and I bumped a skull that fell from the wall. It made a terrible racket that brought everyone's attention in my direction. I held my breath and teetered on the old crate I was standing on. But, the incident was dismissed as being, 'only rats.' Maybe they were right,"

Diamante sighed. "Well anyway, after they were through discussing Karl's future, and turned to leave, Agapito asked my brother about the attempts on your life. My brother's words will destroy him."

Pope Francis was on his feet, shook the tape in the air and said, "Monsignor, your own courage and loyalty to the Church has washed away any and all past errors in judgment. You have my undying thanks, gratitude, and blessing. Yes, quite possibly, you have indeed saved my papacy. And, you will be rewarded. I've got the very assignment in mind."

"Holy Father, I do not wish, nor am I worthy of any reward."

"We'll discuss that later. I'll be the judge, Diamante. And as for you," he pointed his finger at Raphael, "report to Captain Felici of the Vatican Security Force at your leisure. That is, if you're tired of guarding the old stone relic and wish a position guarding another old relic. Cardinal Mumbwa will speak with the captain on your behalf tomorrow. Give it some thought. And by the way, I suggest you contact the historical authorities about the Carcassonne Catacomb."

Raphael was dumbfounded and speechless, and fell at the knees of his pope. Unfortunately, he was also clumsy, and collided with the pope's injured knees. After giving out a loud 'whoop', the pope spent the next two minutes assuring the man he hadn't seriously hurt him, and that all was forgiven.

"Right now, I need to get to a public phone. Raphael, lead the way. And you Giuliano, come, too. You'll be safe at the Vatican."

*****

It was six in the morning, but Cardinal Mumbwa was already at work, with a sleepy eyed secretary manning the outside desk. The phone rang. Who could be calling at this hour? Thinking it might be Chief Santini with news, Thomas picked up the receiver before his assistant could react.

"Good morning Thomas," said the voice on the other end of the line. "Miss me?"

"My God, Dom, are you all right? Where are you?"

"Couldn't be better, my friend. Let's not waste time. Get in touch with Monsignor Lucchesi. Have him call in all his markers with the media. We have breaking news concerning all the nasty rumors. Tell Lucchesi it must be broadcast in prime time. Pope Francis will be talking live. He can do it. Don't have time now to explain. Send a car for me. Here's someone to give you our location. And, oh yes, Monsignor Diamante's with me. Now - here's Raphael."

"Raphael?"

265

CHAPTER THIRTY THREE

"Turn up the damned television!" demanded the bedridden Cardinal Buldini. If his partner in crime, Monsignor Zacchia, hadn't also been glued to the screen, he would have left the man to suffer alone.

At end of the forty-five minute broadcast, the anchor person was doing his normal wrap-up, telling the viewers what they had just seen and heard.

"And there you have it ladies and gentleman. The biggest scandal the Vatican has seen in centuries. The video tape you have witnessed vindicates Pope Francis and his Franciscan brothers. The malicious rumors spread by the head of the CDF, Cardinal Alfonso Buldini, and his accomplices, were absolutely false. You saw and heard it for yourself; the cardinal's and the monsignor's own words also connect them with the assassination attempts on the pope, as well as the kidnaping of Karl Kumbach, and the murder of Cardinal Uden of the Netherlands.

"The chief of Rome's police force informed this reporter just moments ago, that three of Cardinal Buldini's conspirators are dead and another is in custody. Warrants will soon be issued for the arrest of Cardinal Buldini and Monsignor Zacchia."

"Damn that man! Damn that man!" screamed Buldini. "And you Zacchia, you worthless piece of shit, it's all your fault."

The cardinal managed the strength to sit up in his bed. He waved his arms wildly and shook both fists at Zacchia, who was approaching Buldini with fury in his eyes. Before he could get to him, Buldini had already fallen back onto the pillow with a loud gasp. Zacchia, reaching down, struck Buldini across his spider vein cheeks with a force that sent a string of saliva sailing across the mammoth bed. Then, grabbing Buldini around the neck, he proceeded to shake and choke him violently, repeating, "Die you fat bastard - die!"

Suddenly, Zacchia let go of Buldini's neck, his hands and fingers still extended, as the man fell back lifeless. "You cheated me again, you bastard!" He hissed in disgust.

Buldini's own anger had killed him. He had died of a massive heart attack before Zacchia had the opportunity to reach him. Zacchia could hear the pounding on the front door; even in the upstairs bedroom, it sounded loud. It had to be the police. Turning, he hurried towards the small conference room office and the sliding panel leading to the secret passageway; his safety lay beyond the alleyway exit.

*****

Thomas had already left the room smiling. Pope Francis was alone and quite pleased. Lucchesi had done his job well; the media news networks cooperated. It was over. At last.

Dom felt joy and relief, yet sadness. Two friends had died and two others had experienced pain in their efforts to help their Franciscan brother, their pope.

Symon led the parade. One by one, his friends entered the sitting room just off his bedroom to offer their congratulations. Applause and cheers filled the air. Their exuberance managed to lift Dom from out of the depths his mind had threatened to take him.

'Symon, and the seven friars' - Thomas' playful nickname for the group, had pulled their chairs and short sofas into a semi-circle around their leader, who reclined on a large couch, giving his knees a much needed rest.

Dom was glad to be back in his habit, where his scabs had a chance to heal without the restrictions of pant legs. Pandemonium ruled. Everyone was talking at the same time. Nobody could be heard. The scene amused him, as he thought to himself - *everything's back to normal.*

Thomas rushed into the room, out of breath, and with an excitement uncharacteristic of the calm, always in control, constrained cardinal from Africa.

"Dom, Dom, you won't believe it! It's a miracle!" he gushed, in an effort to get his undivided attention, which was hard do under the circumstances.

Dom raised his hand for silence, and everyone's attention turned to Thomas. "I've just returned from the communications office where the students have been frantically attempting to record thousands of phone calls and e-mail messages coming in from all over the world. They're overwhelmed. The equipment is overloaded and jamming. It's a panic over there. I ran all the way to tell you the news."

"Here," said Dom, placing his feet on the floor, "sit next to me, and settle down, you're not a young man any more. Something I learned just recently about myself. What's this earth shaking news you're so excited about?"

"Remember I told you that several of the religious leaders pulled out of our planned global symposium on God? Well, since your broadcast, not only have they changed their minds and pledged their full support, others who had not replied to our initial invitation, now also plan to attend. We're even receiving inquiries from groups we hadn't contacted.

"Members of our religious community who had not as yet responded to your call to partake in St. Francis' life of service, are vowing to participate.

"And, get this. We've heard from the Curia, and so far, from nearly every member of the College of Cardinals. They're calling for an emergency meeting to begin discussions on your proposed reforms. It's a miracle. You're more popular than a rock star."

Everyone burst out laughing. Even Thomas was smiling. With a hand over his mouth, stifling a grin, Thomas remembered, "Oh, I almost forgot. Chief Santini is waiting in the outer foyer. He's got an update on Buldini and Zacchia that he feels we should be made aware of. Shall I have him come in?"

"By all means, Thomas, show him in. And everyone stay where you are. This shouldn't take long. You wouldn't want to miss out on the refreshments I've ordered. We might even ask the chief join us."

Santini marched into the room, twirled his mustache at both ends, and bowed to the pope. "Holy Father, gentleman," he said, failing to acknowledge Symon's presence. "Cardinal Buldini is dead. He suffered a major heart attack in his bed, under suspicious circumstances. And Monsignor Zacchia has vanished. We've checked every route out of Rome, and there's been no sign of him. The only possible lead is that a man resembling his physical description boarded a plane for Zurich before airport security people could be alerted. His passport was in the name of Haans Loewman. The man's description was similar, except his white hair was cropped short like his beard. I'm afraid Zacchia may have eluded us."

The pope thanked Santini for his diligence, and suggested he stay and join him and the others for a glass of wine. The chief respectfully declined, stating that pressing matters would not permit it. As he turned to leave, Symon stepped forward, blocking the chief, and asked to meet him in the foyer. Puzzled, and distrustful, the chief followed Symon.

THE FRANCISCAN

CHAPTER THIRTY FOUR

Plans were being formulated for the gathering of the cardinals, the early summer symposium was scheduled, Pope Francis' knees were well underway to a full healing, as were his palms - and the televised Christmas Mass homily had been inspiring; Thomas had been the proud author.

With the meeting arrangements completed and Christmas behind them, both he and Dom were now hard at work on the pope's New Year's Day balcony proclamation to the world. This year, it was decided to limit the balcony participants: only the pope, Thomas, Symon, the Franciscans, three members of the Curia representing the cardinals, Jima, Monsignor Diamante, and for the first time, select members of the papal household would be present.

*****

It was a pleasant morning. Menacing black clouds had surrendered to a bright blue sky. Even the threatening cold snap that had been predicted decided to swing further north. The new year would be welcomed with a surprising sunny 62-degree day. The balcony had a superb view; from there, one could embrace the entire city. On either side of St. Peter's Square loomed the colonnades, composed of 384 columns and pillars, each 64-feet high. They were staggered, but if a person stood in an exact spot in the square, indicated by two flat stone markers, they would only see one row of columns. From that vantage point, they had been engineered to line up behind each other.

Beyond the long red carpet of tiled roofs were the Castle St. Angelo and the Tiber. Still further, stood long lines of trees which marked the beginning of Rome's expanse of public parks. The number of churches, palaces and monuments seen from the balcony, were too numerous to count. The pope would have a breathtaking view.

Pope Francis and his entourage walked out onto the balcony; a hush came over the square, packed with the faithful and fascinated sightseers. The only sound heard was that of the gentle splashing of water coming from two giant fountains that flanked the plaza.

The pope leaned over the railing, pointed to the fountains, then to his ears, then clasped his hands together in front of him, and silently gestured with his expression and head movement that he enjoyed the rhythmic sound. The crowd understood and respectfully applauded their approval.

He stepped back from the rail and turned to smile at the group behind him. Without warning, one of the invited female kitchen staff sisters rushed forward, brandishing a revolver that had been hidden in her large sleeve.

Everyone seemed to be frozen in time. Now, within six-feet of Pope Francis, she raised the weapon shoulder height and slowly applied pressure on the trigger. For those on the balcony, everything appeared to move in slow motion. Symon was the first to take action. He leapt forward, shielding Dom with his own body.

Surprised, the would-be assassin hesitated for a split second and whispered... "Johnny?"

A single shot rang out. She dropped the gun, clutched her chest, and staggered backward towards the rail. At once, Symon was by her side in time to prevent her from falling over the railing and onto the steps below.

Blood flowed profusely from the wound and from the corner of her mouth. She was mortally wounded. With her head cradled in Symon's lap, she looked up with eyes full of tears, sadness and fear. She labored to speak with her last breath - and said in a raspy, almost inaudible voice, "Johnny, I..., I couldn't. It was you. I did it all for my family. I knew no other way. I..."

Her head rolled to the side. Annette was gone. Symon was the only one to hear her last words. He closed her eyes.

*****

"You've been blessed with a keen sense of character judgment," assessed Thomas. "This time it saved your life for sure. Although it was Symon who momentarily distracted the woman, it was our new friend, Agent Carcassonne, who was alert enough to make the instant decision to shoot."

Dom squirmed in one of Thomas' plush office chairs. He looked uncomfortable and distant. His eyes wandered around the room. He hadn't heard a word Thomas had said. Like all the other offices, halls, chapels, and rooms of every description, this office was also adorned from ceiling to floor with frescoes, oil paintings, tapestries, ornate furniture, sculptures, and gold leaf trimming glittered from every nook and cranny.

Thomas waited patiently. Finally, Dom's attention turned to Thomas and he asked, waving his arms about, "Do you ever feel like you're living in some kind of lost fantasy world? A world that existed once-upon-a-time and the present has passed it by - and you're trapped inside. I do. And it makes me feel uneasy."

The cardinal chuckled, and looked around. "Oh, I've come to accept it. Truthfully, I've been so busy I never even think about all the glitzy trappings. It's what visitors come to expect. They're pretty awesome though, aren't they? In time we'll sell some of them at auction, but retain just enough to please our guests." Then he shook a finger at Dom and said. "What your problem is right now, is that you're missing Symon's company. He was quite a man. Englishman, or not."

"You're wrong Thomas, he is quite a man. He placed his life in harm's way, time and time again, for all of us. If that woman hadn't recognized him and wavered for just a moment, he would have taken the bullet that was meant for me. Not bad for a life long academic. He confessed that he even surprised himself. I hope his cave surrenders what he's searching for."

Dom got up, walked to the door, and then turned to say these last words to Thomas. "Before he left, he phoned Inge. He had originally made plans to visit her for a late Christmas celebration, so she was waiting for his call. He asked her not to open the package he mailed last month. At the time, he didn't know that the earrings he had purchased as a gift were made by the person who had murdered her husband. He told her nothing else about the package. I think he plans to just throw them away. He's bringing gifts for all of them and also personal gifts from me to her and the boys . After a short visit, he's heading straight to Turkey."

*****

Months had passed since the New Year's Day incident and everything was going as smoothly as possible. The first international symposium on God was considered a success. By devoting discussion to only the recognized areas of agreement concerning a supreme being, at least for this conference, most of the leaders and participants went home pleased with the outcome. It was a good beginning.

What most encouraged the Vatican was that all but three of the non-democratic nations who had been most repressive with their citizens were holding pat on their early agreement with Pope Francis. Nearly six months had passed since he had broadcast his plea to the leaders of those nations and their people. Perhaps both sides had discovered the fruits of peace. Maybe hearts were changed. Whatever the reason, it was a time for guarded optimism and continued diplomacy.

*****

"Thomas, it's me, please meet me in the garden at 6AM. Same place. No need for the long johns. See you then," was the message on Thomas' personal recorder on his night stand.

The recorder beeped again. "It's Dom again, just wanted to remind you...some dreams do come true."

CHAPTER THIRTY FIVE

In his absence, every crawling creature imaginable had returned with a vengeance. It took days to tidy up and make his home livable again. As luck would have it, his gear, tools, and food supplies were still intact. But come to think of it, why wouldn't they be? Who, except the ghosts of the past, would be seen dead in this God forsaken land of never ending emptiness. Yet, it excited him, and then on the other hand, it humbled him. God's gift to humanity - time, our way of measuring hours, days, years, and distances, would not seem to exist in this land if it hadn't been for the rising and setting of the sun. Time could not be held or felt with ones hands, tasted or smelled, but it could be observed. Time in it's reality, was change. Change - one could visibly see. This land had not changed in thousands of years. There among blowing dust, craggy cliffs, small clumps of stubborn brush whose roots clung on for dear life, sat a lone figure - smiling and reminiscing.

From the cave's lip he could see the emptiness for miles; the scene was quite different from that of the eternal city as viewed from the papal balcony.

In the past months Doctor Symon Carpenter had asked himself the same two questions repeatedly. "Was it all real? Did it actually happen?" In a vacuum, everything seemed so far away. Just like a wonderful vacation, once home and back to normal, it never seemed to have happened - unless you had photos for proof. Symon had no photos except the images imprinted in his memory. He gently shook his head and smiled again. Yes, it all had happened. There was no denying it.

A melancholy mood dug a foothold in his heart. The smile went the way of the dust at the thought of Uden's murder, Paulo's suicide, the dangers he had faced, Dom's courage - and Annette.

*****

After Chief Santini had followed Symon out into the foyer, he had told the chief that an informant claimed Annette Bordenave was still somewhere in Rome. The chief didn't need to know Symon had called the phone number Annette had given him and that her mother had answered the phone, saying, "No, her daughter was in Rome selling her jewelry."

Days after her death, an anonymous bouquet of flowers and a cashiers draft in the amount of $8,000, marked, *'for the burial'*, had arrived at Annette's home outside Paris.

*****

Symon had spent nearly three weeks visiting Inge, the twins, and praying at Uden's gave. Then he had dropped in on Peter for a week in Tbilisi. He had promised that to Peter at the beginning of his adventure last September. The remainder of that time until now, he had walked the stark, remote desert, and climbed and surveyed most of the rock structure that was home to his two room apartment - the caves.

It wasn't until the last week that the notion had hit him. He had camped in the cave below, and later found the cave above. What if Assuri, hiding in the cave above, found the cave below? Upon seeing the dust from the oncoming would-be captures, could he have turned over his stone table to make it appear as though whoever had once lived there was gone - and then hidden in the lower cave, hoping he wouldn't be spotted?

Assuming that possibility, Symon, for the first time, had searched his own cave for clues. For days, he had tapped and probed the walls, floors and ceiling. Nothing. Then on day four, in frustration, he threw the pickax the length of the cave. As it hit, a large stone in the back wall moved slightly ajar, enough for him to notice. With some effort, he jimmied the rock loose. Inside was a small cracked and brittle leather purse. The flap fell off, exposing a folded sheet. Carefully taking it out, he unfolded the piece, but it began to crumble in his hands, and fell in pieces at his feet. The object had not been as painstakingly hidden and preserved as what was discovered in the upper chamber.

Cautiously, he sprayed the fallen bits with a preserving-fix and allowed them to dry before endeavoring to pick them up and to piece them together as best he could. Several bits, when touched, disintegrated. At first it looked hopeless. But much to his surprise, a number of the larger pieces remained whole. He was able to put them together like a puzzle and decipher a message from Assuri, filling in the blanks with his own thoughts, based on what he envisioned were Assuri's frantic last moments.

The message appeared to have been written quickly; the writing was not as neat and precise as what was found earlier. Nevertheless, the symbols

276

were definitely Assuri's. The swagger of certain symbols was a key. He must have felt the dire need to leave a legacy of his own as a way of preserving the fact that he had lived and served well.

Symon began to read the message, and smiled. Just as he suspected, Assuri had not waited to be captured. His single-minded duty was to his master and the protection of the three volumes of the History of The World. He intended to guard them with his life. He may have been a slave, but above all, he was brave, cunning and resourceful. After eluding the party from Alexandria, he planned to head north to the sea. Today, that would be the Black Sea. One last bit of disturbing reference. He must have become aware of the horrible death of his friend. Perhaps overheard in comments made by men in the cave above. He wrote, *'Hypatia, flower of my heart - dead.'*

*****

Later, seated at the cave entrance and gazing out across the desert, darkness surrounded Symon like a closed fist. He couldn't remember a night in the desert that was so black. Even the stars deserted him this night. He thought about Karl's ordeal. Tired, he returned to the cave, and crawled into his thermal sack. Minutes after laying his head down, he heard a familiar soft whooshing sound. At first, it was some distance away. Must be a Turkish reconnaissance craft, he thought. The sound became louder and louder - closer and closer. It hovered below, just outside the cave entrance. "Either the Turks have found me, or the Vatican's calling me back," he whispered to himself. "The Turks can have me. I've done my time as an unpaid Vatican spy."

Suddenly the craft made a booming, wheezing noise, and within moments there was silence once again. Apparently, the craft had moved on. Relieved, he lay his head back on his arm and closed his eyes.

"Well, don't I even get an hello!" roared a voice from out of the darkness below. At first Symon had thought he had fallen asleep and was dreaming.

And then, there it was again. "Can't a fellow adventurer get some light down here? I can't see, even to move."

Hearing a voice out of nowhere in this God forsaken place was surprise enough, but that voice - it couldn't be. "Dom - is that you?" Symon replied, falling on his face after getting tangled in the sack. Spitting out a mouthful of dirt, he shouted back, "Be right there - give me a minute! And what do you mean - a fellow adventurer?"

Until early morning, Dom, wearing a crisp new khaki-colored pair of cargo pants and matching shirt, sporting two days growth of whiskers, and topped with a white silk skull-cap, explained everything to his stunned, but attentive friend.

When he finished his account, his last words were, "Let's get some sleep Symon, we're in pursuit of the ghost of Assuri. We'll see where the winds blow us. And, oh yes, don't forget the Ashkari monks. Yes, it'll be our *Alpha Search*. I can't wait."

Symon didn't sleep a wink. Dom slept peacefully.

CHAPTER THIRTY SIX

DOM'S ACCOUNT OF HIS FINAL DAYS AS POPE

The sound in Dom's voice on the recorder gave Thomas a feeling of uneasiness. The message, 'Some dreams do come true,' filled him with an unsettling premonition that invaded his heart and mind like an unwanted virus. He tried to shake it off through the night, without success. He couldn't wait for morning.

The Vatican gardens had come alive with color. The trees and bushes had shed their icy shells; the late spring sun had done its job well. Glossy green leaves provided shade; blooming flowers became nourishment for winter-worn eyes. Nature had renewed itself.

*****

Thomas knew where to find Pope Francis. He had walked briskly down the path, unaware it would be a rendezvous with destiny, but slowed his gait upon approaching the meditating pontiff. "I always seem to interrupt your morning prayers," he apologized.

"No you didn't. I saw you coming. Good morning, my friend. Rest your bones," Dom said, patting the bench top. "We have much to discuss, and here, among God's beauty, there's no better place.

"I would imagine you would like to know the reason for my last minute, late night phone message. And, if I'm correct, a full explanation of the post script, *Some dreams do come true*."

The cardinal, after serving as Dom's closest Vatican confidant for some months now, was well aware of his unorthodox style of running the papal office. Nothing would surprise him at this point, he thought, as he shrugged his shoulders and nodded. Dom had his chin on his chest as though in thought, then lifted it up and smiled. "I guess the label of a 'maverick pope' cannot be avoided, or denied, right Thomas?"

Being honest to a fault, Thomas nodded again. No, it couldn't be avoided.

"You know, if Buldini's staff had uncovered that fact, I would never had been selected as his next puppet pope. My past exploits on the behalf of the faithful, and my often heated engagements with my superiors, won me the reputation as a maverick priest. They said the same when I became cardinal. For one reason or another, sometimes by order of a bishop, or by my own choice, I moved from one diocese to another - from one hot spot assignment to another. And all the while, loving every moment of it. The challenges were exciting. I wouldn't trade that experience for anything.

"And then came the papacy. Between you and me, Thomas, it too, has been exciting. You've been a major player; you know first hand. But, there's been sadness, too. And, there's been anger on my part. This experience has taught me much about myself. And, I'm not proud of all that I've learned. With your help, Symon's, and my Franciscan brothers', we've accomplished much. We, together, have begun to rebuild His Church."

Thomas opened his mouth to say something, but Dom motioned with a shake of his index finger not to speak.

"I'm far from being done," he said, and continued. "While shivering on the dirt floor of the Colosseum, waiting in fear that the assassins would find me, I had time to make a life altering decision. I'm convinced it's the right one. "It's something that has occupied my mind for days now."

Dom had Thomas' undivided attention; he leaned forward so as not to miss a single word.

"I'm abdicating the papacy. I'll announce the decision at next week's conference to members of the College of Cardinals. You will become pope by papal proclamation. It's been done before. There's precedent for the motion. And that evening you and I will go live, and broadcast that news to the world. Yes, my friend, some dreams do come true. Your boyhood dream will come true. Finally, a black pope. Your presence will restore dignity to the office; I predict you'll make the best pope yet."

Cardinal Thomas Mumbwa held his breath, his mind desperately trying to comprehend the consequence of Dom's words.

*****

The morning had gone well. Even though the previous shortage of priests had been eased by Vatican III's declaration providing a choice of celibacy or a married life, this particular group of red hats were willing to consider female participation in the priesthood. Willing to consider was the operative statement.

Pope Francis was determined to have the long standing gag order on theologians lifted. Addressing the subject, he argued, "What use is it to be a theologian? Why do we even acknowledge the profession? We allow them to study their craft, but maintain they must remain mute. That's like telling someone they're a carpenter, provide them with lumber and a hammer, and then deny them the nails. What are we afraid of - the truth?

"It's true, humanity has been blessed with many truths, from many sources, but are we certain of the fullness of those truths as they apply to a another day and time? Truths cannot be changed, but perhaps better understood in a new light. Wasn't it our Lord who said he would no longer write the law in stone, but rather in our hearts? Wasn't it Jesus who was aware of the letter of the law, but also followed the spirit of that law? What truths are out there that our finite minds have yet to behold? We must open their mouths and allow them to speak. We are wise enough to sift the chaff from the wheat."

Before the day would end, the ban would be put to a vote, and passed without opposition. The committee overseeing the proposed new democratic organization gave a sterling progress report that pleased the pope.

Just before lunch, Pope Francis reported on the state of the Vatican's efforts to auction some of its treasures to obtain funds for its world charities program. He pointed to Thomas and said, "Cardinal Mumbwa has managed to keep the Vatican Museum viable, while selling-off much of what had been in storage and cluttering our offices and buildings with nothing but irrelevant dust gatherers. The funds will help to feed, house and protect the needy everywhere. And the cherished collection of Vatican treasures will now be spread throughout the world and seen by millions of people who could not have enjoyed them before." That seemed to have pleased the cardinals.

Until the pope mentioned Cardinal Mumbwa, there had been no reference to him, and he had been uncharacteristically silent during the morning session, sitting off by himself, seemingly uninterested in the presentations and discussions. He was the target of conversation and speculation throughout lunch.

*****

At approximately four o'clock, the pope called an abrupt halt to the day's sessions, declaring that he had an important announcement to make.

"My brothers in Christ, those of you who were present during the latest selection process at which time I was elected your pope, are painfully aware that the election was rigged. For those who were not present, you should know that the late Cardinal Buldini pressured many into voting for Cardinal Masone. Of course, his hand picked representatives voted for me as well. What most of you are not aware, since only a handful had been privy to the ballots, is that Cardinal Thomas Mumbwa would have been elected pope if Buldini had not interfered. There's no doubt he was the favorite."

His audience stirred in their seats, stared at each other, then to Thomas, then back to Pope Francis. He observed their bewilderment.

Once again commanding their attention, he went on. "I'm going to ask for your fullest cooperation, without question or challenge. Agreed?"

A sea of red swayed like a wave from side to side, finally acknowledging they would abide by their leader's request. Whatever it was.

"My God-given task is well under way, if not yet completed. His house is being rebuilt. While I am not abandoning my mission, it is, however, calling me in another direction. As of this moment, I, Pope Francis I, hereby abdicate, and by the authority and power of the papacy, appoint Cardinal Thomas Mumbwa the new pope. I would like you all to welcome him in the spirit of solidarity." He pointed with both hands to the group. "Remember, you all agreed?"

They sat like mannequins, stunned; not a sound could be heard. Then a swallow, a sniffle, several coughs, a stirring of hundreds of feet on the concrete floor beneath their chairs, and in unison, they stood and faced Thomas. Applause rang out. Dom smiled. The new pope was crying.

Dom let Thomas enjoy the moment, and after a few minutes had passed, stepped forward and put both his hands in the air to get everyone's attention. When calm prevailed, he motioned for Thomas to join him, saying, "Behold - your new pope." And then asked, "By what name will you be called?"

"Pope Francis II," came an instant reply.

This time, Dom brushed away the tears.

*****

Dom was nearly through the broadcast; he had repeated most of the report he had given to the cardinals earlier in the day, minus elements not germane to the viewing and listening audience. During the presentation, Cardinal Mumbwa, now Pope Francis II, sat attentively at his side; occasionally the television camera would focus in on his reactions, the audience unaware that they were seeing the new pope. But they soon would learn.

Dom carefully, and without emotion, explained his decision to step down in favor of Cardinal Mumbwa, and that the College of Cardinals wholeheartedly accepted the decision. He closed his portion of the broadcast by saying, "Pope Francis II, has the wisdom and foresight of the lovable Pope John XXIII, and the courage of Pope John Paul II.

"These are my last words to you as pope, and perhaps the most significant. Please take them to heart. *'Your physical life here on God's creation is but a moment in time. The spiritual hereafter lasts an eternity. Make the most of the moment.'*

"I'll repeat that," he said, eyes riveted directly on the camera, "it's so important. *'Your physical life here on God's creation is but a moment in time. The spiritual hereafter lasts an eternity. Make the most of the moment.'*"

*****

Pope Francis II concluded with a brief statement of his own, promising a balcony address in the near future. The two men walked back to Dom's chambers without a word. They didn't have to. Dom was the first to break the silence. "Thomas, do me two, no, three favors. The palace behind St. Peter's where the new orphanage is being established, offer Monsignor Diamante the directorship. If anyone should know the pitfalls of living in such a home, he does. Secondly, I told my Franciscan brothers when this all began, that if they wanted the job of Vatican ambassador to their respective homelands, it was theirs. Start with Karl."

"It's done," answered Thomas. "Please stay in touch. Let us know where you are. You have an open invitation here; you know that. And, what's the third favor?"

With the biggest grin yet, Dom sheepishly asked, "Can I get to keep my white silk skull-cap?"

283

EPILOGUE

Hours before the sun had opened its eyes, and with the full moon lighting their way, the ex-friar, professor, seafaring scalawag, pal to the most influential man in the world - and the Franciscan holy man, both followed the footsteps of a Babylonian slave whose tracks had been blown away by the merciless winds over a millennium and a half ago.

Their quest, their *Alpha Search*, would take them to some of the most remote, dangerous and mysterious locations.

With backpacks in place, and their beloved brown habits safely tucked away, they walked stride for stride towards the Black Sea - and the unknown. The spirit of Uden, who remained in their hearts, created an invisible set of footprints.

The moon's smile was uncommonly bright, and the stars appeared to twinkle with amusement.

Watch for *Volume II of The Franciscan Trilogy*
'The Alpha Search' in 2001

Watch for *Volume III of The Franciscan Trilogy*
'The Missing Hair Shirt' in 2002

AUTHOR'S NOTE

The Babylonian priest Berossus' three-volume History of The World from Creation to the Flood was known to have existed, and presumed destroyed in the Alexandria Library fire.